Praise for
Santa Montefiore

'No one does epic romance like Santa Montefiore'
JOJO MOYES

'I couldn't put this book down'
JULIAN FELLOWES

'Fantastic, moving and beautifully written'
TRACY REES

'Enjoyable and engaging, I loved it!'
BARBARA ERSKINE

'A love story to break your heart!'
LIZ FENWICK

'Beautifully written, haunting and enchanting'
FIONA VALPY

'Irresistible! Full of passion, love and loyalty'
CAROL KIRKWOOD

'Everything I love most in a novel, I adored every word!'
JENNY ASHCROFT

'Gloriously compelling, I was glued to every page. I adored it!'
LIZ FENWICK

Santa Montefiore is the international number one bestselling author of over thirty novels and has sold over eight million copies worldwide. Her books have been translated into twenty-five languages. She won an RNA Award for *The Temptation of Gracie* in 2019, which is currently in development for film. Born in England in 1970, she grew up in Hampshire and now lives in London with her husband, historian and author Simon Sebag-Montefiore, their daughter Lilochka, son Sasha, and dog Simba. *The Last Encore* is the final novel in her Timeslider series following psychic detective heroine Pixie Tate.

Santa loves to hear from readers and you can find her at www.santamontefiore.co.uk.

THE LAST ENCORE

Santa Montefiore

ORION

First published in Great Britain in 2026 by Orion Fiction,
an imprint of The Orion Publishing Group Ltd.
Carmelite House, 50 Victoria Embankment
London EC4Y 0DZ

The authorised representative in the EEA is Hachette Ireland,
8 Castlecourt Centre, Castleknock Road, Castleknock, Dublin 15, D15 XTP3,
Republic of Ireland (email: info@hbgi.ie)

An Hachette UK Company

1 3 5 7 9 10 8 6 4 2

A CIP catalogue record for this book is
available from the British Library.

ISBN (Hardback) 978 1 3987 2015 2
ISBN (Export Trade Paperback) 978 1 3987 2016 9
ISBN (eBook) 978 1 3987 2018 3
ISBN (Audio) 978 1 3987 2019 0

Typeset by Input Data Services Ltd, Bridgwater, Somerset

Printed in Great Britain by Clays Ltd, Elcograf, S.p.A.

FSC www.fsc.org MIX Paper | Supporting responsible forestry FSC® C104740

www.orionbooks.co.uk

Dedicated to my very special friend
Bruce Dundas, with love and gratitude
for being there.

I don't solve crimes
That's too easy
I settle souls

Pixie Tate

Prologue
New York

I will find a way . . .

Pixie was in turmoil. She leaned back against the gnarled trunk of the tree and pressed a hand to her chest, but nothing could ease the pain beneath it where her heart ached with a searing longing and a terrible emptiness. Nothing could bring back a moment that had been snatched from her one-hundered-and-two years ago. With all the will in the world she, a proficient timeslider, could not slip back to a precise instant. Metaphysics was not an exact science, it was capricious. That moment was gone forever, like a pearl lost in the ocean.

Pixie, as Constance, had been due to meet Cavill *here*, on Bethesda Terrace in Central Park, but Constance had been murdered and Pixie had returned to her own time. She would never know what he had wanted to tell her, and *he* would never know what *she* had planned to tell *him*.

How could she possibly go on living in a world without Cavill?

She pictured his gravestone in the long grasses outside the church at St Sidwell Manor, and the sight of it, so cold and still, brought her up short. Those dates, branded on her memory, were so *final*. So *dead*. *1857–1943*. It was now September 2014. He had been gone one hundred and seventy-one years. But Pixie had seen him yesterday, in 1912. He had held her hand. He had unbuttoned her glove and brought it to his lips where he had kissed the naked skin on her wrist. And she was sure he had recognised *her*, Pixie, behind Constance's eyes, even though he didn't know it. Even though he couldn't *possibly* know it. But he had, on a subliminal level. She knew he had. The realisation that he loved her had dawned on his face like a beautiful sunrise and revealed itself in his unfettered smile. In his unrestrained joy. After all he had been through – the disappearance of his nephew Felix, the deaths of his sister-in-law Cordelia and his wife Hermione – did he not deserve to be happy?

Yes, he deserved to be happy, but his happiness had once again been snatched from him with Constance's death.

Pixie shuddered as she realised how close she had come to telling him the truth. She was going to meet him on those steps and explain everything. She was going to break the cardinal rule of timesliding by telling him who she really was. But for what purpose? For whose benefit? Certainly not for his. Why would he believe such a thing? How could that knowledge possibly make him happy? She grew uncomfortably hot as the memory sharpened. What had she been thinking? But it had felt so right at the time. She realised now that she had been blinkered by her own selfish longing. Blinded by a burning need to be loved for herself. Not as Hermione, not as Constance, but as *her*, Pixie Tate. She had needed him to recognise *her* behind the eyes, but how was that even feasible?

She closed her eyes and let the tears squeeze between her lashes and trickle down her cheeks. What was the point of loving Cavill, she thought miserably, if she could never stay long enough to be with him? *Was* there a point, or was it simply the fact that her heart, like a magnet, had pulled him to it – would it continue to pull him to it slide after slide? A force greater than the two of them with an unrelenting attraction. Would she ever be free of him? Or were they connected now, doomed to meet for fleeting moments in the past; a love that could never be fulfilled? Was she fated to endure this agony over and over again? In which case she had to put a stop to it, for her sake as well as his. If she had somehow tied her destiny to his, she had to work out a way to *un*tie it.

The sun found a gap in the leaves and shone a golden beam onto her face. It was warm and gentle, and she was immediately reminded of that final carriage ride around Manhattan with Cavill. She pictured him and the knife twisted deeper into her heart. She was seated beside him, and he was gazing at her, his cornflower eyes full of tenderness and recognition. She could almost feel him next to her. She could almost reach out and touch him. She didn't want to open her eyes and lose this blissful feeling. Then a thought slithered into her consciousness like a serpent with the whispering voice of temptation. Couldn't she hold on to that feeling and slide through the veil?

Would her love for Cavill take her back to him?

She could try . . .

Her heart began to accelerate with anticipation. There was no harm in giving it a go. She had no object to link her to Cavill – his sketchbook that she had stolen from St Sidwell Manor was in the hotel – and she had nothing tangible to link her to 1912, but she *did* have the park. She was right here where she wanted to be, a short distance from the Bethesda terrace – surely, she could project herself back to April 21st 1912. If she focused on the park and the meeting they'd arranged for midday, wouldn't the Law of Attraction see to it that her desire was fulfilled? She wouldn't be Constance, of course, for she was dead. She'd be someone else. But maybe she wouldn't need to possess a body at all. She could slip out of her own body and transport herself back, as she had spontaneously done on many occasions as a child when her parents' fighting in the kitchen below had got too much. Back then, she had consistently arrived in a meadow, believing it to be heaven. It was years later that she realised it wasn't heaven at all, that she had actually slipped through time and was in the very same place, only long before her house had been built. Could she not, in the same way, transport herself back to 1912 and simply observe, *as herself*. She wouldn't be able to stay for long, admittedly – that was the drawback of timesliding without acquiring a body, but it wouldn't matter. She'd see him again, and that would be enough – even though he wouldn't be able to see her. To him she'd be even less perceptible than a breeze. Could she bear it?

She could.

With mounting excitement, she took a series of deep breaths, focusing on the rise and fall of her ribcage and the sensation of air entering and leaving her nostrils. Shortly, she felt the familiar heaviness in her limbs and the dizzying feel of her finer, etheric body loosening from her physical body and slowly detaching. She thought of Cavill, and her yearning seemed to lift her up so that she was hovering in the branches of the tree, a wisp of wind, a ray of sunshine. Then she was slipping through the veil.

A Park
Winter

I open my eyes. I am not me, observing, but someone else. I have slid into the body of a young woman, and I'm freezing cold.

My scuffed black boots are embedded in snow. It's thick and twinkling like tiny diamonds. I look down at my dress. It's long and black and very plain. My eyes catch sight of my hands. I spread my fingers wide and am horrified at the rawness of the red skin and the dry, ragged nails. They're the hands of a scullery maid, or someone whose job it is to scrub with water and harsh soap. No Fairy Liquid for these hands, or rubber gloves. I gaze about me. I believe I'm still in Central Park, but it's very different. The trees around me are young and spindly, beyond them I see a wide track upon which horse-drawn sleighs glide over the snow. Elegant women walk side by side in long cloaks and hats, their hands buried in fur muffs. A man pulls a child on a wooden sled. The child is giggling happily. A dog trots behind, then gets distracted by a pleasant smell and cocks its leg on a lamppost. My breath fogs on the air. Above me the sky is a pale, duck-egg blue. I see no skyscrapers, only trees, shivering in the cold as I am.

I walk through the snow, trying to work out where I am – if, indeed, I'm in New York at all. I don't have a muff, only some sort of hat. I'm freezing. As I emerge over a mound I see on the other side of it a large, frozen lake. Dozens of people are ice skating: boys in breeches and caps; men in frock coats and hats; women, arms linked, moving slowly over the ice in their long skirts, short jackets and bonnets. Beyond them an enormous, yellow stone building with three pointed gables stands alone. It looks vaguely familiar, but I have no idea what it is.

It's then that I spot a newspaper discarded on a wooden bench. I seize it. It's *The Evening World*. To my disappointment I read, New York, Saturday December 7, 1889.

Join the Nellie Bly Guessing Match

And You May Take

That Free Trip to Europe

I have no idea what that means. I do know, however, that in 1889 Cavill is in England. Why has the Law of Attraction brought me here if *he* is in St Sidwell?

I sit down in frustration. It's clear to me that I cannot engineer my slides. I don't know whether that's because I don't know how to, or because I'm not meant to, or because I don't have something of Cavill's to link me to him. Perhaps I've been overthinking and Cavill's presence on the *Titanic* was nothing more than a wonderful coincidence. One which won't be repeated. I slump over the newspaper in despair. How will I ever see him again? I cannot accept that I won't. That I *can't*.

'Mary! Mary Connor . . . !' I lift my eyes to see a young woman with a red face glaring at me. She's wearing the same sort of dress as I am, and she's shivering too. 'Would you come now please!' she exclaims crossly in an Irish accent. 'I've been looking all over for you.'

There's no point staying another minute in this time and place. Besides, I'm numb with cold.

I close my eyes and will myself home.

Chapter One
London, 2014

'You're crazy!' Ulysses exclaimed. 'And you waited until now to tell me?'

It was dusk. A blood orange sun was dropping slowly behind the buildings, plunging the street below into purple shadow. Pixie and Ulysses sat on the terrace outside their apartment in Little Venice, wrapped in coats and hats for it was now mid-October, and November was edging closer with its cold winds and shorter days. They'd been back in London for three weeks. They both missed New York, but for entirely different reasons. Pixie pined for Cavill; Ulysses yearned for Henry. While Pixie's pining was futile, Ulysses' yearning was productive – he seemed to be constantly texting and FaceTiming, and laughing out loud at jokes to which Pixie was not privy. She found it annoying. Ulysses, who claimed not to be interested in love, was clearly smitten with Henry Stirling whom he'd wasted no time in seducing at the Aldershoff Hotel. Pixie, who wanted only to be loved by Cavill Pengower, was still coming to terms with the fact that she could never have him. Ever. It seemed so unfair that Ulysses should be rewarded for his carelessness, while Pixie should suffer for her honest heart.

It was over a glass of wine on this copper-coloured evening that Pixie confessed to her friend that she had tried to timeslide back to 1912, without Ulysses there to protect her. 'Can you imagine if someone had disturbed you! What would you have done then? Would they have known what to do when you began to writhe around on the floor in a fit?'

Pixie shook her head and shrugged. 'You're so dramatic, Ulysses.

I was in trance for a minute, no more. No one came near me.'

'I'm not dramatic, I'm passionate,' he exclaimed, his Brazilian accent giving the word 'passionate' a sensuality it didn't have in English. He grinned, his teeth white against his olive skin, the green of his eyes accentuated by the last rays of sunshine that caused them to shine like tourmaline. His smile was winning, as were his indecently good looks, and Pixie couldn't help but smile back.

'It's all right for you. You have Mr Stirling – Henry – on the phone whenever you want him. I can't call Cavill, ever.'

'Give it up, Pixie,' said Ulysses seriously. 'You're wasting your life on a man who doesn't even exist. You might as well love a movie star.'

She took a sip of wine. 'I thought I could slide back to a specific time and place. I just wanted to see him one more time. It was worth trying . . .'

'Not without me,' he cut in crossly.

She glanced at him slyly. 'I knew you'd try to persuade me not to.'

'So you went behind my back?'

'Yes.'

'You little devil.'

She laughed, but her joy turned quickly to worry. 'Okay, so it was foolish, but at that point I was desperate. I thought I'd never see him again. I thought I'd lost him forever. But what if I haven't lost him at all? What if I've actually started something that I don't know how to get out of?'

Ulysses frowned. Pixie often seemed to speak a language he didn't understand. 'What do you mean? Started what?'

'I mean, what if in falling in love with Cavill I've somehow tied our destinies together? Maybe it wasn't a coincidence that I met him on the *Titanic*, after all. What was he doing on the *Titanic*, for goodness' sake? What if *I* drew him there? *Me.* What if I draw him to me on *every* slide?'

'That's impossible. If you slide back to, say, mid-nineteenth century, he won't have been born.'

'But that's the thing, am I destined to always slide back to *his* time? Will the Law of Attraction assign me jobs that take me *there*. Is this going to go on and on and on . . . ?'

'Isn't that what you want? You said you wanted to see him one last time. Well, maybe your prayer has been answered.'

She shook her head and her brow creased into small furrows. The truth was she wasn't really sure *what* she wanted. She wanted Cavill in her own time, as Pixie, but only magic could make that happen, and she didn't believe in magic. She sighed heavily. 'I don't want to meet him again as someone else. I can't do that to him. I possessed Hermione and he fell in love with her and married her. She died. I possessed Constance and he fell in love with *her*, and *she* died. Poor man – the women he loves, leave him. *I* leave him. Is that fair on him, just to satisfy my own longing?'

'Are you suggesting that he's going to fall in love with you every time you slide into his world? That every woman you take over is going to become the object of his desire? It's only happened twice. Maybe the third time you'll take over someone who isn't his type!' He grinned triumphantly as if he'd solved the problem.

'It's not about how she looks, it's about *me*,' she insisted, frustrated suddenly that he wasn't keeping up. 'It's about who she is on the inside. Don't you get it? It's a soul connection. It's me that he loves! At least, I hope that it is.'

'It's far-fetched if you ask me.'

'The point is, it's not fair on him to put him in that position time and again, nor me for that matter. I can't return to the past as another woman and hope that he'll eventually see through her eyes into my soul. I have to put an end to it.'

Ulysses raised his glass. 'Now you're talking sense, Pixie.'

'So, how do I do that?'

'Well, if you *are* somehow drawing him into your slides, perhaps you shouldn't timeslide at all.'

She cocked her head. 'That's ridiculous. It's my job. I have to timeslide.'

'Get another job. There are a thousand things you could do.'

'Like what? Sit in an office in front of a laptop? You know I can't do that. This is the only thing I know how to do. And I'm good at it. Besides, I feel a responsibility towards those earthbound spirits I help. It gives me pleasure seeing them letting go of their misery and heading off into the light. They need me.'

'Then take on jobs that don't require timesliding. At least for the moment. Give yourself a rest. Perhaps, if you get over Cavill, you'll stop drawing him into your slides. Maybe you're right, the person responsible for his participation in your slides is *you* and your dogged pining.'

She thought about that for a moment. Then she said, 'You know, I feel there's more to it. That there's a *reason* we keep meeting. Like it's destiny. There's something important I need to learn from him, and he from me. Like life – only played out in a different time. On another level. It's still life, isn't it? Maybe we learn from our dreams too.'

He chuckled and drained his glass. 'You're reading way too much into it, if you ask me. You slid back to 1895 and fell in love. That's not so crazy. Why *wouldn't* you fall in love? It's just a shame he's dead now. But there's nothing significant about it. It's just unlucky. You'd be better off falling in love with someone in your own time.'

His phone buzzed with a call. He lifted it off the little table between them and grinned happily. 'Sorry, Pix. New York calls.' He put it to his ear. 'Hey you,' he said, getting off his chair and wandering inside. Pixie felt herself bristle with resentment. Why couldn't *she* find a man who called her and said, 'Hey you'?

The sun dipped behind a building, and she was plunged into shadow and cold. She went inside, closing the glass door behind her. She could hear Ulysses' laughter from his bedroom. His happiness made her heart heavy. She wasn't sure whether that was because she was jealous he was in love, or because she felt excluded. Ulysses always had a man on the go, but Henry Stirling felt different. Ulysses' laughter sounded different too. It resonated with an intimacy she hadn't heard before.

She went into her bedroom and perched on the edge of the bed. Still in her coat and bobble hat she felt cold, and lonely. She felt *terribly* lonely. She rubbed her hands together to warm them and glanced warily at the drawer of her bedside table. Her stomach tightened with anxiety just thinking about what lay inside it. But like the tongue that craves the aching tooth, she reached out to open it. Inside was a pile of letters. On her return from America, she had stopped throwing away her mother's attempts at communication. Instead, she now kept them in a drawer, unopened. She hadn't read a single one. She knew what they contained, and she didn't want to hear it. The postmark was Manchester. Fortunately, that was quite a long way away. She didn't think her mother would suddenly turn up on her doorstep. If Pixie ignored the letters, her mother might stop writing them and disappear.

At that thought she felt her throat tighten with anguish. She'd like to have a mother, only not *her* mother. Not a mother capable of plunging a knife into her husband's chest, a mother who was so selfish as to deny Pixie a father. No, she wished she had a mother like other people's mothers. A mother who was soft and gentle and loving. Her eyes stung with tears. She closed the drawer, hiding the letters in darkness.

She did not want *her* mother.

The following morning Ulysses received a call from the College of Psychic Studies in South Kensington. 'There's an earthbound spirit in a house in Battersea that needs to be removed. A simple job for Pixie,' said the receptionist brightly. 'Do you think you can head up there today?'

Ulysses was a journalist by trade and worked at home, in the flat in Little Venice that he and Pixie had shared since leaving university six years before. Accompanying Pixie on her visits was something he was able to juggle between assignments. As it happened, he'd just submitted an article for *The Sunday Times* about public demonstrations in his home country, Brazil, and was free. He took down the address then texted Pixie, who had gone out to buy groceries.

Pixie received his message in the vegetable aisle. She read it with interest. Secretly, she hoped she'd be required to timeslide, but recently her jobs had been far too easy for that. Simple souls who were keen to be shown the way home, not Linguinis, as she and Ulysses called the ones who were too traumatised to leave, or simply didn't want to go. Those spirits very often didn't know they were dead. She hoped and feared in equal measure that she'd slide back to Cavill, that her theory about having tied their destinies together was true. If only to see him one last time.

Pixie and Ulysses arrived at an ordinary terraced house in Battersea just before midday. It was an overcast, windy morning. After having rained in the night the pavements were littered with sodden leaves, the branches of the trees wet and glistening. It was cold. Winter seemed to have come early. Pixie, in her customary bobble hat and grey coat, shivered on the doorstep as Ulysses, handsome in a black beanie and peacoat, pressed the bell.

Shortly, a young woman opened it. 'Thank God!,' she exclaimed in what sounded like a German accent, and invited them in. 'My son's been complaining of a man in his bedroom cupboard. He won't sleep in there anymore. We're at the end of our tether. I hope you can sort it out.'

The woman introduced herself as Adelaide Bauer. She was petite with long blonde hair tied in a low ponytail, sharp cheekbones, and pretty hazel eyes that gazed at Pixie with hope. She wasn't at all surprised by Pixie's pink hair. She was, however, surprised by Ulysses' extraordinarily handsome face. When she settled her gaze on him she blinked a few times in quick succession, then turned away sharply. Pixie was used to people's strange reactions on seeing him. Sometimes, he was just too dazzling to look at.

Adelaide offered them coffee, but they declined. Ulysses was very picky about coffee. Coming from Brazil he liked it strong, and it had to be exceedingly *good* coffee, certainly not instant, and definitely not from a capsule. Pixie drank tea but preferred not to drink while she worked. If she was required to timeslide, she couldn't be interrupted by needing the loo. 'Can you show us the wardrobe,' she asked, and followed Adelaide up the narrow staircase.

The house smelt pleasantly of baking bread and was decorated in fashionable pale grey, taupe and cream. The carpet was seagrass, and black-and-white photographs of glossy, smiling children hung on the walls. Adelaide seemed to have a happy family life. Conversely, the energy in the house was negative, giving it a hard feel, which Pixie picked up immediately. Ulysses, who was insensitive to vibration in spite of having explored metaphysics and the paranormal with Pixie and a group of like-minded people at university, felt nothing but the warmth of a heated home.

Pixie didn't need Adelaide to show her the bedroom. She knew instantly where the spirit resided. Adelaide opened the door and walked in and folded her arms. It was chilly and the energy was off. There was a child's bed covered with soft toys, a chest of drawers beneath a sash window, and, against the wall, the antique wardrobe in which the child claimed to have seen the ghost. Pixie nodded. 'Your son's right,' she said. 'There *is* a spirit in there. The spirit of a man.'

Adelaide looked horrified. 'You can see him?' she exclaimed.

'I can. But you needn't be afraid. He's more frightened of you than you are of him.'

'Why won't he go away?'

'Because he's stuck.'

'Stuck in the cupboard?'

'No, stuck in limbo. He's hiding in the cupboard because he's afraid of *us*.'

'Good Lord. Can you get rid of him?'

Pixie nodded again. 'I think I can. Why don't you go downstairs and make yourself a cup of coffee. Ulysses can go with you. I can do this on my own.'

Adelaide looked panicked. Pixie wasn't sure which terrified her more, the ghost in the cupboard, or handsome Ulysses standing beside her.

Ulysses smiled, which startled Adelaide all the more. His smile was stunning. 'Might I have a cup of tea?' he asked. 'Pixie won't be long. Spirits in cupboards are usually easy to move on.'

Adelaide laughed nervously. 'Do you get many spirits in cupboards?' she asked.

'You'd be surprised,' Ulysses replied.

The two of them left the room. Adelaide closed the door behind them.

Pixie sat on the bed and folded her hands in her lap. She closed her eyes and took three deep breaths. She centred herself, allowing the material world around her to gradually recede, and connected to her inner world and her psychic sense.

She tuned in to the man, who was now standing outside the cupboard. Old and bewildered, he was trembling with fear. He looked as if he was wearing a dressing gown and slippers.

Can you hear me? she asked in her mind.

You're English, he said, his voice thick with relief. *Have they gone?*

Who?

The Germans.

The Germans? Pixie suddenly understood what had happened, and she realised too, with a sinking heart, that she wasn't going to have to slide. There was no mystery here. *What year is it?* she asked, pushing the thought of Cavill from her mind and focusing on the job.

February 1941, he answered without hesitation.

And the Germans are bombing London, Pixie cut in.

They're in the house, he said anxiously. *They're here in the house.* He meant Adelaide and her family, of course.

What's your name? Pixie asked.

Alfie Hancock.

Listen Alfie, she began gently. She was going to have to tell the poor man that he was dead. He obviously had no clue. Most likely the house had been hit by a bomb and he'd been killed so quickly, he hadn't registered that he'd died. *Do you know how long you've been in that cupboard?*

I don't know, he answered vaguely.

You've been in that cupboard for a very long time. You've been in this house for a very long time. Do you know how long it's been since you left the house?

He thought about it. When he eventually spoke, his voice quivered with fear. *I think I've lost my mind. I don't know when I last left the house. I don't know when I last had a bite to eat.*

But you're not hungry, are you?

No. No, I'm not hungry.

There was no easy way to break it to him. *Alfie, you haven't lost your mind. You have nothing to be afraid of. The Germans who are living in this house are friends. The war ended nearly seventy years ago. It's 2014 now and we're allies with Germany.*

I don't understand.

You're no longer living as you were before. You must have lost your life in the Blitz. I imagine this house was hit by a bomb that killed you.

He looked at his hands in astonishment. *How can I be dead if I can see my body? I couldn't see my body if I was dead, surely.*

You're in your spirit body, Alfie, she told him kindly. It was always a challenge to tell someone they were 'dead', when they felt very much alive. *It's time to go home. Your loved ones are waiting to welcome you. They've been waiting a long time, I suspect. Don't you think you should go to them?*

So this is death, is it? I don't know what to make of it. I do remember a loud blast, a bomb . . . His voice trailed off. *I hid in the cupboard.*

You can leave the cupboard now, Alfie. There's nothing to fear.

Pixie focused then on her chest where her heart centre was now glowing with an expanding light. Out of that light she created a door. *Can you see a door of light, Alfie?* Not for a moment did she take her attention off it but held it steady and bright with her mind.

Yes, yes I can. Well, I'll be damned. Has that always been there?

Light has always been there, Alfie. It's been trying to find you. But you haven't been able to see it because of your fear. You need to walk through that door now, into the light.

Marjorie!

Pixie noticed then the figure of a woman, hovering in the doorway. She had a kind face and a wide smile, and glowed brightly, like a lightbulb. She held out her hands. *Come on, Alfie. Goodness me, you're a stubborn old man, aren't you?*

Marjorie. Dearest . . .

With that, Alfie Hancock moved seamlessly into spirit.

Pixie was moved. She opened her eyes and rested there a while on the bed, as the world around her grew solid again. It was always gratifying when a lost soul found its way home. She'd hoped she might be required to timeslide, but it hadn't taken much to move Alfie on. He'd wanted to go, once he realised he was dead. Most did. It was only in unusual cases where spirits lingered.

She got up and took a deep breath. The room felt different now. The energy was soft and warm. She knew the child would be happy to sleep here again. She'd done her job well and was satisfied.

She was, however, disappointed it had been so easy. She thought of Cavill again and felt forlorn suddenly. She knew she should leave him alone and not desire to slide back to see him, but the craving in her did not abate in spite of her reasoning. In spite of the logic. She missed him terribly. It was an ache in the core of her heart that was constant and acute and deaf to all argument.

She found Ulysses and Adelaide chatting at the kitchen table. Adelaide had clearly got over her awkwardness and the two of them were talking with the ease of old friends. Ulysses hadn't touched his tea, which didn't surprise Pixie at all. He never drank tea. Adelaide looked up at her hopefully. 'Did he go?' she asked.

'He did,' Pixie replied. 'He wanted to go once he realised he was dead.'

'How can a person not know they're dead?' Adelaide asked.

'If they're killed very quickly and unexpectedly, they often don't realise they're dead,' Pixie explained. 'Some see their lifeless bodies and understand right away, others are met by guides from the spirit world who come to take them home. Sometimes, like in Alfie's case – that was his name, Alfie Hancock – they're in such a state of bewilderment that they can't see their guides and loved ones. They remain stuck, like being in a dream. Only they don't know they're dreaming.'

'When did he die, do you think?' Adelaide asked.

'In the Blitz. He was still in his dressing gown.'

Adelaide thought about this a moment. 'How come they're dressed if they don't have bodies?'

'They don't have *material* bodies, but they have *etheric* bodies. It's a subtler body than this one, so when we die we slip out, a bit like a butterfly from a chrysalis, leaving our material bodies behind. This etheric body is invisible to most people. Think of it like a radio wave, or ultra-violet light; we know it's there, but it can't be seen with the naked eye. Alfie was in his dressing gown because he *believed* himself to be in it. The etheric body is simply energy. And energy can be manipulated with the mind. As spirits we don't have genders, or ages, but we can appear as we want by using thought. That's why when spirits come back and visit us, they usually take the form of the person they were when they were at their happiest, or a form they know will be recognised. Alfie didn't know he was dead and was still taking the form of the old man he was when he died, because that's who he believed he was.'

'I'm glad I can't see them then,' said Adelaide with a shiver. 'I'd hate to see ghosts.'

'I'd love to see spirits,' said Ulysses. 'In spite of trying, I've never seen anything remotely ghostly.'

Pixie laughed. 'That suits me fine,' she said. 'I'd hate to have to compete with you for jobs.'

Adelaide went up to the bedroom to see if she could sense the change in energy. 'It certainly feels warmer,' she said to Ulysses and Pixie, looking around in fascination. 'I hope Joshua feels the difference too. His father and I would rather like our bed back.'

'If you don't get your bed back,' said Ulysses, 'It will have nothing to do with the energy in this room, and everything to do with the comfort of your bed!'

Adelaide laughed and accompanied them downstairs.

'That's one happy client,' said Ulysses as they left Adelaide waving them off on the doorstep. Pixie turned to look at the house. The entire row looked like it had been built in the 1950s, which fit Alfie's story. She knew from studying history that Battersea had taken quite a hit during the Blitz.

They walked up the road towards the bus stop. 'I'm going to go and see Avril,' she told Ulysses suddenly.

'Oh dear,' Ulysses groaned. 'I knew this was coming.'

She laughed. 'You don't know why yet.'

'Yes I do. You want to find a way back to Cavill. You know you shouldn't, but you can't help yourself. You're blinded by love.' He looked across at her and smiled. 'I know you so well, Pixie!'

Her smile dropped. 'Well, I want to end it, you know.'

'You want to see Cavill one final time.'

Pixie stopped walking and pulled an anxious face. 'Is that wrong?'

He put his arm around her, drawing her close. 'It's unwise, Pix,' he replied affectionately.

'It's something I have to do.'

'I know.'

'Will you come with me?'

'Do you need me?'

'Yes.'

'Then I'll come. But if you do manage to slide back and find him, you must end it, okay? You have to promise me that. Then you have to start living in the present, join a dating app or something. Find a man in your own time. Do you promise?'

'I promise.'

'Very well.' He sighed dramatically. 'The things I do for love!'

Chapter Two

Avril Merivale lived in a red-brick, terraced house on a cherry-lined street in Chiswick. She worked at the College of Psychic Studies, which is where Pixie originally met her after leaving university and signing up for her tarot course, but since then the two women had formed a strong friendship, forged in Avril's unique understanding of the ancient art of time travelling, and Pixie now visited her in her home.

Avril was a warm, demonstrative woman with a big personality, a generous heart, and a penchant for bright colours and playful jewellery. Her home was full of giant amethyst caves, wind charms and dream catchers, but Avril was no cliché, nor was she a caricature of the archetypal fortune teller; she just had a good sense of humour. In actuality, Avril was wise beyond her sixty-one years, pragmatic, sensible and straight-talking. Above all, she had an extraordinary psychic ability, which she used to enlighten spiritual seekers, or to advise those who simply needed guidance in their lives. Pixie had a very specific question in mind, and Avril was the only person to whom she could turn to answer it.

Pixie and Ulysses arrived in the afternoon, buffeted along the street by a robust wind that tore the leaves from the trees and sent them flying like orange paper aeroplanes into the damp air. Avril saw them approaching up the wet pavement and opened the door before they had time to ring the bell. She was dressed in a long, multi-coloured Jacquard cardigan, her cropped hair dyed ash white, a pair of silver glittery spectacles hanging on a beaded string over her ample breast. She greeted them enthusiastically and showed them into her cosy kitchen where a pink scented candle burned on the round table and a scarlet kettle steamed on the sideboard. She had laid out coffee cake and biscuits in anticipation of their visit, along with pretty china teacups and saucers that didn't match.

'What can I get you?' she asked, directing her question at Ulysses, because she knew Pixie would drink mint tea while Ulysses, being notoriously fussy, would more likely have a Coca-Cola or cordial. Ulysses considered it a moment, pulling out one of the spindle-back chairs and sitting down.

'I'll have elderflower cordial and cake,' he replied.

'I'm longing to hear how the timesliding is going, Pixie,' Avril said, pouring boiling water into the teapot and popping in a handful of fresh mint. 'I suspect that's why you're here?' She looked at Pixie and arched an eyebrow. 'I would even go as far as to predict that you're wanting to take it a stage further.'

Pixie was surprised. '*Is* there a stage further?' she asked, hope flaring in her chest.

'Of course.' Avril put the teapot on the table and went to the cupboard to fetch a glass for Ulysses. 'There's always a stage further. Everything has its time, and you weren't ready for the next stage. I imagine you are now. That's why you're here.'

Ulysses caught Pixie's eye and pulled a startled face. Pixie ignored him and poured the tea. 'I *am* here to talk about timesliding,' she said.

'Exciting!,' Avril exclaimed. 'I didn't think it was purely a social visit.'

'Well, it's that too,' said Pixie. 'Obviously!'

Avril smiled. 'I know that. But all the same, let's get the pleasantries out of the way while I add a sprig of mint to Ulysses' elderflower cordial. Don't hold back on the cake, love, you'll be doing me a favour if you eat it all. Then we can cut straight to the chase.'

They chatted while Avril busied herself making Ulysses' drink, then she joined them at the table, knitted her fingers and gave Pixie her full attention. 'Right, Pixie, I'm all ears.'

'Okay, so let me fill you in. It's been quite rocky to be honest.'

'Take your time, don't cut any corners. I want to hear the full story.'

Ulysses spoke through a mouthful of cake. 'It's quite a story,' he said, widening his beautiful eyes. 'No one else but you would believe it.'

'That's what I'm here for,' Avril replied.

Pixie launched into her adventure without inhibition. She described her two most recent slides from the beginning – from 1895 when she arrived at St Sidwell Manor as a governess and fell in love with Cavill, to 1912 when, as Constance, she experienced being murdered on the stair in the Aldershoffs' mansion in New York and missing her rendezvous with Cavill the following morning.

Avril's face grew serious as she took it all in. Having taught Pixie how to hone her ability to time travel she felt she had a responsibility to guide her in doing it safely and sensibly. It sounded like Pixie had allowed her feelings for Cavill to get way out of control, and that was concerning. Ulysses, who hadn't heard all the details of Pixie's experience on the *Titanic*, stopped eating cake and listened with rapt concentration and an open mouth, punctuating her tale with gasps of 'No!' and 'Holy moly!'

When she finished, Ulysses burst into exclamations. 'That is some crazy shit, Pixie! You never told me about Mr Rowland and Orlando, and Mrs Brown! You also failed to mention that Constance was a suffragette. That's insane!'

'I didn't have time to tell you everything,' she replied.

'You had time, you just didn't have the will,' he returned, a trifle petulantly.

Avril put a calming hand on his. 'I imagine this must have needed a lot of processing, Ulysses. Occasionally, a little time is required before such things can be shared.'

He shrugged defensively. 'I'm glad I came today, otherwise I might never have heard the full story.'

Pixie rolled her eyes. 'Ulysses fell in love too, you know,' she added with a grin. 'In New York.'

The thought of Henry Stirling caused his face to soften. 'This isn't about me,' he said, but his mouth curled into a smile.

'We're in this together,' Pixie replied. 'So, yes it is. It's about us both.'

'What a pair you are,' said Avril, chuckling with amusement.

'Well, he's the lucky one,' said Pixie. 'Henry Stirling is a living person. Cavill Pengower died in 1943.'

'Naturally, you want to get back to him,' Avril stated.

Pixie was embarrassed to admit that she did. She sipped her tea a moment, then she put down the cup and sighed, deliberating how best to explain what she *really* wanted when she wasn't even sure herself. 'Okay, so I believe I've started something with Cavill, which has gained a certain momentum. The old wise woman in St Sidwell told me that love will always bring me back. I realise now that her words have more significance that I realised. You see, that's what I think happened when I slid back to the *Titanic*. Cavill was on it because I somehow caused him to be there, by a combination of the Law of Attraction and my desire.'

Avril nodded slowly, her mind swiftly weighing up the possibilities. 'You're suggesting that if you hadn't taken that job and slid back to the *Titanic*, Cavill wouldn't have been on it?' she said. She narrowed her brown eyes thoughtfully. 'But what if it's the other way around? The entire slide was engineered around Cavill being on it? He was always on it, only the Law of Attraction found you a case that linked into it, thus drawing you to *him*.'

Pixie considered that, and after a moment's pause concluded that both scenarios were entirely possible. 'It could be either way, couldn't it?' she agreed. 'Either *I* was drawn to Cavill, or *he* was drawn to *me*. The question is, am I going to attract slides to *me* that include *him*, or pull *him* into my future slides? Are our destinies forever entwined? Do I have to somehow undo it in order to be free of it?' She frowned as the thought of never seeing him again caused something in her heart to pinch. Instinctively, she put a hand to her breast and rubbed her sweater. 'Obviously, I want to see him again and I don't want to finish it, ever. But I can't slide from person to person and meet Cavill every time as someone different. That's mad. I can't do that to him, and I can't do that to myself. You can't imagine how horrible it is to see him and for him not to recognise me. And to not be able to tell him the truth of who I really am. It's agony. I want to tell him, but I know he'll think I'm crazy. What do I do, Avril? Tell me what I should do?'

Avril got up to make a fresh pot of tea. She stood by the counter until the kettle boiled, lost in thought. Pixie and Ulysses sat in silence – Pixie chewing on her thumb nail, Ulysses glancing at his phone in the hope of a text from Henry Stirling. He was not disappointed. His thumbs moved quickly over the tiny keyboard in response.

Shortly, Avril returned to the table with the teapot and refilled their cups. Then she sat back in her chair and nodded reflectively. 'Right, we need to consider this carefully,' she began slowly. 'There's no manual on how to timeslide, so we're feeling our way. This is what we know. Rule number one, you do not change anything in the past that might impact the future. What you think is a small change, might end up having a massive consequence down the line. It's a definite no-no.' Avril gave Pixie a hard stare.

'I'm aware of that,' said Pixie sheepishly. 'And I'm aware of having already altered Cavill's destiny.' She lowered her eyes. 'Potentially twice.'

Avril's expression softened. She did not look at Pixie with condemnation, but with compassion. 'There's a strong possibility that by falling in love with Cavill, and obviously changing his destiny by inspiring *him* to fall in love with *you*, you have set a powerful energy in motion that is simply going to build and build until it fulfils itself.'

'What do you mean "fulfils itself"?' Pixie asked.

'You won't be free of each other until you allow your love to fully and honestly express itself. Imagine you are both magnets attracting one to the other. The women you embody, Pixie, are obstacles to those two magnets joining as they should. In order for this love to fully and honestly express itself, Cavill needs to know that he loves *you*, Pixie. Does that make sense?'

Ulysses looked blank.

Pixie nodded thoughtfully. 'But that would mean he'd have to believe me,' she said, heart shrinking at the thought of coming clean and not being believed. 'I don't know that he'd do that. I mean, why would he? It sounds so science fiction.'

'He must recognise you on the level of your soul,' said Avril gravely. 'This is no ordinary love story, Pixie. You've slid back in time. You've *played* with time. And you've tied his destiny to yours. It's only natural that there are going to be consequences.' Her face mellowed. 'Look, I'm not condemning you. I'm just trying to explain that timesliding is a gift that comes with great responsibility. And you're only human. Yes, you've broken that rule various times, in small ways which you couldn't help, and in big ways, which you could help. I'm not criticising you. I'm just telling you how it is. Love makes us all do things we know we shouldn't do. But we have to stand up and face the consequences of our actions. It's the Justice card in the tarot deck. You have to stand up now and face yours.'

Pixie nodded. 'So there's a strong chance I'll meet Cavill again,' she said, half-dreading it and half-longing for it.

Ulysses interrupted. 'Tell Avril your theory about there being a purpose to your relationship with Cavill. You've put his life on a different path, but perhaps it was meant to be.'

Pixie inhaled deeply. 'Okay, well, it might be way off the mark. Even *you* dismissed it as stupid, Ulysses,' she said.

'I never said it was *stupid*,' he corrected.

'Well, you dismissed it.'

'What do *I* know?' He shrugged. 'Avril's the master. Ask *her*.'

Avril smiled indulgently. 'Go on, Pixie. Put it out there. This is a safe space, after all.'

'Okay.' Pixie began slowly. 'So, there's no such thing as coincidence, right? We all agree on that. Everything that happens in our lives is for a reason, to learn and grow. So, what if, right at the beginning, I drew Cavill into my experience, and *he* drew me into *his*, for a reason, because we have something we need to learn from each other?'

Avril nodded. 'Go on.'

'I've been given this gift to help lost souls find their way home.

That's my purpose. But what if my gift is designed also to teach *me* in the process.'

Avril nodded again. 'You're not wrong. I have no doubt that you learn life lessons in everything you do, whether in the present or in the past. In the grand scheme of things, they're the same thing. There is no time, we just perceive there to be. In order for us to live life here on earth, time has to be experienced as linear, cause and effect, birth to death. But, really, the past, present and future are all one. So, whether you're experiencing life a hundred years ago, or here today, you're still in the now. There is only ever the now. When you're sitting in trance, Pixie, in 2014, and projecting yourself into 1895 or 1912, you're still experiencing life in the *now*. The lessons you're being given, and those you're giving, are as valuable and important in *that* dimension as they are in *this* dimension. So yes, you and Cavill have a destiny to carry out. I do believe there's a meaning to it. In which case, you will very likely meet him again in another slide.'

'That's what I suspected. And what do I do when we meet again?'

'Well, this is what I think will happen. You've set a dynamic in motion, which will continue to roll until it has served its purpose or brought itself to fruition. So, when you next slide, I think you'll slide back to Cavill again – and perhaps again and again, until the situation is resolved. Maybe this is going to be your most challenging case. Not to settle lost souls, but to settle *your* soul, and *his*.'

'I feel like a lost soul right now,' said Ulysses, screwing up his beautiful face.

Pixie laughed, eyes very blue suddenly as her enthusiasm steadily mounted. 'I get it.'

'I don't,' said Ulysses. 'When you tried to slide back to a specific time and place in New York, it didn't work, did it?' he reminded Pixie. 'Why will it work now?'

Pixie frowned, deflated suddenly. 'He's right. Why will it work now? When I tried to slide back to the Bethesda terrace in Central Park, I found myself in 1889 not in 1912.'

'So, you need to take timesliding to the next stage,' said Avril simply.

'Ah, the next stage,' echoed Ulysses.

'What's the next stage?' Pixie asked.

'Engineering your slides. Being specific. Being the Chariot in the tarot deck. The one holding the reins, controlling, willing, manifesting.'

'That's sounds exciting!' said Ulysses, helping himself to another slice of cake.

'How do I do that?'

Avril shrugged. 'I'm not entirely sure. But let's consider timesliding per se. As a child, you basically slipped out of your body, and soul-wandered into the past. You were still you, in a finer body, in the same place, only years before. You time travelled. Then you refined it, by linking into an object that connected you to someone in the past and putting out your desire in a focused thought, and allowing the Law of Attraction to fulfil that desire. You discovered that you could last longer in the past if you inhabited another person's body. Due to your vibration being that of a woman, you could only possess the body of someone with a similar vibration. Not a man, or an old person, or a child, but a young, or relatively young, woman like you. Those things you have learned. But now you need to refine the process. But you have to bear in mind that it's not completely in your control. This might be a bit complicated, so I want you to listen very carefully.'

Pixie folded her arms on the table and leaned forward. Ulysses just continued to eat cake. Avril had already lost him around the moment she started talking about vibrations.

'Where we put our attention, our energy follows. So, when you focus on Cavill, your energy radiates out to him. That energy draws you to him. Now, as we know, that happens in life, all the time. It's how we create our reality. Our thoughts and beliefs manifest our world. But most people would say that if that were true they'd create a nicer world for themselves, but how many people are able to control their thoughts? Fear and anxiety invade and manifest, and much of the time we get what we fear, not what we desire. The point I'm making is that you focused on the Bethesda steps in Central Park and tried to will yourself there with the power of your desire. But, like our underlying fears and anxieties, you knew deep down that there was no purpose to that. You knew that it would achieve nothing. Constance was dead. You couldn't possess the body of someone else and turn up and say, 'Hey, Cavill. Look, it's me, in the body of someone else, again!' Deep down, you knew it was futile, and that knowledge prevented it from happening. You timeslid randomly with no real objective, just an uncontrolled and desperate longing.'

Pixie nodded slowly. 'I suppose that could be right.'

'You need to focus on what you want to achieve with the next slide and leave the Law of Attraction to fulfil it. Don't concern yourself with the how. That's not your job. If you try and manipulate the how, you'll just limit what the Law of Attraction can achieve. You don't know better, so leave it to a force that does.'

'So, how do I do it?'

'Do you have something of Cavill's – something to connect you to him? A photograph . . . a . . .'

Pixie's eyes lit up. 'I have his sketchbook of birds,' she said with a rush of excitement. 'I stole it from St Sidwell Manor.'

'That was so bad,' Ulysses muttered.

'Good!,' Avril exclaimed, ignoring Ulysses. 'When you next embark on a slide, hold the sketchbook and put out the desire of what you want to achieve. You want your relationship with him to reach its conclusion so that you can sever the link. You want the next slide to take you back to him so that you can resolve it. So that you can end it. If you focus hard enough, the power of your intention might draw to you a case that will enable you to fulfil that desire. Then, when you slide, link into the sketchbook as well as into whatever it is that links you to the case and leave the rest to the Universe.'

'But couldn't I just link into Cavill's sketchbook *without* having a case?'

'It's possible. But the past two slides where you've encountered Cavill have been linked to cases of altruism, haven't they? What you've set in motion with him might be tied to that energy. I would maintain it if I were you. Keep it consistent, otherwise you might slide back to before 1895, which would really complicate things.'

'I hadn't thought of that,' said Pixie.

'Listen, it's unchartered. We're both learning on the job, so to speak. There's no one who has done this before to whom we can go for advice. As far as I'm aware, you're the only modern-day timeslider out there. But energy and vibration are important. You have to stay within that flow and allow it to carry you forward. It's like a rip tide. You're in it. You have to stay in it. Otherwise, if you shift out of it, you'll lose the momentum and drift.'

'So, you're saying that my next slide might very well take me to the next chapter in Cavill's and my story?'

'I think every slide will, until you end it.' Avril narrowed her eyes, tuning into an intuition that had suddenly come. 'I sense your next slide will take you back to the southwest, possibly Cornwall.'

'To where it began,' said Pixie wistfully. She rubbed her hands together with nervous excitement. 'Very well. Rock on the next chapter.'

'Let's hope it's the *final* chapter,' said Avril firmly.

'Me too,' Ulysses agreed. 'It's like a pig on a spit that never cooks, going round and round and round.'

'Thanks for that, Ulysses,' said Pixie dryly.

They all laughed.

'I just want you to have a relationship that's satisfying and fulfilling, Pix,' Ulysses explained, looking at her fondly. 'And *real*,' he added with emphasis.

'Okay,' said Pixie, picking up her teacup. 'I will put out the intention and leave the Universe to do the rest.'

'Good,' said Avril. 'And let me know if it works. And Pixie . . .'

'Yes?'

'Don't get lost in your slides. Don't ever forget who you really are and what you're there to do. It's not a game. The consequences are serious. This time you have to end it. I can't tell you how to do it. You'll know what to do when you're in the moment. But you *must* end it.'

Pixie felt a stab to her heart. The word *end* was so final.

Chapter Three
Seacombe, Cornwall

There was a high wind the night Shakespeare's *Macbeth* opened at The Aphrodite Theatre in Seacombe. It raced around the sandstone walls of the sturdy Edwardian building, moaning like a demon, rattling the sash windows and agitating the twin towers that remained unmoved beneath their domed hats. Drizzle danced in the golden halos of the streetlamps and soaked the pavements as punters navigated their way around puddles in their hurry to reach the big wooden doors that opened promptly at six thirty.

Joseph Lightwater, the director, popped into the foyer to gauge the temperature and was delighted by the sight of so many people. In his mid-fifties, he was of average height and stockily built, with a slight paunch he was wont to pat after a hearty meal and a pint of beer in The Wily Fox. His greying hair was receding in the usual places and the deep lines on his brow exposed a tendency to worry, but his light blue eyes were bright with vigour and his full lips quick to smile. Trotsky-style spectacles and thick stubble gave him the intellectual air of a dedicated creative, and the brown corduroy jacket he wore over jeans and trainers had been patched at the elbows, for Joseph rarely spent money on himself, and certainly not on fashion. After a successful run of comedy, he'd been a little apprehensive about producing such a serious play, but it didn't seem to be putting anyone off. Neither was the weather. He'd been down on the beach that morning walking his dog, and the wind had almost blown them both away. The gale had picked up and by late afternoon the rollers that had come crashing onto the coast were the biggest he'd ever seen. However, he knew it wasn't simply the play that was drawing people to the theatre that stormy night, but the leading lady, Isadora Nash, who was an American film star of international fame. Still beautiful at forty, and apparently very much in demand, she had declared on a recent podcast that she wanted to go back to her roots and do a season of theatre. On hearing that, Joseph had immediately called her agent. The fact that his theatre was in a provincial town in Cornwall seemed to work to his advantage for the agent told him, earnestly, that Isadora didn't want the glamour of New York or London, but something gritty and authentic – he decided to take that as a compliment. There was, however, nothing gritty and authentic about Isadora Nash, but what did that matter when her name would fill the theatre night after night? Theatres, these days, struggled to make ends meet. To Joseph Lightwater, for whom the theatre was a lifelong passion, Isadora Nash felt like a gift from God.

The gift from God, Joseph soon discovered, was an exceedingly difficult woman. He had met many actresses in the thirty odd years he'd been in the business, and besides the occasional diva, most were charmingly eccentric. Isadora, unfortunately, was a toxic combination of insecurity and arrogance – nasty to women she classed as competition and haughty to those she deemed unimportant. She wafted around backstage with the entitlement of a multi-award-winning actor. The truth was that in spite of the many films she had starred in, she had never won a single accolade. That must have irked, Joseph reflected. He knew that people who felt they hadn't quite made it were always unhappy, and unhappy people were never nice. The likes of Meryl Streep and Dame Judi Dench were, apparently, delightful.

As he made his way backstage, he dismissed Isadora's tricky character as inconsequential. She was a good actor and would make a compelling Lady Macbeth, and that was all that mattered. The audience would love her, even if the company didn't.

Joseph loved the buzz of a theatre an hour or two before the curtain went up. He adored the heightened energy as the crew raced about doing the final checks on lighting and sound; the stage management team made sure that everything was in its place on stage, and in the wings at the ready for the various scene changes; wardrobe and make-up were busy attending the actors; and Madge, the octogenarian beverages manager, who had worked at The Aphrodite since she was a girl, moved slowly up and down the corridors pushing a trolley of tea, coffee and sandwiches which she made herself in the kitchen at the back.

Joseph savoured the unique smell: a mixture of historic carpet, paint, wood, stale perfume, dust burning on the hot lights and, embedded in the fabrics, cigarette smoke from the time when smoking was permitted inside. A theatre smelt like nowhere else, and it took him back to his am-dram days when, as a boy, he had started at the bottom at a small theatre in Exeter doing everything from sweeping and shifting furniture to assisting stage designers with a pot of paint and a big brush. He'd tried his hand at acting but had never been good enough to qualify for a leading role – or, indeed, any role. So, he'd worked his way up to the coveted position of assisting directors, quietly harbouring the dream of one day becoming a director himself. At last, at the ripe age of thirty-two, he'd put on his first play, Oscar Wilde's *The Importance of Being Earnest*, in the theatre in Exeter where he'd grown up. He'd befriended Rupert Everett while working on the set of *Another Country* eight years before and managed to persuade him to play the lead. Rupert, riding high on a heady wave of global acclaim, was both generous-spirited and shrewd. He'd waived his fee in exchange for a small percentage of the takings and guaranteed that the production was an enormous success. It had been a win-win for both of them. From that moment on, Joseph had produced and directed plays. He knew he never wanted to do anything else.

His big break came when Emma, his wife of fourteen years, had declared that she wanted to move to Seacombe for the sake of their two children who she believed would benefit from provincial life and sea air. Joseph, whose work took him to theatres all over the country, wasn't keen at first to move out of their comfortable townhouse in Exeter where his roots had been laid down since childhood. But on the day Emma dragged him to visit possible homes in Seacombe, he had just happened to be having a pint in the local pub while Emma nipped into the chemist, when he'd noticed an elderly woman at the table behind him. Initially, she drew his eye because of her charisma – she was like an old lighthouse whose beacon still shines brightly and is impossible to ignore. Then the emphatic way she moved her hands combined with the rich timbre of her voice had further piqued his interest. He just knew she had trod the boards. He cocked an ear and listened. It wasn't long before he was proved right. 'I'm going to sell the theatre,' she said with a dramatic sigh typical of someone for whom small gestures exaggerated on stage had become second nature. 'I've run out of steam and the place just loses me money. I'm going to retire to my house by the sea and ruminate on the good old days.'

Joseph had swung round and introduced himself. With his genial smile and boy-next-door good looks, he was the sort of man people found approachable and immediately likeable. The woman's beady chestnut eyes had lit up and she'd taken him in with interest. 'Leila Frost,' she had said in a gravelly voice, and put out a hand. Her long nails were scarlet to match her lips, her hair an unruly mop of greying brown curls. When she smiled there was an echo of mischief in it, and Joseph guessed she must have once been a formidable flirt. Her companion was a plain, scrawny woman with platinum blonde hair pulled into a tight bun and sharp blue eyes who, at sixty-five, still edited the local newspaper. Infected by his charm and vitality, they had invited him to join their table. He'd accepted enthusiastically, pulled up a chair and ordered himself another beer and a couple of glasses of Pinot Grigio for the ladies. By the time Emma returned with her paracetamol Joseph had accepted Leila's challenge to revive her theatre. His first play would be his lucky play, *The Importance of being Earnest,* only without Rupert as the lead. By then Rupert had moved on to bigger and better things.

Twelve years later Joseph was still there.

Joseph knocked on the wooden door, distinguishable from all other doors by the illustrious name emblazoned in big black letters on the brass nameplate: Edward Rye, aka Macbeth. 'Come in, my dear Joseph,' came a booming voice in crisply articulated Received Pronunciation.

'Hi,' said Joseph, poking his face around the door.

'Come in, come in,' Edward exclaimed heartily. He was made up and ready to go on stage. His face with its large, bulbous nose, assertive chin and hooded grey eyes was mud-spattered, his clothes those of a medieval soldier. He had grown his beard especially for the part, and it was clipped and shaped to look suitably regal. In one hand he held a can of Coca-Cola, in the other *Citizens* by Simon Schama; both looked incongruous against his eleventh-century garb. He put the book down on the dressing table cluttered with the grubby script, his mobile telephone and various pots, tubes and cotton wool balls, and looked at Joseph with the invigorated gaze of a man who comes alive in front of an audience, *any* audience. 'What bringeth you to my door, my good man?' he asked in the voice of Macbeth. 'Sit down, sit down, my dear fellow.'

'I just wanted to wish you luck,' said Joseph, taking the chair in the corner of the dressing room and crossing one leg over the other, revealing a stripy Paul Smith sock in red, yellow and green. 'Not that a seasoned actor like you needs luck,' he added, for Edward was a veteran of the stage.

'I just need my dear beloved wife to do what she is paid to do and play her part,' he said. Then becoming Edward again, he added in an accent closer to Estuary English, 'She's a bloody nightmare. Remind me never to work with her again!'

Joseph laughed uneasily. He wanted to say that thanks to Isadora the theatre would be full for the entire run, but knowing Edward to be sensitive, he said instead, 'The two of you are a formidable team. You might not like her very much *off* stage, but the chemistry *on* stage is insane.'

'That might be true, but really, rehearsals have been a trial for all of us, but mostly for me.'

And me, Joseph wanted to add. In fact, when it came to Isadora's demands, ninety-nine per cent of them were directed at *him*. 'Look, you're a professional and you're doing a great job. I appreciate it. The play is going to be great. This is the best cast I've ever worked with.' Which wasn't true, but Joseph wasn't in the business of telling the truth when the success of the production depended on the odd white lie. 'Isadora will calm down once she gets into it. The first night is always tense.'

'Well, she could do with a bloody reality check. We're not so impressed with her here.'

'I know, but a lot of people out there are, and they're buying tickets.'

Edward took a swig of Coke, swallowed, then burped unselfconsciously. 'She thinks she's going to earn brownie points in Hollywood by working in a provincial English theatre for peanuts.' He grunted with disdain. 'Good luck to her, I say.' He chortled bitterly. 'If she really wants to earn respect she should be more professional backstage and less of an arse.'

Joseph looked at his watch. It was seven fifteen. He got up. 'I'll go and check on her,' he said.

'Into the lioness's den,' said Edward with a snigger, picking up his book.

'You just concentrate on what you're doing and leave her to me. Leila will be in the front row.'

'Lovely Leila,' Edward gushed. 'Now that's a classy dame, if I ever saw one. Give me ten Leilas for one Isadora.'

'Break a leg,' said Joseph.

Joseph closed the door and took a breath. It wasn't good that everyone was already losing patience with the leading lady. They'd just have to bite their tongues and be professional because Isadora wasn't going anywhere. In fact, the idea of her walking out was a nightmare he couldn't bear to contemplate. People had booked their tickets way in advance just to see her, and it was a sell-out. She might not have won the respect of her colleagues, but she was incredibly popular with people who knew her only from a distance. To them, her diva-ish antics, which were regularly reported in the press, just made them all the more curious to watch her perform.

Isadora's dressing room was a few doors down from Edward's, and the largest and most comfortable in the building, naturally.

Joseph gathered himself for a second before knocking, his fist poised in front of the brass name plate. Isadora's whims and complaints were only half the problem, it was the sugary way she expressed them that grated the most, because it was so insincere. It was a challenge not to let his impatience show. He took a deep breath and knocked.

A moment later Isadora's long-suffering assistant, Lezli, opened the door and her elfin face appeared pale and gaunt in the gap. On seeing Joseph, she turned her head and informed her boss. 'It's only Joey,' she said in her Chicago drawl. That also grated; no one called him Joey.

'Joey, come on in, sweetie,' came Isadora's treacle voice. 'I need some love. I'm feeling like a Christian at the Colosseum.' If that were the case, Joseph would feel sorry for the lion.

He stepped into the room. He was hit by the powdery smell of Isadora's perfume and the cloying scent of Elnett that Joanne, the make-up girl, was generously spraying onto her hair in a sticky mist. Isadora was resplendent in a green velvet dress, sitting at her dressing table in front of a mirror framed with bright round light bulbs. The dressing table was cluttered with bottles of make-up and brushes, a half-eaten box of pastel-coloured macaroons from Ladurée in London, and an empty crystal champagne flute. Extravagant bouquets of flowers, still in brown paper and cellophane and tied with silk ribbon, had been placed in glass vases around the room. 'All good?' he asked hopefully.

Isadora looked at him through the mirror and wrung her hands. Even caked in stage make-up she looked beautiful with her high cheekbones and beguiling kitten eyes. 'I'm so nervous,' she said, hunching her thin shoulders and giving a little shiver like a greyhound in the starting block. Joseph was used to this act. Playing the ingenue, while sucking the energy out of everyone like a vampire.

'You're going to be great,' he gushed, indulging her need for constant reassurance.

'Yes, you are, sweetie,' Lezli agreed in the effortless manner of a professional fawner. 'You're made for this part.'

'It's a full house,' said Joseph. 'The theatre is packed!'

'They've all come for you,' Lezli added.

'Have they?' Isadora's moonstone green eyes widened with disingenuous self-doubt. 'The press too?' Her scarlet lips extended into a tremulous smile as she stared wistfully at her reflection, as if seeking confirmation that she was still beautiful. More beautiful, at least, than the three younger women who were taking the parts of the witches. She put her fingers to her cheek and narrowed her eyes. 'Oh, my Lord, I hope the press are kind. I haven't been on stage since I was a girl. It's daunting, you know. I forgot how daunting it is. I feel judged already.'

'The press will love you,' said Joseph, glancing at his watch.

'Joanne, do I need a touch more blush, do you think?' she asked.

Joanne stood back and appraised her face with a critical air. 'I don't think so,' she replied.

'I do,' said Isadora, her voice hardening. 'Touch it up a little. I don't want to look like a corpse.'

'You could never look like a corpse,' gushed Lezli, on cue.

Joanne reached for the blush and brush. 'Okay, just a little,' she said as Isadora tilted her face expectantly.

'I'd better go,' said Joseph, making for the door. 'Break a leg, Isadora,' he added.

'Thanks, Joey, darling,' she replied in her little girl voice. As he left the room he heard her practising her lines in a flawless English accent. '*Come you spirits that tend on mortal thoughts . . . Come to my woman's breasts . . . Come, thick night, and pall thee in the dunnest smoke of hell.*' She might be a pain to deal with, he thought, but she sure could act.

Joseph made his way swiftly to the back of the auditorium. The place was crammed. The air thick with body heat and perfume, and the low murmur of idle chatter. His wife Emma was in the stalls somewhere. She'd come with Leila. After weeks of listening to her husband complaining about his leading lady, Emma was curious to see whether hiring her had been worth all the stress. Joseph hadn't shared his grievances with Leila. He didn't want to worry her. As far as she was concerned, everything was running smoothly, and he was doing a tremendous job.

He settled into his seat in the back row, gratified by the sight of so many people. At last, the lights went down, the voices hushed, and the red velvet curtains lifted to reveal a dark, foggy stage. This was one of the moments Joseph loved the most. That brief pause before the action starts, when the audience holds its breath, not knowing what it's going to see. In this case, three ghostly faces illuminated suddenly in an eerie blueish glow, to the unsettling sound of dissonant music. The witches. The three young women who had been on the receiving end of Isadora's sharp tongue. Joseph had had quite a trial pacifying them each time Isadora, in her sweet, girlish voice, insulted them. Isadora knew exactly how to wound, and exactly how to act the victim when accused of being a bitch. She was a master at turning the tables with wide-eyed innocence and claiming ignorance of so shrewdly calculated strikes. Joseph pushed those thoughts aside and concentrated on the play. It didn't matter what politics seethed behind the scenes. It only mattered what happened on stage.

The audience fell into rapt silence. The witches were mesmeric. Cawing, crying, moaning. Even Joseph couldn't take his eyes off them. Their hair was wild, their eyes black and feral, their movements in their white robes fluid and other-worldly. He felt his spirits soar. This was brilliant. They were beautiful and terrifying.

When Macbeth strode onto the stage, he did so with the self-assurance and charisma of a seasoned actor, and Joseph was pleased he'd managed to book Edward Rye who had trained with the Royal Shakespeare Company. He was, without doubt, one of the most professional stage actors he'd worked with. '*So foul and fair a day I have not seen . . .*' His voice had a deep resonance and the kind of gravitas that inspired confidence. Joseph was pleased.

The moment the witches vanished, there was an audible gasp from the audience. Joseph chuckled quietly to himself; he had a clever lighting technician, too. However, the loudest gasp was reserved for Isadora Nash, who, delighted and thrilled to have caused such a positive reaction, visibly grew an inch. She lifted her prettily pointed chin, straightened her elegant shoulders, narrowed her feline eyes and basked in the radiance of the spotlight, which loved her as much as she loved it. In her white hands she held Macbeth's letter. She took a breath, then her scarlet lips parted, and she spoke. Her voice was no longer the sweet, girlish voice of Isadora Nash, but the strong, steely voice of Lady Macbeth. Joseph nodded, acknowledging his brave and clearly brilliant idea of casting her.

It was at that moment, as she began her first soliloquy, that the chair behind her began to move.

It caught Joseph's eye immediately. He sat up in alarm. It *definitely* moved. Not far. It couldn't have been more than a foot, but it definitely moved. He frowned and blinked a few times. It was now perfectly still. Perhaps he had imagined it. Then he wondered whether it was a prank. One of the witches, insulted by Isadora, exacting a subtle revenge. Isadora continued to recite her lines, oblivious. Joseph slid his eyes around the audience, but no one else seemed to have noticed. He sighed with relief and sat back in his seat. He realised he was sweating and wiped his brow with his hand. Ridiculous. It must have been a trick of the light. He focused his attention on Isadora again and forgot about the chair.

'Glamis thou art, and Cawdor; and shalt be What thou art promised: yet do I fear thy nature; It is too full o' the milk of human kindness . . .' Isadora was a captivating Lady Macbeth, Joseph reflected. She was really getting into her stride. He was beginning to relax too, allowing himself to be drawn into the drama unfolding on stage, when the chair moved again.

This time it made a scraping sound, which could not be ignored, and traversed more than a foot. Maybe even four. A rumble of confusion rippled through the auditorium. The whispering sound of muttering rose into the air which had suddenly begun to feel strangely cold. Isadora faltered, gathered herself, and continued. From where she was standing she had no view of the moving chair. Furious, suddenly, that someone was clearly playing a prank, Joseph hurried out the exit and raced backstage, his fury escalating fast.

'What the devil is going on?' he hissed to the stage manager and cast members hovering in the wing. By the way they had gathered there in a huddle, he knew they'd seen the chair move as well.

'I swear it moved by itself,' Toby, the stage manager, whispered. He was holding a clipboard and wearing a headset over his floppy blond hair.

'Chairs don't move by themselves,' Joseph snapped. 'Where are the witches?'

'In their dressing room,' Toby replied, turning his attention back to the stage. He suddenly took a sharp intake of breath.

Isadora cried out.

The audience gasped. Joseph looked onto the stage in time to see the letter she'd been holding flying into the air and then floating slowly towards the floor like a falling leaf. 'What the hell . . . ?' he began.

'*That* moved by itself,' said Toby in wonder, his face blanching to a shocked white. 'No doubt about it!'

Isadora glanced desperately into the wing. Joseph made a rapid gesture with his hand to encourage her to carry on. She blinked a few times, took a shallow breath, and continued. But she was no longer in her stride and the rigid voice she'd adopted wilted into her little girl whimper.

It was a disaster.

The act limped on. But all eyes were on the chair, in anticipation of it moving again.

Joseph hurried to the witches' dressing room. He entered without knocking to find them sprawled over the sofa and chairs, gossiping. They obviously had no clue as to what had just happened on stage. But Joseph was sure, nonetheless, that they had something to do with it. 'Which one of you is responsible for the moving chair?' he demanded, looking sharply at each witch in turn. He suspected, however, Witch One, because she was Isadora's understudy and therefore had the most obvious motive. 'And the letter,' he went on. 'It just flew out of Isadora's hand . . .' The trio stared at him in bewilderment.

'What?' Witch One crinkled her nose. 'I don't know what you're talking about.'

Joseph looked from Witch Two to Witch Three. 'Well? Chairs

don't move on their own and pieces of paper don't just fly out of people's hands!'

'What?' Witch One repeated. She stood up in agitation. 'Are you saying someone whipped the letter out of Isadora's hand?'

'And a chair moved on its own?' Witch Three interjected.

Joseph didn't know what to make of them. By their reactions it was pretty clear that this was the first they'd heard about it – but then acting was what they were good at. 'Yes, it's obviously a prank. I thought it might be you.'

Witch One giggled, then bit her lip. 'Poor Isadora,' she said sarcastically.

'I wish I'd thought of that,' said Witch Three. 'Brilliant.'

'It's not funny!' Joseph barked. His whole body was cramping with panic. He inhaled through his nostrils like a bull. He pointed a finger at them in turn. 'If I find out that any of you . . .' He gave Witch One the sharpest stare.

'Look,' said Witch One seriously. 'We're playing the parts of witches, we're not *really* witches. How are we supposed to move a chair and do whatever was done to a piece of paper, from *here*?'

'It flew out of her hand,' Joseph corrected.

'As if by magic,' said Witch Two, then her face softened. 'Sorry, Joey, wasn't us.'

'And don't call me Joey!' he snapped.

He stormed out and returned to the wing, his heart in his mouth. It was Act I scene 7 and Edward was back on stage, with Isadora, and the audience was silent once more, and engrossed. Edward, with his magnetism, had managed to raise the tone. He had raised Isadora too, restoring her to the formidable Lady Macbeth. But Joseph couldn't relax. He stood in the wing, arms folded, eyes darting about the stage, expecting the worst.

But the worst didn't happen.

During the interval the cast and crew gathered behind the curtain. Normally, the conversation would have been about their performances and any tweaks that needed to be made. But this time no one could talk about anything but the moving chair – of which Isadora had been ignorant – and the flying piece of paper, which she simply couldn't explain. The atmosphere was tense. Each member of the company glanced shiftily from one to the other. No one was above suspicion. The air was unusually cold on the stage, as if someone had opened the door of a giant fridge, and Isadora folded her arms and shivered. 'Someone tried to sabotage my scene!' she exclaimed tearfully, bottom lip trembling. 'There's no other explanation. Nothing happened in anyone else's scene. Why in mine?'

'How could someone make a chair move?' asked Clare, one of the stagehands. She lifted it up and looked at it closely. 'It doesn't make sense. But I saw it with my own eyes.'

'We *all* saw it,' said Toby gravely. 'Well, everyone except Isadora,' he added, glancing at her anxiously, anticipating a meltdown.

'What are the press going to say?' Isadora wailed. She turned to Joseph, eyes flashing suddenly like those of a feral cat. 'You fix this, Joey, and you fix it good!'

'I'll fix it, don't worry,' he said, knowing the best way to deal with an angry Isadora was with a gentle touch. 'You go out there and be the best Lady Macbeth that's ever been, and the press will rave about you. The moving chair and flying letter were nothing to do with you. I'll find out who did it and have their bloody guts for garters!'

Isadora turned on the witches. 'I know who it was, and it wasn't funny. You English have a strange sense of humour. This is my career on the line. If you do it again, I'll do more than have your guts for garters, I'll fucking ruin every one of you so you never work again!'

Chapter Four

'There are always mishaps in the theatre,' said Leila when she and Emma met Joseph backstage after the play had finished. Isadora had flounced off in a huff in spite of the standing ovation she had received from an ecstatic audience. Edward had gone for a drink in The Wily Fox with the witches, most likely to bitch about Isadora, and only members of the crew remained, clearing up and preparing for the following day.

'I didn't notice the chair,' said Emma, ever the tactful wife. 'And I'm sure many people thought the flying letter was something to do with the witches.'

Joseph sighed. 'Everyone knows *Macbeth*, darling,' he said.

She put a hand on his arm. 'A silly prank then. But it didn't ruin the play. Everyone loved it. It was brilliant.'

'Yes, Joseph, it *was* brilliant,' Leila echoed enthusiastically, pulling her faux fox-fur coat tighter about her body. The place still felt cold. 'I must say, Edward was superb,' she continued. 'As for Isadora Nash, after a momentary wobble, she was back on the horse and flying over the jumps. A true professional.'

'It won't happen again,' said Joseph resolutely. 'I think I've made that clear to the cast. Whoever did it won't dare repeat it.'

Leila pulled a face that revealed she knew more than she let on. 'You don't want to make enemies in theatreland,' she said quietly. 'If I were Isadora, I'd be a little more considerate of my co-actors.'

Joseph looked at his wife. Emma shrugged; *she* hadn't said anything. Leila grinned shrewdly. 'I've been in this business long enough to sniff a situation when its brewing. I'm like a bloodhound.' She tapped the side of her nose with a red talon.

'Well, let's just say she's taken a bit of settling in,' said Joseph cagily.

'And this won't help,' Emma added. 'Poor you, darling. Still, you got a standing ovation, and everyone went home happy.'

'Except Isadora,' said Leila, arching a thin eyebrow.

'Tomorrow is another day,' said Joseph optimistically.

The following morning Joseph was thrilled to see the number of positive reviews both online and in the local newspaper. There were various mentions of the flying letter, but most assumed it was witchcraft: '*those devious and beautiful witches*'. One person on Twitter suggested it was a ghost, calling it the '*phantom of the theatre*'. Isadora was described as '*compelling*', '*mesmerising*', '*deliciously evil*', and Edward as '*an old hand*' and '*magnetic*'. Joseph walked his yellow labrador up the beach with a spring in his step. The sky had been washed to a sparkling blue and beneath it the sea was calm. The waves broke onto the sand in reams of gentle foam, and seagulls squabbled benignly over small creatures left behind by the tide. Joseph felt good. All would be well. He threw the rubber ball for his dog and watched him scamper after it, scattering sand and seagulls into the air.

That afternoon the cast arrived as normal, but there was a distinctive froideur backstage. Isadora flounced into her dressing room, barked at Lezli, shouted at Joanne, and scolded Madge for serving up cold coffee and dry cake. Madge left the room in tears, while Lezli, who was used to Isadora's outbursts, tried to smooth it over with Joanne and made a mental note to give Madge a bunch of flowers from Isadora as an apology – if she took a dollar for every reconciliatory gesture she'd made on behalf of her boss, she'd be a very wealthy woman.

Isadora, despite the good reviews, was anxious about tonight's performance. 'If they play around again, I'll fucking kill them,' she growled to anyone who was listening.

Edward called Joseph to his dressing room. 'My dear Joseph, the witches are as blameless as lambs,' he said, owning his big chair like a king on his throne while the make-up artist applied thick foundation to his face with a sponge.

Joseph hovered in the doorway. 'It could be anyone really, couldn't it?' he said, putting his hands in his pockets. 'Isadora hasn't made an effort to win friends around here.'

'They've made their point. I think they'll leave her alone now,' said Edward.

Joseph nodded. 'Well, I'm staying backstage tonight, and everyone is going to be vigilant. They'll be very stupid to try it a second time.'

Once again, the theatre was full to capacity. Emma and Leila returned out of curiosity. Leila had brought her theatre glasses to better watch the stage for skulduggery. 'If anything untoward happens tonight,' she said with a grin, 'I won't miss it.'

'I can't imagine anyone's going to do anything foolish a second time. The whole cast and crew will be watching,' said Emma, who was always ready to see the bright side of a situation. 'Love or loathe her, Isadora is certainly drawing a crowd.'

'That genius husband of yours,' said Leila happily. 'The best thing I ever did was go to the pub that night.'

Emma laughed. 'I think it was the best thing *he* ever did as well,' she laughed. 'You and he were destined to meet. You're the perfect team.'

'There is no such thing as chance,' said Leila. '"*It is not in the stars to hold our destiny but in ourselves.*" So sayeth the great bard.'

When the curtain went up, the bewitchingly lovely faces of the three 'Wayward Sisters' were illuminated like ghosts in fog. The auditorium went quiet as the chilling, discordant music filled the theatre once again. Emma pulled her shawl about her shoulders; the fake fog was freezing. When Isadora made her first appearance, Leila put her glasses to her eyes and watched the stage closely.

Joseph stood in the wings with Toby. His heartrate had gone up and he felt his insides clench with apprehension. The witches had gathered in the wings on the opposite side of the stage with other cast members. Everyone trained their attention on the chair and the letter. Only Edward remained in his dressing room; he was certain the events of the night before were not going to be repeated.

Isadora was in character. She owned the stage, and the role. She was Lady Macbeth, with all the evil vitality of a scheming conspirator. Her voice was steady, her movements confident. She betrayed nothing of the inner turmoil that raged beneath the surface. It was as if she was daring the perpetrators of the prank to try it on a second time, only so that she could disregard them.

Just as she was reaching the pinnacle of her soliloquy the chair moved.

Leila's mouth fell open. She gasped. 'Bloody hell!'

Emma leaned forward in her seat and blinked to check that she wasn't hallucinating. Joseph was furious. How could this be happening a second time? The chair didn't just move but slid a good five feet across the stage. It was a deliberate sabotage of Isadora's first scene. A calculated disruption.

But Isadora, as before, didn't notice and carried on. '*Thou wouldst be great, Art not without ambition, but without The illness should attend it.*'

With those words, so skilfully articulated, the letter was snatched by an invisible hand and carried high into the air. Isadora caught her breath and watched it helplessly as it flew out of her reach. Then, as it began to float slowly down, rocking from side to side like a feather on the breeze, she lunged for it and grabbed it with the furious determination of a beleaguered actor to reclaim the scene. The audience erupted into wild applause.

Encouraged by the rousing sound of clapping, she valiantly carried on. Defiant this time. Her voice harder than ever.

Emma shivered. Leila was so transfixed by what she was witnessing that she didn't notice the cold. But Isadora did and she shivered too. '*The King comes here tonight,*' said the Messenger, distracting the audience from the chaotic props that seemed to have a life of their own.

But whoever was playing tricks was not yet finished. '*Nor heaven peep through the blanket of the dark,*' said Isadora in a stirring voice.

Then the lights went out. The theatre was plunged into darkness so black, only the neon glow of the red exit signs could be seen. Murmurs of panic rose up from the stalls.

'Shit!' Emma exclaimed.

Leila lowered her glasses and looked around. 'What the hell is going on?' she muttered, unamused now.

Joseph sprang into action, giving orders as calmly as he could, trying to keep everyone from panicking. On his instructions, Toby made a hurried announcement over the loudspeaker, telling the audience to remain in their seats, informing them that it was merely a technical hitch and that the play would be up and running very soon. But some feared it was a terrorist attack and left the theatre at a run.

It must have only been a few minutes before the lights went on again, but it felt like ten. The audience clapped once more and Isadora, who was now red-faced with fury, was persuaded to go back on stage, at which point the audience got to their feet and clapped even louder. She soaked up the support, raising her hands as if playing the part of Evita on the balcony of the Casa Rosada.

Then the chair didn't just move but was lifted into the air by an invisible force and dropped onto the stage with a loud crash. The audience was stunned into silence. The clapping stopped. The cold had now spread into every corner of the theatre so that it wasn't just Emma who was pulling her shawl about her, but other members of the public too. Even Leila shrank into her fox fur. A feeling of fear spread through the crowd like a virus, infecting them one by one. The muttering turned into exclamations of fear.

Isadora hurried into the wings. The curtain came down. By now people were getting up and flooding the aisles. Joseph strode onto the stage. 'I'm very sorry, but we're going to have to take a short break while we sort out a few technical issues,' he shouted, but no one was listening. They were making for the doors. There was nothing for it. He withdrew backstage and reluctantly told Toby to instruct the front of house to refund tickets to those who didn't want to stay.

No one wanted to stay.

It was an absolute catastrophe.

Behind the curtain the stagehands were clearing up the broken chair in bewilderment.

'I tell you, something strange is in this theatre,' Isadora exclaimed tearfully. 'The letter just flew out of my hand as if someone grabbed it. There was no string attached to it. Nothing.'

'And the chair,' said Witch One. 'That wasn't special effects.' Witch Two and Witch Three nodded in agreement.

Nigel, the lighting technician, claimed to have touched nothing. 'I didn't turn them off and I didn't turn them back on,' he said firmly, scratching his curly head with a pudgy hand. 'It happened all by itself.'

'It's a ghost,' came a quiet voice. There was something about the soft Irish accent that made them all to go quiet. They turned to see Madge, diminutive in a pale yellow overall and tortoiseshell-framed spectacles, walking slowly onto the stage. 'Can you not feel the cold?' She rubbed her small hands as if to demonstrate.

Joseph put his hands on his hips and shook his head. 'Now Madge . . .' he began. He had heard the old lady speak of the theatre ghost before and had laughed it off. But it wasn't funny now. He didn't want her spooking the cast. 'Every old building is supposedly full of ghosts,' he added. 'But I can assure you there are no such things.'

Madge ignored him. 'They always drop the temperature when they come,' she said, her voice low and steady. 'Did you not see the way the chair moved? That's not easy for them to do, them being so fine and the chair being so dense. They find the lights easier to manipulate because they themselves are made of electromagnetic energy.' She looked at Isadora and narrowed her pale blue eyes. 'It's *you* they want to scare,' she said darkly.

Isadora's face twisted into an indignant knot. 'What the . . . ?'

'Oh yes, they made that very clear, did they not?' Madge went on.

'What are you talking about?' Isadora retorted, looking at Joseph for support.

Madge lifted her chin. 'Sure, the letter was snatched right out of your hand, was it not? And the chair, well, when the audience clapped for you, the ghost was having none of it. I'm afraid the ghost wants to scare you, and it's doing a fine job of it.'

Isadora folded her arms defensively. 'Look, are you getting back at me for complaining about the coffee? Is it *you* who's playing tricks on me?'

'Now, look here, Isadora . . .' Edward cut in.

Madge chuckled. 'You wish it were me, Miss Nash. I'm easily dealt with. But no, I couldn't perform such feats of superhuman power, even if I wanted to. Only something supernatural could do that.'

'Come on,' Joseph interrupted with an uneasy laugh. 'I don't think any of us truly believes there to be a ghost.'

'I do,' came a voice he recognised from the back. It was Emma. Everyone turned to look at her. She curled a tendril of brown hair behind her ear and smiled apologetically. 'I'm sorry, darling, but I agree with Madge. It's the only explanation.'

'But you don't think it has anything to do with *me*?' said Isadora indignantly.

'I don't know,' Emma replied, shaking her head. 'But I don't think anyone here is responsible for lifting a chair off the ground and . . .'

'I've heard many accounts of people seeing ghosts over the years, but I've never seen one myself,' interrupted Leila, who was standing at the back with Emma. 'When it comes to the paranormal, I like to keep an open mind. I agree with Madge, however. There is no other explanation, unless the special effects team have pulled off something extraordinary.'

'We don't have a special effects team,' said Joseph flatly, feeling undermined. 'Just lighting and sound.'

'It's not me,' said Nigel, for the second time. He put up his hands as if in front of a gunman. 'Not guilty!'

'Really!' Joseph exclaimed impatiently. 'We've never had a whiff of a haunting in all the years I've worked here, so why would this ghost suddenly come out and sabotage Isadora's performance now?

Can't you see how ridiculous that sounds? People who believe in ghosts are simply using something otherworldly to explain something inexplicable.'

Madge shrugged. 'I've seen her many times and sensed her presence about the place, but why would I want to scare people? I keep those things to myself. But why she's chosen to create mischief now is a mystery. However, I can tell you that monkey business on stage was not done with human hands.'

Isadora turned on Joseph. 'What are you going to do about it, Joseph?' He noticed he was no longer Joey. 'You gotta sort it out, and fast, or I'm walking.' She glared at the witches and shook her head. 'I know it has something to do with you three. I can feel it in my gut.'

Witch One glared back at her. 'You know what, Isadora, every one of us here has reason to be pissed off with you, but none of us has the capability to lift a chair off the stage, cut the lights and snatch a letter right out of your hand while we're nowhere near you. It's not possible. So keep your stupid accusations to yourself. We had nothing to do with any of it.' She turned to Madge who was standing quietly with her hands in the big pocket of her overall. 'Madge is right. There's a ghost in here and it's pissed off with you, too, and I don't blame it!'

Joseph put up his hands. 'Now everyone calm down,' he said, sensing the situation spinning out of control.

Isadora pursed her lips and inhaled sharply through her nostrils. 'I'm not going to stand here being insulted!' she snapped. 'Sort it out, Joseph, or I'm not coming back.' With that she stalked off the stage.

Leila walked up to Joseph and patted him on the arm in a motherly fashion. 'She'll come back,' she said reassuringly. 'She's behaving exactly as one would expect an actor of her kind to behave. But something needs to be done.' She turned to Madge. 'You seem to know a lot about ghosts. What should we do?'

Madge nodded knowingly. 'Sure, I know a fair bit. I grew up with ghosts and the like. There are plenty of them around if you have the ability to see them. Poor lost souls, they are. You need to get a medium to come and move it on.'

Joseph sighed in exasperation. This was farcical. There simply wasn't a ghost in the theatre. Ghosts didn't exist. But he realised by the fearful faces of the company that doing nothing wasn't an option. At least, he had to appear willing to do whatever was necessary. 'A medium?' he repeated in a weary but resigned tone of voice. 'And where do I find such a person? Google?'

Madge laughed, not unkindly. 'Oh, no, Joseph. You need the real McCoy, not some charlatan out to make a quick buck. I have a friend in St Sidwell who told me of a haunting at the big house there a short while ago. They sorted it out good enough. A young woman with pink hair came down from London. They found her through the College of Psychic Studies. You know the place. Arthur Conan Doyle himself was president of the college in the twenties, so I'm told.'

'The author?' said Emma. Madge nodded.

'I think I'd rather call in Sherlock Holmes,' said Joseph wryly.

'No, no, this is a case for a spiritualist, not a detective,' said Madge seriously. 'You need someone who knows about the paranormal. This is no criminal, Joseph. This is a ghost.' She rolled her eyes about the stage. 'And it's still here. Can you not feel it in the chill?'

All eyes followed hers, but besides the unusually cold temperature, no one sensed anything out of the ordinary.

'Very well. I'll get on to it,' said Joseph grudgingly. 'I'll call the college first thing in the morning.'

'What do we do about tomorrow night?' asked Witch One. She grinned raffishly. 'If Isadora's gone off in a huff, well . . .'

'The show goes on,' said Joseph abruptly. 'If she doesn't come back tomorrow, you're on, Rebecca, and you, Samantha,' he said, turning to one of the other actors, 'will be Witch One, so be prepared.'

Rebecca nodded eagerly. 'Let's hope the ghost doesn't have a problem with *me*, then,' she said, and shivered not with cold, but excitement. As Isadora's understudy, her moment had come.

'What a bloody nightmare,' said Joseph once he was home alone with Emma. 'Do you really believe it's a ghost?' He poured two large glasses of wine and then went and plonked himself down at the kitchen table

'Well, you're right about every old building having a story of a resident ghost,' she replied. 'People love tales of hauntings. But if it's not a ghost, how do you explain it all? The chair, the letter, the lights?' She leaned back against the sideboard and took a sip. 'I've heard Madge mention the theatre ghost, we all have, but beyond the occasional sightings, there's never been anything physical. I'm not sure why the ghost would choose to make mischief now. I mean, to actually disturb a scene is quite radical.'

'Which is why it's not a haunting,' said Joseph, hoping his wife was beginning to see sense. 'Even if there was a ghost lurking about in the shadows, it wouldn't suddenly, after decades of lying low, come out of the shadows and throw a chair into the air. Come on, darling, surely you can see the logic of that!'

Emma cocked her head as she considered his argument. 'You do have a point,' she conceded slowly. 'But it doesn't matter what you believe, you still have to be seen to be dealing with it or you'll lose the trust of the company.'

'Do I really have to call in a medium?' Joseph asked. 'It's just ridiculous.'

'Call the pink-haired woman as Madge suggested. You've got nothing to lose.'

'My reputation,' he said with a wan smile.

'Don't be silly. No one cares. You're expected to be a little mad in the theatre!'

He laughed with her. 'I didn't think it would be this complicated hiring a Hollywood star.'

'It shouldn't be, but Isadora is temperamental, for sure.'

'She's a good actress though.'

'She's not a nice person, darling,' said Emma sensibly. 'She's created a horrid atmosphere at the theatre, and no one likes her.'

'She's bringing in the punters,' he argued.

'If the actors are good enough, word of mouth will bring them in.'

'I wish that were all it took.'

'Do you really think Isadora will pull out of tomorrow's performance?' Emma asked, rather hoping she would. She was curious to see whether the strange occurrences on stage would happen with the understudy. Did the 'ghost' have a problem with Isadora as Madge had suggested?

'No, she'll flounce on stage at the last minute after having made us all sweat. I guarantee it.'

Emma grinned over the rim of her glass. 'You've got the measure of her then.'

'I have,' he said with a shrug. 'She's a diva. It's expected.'

'Or she'll let Rebecca take the part and see if the weirdness happens when *she's* on stage. If it doesn't, she'll accuse Rebecca of deliberately sabotaging her performance in order to get the chance to play Lady Macbeth. We don't want Isadora slagging off the company in the press.'

Joseph shook his head in despair. 'Oh God,' he groaned. 'What the hell have I got myself into?'

That night Joseph couldn't sleep. What had begun as a triumphant first night had collapsed into disaster. He went out into the garden in his dressing gown and slippers and gazed on to the moonlit harbour that shimmered in the horseshoe bay beneath him. The sky was a rich indigo blue, twinkling with stars. The black water beneath it glittered prettily. Sailing boats slept peacefully in their berths, their masts lit up resembling spindle sticks. A gentle breeze carried on its breath the salty smell of brine and heather. Joseph inhaled deeply. He had grown to love that smell. He bent down and patted his dog, who sat to heel. 'You have a nice life, Benny,' he murmured fondly. 'Nothing to stress you out, is there? As long as you have food and walks and affection, you're all right. Why is life so complicated for us humans? I should never have hired Isadora. What a bloody mistake that was. Rebecca's a better actor if I'm honest. What was I thinking?' Benny gazed up at him adoringly, which made Joseph feel a little better.

But he *knew* what he was thinking. It was getting harder to fill the theatre, what with the increasing popularity of streaming television channels such as Netflix and Amazon. He'd thought that a famous Hollywood star would attract a new audience, a younger audience, and he hadn't been wrong; Isadora Nash was certainly famous. However, no one had told him how difficult she was to work with. If he'd known, he wouldn't have risked it.

As for ghosts. He rolled his eyes and sighed loudly. 'What bloody next?' he muttered out loud in exasperation. He looked down at Benny. 'Will the witches fly off on their broomsticks?' He laughed and Benny got to his paws and wagged his tail. 'You like the sound of that, do you? Well, I'm going to look a right idiot when I call the College of Psychic Studies tomorrow and hire a medium. A pink-haired medium to boot! What will you think of that?' Benny, assuming by the tone of his master's voice that he was going to be taken on a midnight walk, began to bounce about excitedly. 'All right,' said Joseph, thrusting his hands into his pockets and setting off towards the path that wound its way from the bottom of the garden to the beach below. 'A midnight walk will do me good.'

The following morning, he called the College of Psychic Studies and requested the medium with pink hair. Fortunately, they had only one of those on their books and she was called Pixie Tate. 'She's the best,' the receptionist told him proudly. 'She never fails. She has an extraordinary gift.' Joseph made all the right noises and didn't let on that he thought the whole thing utterly ridiculous. The receptionist explained that Pixie worked with a colleague called Ulysses Lozano, and that they'd require a bed for the night as they'd be travelling down from London. Joseph explained that he needed her to come at once, preferably today, and that he'd put them up in the local hotel which was a two-minute walk from the theatre. The receptionist rung off and then called him back ten minutes later to confirm that Pixie Tate and Ulysses would arrive on the 16:45 Penzance train from London.

Joseph had a sinking feeling. If Pixie Tate was the best, then why was he able to book her so quickly? It didn't bode well. He was massively irritated. It wasn't the cost that irked him – her rate was reasonable – it was the fact that he was paying for her to do nothing more than appease the company by waving a magic wand or something. He could do that himself!

But Pixie Tate and Ulysses Lozano were coming down on the train and he was going to have to go through the motions of welcoming them warmly. *For God's sake*, he thought crossly as he left the house to get into his car. *I'm a producer and director, not a bloody actor!* And with that annoyed feeling seething inside him, he set off for the theatre.

Chapter Five

When Ulysses told Pixie about the next assignment, she knew right away that this was *the one* – the one she'd been waiting for. She hadn't been required to slide since New York, but she sensed, intuitively, that this time she would. That this was going to be the slide that reconnected her with Cavill. It *had* to be. It was too much of a coincidence that the theatre was in a town in Cornwall near St Sidwell. In fact, when she looked it up on Google Maps, she could see that it was merely twenty miles from St Sidwell, a little further up the coast.

Pixie had put out the desire to reconnect with Cavill and now the Universe had responded, loudly. She slipped Cavill's sketch-book into her carpet bag and set off with Ulysses to Paddington Station.

As she sat in the train idly watching London whizzing past her window, it crossed her mind to pay the Talwyns a visit. It would be nice to see Tabitha again. The child had the makings of a gifted psychic, and Pixie was keen to encourage her. But then the thought of returning to the house where Pixie had met and fallen in love with Cavill caused her heart to burn with longing and she changed her mind. It would be foolish to go back, she conceded, especially as his gravestone stood outside the church on the estate, a cold reminder of the years that separated them. She couldn't bear to see that again.

She couldn't bear to return to the place where little Felix Pen-gower had died, either. Even though it had happened over a hundred years ago, the memory of that traumatic slide still haunted her when she recalled it, which she made every effort *not* to do, but the mind was an uncontrollable thing, and often it caught her unawares and took her back down that dark and terrifying path. It had been agonising to have to stand by and allow events to unfold when it had been in her power to prevent them.

No, it would be unwise to revisit St Sidwell Manor. Too much had happened there, and the wounds to her heart were still open.

Ulysses took his AirPods out of his ears and gave Pixie a knowing look. 'I know you've brought the sketchbook you stole from St Sidwell,' he said, and grinned mischievously. 'And you're going to try and use this slide to reconnect with Cavill.'

'That's right,' she replied. 'I have to shut it down, somehow. Even *you* told me that that's what I have to do.'

'But are you actually going to go through with it?'

'If this slide takes me back to him, I'll end it. I promise you that. I'll end it for both of us.'

'How? When he won't know who you are. You can't tell him the truth. That would be crazy. Anyway, he wouldn't believe you.'

Pixie sighed and turned her eyes to the window where the grey city had been replaced by fields of long grasses, leafy hedgerows and trees of orange and red. 'To be honest, I don't have a clue. I'd like to tell you that I have it all planned out. But I don't. I really don't know how I'm going to do it. I just know that I must. If I want to let him go so that I can live my life, and leave him free to live his, I have to sever the connection somehow.'

Ulysses frowned. 'He's finished his life, Pixie. He finished it about seventy years ago.'

She looked at him and her bright blue eyes shone obstinately. 'You're looking at it as linear, Ulysses. Life is not linear. It just appears linear so that we can do whatever it is we need to do here on this planet. As I told you, there is no past, present or future . . .'

'I know,' he interrupted briskly. 'Everything is happening all at once. Christ, that does my head in!' He slotted his AirPods back into his ears. 'I can't deal with that. Sorry, Pix. It's too complex for my simple, earthly mind to comprehend. But I hope you do finish whatever it is you have going with Cavill. Because you're not really here, are you?' He gave her a meaningful look.

'What do you mean, I'm not really here? I'm here,' she replied defensively. But she knew what he meant. Her mind was in the past, with Cavill. It was *always* in the past with Cavill.

'You need to commit to *this* life, Pixie. It's full of beautiful things, but you're not seeing them right now. In fact, you're wasting every precious moment, pining like a dog for someone who doesn't exist. You'll never fall in love if you don't open yourself up to it.'

She smiled at him in amusement. 'For a man who said he'd never fall in love, your fixation with Henry looks very much like love to me.'

Ulysses dropped his eyes to his phone. 'I don't know what it is. But Henry's not like others,' he admitted bashfully. Then he lifted his gaze to meet hers. 'If *I* can fall in love, then so can you, a *second* time.'

She folded her arms. 'I know I'll never find anyone like Cavill.' Her eyes drifted to the window again. To the immense sky and beyond, to where all truth lay hidden.

'No, you won't, Pix. Of course you won't. And you wouldn't want to. How miserable for a man to love you in the shadow of the great Cavill Pengower! No one can live up to him. Because, if you're truly honest with yourself, you never really knew him in the first place. You've put him on a pedestal and created this perfect man. The Cavill Pengower in your memory probably doesn't exist at all. Probably never did. No, you need someone different. Someone real. If the Universe can bring *me* Henry Stirling, it can bring *you* someone too.'

She chose to ignore what he had said about Cavill. How could she explain such a deep knowing, such a profound connection? It had nothing to do with the amount of time they'd known each other. What she felt about Cavill was timeless. 'Perhaps,' she replied flatly.

'And by the way, I'll be heading out to New York soon, to see Henry.'

'Really?' Pixie felt a wrench in her stomach that brought her sharply back to the present. 'When?'

'In a week or two.'

'That *is* soon,' she said, trying to look as if she didn't care.

'It's getting serious, Pixie.' He grinned and began scrolling down his playlists for the right tunes to listen to.

Pixie felt low suddenly. The thought of London without Ulysses, even for a few days, made her feel quite desolate. Besides him, she didn't have any friends of her own. The people she hung out with were *his* friends.

She turned her attention back to the window, only to be assaulted by one negative thought after another. What would happen to *her* if Ulysses decided to go and live in America? She'd be on her own; totally alone. What if she never got over Cavill? What if she never met anyone else? What if Ulysses and Henry became a solid couple and there was no room for her? *What if, what if, what if . . .*

The train was late. When they arrived at the station it was already getting dark. Emma Lightwater was waiting to meet them in a belted red coat and floral scarf. Her long brown hair was swept up into a velvet scrunchie. She recognised Pixie at once due to her pink tresses. But she had imagined someone taller. Pixie was surprisingly small and slight, like an elf, in a long, bohemian cardigan worn over jeans, and a shabby carpet bag hooked over one arm. Beside her – and striding down the platform with an air of great confidence, was the most handsome young man Emma had ever seen. Truly, he looked like a movie star. Put him on the stage, she thought to herself, and you'd have all the women in Cornwall fighting for seats, and many of the men too!

'Pixie,' she called out and waved. Pixie and Ulysses both smiled in acknowledgement and made their way swiftly towards her. 'Hello! I'm Emma, Joseph Lightwater's wife. Lovely to meet you. And you must be Ulysses Lozano,' she added with a blush. Really, she was old enough to be his mother! But he was so handsome, she didn't know where to look! She shook their hands enthusiastically.

'Thank you so much for coming all this way. I can't begin to tell you what's been going on at the theatre.'

'I'm dying to know,' said Pixie. 'It sounds like you've had a dreadful time.'

'It's been crazy. Really, I've never known anything like it, and Joseph has been the director at The Aphrodite for twelve years. Come, I'll drive you to the hotel and then take you straight to the theatre. Is there anything you need? Are you hungry? Did you eat on the train?'

Pixie reassured her that they were fine, but Ulysses requested a sandwich. 'I'm ravenous,' he said, and his smile was so dazzling that Emma resolved to find him the most delicious sandwich in Seacombe.

Emma drove a navy-blue Volvo. It was clean and smelt of leather with a subtle undertone of wet dog. As she drove the short distance to the hotel, she filled them in. 'My husband thinks it's someone playing a prank on poor Isadora Nash, but I saw the chair rise off the floor with my own eyes. If someone's playing a prank, they're an extraordinary magician.'

'Isadora Nash,' said Ulysses from the back seat. 'I've seen lots of her films. I like her. She's a character.'

'You'll find that none of the cast or crew like her. She's a bit of a diva, I'm afraid.'

'And nothing like this has ever happened before?' Pixie asked. She was more interested in the spirit than in Isadora Nash.

'Not in my experience. No paranormal activity whatsoever,' said Emma. 'But there's an old Irish lady who has worked at the theatre since she was a child, which is probably over seventy years, called Madge Boylan. She's often mentioned the legendary theatre ghost and claims to have seen it mulling about the place. But no one takes Madge seriously. You know, she's old and a bit dotty. In a nice way. Besides her, I don't think anyone else has seen anything otherworldly.'

Pixie nodded slowly. 'What does Madge do?'

'She makes the tea and cakes, and sometimes helps out in the costume department, although her sewing leaves much to be desired.' Emma laughed fondly. 'She's as much part of the place as the stage itself, so we find things for her to do to keep her involved. It's been her life. She seems to know a lot about the paranormal. She was the one to point out that what happened on stage was the doing of a ghost and not someone living, which is what my husband thinks. In fact, Madge was the one who recommended we call *you*. She knows someone in St Sidwell who told her about you sorting out a ghost in the big house there a while back.'

Pixie was astonished. That was another coincidence – which *wasn't* a coincidence. She felt a frisson of excitement. There could be no clearer sign that she was about to be reunited with Cavill. The anticipation of sliding back to him caused her spirits to soar. 'Really, she knows someone in St Sidwell?' Pixie asked.

Emma nodded. 'That's what she said. Did you, in fact . . . ?'

'Yes, I released an earthbound spirit there last January.'

'That's what Madge said. She said you had pink hair.'

'Well, she's right about that,' Pixie laughed.

'Madge thinks it's definitely a ghost and that it doesn't like Isadora. Well, I can't say anything about that, but it didn't interrupt anyone else's scenes,' Emma went on.

'Has Isadora experienced anything like this before?' Pixie asked.

'Not that I know of.' Emma drew up outside the hotel. 'But you can ask her. We've put her up here too.'

Brambling House Hotel had once been a stunning private home. Built in the eighteenth century it was harmoniously proportioned with big sash windows, a pale stone façade and a pillared front door positioned beneath a half-moon transom window. Inside, however, the good taste had been squeezed out of it, like juice from a delicious orange. Bent to the will of a local authority completely lacking in taste and sensitivity, there was precious little of the original building left. Health and Safety had sacrificed beauty at the altar of utility and practicality, and the result was disappointing for Pixie and Ulysses who loved history, especially historic buildings. It wasn't the Aldershoff, but it was nonetheless comfortable with big beds, crisp white sheets and clean en-suite bathrooms.

As they returned to the hall where Emma was waiting for them on the sofa, flicking through *Country Life* magazine, the door opened and in swept Isadora Nash in a cream-coloured leather trench coat, wide-legged cream trousers and black leather boots. She wore a matching cashmere polo neck, oversized dark glasses and a berry-red fedora. Her blonde hair was tied in a ponytail and falling down her back. If she wanted to shout '*movie star*', she could not have dressed more appropriately. She was followed by her assistant Lezli, straining beneath the weight of a large number of shopping bags. When Isadora saw Emma, she sighed melodramatically and took off her dark glasses. 'I've spent the day shopping,' she declared. 'Not much to buy around here – it's hardly Rodeo Drive – but I needed retail therapy. I've been so upset. I didn't know what else to do with myself!'

Emma dropped the magazine onto the coffee table and stood up with the hastiness of a private in front of a field marshal. 'Can I introduce you to Pixie Tate, Isadora?' she asked. 'She's the medium who's come down from London to get rid of the ghost.'

'If it *is* a ghost,' said Isadora sulkily, looking sceptical. She didn't put out her hand. It was as if she considered Pixie staff, and she didn't bother with staff. Ulysses, however, was altogether different. On seeing him, tall and absurdly handsome, Isadora's face opened into a radiant smile. 'And you are?' she asked, extending her hand.

'I work with Pixie. Ulysses Lozano, at your service.'

Isadora let out a light, tinkling laugh, like a pretty bell. 'You can be at my service any time, Ulysses Lozano,' she said, and gave him the full benefit of her kitten eyes.

Emma felt embarrassed for Pixie, but Pixie didn't look in the least surprised to see Isadora fawning over Ulysses. 'Perhaps you'd like to have a quick word with Pixie before I take her to the theatre,' she suggested.

It was as if Isadora hadn't heard. 'Let's all go and have a cup of tea, as the English love to say,' she suggested, without taking her hungry eyes off Ulysses. She threaded her hand through the crook of his arm and led him off towards the dining room. 'If you've come all the way from London, you must be starving. Did you come on the train? I imagine the food on the train is gross. Let's go and demand a full English tea in the dining room.'

Emma did not bother to go and buy Ulysses a sandwich and Lezli went to put the shopping in Isadora's suite, which was the best set of rooms in the hotel.

Emma, Pixie, Ulysses and Isadora settled into comfortable armchairs positioned around a table in front of a large bay window, and Isadora waved over a waiter and ordered tea, scones, clotted cream and jam. 'There's nothing to do here but eat,' she exclaimed cheerfully. 'I've put on five pounds, and I've only been here a couple of weeks.'

'Then you should thank the scones, because those five pounds suit you,' said Ulysses, and Pixie gave Emma a knowing grin; Ulysses, although gay, flirted with anything that had a pulse.

Isadora laughed again. In the dazzling glare of Ulysses' beauty, she seemed to have forgotten all about the unfortunate mishaps on stage. Shortly, the waiter returned with a tray of pretty china cups and a matching teapot, a three-tier cake stand laden with little sandwiches and not so little scones, still warm from the oven. While Ulysses tucked into a scone with the relish of someone who hadn't eaten for weeks, Pixie took the opportunity to ask Isadora some questions.

'Can you tell me exactly what happened to you on stage?' she said.

Isadora brought the teacup to her scarlet lips and took a dainty sip. Then she put it down with a clink and began to describe in great detail, and with a sudden explosion of self-pitying vitriol, what had occurred. 'You don't have to be Sherlock Holmes to work out that it's either that horrid old crone Madge, or the three witches. Rebecca Shaw is Witch One and she's my understudy. No points for guessing who's taking my place in tonight's performance.' She lifted her immaculately plucked eyebrows provocatively. 'You have to look for a motive, you know, and those two women have the mother of all motives. Madge is cross I complained about her cold coffee and dry cake, plus I've caught her on various occasions having strange conversations with herself, so she's probably worried I'm going to report her as mad. And Rebecca wants to play Lady Macbeth. The thing is I can't work out how it was done.' She tossed her head dismissively. 'It doesn't matter. The fact is, my scene was sabotaged, two nights in a row. I'm an A list Hollywood star! This shouldn't be allowed to happen!'

Ulysses grinned empathetically at Isadora through a mouth full of clotted cream and jam. Pixie ignored her dramatics. 'Did you notice a change in temperature?' she asked. Emma nodded, for she most certainly had noticed.

'They did that too,' Isadora complained. 'They not only turned out the lights, but they did something to the heating as well. It was freezing. Like we were in a refrigerator. If they didn't manage to scare me away, they certainly succeeded in freezing me out.'

'It sounds to me like you have an earthbound spirit,' said Pixie, directing her words at Emma, because Isadora was no longer listening. She was laughing at Ulysses, who was playing the clown with another scone.

'What exactly is an earthbound spirit?' Emma asked, intrigued. She'd always been curious about the paranormal and was delighted now to have the opportunity to talk to someone who knew things.

Pixie left Isadora and Ulysses to their banter and answered Emma directly. 'Okay, so when we die, our souls rise out of our bodies and most usually move on into the next dimension. From there, we can return to the earth plane whenever we fancy, to be around those we love who are still here, or simply to explore. Those spirits are very bright, radiant beings, full of love. Souls who are *not* able to move on into the next dimension, because they don't want to, are fearful of what they might find there, or because they died traumatically and haven't realised that they're dead, remain bound to the earth plane but without their bodies. They're called earthbound spirits. To sensitives like me who can see them, they're not bright and radiant, but dull and lacklustre. They're on the whole distressed and confused. Those souls often create mischief, like *your* spirit, which is often interpreted as malevolent. But most of the time they're just unhappy and trying to get our attention because they need help.'

'Can't they go to the next world on their own?'

'Not in that state, no. They need our help to raise their vibration. Guides on the other side are helping too. Think of it as a dream. When you're dreaming, you don't know you're dreaming. Your dream world is confusing and uncomfortable, but you don't know you can leave it. You get lost in your dream. That's what it's like for earthbound spirits. They don't know they can leave, and if they decide they want to leave, they don't know how to do it. That's where I come in. I'll link into your earthbound spirit and hopefully help it move on.'

'Where does it go?' Emma asked, glancing at Isadora who was now suggestively sucking on a chocolate strawberry and giggling flirtatiously at Ulysses.

'I don't know, because I haven't been there. But I believe it to be a place of love and beauty. I think it's best not to try and understand it. Imagine an ant on a leaf. That ant can't imagine what it's like in this dining room, with our teacups and scones. Likewise, the spirit world is beyond our comprehension. Suffice to know that there's a reason that we're here, and when we return home, we'll likely wake up as if from a dream, and things will be a lot clearer. Right now, we just have to commit to the reality as we're experiencing it, like the ant on its leaf, and live the best lives we can.'

Emma smiled. She liked Pixie. She was straight-talking, wise and open-minded, and not at all dogmatic. 'Let's go to the theatre and see if you can sense the ghost,' she suggested eagerly. She hoped Pixie would pick up something that confirmed the presence of a spirit. 'Shall we leave Ulysses here?'

Ulysses overheard and snapped out of the game he was playing with Isadora. 'I'm coming,' he said, dropping his napkin onto the table. Then to Isadora, 'You coming, too?'

Isadora vigorously shook her head. 'I'm not going back on stage until the old crone and the witches have been fired. They're probably in it together. A little plot they've cooked up to get rid of me. I don't have to put up with that shit, so I won't.'

Emma got up and laughed nervously. 'You must do exactly as

you want, Isadora,' she said with patience honed over many years of living with a creative and moody husband. 'I'll let you know what happens.'

Isadora remained in her seat and called over the waiter to order a fresh pot of tea. 'It's cold,' she said curtly, holding out the teapot. 'Bring another and make sure it's piping hot.' Then to Pixie. 'I wish it *was* a ghost, but I think you'll discover that the perpetrators of those horrid pranks are only too human. Jealous humans. I've encountered jealousy all my life. But that's the price you pay for success.' She gave a little sniff. 'There's always someone trying to bring you down.'

Pixie wondered whether she ever looked in the mirror and recognised that *she* was part of the problem.

Chapter Six

When Pixie entered the theatre she felt the spirit's energy at once. It wasn't just the air that was hardened by the usual chill that denoted a spirit presence, but a closer, more direct feeling, like she was being watched. It caused the hairs on the back of her neck to bristle. She followed Emma slowly into the foyer and swept her eyes over the crimson-and-gold patterned carpeting, the shiny wooden ticket booth and souvenir shop, and the staircase at the other end. She narrowed her eyes, suspiciously. Someone was most definitely watching her.

The skin on the back of her neck began to itch and she put a hand there to scratch it. Her eyes were drawn again to the stair. What she saw there took her by surprise.

She caught her breath and stopped dead in her tracks.

Standing in the middle of the staircase was what looked to Pixie like a hologram of a young woman. She was wearing a drop-waisted dress, cloche hat and round-toed shoes with a T-strap. Pixie recognised the fashion at once as being typical of the 1920s.

The woman, on realising that Pixie could see her, stared back with astonishment. The spirit clearly wasn't used to being noticed, Pixie reflected. Pixie wasn't used to being observed so blatantly, either. They remained frozen, the two of them, gawping at each other.

Ulysses put a soft hand on Pixie's arm. 'What do you see?' he whispered, following the direction of her gaze and finding nothing but the empty staircase.

Emma spun round. 'Are you seeing something already?' she

asked, blanching. Talking about ghosts had been quite fun until that moment. Now she was back in the theatre with the very real possibility of coming face to face with one, she was afraid.

Pixie nodded slowly without taking her eyes off the spirit. 'There's a young woman on the stair,' she said quietly. As she uttered those words, the woman vanished. 'Now she's gone,' she added in a normal voice. 'I think I scared her away.'

'Goodness, that was quick,' said Emma.

'Well, there's no doubt now that you have an earthbound spirit,' said Pixie with satisfaction.

'Can you ask her to leave?' Emma said hopefully.

'I'll try,' Pixie replied. 'But first I'd like to speak to Madge, if I may.' The fact that this old woman knew about the haunting at St Sidwell was intriguing.

Emma ushered Pixie and Ulysses backstage and introduced them to her husband. Joseph was used to creative, often eccentric people and wasn't at all fazed by Pixie's pink hair. He greeted them with politeness, but hoped they'd quickly do their thing then return to the hotel so he could get on with tonight's performance. Rebecca was in the middle of rehearsing some of the more demanding scenes with Edward, and Joseph was keen that nothing disturbed her flow. After the drama of the night before, it was imperative that nothing went wrong tonight.

'Pixie has already seen the ghost,' said Emma excitedly, regretting the words as they tumbled out, because Joseph didn't believe in ghosts and thought mediums and psychics were charlatans.

'I'm sure she has,' said Joseph, trying to keep the cynicism out of his voice. But Pixie picked it up and chose to ignore it; it made no difference to her whether people believed her or not. She wasn't here to convince or convert. She was here to help lost souls find their way home, and that was all that mattered. 'I'd be grateful if you could get rid of this ghost before tonight's performance,' he said loudly, keen to be overheard so that the cast and stage crew would know that he was doing the right thing.

'I'll try my best,' said Pixie, which was all she could ever do.

Ulysses was more assertive. 'Of course she will,' he said confidently. 'Pixie succeeds where all others fail,' he added with a smile, and even Joseph couldn't help but smile back at such a charming face.

Emma, like a fly in the glare of a bright light, was momentarily distracted by Ulysses. Then she remembered Madge. 'Darling, Pixie would love to have a chat with Madge. Is she about?'

'She's in the kitchen,' Joseph replied. He was about to ask why Pixie needed to speak to the woman who made the tea, when Samantha, the new Witch One who had been promoted from lady-in-waiting to Lady Macbeth, interrupted.

'Can I have a quick word, Joseph?'

Emma found Madge in the kitchen making sandwiches. She was humming to herself as she stood hunched over the sideboard laying out slices of bread and scooping a knife into a big pat of butter. Madge stopped what she was doing when she saw the trio in the doorway. She recognised Pixie at once on account of her hair. 'You're the medium, aren't you?' she said, smiling cheerfully and wiping her arthritic hands on her apron. 'It's a good thing you're here,' she said. 'We can't have a repeat of last night or the entire cast will leave.'

'Do you have a moment?' Pixie asked. 'I'd love to ask you a few questions.'

'Of course. Be my guest and take a pew. I'll continue with the sandwiches if you don't mind, or everyone will complain. Although, no one has complained quite so rudely as Miss Nash,' she added tersely. 'Perhaps it's an American thing.'

'It's an Isadora thing, I'm afraid,' said Emma, sitting down at the rectangular wooden table and gesturing at Ulysses and Pixie to join her.

Pixie sat down, put her elbows on the table and tented her fingers. 'I gather you know something of the haunting at St Sidwell Manor, Madge,' she began.

Madge nodded keenly. 'Oh yes. My friend works there . . .'

'You know Elsa Tregoning?' said Pixie excitedly. It couldn't be anyone else.

'I do. Her late husband, Gerren, and my husband, Jacob, were childhood friends.'

'So you know St Sidwell Manor?'

'Oh, indeed I do. A beautiful house it is. Of course, it's different now that it's owned by a family. It was a sad place before, when Mrs Delaware lived there.'

Pixie knew that first hand. As soon as she persuaded the sad spirit of Cordelia Pengower to move on, the energy lifted, and the house felt warm and welcoming once again. She wanted to talk about the Talwyns, and ask after Tabitha, but she realised time was of the essence, the play would start soon. 'How long have you worked here, at the theatre?'

'Since I was a teenager. I was born in West Cork, but my father moved us here to Seacombe when I was fifteen, in 1946. He was a carpenter. They employed him here at the theatre. It was amateur drama in those days. A little chaotic, but grand. He made sets. I used to come and help him in my spare time. I was quite good with a paintbrush and a hammer. Mam was a seamstress. A good one, too. She had to be. She had nine mouths to feed.' Madge began to lay pieces of shredded chicken onto the thickly buttered bread. 'She made costumes, and I helped her from time to time, but I wasn't good at sewing. My fingers don't have the patience for that kind of work. What I liked to do was keep the theatre clean and tidy, and watch the rehearsals. I was never going to be an actress myself. I didn't have the talent. But I liked to watch. Plays take you into a different world, don't they? And no two nights are the same.'

'Tell me about this spirit, Madge.'

Madge put down her knife and came to the table, where she hovered with her hands on her hips. 'I'll tell you right now that she's a woman. Nessa Blunt.'

'How do you know that?' Emma asked. In all the twelve years that Joseph had worked here, Madge had never once mentioned a ghost named Nessa Blunt.

'I didn't like to say. People get the wind up them when you talk about ghosts. But Nessa Blunt haunted this place when my father worked here and has haunted it ever since. I see her from time to time, bless her heart. I like her company. She's a benign creature. At least, she *was* a benign creature until the arrival of Isadora Nash. Back when I was a child everyone seemed to know about her. Now I'm the only person who does. I've been here nearly seventy years. I'm like a piece of furniture.'

'That sounds like the woman I saw on the stair when I came in,' said Pixie. 'She was wearing one of those flapper dresses from the 1920s and a cloche hat.'

Madge's eyes widened with interest. 'That'll be her,' she said emphatically, forgetting all about her sandwiches and pulling up a chair and sitting down keenly. 'She died here in the fire of 1923,' she added. 'Ninth of May to be precise. There used to be a framed newspaper article on the wall. I don't know what happened to it. The fire was front-page news.'

Emma knew nothing of the history of the theatre, but she did know that the interior was Art Deco, her favourite style.

'How much of the theatre was destroyed?' Pixie asked.

'The inside. It was gutted like a hare,' said Madge.

'That makes sense,' Ulysses cut in. 'The façade is Edwardian.'

'Tell me what you know about Nessa Blunt,' Pixie asked.

'Not very much, I'm afraid. My father was touched by the four winds, if you know what I mean. He loved ghost stories and was an admirer of Sir Arthur Conan Doyle. If there was ever a strange noise, or it got particularly cold, he'd say: "That's Nessa Blunt." Everyone here knew about Nessa Blunt.'

'Who was she?' Pixie asked.

'Well, Da worked here in the late forties and fifties, which was long after the fire. But she was an actress. It happened during a performance, apparently.'

'Was anyone else killed?'

'Not that I know of. Just Nessa Blunt. Poor lamb.'

'And did they find out how the fire started?'

'Oh yes,' said Madge. 'Nessa herself started it.'

'Nessa started it? And she died in the process?'

'She did.'

Pixie thought that sounded a bit odd. Surely, if you start a fire, you make damn sure you get out alive. She narrowed her eyes thoughtfully and nodded slowly. 'Okay, I'll see what I can get out of her.'

'How do you do that?' Emma asked. 'I mean, will you talk to her?'

'Yes, I'll just talk to her.'

Emma grinned, eyes gleaming with fascination. 'That's pretty wild.'

Ulysses laughed. 'If only you knew what else she can do.'

Pixie flashed him a look. 'She might not respond,' she said quickly, before Ulysses forgot himself and spilled the beans about her timesliding. 'Spirits aren't always forthcoming. But she might be keen to leave, so you never know.'

'I think you'll find she likes it here,' said Madge. 'I like having her around, too. She keeps herself to herself, or at least she did until the opening night two days ago. I'm not sure why she's suddenly decided to make a menace of herself now.'

'Most spirits want to move on,' Pixie added. 'That's my job, to help them find their way home. I suspect she's unhappy and her mischief-making is a cry for help.'

Madge looked unconvinced. 'Oh, I don't think she's after help. She's after something more sinister than that.'

'Where will you do it?' Emma asked Pixie.

'Is there somewhere I can sit in quiet?'

'The VIP room?' Madge turned to Emma. 'There's no one in there tonight.'

Emma nodded. 'Good idea. Come, I'll take you there now. Madge, you'd better get on with those sandwiches.'

Pixie got up. 'Thanks, Madge. You've been very helpful.'

Madge pushed herself up off the chair with a sigh. 'I can't help feeling a little sad, though, at the thought of you encouraging her to move on. Nessa's part of the place. It won't feel the same without her.'

'Which will be a good thing!' said Emma firmly. 'I'm not sure I like the sound of a ghost haunting this place, nor do I like Joseph's productions to be interrupted.'

'That has never happened before,' said Madge. 'Nessa is usually as quiet as a breeze.'

'Well, something has made her assert herself,' said Pixie. 'And I need to find out what that is.'

'Isadora Nash,' said Madge firmly, her face hardening. 'That's what you'll find out. That it's Isadora Nash. Nessa Blunt wants her to leave.'

Emma led Pixie and Ulysses down a dark, narrow corridor, through a little wooden door, up some steps and into a scarlet room that contained a round table, red upholstered armchairs, a bar and stools, and a large shiny Art Deco sideboard. On the walls black-and-white photographs of stage performances and portraits of actors were hung in tight collages. 'This is our VIP room,' Emma told them proudly. 'So, you can be our VIPs tonight.'

'What a cool room,' said Pixie, looking around warily. The hairs on the back of her neck bristled again. They were not alone. 'Ulysses, I don't need you for the moment,' she added quietly.

Emma looked surprised. 'Oh, right. What do you do when you *are* needed?' she asked Ulysses, curious to know how mediums worked.

'I keep her safe when she's in trance,' he replied. 'You don't want to disturb her when she's miles away.'

Emma laughed. 'I see. It's like waking a sleepwalker, then. You know, apparently, if someone is dreaming of being hit by a train and you go and shake them, they actually die.'

Pixie frowned cynically. She'd heard that before and didn't believe it. However, timesliding wasn't dreaming, and the consequences of being shaken out of it and wrenched back to the present were truly hazardous. 'If I need to go into trance, Ulysses, I'll come and get you,' she said.

'He can watch the play from the back row with me,' Emma suggested.

'I'll come and find you when I'm through,' said Pixie, watching her close the door softly behind them.

*

Alone in the room, Pixie sat down on one of the upholstered armchairs and closed her eyes. She took a few breaths and centred herself, shutting out the three-dimensional world and tuning in to the higher vibration of spirit. It wasn't long before Nessa Blunt stood before her. She was so confident of her place here in the theatre that Pixie did not need to work hard to sense her. In fact, she opened her eyes and saw the spirit so clearly that she could even make out the long string of pearls that hung over her blue dress. *Nessa?* When Pixie communicated with spirits she did so telepathically.

Who are you? Nessa replied. She seemed equally astonished to be able to communicate so easily with Pixie.

I'm Pixie Tate.

You're not an actress, are you?

No. I'm a medium.

Nessa laughed somewhat scornfully. *I've met a few of those and disregarded them all.*

So you know what you are?

I'm not dim. Of course, I know what I am.

Then don't you want to go home?

I am *home.*

This is not your home, Nessa. You no longer belong in this world, but in the next. Trust me, the next world is a much nicer place than this.

How do you know? Have you been there?

No, but I've spoken to a good many spirits who have.

Well, I'm not going anywhere.

Are you afraid?

No.

Then what's stopping you from moving on?

I like it here.

Don't you get lonely?

She shook her head *No.*

Do you like watching the plays?

Some of them.

Is that what you did when you were alive?

I was an actress, and a good one too!

Is that why you're disrupting the performances, because you want to be part of them?

Nessa's face hardened. *I want to ruin them.*

Why?

She folded her arms guardedly. *I just do.*

Wouldn't you rather be in a place of love?

What's love ever done for me? she snapped.

Pixie sensed she had touched a nerve. *Earth is a harsh school, Nessa,* she said gently. *Life is hard. It's full of suffering, so that we learn and grow. If it was easy, no one would learn anything. But home, where the light is, is full of love. You cannot imagine how much love there is there. Why don't you go and find out? You'll be astonished. And you'll be happy.*

I'm happy here, aren't I?

I don't think you are. Happy people don't do mean things.

She deserves it.

Isadora Nash?

She's not happy either. She does mean things.

She's learning and growing as we all are, Nessa. She's treading her own path. Making mistakes and having the opportunity to learn from them is what life is all about. Leave her to live it. It's not your place to judge her. And go to the light to continue with your *life. Death is not an end, only an end to this earthly experience. Life will go on in Spirit. Those whom you love are waiting for you with open arms.*

You don't know what you're talking about. There is no one who loves me there.

I think you'll be surprised.

No one loved me when I was alive. Why should they love me when I'm dead?

Your life here was like a play. You only knew the cast members who were in the play with you. When you go to the light you'll be reunited with those you did other plays with. And you've performed in so many other plays. Trust me, there are lots and lots of souls who love you, just waiting in the wings.

You talk a lot of tosh, you know.

Try me. Go on. If you don't like it, you can come back.

Nessa chuckled bitterly. *They've tried that one on me before. I didn't fall for it then and I won't fall for it now. I'm no fool, Pixie Tate. I'm staying right where I am, and you can't do anything about it.*

Did you start the fire? Pixie asked, trying another tack. Maybe being direct was a better approach.

What's it to you if I did or did not? It was a long time ago. I'm aware of the time that goes by. I've seen people come and go. But I'm always here. I'll always *be here. It's where I want to be. Where I'm happy. I always wanted to be in the theatre. I wanted to be a great actress. I was never given the chance. Well, they're noticing me now, aren't they? If I were alive I'd be Lady Macbeth. I'd make a fine Lady Macbeth. But no . . . I wasn't even cast as a witch! Shame on them all!*

And with that she disappeared, leaving a cloud of defiance behind her.

Pixie knew she was going to have to slide. Not only did she sense that there was something deeply painful lurking in Nessa Blunt's soul, but she sensed, too, that this slide was going to be significant, that somehow she would draw Cavill into her adventure, just so that she could end it. The very thought of ending it caused her heart to contract, but her dread was tempered by the anticipation of seeing him one final time. If they did manage to reunite once more, she knew she must be grateful for that.

However, it was late. There wasn't time tonight and after the long journey from London Pixie was too tired to attempt a slide. She would need all her energy to pull this one off.

She got up from the chair and made her way down the corridor the way she had come. At the end she opened a door that led directly into the auditorium. The lights were dimmed. Only the footlights were on, illuminating the actors now performing on stage. She crept quietly to the back of the packed theatre and looked about for Ulysses. After a while of scanning profiles, she saw him sitting beside Emma. There was a spare seat beside him next to the aisle. She made her way towards it.

'And?' Ulysses whispered when she sat down.

Pixie shook her head. 'I'm going to have to slide,' she replied quietly.

'You were always going to have to slide,' he returned, and his teeth shone white through the dark as he grinned. 'You knew that the moment you took on the job.'

She nodded. 'I suspected, but now I know.'

'Do you think she'll disrupt the play tonight?'

'We'll soon find out,' she replied. 'She seems determined to make a nuisance of herself, and I fear I might have made the situation worse!'

Emma began to fidget. Rebecca, as Lady Macbeth, was now moving to centre stage. Emma watched the letter in her hand, and the chair behind her, for any sign of movement. So far, there was none. Rebecca was rising to the occasion with aplomb. If she had any worries about ghostly mischief she did not let them show.

That I may pour my spirits in thine ear . . .

Rebecca finished her soliloquy without any disturbance. The Messenger strode onto the stage and the scene continued. Emma breathed a sigh of relief and stopped fidgeting. She realised then that the theatre was warm, hot in fact, and it struck her as significant. Hadn't Madge said that spirits lower the temperature when they come into our world? It had certainly been very cold the two times the ghost was supposed to have made mischief on stage. She watched Rebecca with interest. She seemed to grow an inch as her confidence swelled. She was showing what she could do. That she was just as accomplished as Isadora.

A doubt slithered into Emma's mind then. Was Rebecca the culprit? Could her poise be attributed to the fact that it was *she* who had somehow caused those crazy things to happen? Certainly, that was the way Isadora would see it. Or had Pixie Tate managed to move the spirit on already? Emma glanced at Pixie, having noticed her coming and sitting beside Ulysses. Pixie turned and caught her eye. Emma gave her a thumbs-up sign and a hopeful smile. Pixie responded with a thumbs-down and a hopeless smile. Emma was baffled. She couldn't understand it. Unless the ghost had gone on its own – if there *was* a ghost. Emma now began to doubt.

Joseph stood in the wings with his arms crossed, watching the performance closely. His entire body was rigid with anxiety. He was aching all over. But so far, so good. He didn't imagine for one moment that the pink-haired medium had removed the ghost. It just meant that whoever had interrupted the play the two previous evenings had decided not to do it tonight. His suspicion fell on Rebecca. She was the only person with a real motive to be rid of Isadora. And here she was, playing the lead, which was every understudy's dream. Though, how she had managed to whip the letter out of Isadora's hand and lift the chair right off the ground, when she had been in her dressing room all along, mystified him. Certainly, she could not have carried out those things on her own. She needed an accomplice. But who? He thought of Nigel the lighting technician but swiftly dismissed the idea as ludicrous. There was nothing in it for Nigel. Joseph tried to think of who else might have aided her, but no one seemed likely. And he didn't believe in magic. Yet, as the play carried on and the cast and crew began to relax, he found himself wondering if Pixie Tate had actually managed to rid the theatre of whatever strange phenomenon had plagued it. Was it possible that some supernatural being existed?

Whichever was the case Pixie and Ulysses would leave in the morning. Job done.

Isadora could return to the stage tomorrow, although the fact that she hadn't performed tonight hadn't affected turnout. No one had cancelled their booking. If anything, more people had flooded to the theatre out of curiosity, in the hope of seeing otherworldly things happening on stage. The place was full to bursting. It was standing room only. The papers and internet had been full of the strange technical faults, which had fuelled people's curiosity. There had even been a queue at the theatre doors for last-minute tickets. He wouldn't tell Isadora that!

*

During the interval Emma, Pixie and Ulysses found Joseph backstage. He smiled with relief when he saw them. 'Well, you got rid of it,' he said with convincing enthusiasm, rubbing his hands together. 'You've done a fine job. I'll drive you to the station first thing tomorrow morning.'

'Not so fast, darling,' said Emma, scrunching her face as she anticipated his reaction to the bad news she was about to deliver. 'Pixie says the ghost doesn't want to leave.'

Joseph looked startled. 'Well, nothing untoward has happened so far, so perhaps it's gone of its own accord.'

'Apparently not,' said Emma.

'Oh, well. That's a shame.' Joseph looked from his wife to Pixie and wondered whether he'd manage to put them on the morning train all the same.

'Pixie is going to have a go at removing the spirit tomorrow morning,' said Emma.

Joseph's heart sank. He hoped they wouldn't require another night in the hotel. Two bedrooms at Brambling House did not come cheap. 'Ah, okay.' He hated having to go along with this farce. 'Right, well, I'll drive you to the station after that, then.'

'Thank you,' said Pixie.

Joseph turned to his wife. 'Can I have a quick word, darling?'

'We'll go to the bar and have a drink,' said Ulysses. He could do with a glass of wine.

Pixie could too. 'See you back in our seats,' she said, and followed Ulysses towards the bar.

Joseph lowered his voice. 'You know there *is* no ghost,' he said. 'It's no coincidence that nothing untoward happens when Rebecca's on stage.'

'That's ridiculous,' said Emma. 'How could she have done it? She's not a magician – or a witch,' she added with a chuckle. 'And wouldn't it be too obvious? Isadora's scenes are sabotaged, but not Rebecca's. If she wanted to incriminate herself, that's a fine way to do it!'

'She did it somehow.'

'Do you really think she's that stupid?'

'Well, it would be a bit foolish, I agree with you. She could be double bluffing, of course.'

'Give Pixie a chance. She says she hasn't got time to do it tonight. It might take a few hours and it's late.'

He sighed loudly to show his reluctance, but his wife was looking at him with those big, pleading eyes and he knew he couldn't say no. 'Okay, whatever you want. But Isadora can return tomorrow as Lady Macbeth. No buts about it. Perhaps the game's over now and whoever was responsible has given up.'

'Let's hope so,' she replied. She was about to tell him about Madge and Nessa Blunt, and the vision Pixie had seen on the stair, but she stopped herself. It would be a waste of breath, and she didn't fancy arguing.

'I think it'll be fine now. I feel it in my bones,' he said, glancing at his watch. 'Right, better get on.'

'Good luck,' she said and went to the bar to join Ulysses and Pixie.

No sooner had the second act started than Pixie noticed the temperature drop in the auditorium. The place was full of warm bodies, but the air grew suddenly chilly. She narrowed her eyes and linked into the vibration on stage. It was like reading between lines on a page or being alert to the silence between words. It wasn't long before she perceived Nessa Blunt, between worlds. She was mirroring Rebecca's Lady Macbeth. Whatever Rebecca did, Nessa did it too. Of course, no one else could see her. Only Pixie. Pixie turned to see Emma wrap her shawl about her, so she too had noticed the cold. Pixie ran her eyes about the auditorium and noticed members of the audience putting on sweaters or folding their arms to keep warm. No doubt they would put the chill down to a problem with the heating, but Pixie knew better than that.

She was fascinated by Nessa's invisible performance. It was clear that she had wanted to be the leading lady during her life and was now acting vicariously through Rebecca. But what Pixie couldn't understand was why she had made a menace of herself on stage while Isadora played Lady Macbeth, but not while Rebecca played her. It didn't make sense. What was it about Isadora that incited her wrath? Sure, Isadora wasn't very nice to work with, but could she be punishing her simply for that? Or was there something else? Pixie didn't think that Nessa was going to be forthcoming with that information. But if Pixie could slide back and discover what secret she was hiding, perhaps she'd be able to persuade her to move on into the light. She had done it before many times. She didn't doubt that she could do it again.

When the play ended and Rebecca came on stage to take her bow, Pixie watched Nessa stride out in front of her and take an extravagant bow of her own. The spirit stood before the audience, believing perhaps that they were clapping for *her*, and kissed her fingers, throwing her hands wide as if tossing those kisses into the adoring crowd.

Chapter Seven

In order for Pixie to timeslide with any accuracy she knew that she would need to link into something of Nessa's. It could be anything; a photograph, an object, something that had belonged to her, even something she might have borrowed. Pixie thought of the letter in the play that Nessa had snatched out of Isadora's hand, on two occasions. It hadn't belonged to her exactly, but she had affected it with her energy. Might there be a strong enough connection there for it to work?

As Pixie moved into the stream of people making their way up the aisle towards the exits, Emma tapped her lightly on the shoulder. 'Well, nothing strange happened tonight,' she said hopefully when Pixie turned round. However, an uneasy feeling was building in her gut. What if there wasn't a ghost, after all? What if the culprit had been Rebecca all along? It seemed too obvious to be true, but the evidence seemed to be pointing at her. What was the saying? If it looks like a duck, walks like a duck, quacks like a duck, then it very likely *is* a duck. She hoped Pixie would give her a convincing explanation to believe otherwise.

'I'm afraid your earthbound spirit was on stage throughout the entire performance, playing Lady Macbeth alongside Rebecca,' Pixie told her gravely.

It sounded so outlandish that Emma wasn't sure whether to believe her. But the temperature had certainly dropped again. That, she couldn't deny. And she didn't think Pixie had the face of a fraudster. She fought against the doubts rising within her. 'Really?' she replied, longing for Pixie to give her some evidence to prove it.

'I just don't know why she sabotaged Isadora's performance and not Rebecca's,' Pixie mused ponderously. 'Maybe she didn't feel like ruining it tonight. Perhaps she just wanted to act. It could be that simple.'

'It's very odd,' said Emma, mulling over the same arguments whirring around her head. 'I mean, why has she decided to haunt the place now after having been quiet for decades?'

'I don't know,' Pixie replied. 'That's a very good question. I'm going to have to find that out. Might there be something of hers tucked away in an attic somewhere that I can use to connect to her? A photograph. Something she owned or borrowed. Something she touched.'

Emma wracked her brain. 'Gosh, I don't know. I can't imagine. Wasn't everything destroyed in the fire that killed her?'

'Probably,' said Pixie. She was about to suggest she borrow the letter, when Emma's face lit up with an idea.

'How about I put you in touch with Leila Frost?'

'The actress?' Pixie said. Leila Frost was one of those famous names from the past like Natalie Wood and Catherine Deneuve.

'Yes. She owns the theatre. She might have some relics put away somewhere. We can ask her.'

'That would be brilliant,' said Pixie.

Emma smiled, happy to be of help. 'I'll call her and let you know as soon as I hear back.'

They parted in the foyer and Pixie and Ulysses walked the short distance back to the hotel. Stars shone crisply in the navy sky and in the midst of them glowed the full moon, like a dazzling silver ball, illuminating the streets of Seacombe almost to the brightness of day. 'It's the Hunter's Moon tonight,' said Pixie, noticing how its round face was reflected in the water that collected in puddles along the side of the road. 'It's beautiful, isn't it?'

'Trust you to know your moons,' said Ulysses with a chuckle. 'I don't know one from the other.'

'Well, let me educate you then. It's called the Hunter's Moon because it's so bright and lasts so long, giving hunters time and light to go after their prey.'

'Fascinating,' he replied.

'Are you being sarcastic, Ulysses?'

'Absolutely not. I take you very seriously, as you know.'

Pixie laughed with him. 'Nessa Blunt was on stage tonight, acting the part of Lady Macbeth.'

'Now *that* is fascinating,' he said. 'But why didn't she ruin Rebecca's scenes?'

'My question exactly. Either she couldn't be bothered, or she likes Rebecca.'

'Do you think she's taken a dislike to Isadora?'

'Maybe, but this theatre has been going for years. There must have been many Isadoras treading those boards. Why hasn't she appeared before?'

'That's where you come in, Pixie, with your extraordinary superpower of being able to slide through time. I wish you'd let me write the article.'

'No one would believe you. Or me.' She smiled at him and slipped her hand round his arm. 'And what would be the point? What would it achieve?'

'Fame,' he replied simply.

'For you?'

'For us both.'

'I can't think of anything worse.'

'Money?'

'When has money ever made anyone happy?'

'Unhappy rich people just don't know how to spend it.'

'So what would *you* do with your riches?'

'Travel the world in first class,' he replied without a moment's hesitation. 'And I'd stay in five-star hotels like the Aldershoff.'

Pixie grinned and squeezed his arm playfully. 'I'm sure Henry Stirling would put you up for free.'

'I think he probably would,' Ulysses agreed. 'But when I visit him in New York, I'll be staying in his apartment.'

'I hope the room service is good.'

'Oh, I think the room service will be more than adequate. I like a personal touch! So, what would you do?'

'If I had an endless supply of money?' She considered it a moment. 'I'd buy a big farm and rescue dogs.'

Ulysses scrunched up his nose. 'Really?'

'And donkeys. I'd rescue donkeys too. And pigs.'

'Pigs?'

'In fact, I'd have a great big farm with loads of rescued animals. Animals are much nicer than people.'

'Than *most* people. I think you're right about that.'

'Good. You can help me muck out, then!'

'With that sort of money, you can have a whole army of mucker-outers!'

When they arrived at the hotel, they went straight to Ulysses' bedroom and ordered room service. Then Ulysses put on *Mamma Mia!*, and they snuggled up in the big bed to watch it.

'All that money and you'd buy a farm!' Ulysses said, drawing her close. 'Really, Pix, you never cease to surprise me!'

Joseph met Isadora in the hotel bar. He knew he had to keep her sweet if he wanted her to honour the terms of her contract. He was aware that she wouldn't hesitate to break it if she felt she had been badly treated, and she'd have a very good case; there was nothing about ghosts in the small print!

They sat at a round table in the corner. The lights had been turned down low. Piano music played softly through a speaker. Clusters of guests chatted quietly at other tables and a young couple perched on stools at the bar, drinking champagne. Isadora had not aroused interest. She had tied her hair back, and without dark glasses, lashings of make-up and lavish clothes, she didn't stand out.

'So what happened, Joey?' she asked once the waiter had brought her a Manhattan cocktail and Joseph a glass of Argentine Merlot.

Joseph plunged his fingers into the bowl of peanuts and held the wine glass to his lips. 'Nothing happened,' he said, and took a gulp, wincing in anticipation of a rant.

'You see!' she hissed, eyes widening with outrage. 'Rebecca is *so* obviously the culprit. You'd have to be an idiot not to see it.'

'You have a point,' Joseph agreed.

'All that talk of ghosts is ridiculous. I don't know how she pulled it off, but she did. And now she's playing *my* part.' She pursed her lips crossly. 'Did she get a standing ovation?'

'No, nothing like what the audience gave you,' he said, which was true. 'You're an A list star, Isadora. There's no comparison. Rebecca can't compete with that.'

'She's giving it her best shot!' she replied with a sniff.

'Listen, you come back tomorrow, and I'll give Rebecca the night off. She can go and make herself scarce somewhere on the other side of town.'

Isadora took a sip of her cocktail. 'Okay,' she replied, appeased. 'I don't want her anywhere near the theatre.'

'I promise.'

Satisfied that she had triumphed, she changed the subject. 'That Ulysses is hot,' she said, her scarlet lips curling into a smile.

Joseph frowned. 'Listen, Isadora, I'm not into this ghost stuff, but I'm covering all bases, for *you*. I take this very seriously. You are my priority right now and I'll do everything it takes, even if it means summoning ghost hunters all the way from London.'

She laughed and Joseph relaxed and took another handful of nuts. 'I appreciate it, Joey. I do.' Her voice was little girl lost. 'It's not that I don't believe in ghosts. I once stayed in a really old house in Virginia, and I swear a ghost tried to get into my bed. Imagine, Joey. It actually tried to get into bed with me!'

Joseph chuckled and gave her a cynical look. 'Are you sure it wasn't another guest?'

'I know what it sounds like, and believe me, I've had a few of them too. But no, I turned on the light and there was no one there. But I had felt the mattress sink and the covers move, and I got the real feeling that a big, burly man was trying to get in.' She shrugged. 'You see, I've had the odd encounter with the paranormal, so I don't doubt the existence of poltergeists and the like. I just doubt *this* one.' She took another sip. 'Are they a couple?'

'Who?'

'Ulysses and . . . what's she called? The plain girl with pink hair.'

Joseph was stung by her rudeness, so casually delivered. He was going to disagree with her, for in his opinion Pixie Tate was pretty, but he let it go. There was no point in arguing with Isadora. 'I think you'll find Ulysses is gay,' he said.

Isadora's face crumpled with disbelief. 'No, he can't be. He was flirting with me.'

'Well, if anyone can turn a gay man straight, it's you, Isadora.'

She gave a shallow laugh. She was clearly disappointed. 'Gay! God, why are all the best-looking men gay? It's so unfair.'

'Besides, they're leaving tomorrow,' said Joseph, dreading Emma telling him that they needed another day to rid the theatre of the ghost.

'Shame. I was really getting somewhere,' Isadora mused, and drained her glass.

'I'm surprised a beautiful woman like you is unattached,' he said.

'You heard of the triangle theory, Joey?'

'No,' Joseph replied.

'Imagine a triangle divided into horizontal sections. At the bottom, in the longest section, are all the rats and toads and squirrels and mice. Millions and trillions of them. And they all find each other. Easy; they're on the same level of the food chain. The great masses,' she said with disdain. 'Then as you go up, you get more layers. With each shortening layer you get classier animals, until, right at the top, in the little triangle, you get the beautiful lions and tigers. *Extremely* rare. It's hard to find creatures at the very top of the food chain, you see. So, to answer your question why a beautiful woman like me is unattached? Well, I'm waiting to find another lion or tiger, or a rare Canadian lynx. Being at the top of the food chain can be lonely.' She put her glass on the table. 'Order me another, Joey.' She patted his hand and gave him a pitying smile. 'You're so lucky you and Emma are not in that little triangle at the top of the food chain, Joey. You don't know how isolating it can be.'

*

Pixie lay beside Ulysses watching *Mamma Mia!* on the big television screen. She'd had a large glass of red wine and was now feeling sleepy and a little emotional. The film, although a comedy, pulled at her heart for two reasons. One, because it was about love, and she was on the point of sliding back to Cavill and drawing to a close whatever force it was that was bringing them together. Two, because the relationship between mother Donna and daughter Sophie was so touching that the mother-shaped hole in her heart ached with ever more emptiness and loss. She had never known that kind of tenderness from a mother, and the music made her pain even more acute because it was so beautiful.

As uplifting as the ending was, Pixie felt drained. She put her head on Ulysses' chest and closed her eyes as he wrapped his arms around her. 'Probably not the best choice of film,' he said and kissed her head.

Pixie's eyes filled with tears. 'I wish I had a mother like yours,' she said, and the emptiness she always carried inside her echoed louder than ever, demanding to be heard.

He squeezed her hard. 'I wish you did too, Pix. I wish you just had *parents*, full stop.'

There was a long pause as she took a deep breath. She felt secure there, in his embrace; safe and understood. 'I never talk about them, because it hurts so much. I suppose, I convince myself that if I don't think about what happened, it ceases to be a reality. But I know I should talk about them. I should acknowledge what happened and accept it. It's healing to release these things into the light and not allow them to fester in the dark. I think I want to talk about them, after all.'

'I'm here, Pix. Whenever you're ready,' he said.

'I'm ready.' She sat up and shuffled round to face him. 'Now.'

He picked up the remote and turned off the television. 'I'm all ears,' he said seriously.

Pixie sat cross-legged and took the full, rousing breath of a swimmer about to dive into very cold water. Then she began slowly, dropping her gaze into her hands fidgeting in her lap. 'I know little about my father because I was six when he died, but my maternal grandmother told me that he was an abusive alcoholic. I don't believe her, of course. The few memories I have are of him reading me bedtime stories and putting on all the voices.' She smiled wistfully at one of the only tender memories she retained. Then her smile vanished into a frown. 'Mostly, I remember them fighting. My mother shouting at him in a high-pitched, violent voice, and his low voice trying to calm her down. I was always sent up to my room, but I heard everything because the house was small. The memory that shines brightest is of my father bleeding on the kitchen floor and my mother standing over him with a big knife, dripping with blood. It kind of eclipses all the other memories. I remember her face. The horror on it.' Pixie sighed and shook her head. 'I don't remember feeling anything. I kind of remember it all with a distance, as if it belongs to another life. I can see the bright red colour of his blood as clearly as that red cushion, but I don't remember how I felt. And I don't recall what happened next. It's like a black hole. A black hole that swallowed everything into it, including me.'

Ulysses took her hands. 'I think that's enough for anyone to bear, don't you?' he said kindly.

She nodded and took another full breath. It felt better to have shared that moment. To have prised it out from its hiding place and brought it into the light. It didn't appear so frightening now. She looked at him steadily. 'My mother has been writing to me,' she told him. 'She's out of prison now and trying to get in touch. But I don't want to see her. I can't. I don't want to see the woman who stole my father. Who *killed* my father.' She felt her heart accelerate and the knot in her stomach tighten with anxiety as she uttered those terrible words. 'Who *murdered* my father. I don't want to listen to her lies.'

'Have you ever tried to slide back to see what really happened?' he asked.

Pixie shook her head. 'I couldn't. I mean, I just couldn't go back there. I imagine my aversion to it prevents it from happening. It's absolutely visceral.'

'And your father has never appeared to you in spirit?'

'No. Everyone else does, but he never has. I don't know why.' She shrugged sadly. 'It's not easy making contact with the living. Maybe it's too hard for him to get through to me.'

'Come here, Pix,' said Ulysses, pulling her into his arms. She lay against him and cried softly into his cashmere sweater. 'You're brave to have told me. Very brave. You're always solving everyone else's problems and sharing your wisdom to help others. What you need is someone to solve *your* problem and to give *you* some wisdom.'

'I have you, Ulysses,' she said.

'You do. You have a hundred per cent of me.'

She smiled sadly, knowing that wasn't exactly true. 'But you'll go off and live in New York with Henry.'

'Whoever said I'm going to go and live in New York?'

'Well, you can't have a relationship if you live on opposite sides of the world.'

'If I go and live in New York, then you'll come with me.'

'Really?'

'Really. We come as a pair. Any man foolish enough to want me, will have to take you too. Two for the price of one. Great deal. Couldn't do better.' He laughed. 'But with my love comes my honesty, Pixie. I think you need to hear what your mother has to say. No, don't stiffen. There are always two sides to a story, and you haven't heard her side. In fact, you haven't heard either side. You've just held on to the vision you saw in the kitchen and jumped to conclusions.'

'I don't think I jumped to the wrong conclusions. My mother went to prison for years for killing him,' Pixie objected.

'Sure, but she's your mother. Listen to her and then reject her if you want to. But I think it would be healing for you to meet up with her and take that decision based on a calm, grown-up conversation. You're a deeply spiritual person, Pixie. Surely, you would tell anyone in your position to find it in their heart to forgive.'

'I don't think I *can* forgive her.'

'I suspect you'll be amazed at what you're capable of. How many times have you told me that we're here, on this planet, to learn and grow? That we're faced with challenges we must meet head on?

Do you really want to leave this world having fallen at this hurdle? You'll kick yourself when you arrive in the next world without having settled things with your mother. You really will.'

Pixie took a deep breath. 'I'll think about it,' she said, but her every instinct recoiled.

'Okay. And if you want me to come with you, I will.'

'Thank you, Ulysses.'

'Pleasure, treasure.'

'I don't know what I'd do without you.'

He smiled into her hair. 'You always say that, but I don't know what I'd do without you either. I love you very much, don't ever forget that.'

They were interrupted by a loud knocking on the door. 'Who the hell is that?' Ulysses exclaimed.

Pixie lay back against the pillows as Ulysses climbed out of bed. He went to the door and opened it. To his surprise it was Isadora. She looked younger without make-up, with her hair pulled back and dressed in a simple cream-coloured V-neck sweater, washed denim jeans and bare feet. Her toenails were painted Barbie pink. 'Isadora?'

Pixie sat up in alarm. What was *she* doing here? Then it dawned on her. Isadora wasn't here on a social call.

'Hi, Ulysses,' Isadora purred, gazing up at him from beneath long lashes. 'I was wondering whether you'd like to watch a movie.'

'Actually, I've just watched one, with Pixie,' he replied.

Isadora's eyes strayed beyond Ulysses to the big bed where she could just make out the mound of feet beneath the covers. Her face went pink. She stiffened like a cat that spots another cat on its territory. 'I see,' she replied tersely. 'Well, that's a shame. What did you watch?'

'*Mamma Mia!*,' Ulysses replied.

Isadora narrowed her eyes. Then her shoulders dropped, and she laughed. 'Are you gay, Ulysses?' she asked.

'I am,' he answered.

She put a hand on his arm. 'Well, that explains everything.' She lowered her voice. 'You know, if you change your mind, I'm in room 203. I've been known to turn men like you, and we lions must stick together.' With that she gave him a wink and then wandered off, a little unsteadily, down the corridor.

'What was that about lions?' Pixie asked when Ulysses returned to the bed.

'Beats me,' he replied. He grinned mischievously at his friend. 'I think you'd better stay the night in case she comes back.'

Pixie knew Isadora wasn't going to come back. 'Thank you,' she said, and smiled.

He returned her smile, acknowledging that she saw right through him. He couldn't hide anything from Pixie. 'I don't want you to be alone tonight,' he said seriously. 'I want you where I can keep an eye on you.'

The following morning Pixie awoke to the whisper of Ulysses' soft breathing. It was a comforting sound and one she wished she heard every morning. She lay on her back, staring up at the ceiling, recalling their conversation of the night before. Ulysses was her best friend – her *only* friend – but it was inevitable that he would settle down one day with someone else, and where did that leave her? Alone. The reality was that if he went to live in New York to be closer to Henry, even if it was just for the odd month here and there, she wouldn't be able to go with him. Henry wouldn't want her hanging around. Nor would it be possible for her to work there. Inevitably, their relationship would have to change. She couldn't bear to think of it. She couldn't bear to lose him. Without Ulysses she had no one.

Her mother slipped into her mind then, but before she could grab Pixie's attention, Pixie turned her thoughts to the day ahead and to her mission, thus blocking her out. Pixie had become adept at blocking out her mother.

Pixie had brought with her Cavill's sketchbook of birds in the hope of sliding back to him. Could it be true that unless she finished what she had started with Cavill, she'd pull him into every slide? Was love that powerful? As much as she longed to see him, she didn't want to meet him as someone else. If only she could meet him as Pixie. What a cruel fate it was to love a man who lived in another time, she reflected unhappily.

She dragged herself out of bed and padded softly into the bathroom. It amused her to see Ulysses' lotions and potions lined up in neat rows by the sink. He had more pots of cream than she did. She lifted the bottle of cologne to her nose and sniffed it. Sandalwood, cedarwood and spice. The smell was so Ulysses that it brought him to her in a wave of memories. She closed her eyes and savoured them. She didn't want anything to change. But change was one of the only things in life one could be certain of.

She left him sleeping and went to her own bedroom to shower and dress. When she turned on her telephone she saw she had a message from Emma. *Leila has something that might connect you to Nessa Blunt. Meet me at the theatre at 10 a.m.*

Pixie was in the dining room enjoying breakfast when Ulysses appeared. He looked smart in a pair of khaki jeans and a cornflower-blue shirt, a cashmere sweater thrown casually over his shoulders. He had an effortless style, but he always stood out and drew every eye in the room. He strode confidently over to her table and sat down. 'Bom dia, Pix,' he said, flicking out the napkin and laying it over his lap. 'I slept like the dead. You? Anything go bump in the night?'

Pixie laughed. She had long learned how to shut out those beings that might disturb her. 'We have a meeting at the theatre at ten, so you'd better hurry up and eat.'

'You should have woken me!' he exclaimed, glancing anxiously at the buffet.

'You know one should never try and wake the dead,' she replied dryly.

He pulled a face then made his way to the table of pastries. For a man who did not usually have more than a cup of strong coffee in the morning, the choice of delicious things to eat was too good to resist.

*

They arrived at the theatre just before ten. Pixie carried her carpet bag which contained Cavill's sketchbook in anticipation of her inevitable slide. As she pushed open the heavy door, she cast her eyes to the stair but there was no spirit to greet her today, only Emma and Leila waiting for them in the foyer. When Leila was introduced to Pixie, she shook her hand with a firm grip and exclaimed, 'I'm open-minded, but I'm yet to be convinced of the existence of ghosts!'

Ulysses laughed. 'If anyone can convince you, it's Pixie,' he said.

Leila might have been elderly, but she was not immune to the charms of a beautiful young man. 'I'm sure *you* could convince me of anything,' she added, giving him a raffish smile.

'I was just telling Leila about Nessa Blunt . . .' said Emma.

'I've heard stories over the years about a resident ghost, but I've never seen or heard anything,' Leila interrupted. 'And I've owned this theatre for over twenty years! But I do know about the fire.'

'There must be records somewhere,' said Pixie. 'In the local library?'

Emma nodded eagerly. 'Great idea. It would be interesting to compare historical records with what *you* find out,' she said. If they matched, she'd have ammunition for Joseph, who was adamant that Pixie was a fraud and that there were no such things as ghosts. As it was *she* who had encouraged him to enlist the help of a medium, she very much wanted to prove that she hadn't been imprudent.

'I know something of the history, however,' Leila continued. 'The theatre was built in 1901 by a local man called Randolph Brown who built it for the woman he loved, called Aphrodite Allen. She was an English actress whose real name was Jane. It's a rather romantic story, a man building a theatre so the woman he loved could perform in it. Naturally, it was amateur dramatics in those days, and nothing came of Aphrodite Allen. I doubt the theatre ever made much money. It was a labour of love! It limped on during the Great War and was then sold in 1920 after Randolph died of pneumonia. I'm not sure what happened to Aphrodite. Without her sponsor she vanished into thin air, never to be heard of again. Anyway, you know about the fire in 1923. Poor old Nessa Blunt. Emma tells me she's the ghost.'

'I believe so,' said Pixie.

'Gripping!' Leila exclaimed, giving the gravelly laugh of an erstwhile smoker. 'Come, let me take you to the costume department. It's a veritable Aladdin's cave down there.'

Leila led them downstairs, explaining as they went how, when she bought the theatre, she had inherited all the paraphernalia that went with it. Not only were there costumes and props, sets, lights and scripts, but also boxes of knick-knacks and trinkets. 'Everything is kept in the bowels of the building and right at the back. I couldn't tell you if any of it belonged to Nessa Blunt, but I can tell you that none of it was destroyed by the fire. As you will see, the room is underground. Miraculously, it escaped intact. I'm sure, if she did indeed exist, she would most certainly have worn many of the costumes, wigs and jewellery.'

'The question is *which*,' said Ulysses.

But Pixie wasn't at all doubtful. She knew that when she saw something of Nessa's, she would know.

Leila opened the door, and they entered a large rectangular room that smelt strongly of damp, and dusty old fabrics. She switched on the lights. 'Wow!' exclaimed Ulysses, looking around keenly at the low ceiling, uneven white walls and wonky wooden floor. 'This room is very old.'

'Oh, I should think it dates back to when the theatre was built,' said Leila. 'I bet you'll find some of these costumes do too!'

Pixie wasted no time in rifling through them. She knew she would intuit when she touched something that had a connection to Nessa Blunt. Emma and Leila stood chatting with Ulysses, but Pixie was now focused on her quest and heard nothing of their conversation. She felt Nessa's energy and sensed they were not alone.

'Oh, it's chilly in here,' said Emma, folding her arms.

'We're in the bowels of the theatre,' Ulysses repeated. 'I don't imagine it's heated down here.'

But Pixie knew better.

Leila spied a motheaten fur stole on one of the rails and draped it over her shoulders on top of her faux fox coat. 'I bet the heating has gone on the blink again,' she said, giving an exasperated sigh. 'Probably a dreaded air lock. These old buildings are frightfully difficult to maintain.'

Pixie moved swiftly through the rails of costumes. She flicked past velvet breeches and brocaded jackets, silk dresses and satin shirts. There were costumes for every type of play, from pirates to paupers, kings and queens to court jesters, flapper dresses to flared trousers. She sensed nothing of interest among them. She moved on to the shelves of cardboard boxes. Her fingers lightly touched their labels: tights, brooches, tiaras, buttons, buckles, belts, garters, necklaces . . . her fingers stopped there. *Necklaces.* She took the box down and lifted the lid. Inside was a tangle of beads, fake diamonds and pearls. She immediately seized upon the pearls with a jolt of excitement. When she had seen Nessa Blunt the day before, she had been wearing a long string of pearls. Pixie lifted it out. The hairs on the back of her neck bristled, and not from the cold. She clutched the pearls in her fist, feeling ever more strongly a connection to Nessa.

She knew she would know.

'I have what I'm looking for,' she told the trio.

'Thank God for that,' said Leila emphatically, making for the corridor. 'Now let's go somewhere warm!'

'What happens now?' Emma asked.

'I need to use that VIP room again,' said Pixie. 'I'll link into Nessa's energy with these pearls, and hopefully find out what it is that's keeping her here. If I do my job well, I'll use that information to encourage her to move on.'

'It always works,' said Ulysses confidently.

Pixie wasn't so blasé. 'Until it doesn't,' she added. 'I can only do my best.'

Emma showed Pixie and Ulysses into the VIP room and then left them alone. Ulysses locked the door so they couldn't be disturbed and then looked around for the most comfortable chair; he knew he was likely to be there for at least a few hours. He put his laptop on the low table and settled into the upholstered chair beside it to watch one of his favourite Ingrid Bergman movies.

'Okay, Pix. This is it. Go back and finish what you started,' said Ulysses, putting on his headphones.

Pixie nodded. She thought of Cavill, and a sliver of doubt slipped into her consciousness. What if she didn't draw him into her slide? What then? What if Avril had got it wrong? What if they both had? She smothered the doubt with the light of hope. In order for it to work she had to believe it with all her heart.

Pixie knew Nessa was with them. The temperature had dropped, and she felt the spirit's prickly energy upon her skin. It was full of scorn. She knew Nessa was determined to defy her. But Nessa didn't know what Pixie was capable of. As Pixie relaxed on the straight-backed wooden chair she had chosen, the sketchbook on her lap, the string of pearls resting gently in her hands, she felt a small sense of smugness, for Nessa had no idea that Pixie was going to travel back to when she was alive. She couldn't even imagine it. Timesliding was a powerful tool. The only tool, perhaps, that might give Pixie the information she needed to outwit this most stubborn of spirits. She closed her eyes and took a few deep breaths, focusing on the rise and fall of her chest. She imagined a silver chord coming out of her solar plexus and wrapping around the sketchbook and pearls, and then she put out the intention with as much clarity of thought as she could. *Take me to Cavill so that I can end what I have begun, and give me the information I need to settle the soul of Nessa Blunt.*

With that thought, she felt herself slip out of her body. She saw the room, Ulysses watching his movie, and Nessa Blunt, standing in the corner in her string of pearls, watching her in bewilderment.

But then Pixie was a wisp of vapour, rising into the air and slipping through the veil of time, and Nessa the spirit could see her no more.

The Past

Chapter Eight

I open my eyes. The first thing I notice is an open letter in my hand. Written in black ink are the words: *Let me explain. Meet me in the usual place at midday.*

I stare at it. I have no idea who the letter is from or where 'the usual place' might be. I don't even know who *I* am. I take a deep breath to steady my nerves, which are buzzing with the evident challenges of this new adventure. What should I do? Someone's going to be mightily disappointed when I don't show up!

Firstly, I need to get my bearings, and quickly. I look down at my clothes. I'm wearing a pale blue drop-waisted dress that reaches below the knees, typical of the 1920s. It's made of soft cotton and embellished at the breast with a blue-and-white bow. I'm wearing stockings because I can feel the garters holding them up just above the knees – tights are yet to be invented. I'm wearing some sort of undergarment, but it's not as restricting as a corset, and possibly French knickers, which make me feel strangely naked beneath the skirt. The outfit is comfortable, unlike the stiff Edwardian clothes I had to wear in my last slide. I notice the T-strap brown shoes on my feet and the slender ankles above them. In fact, as I lift the skirt to take a closer look, I notice that my legs are pretty awesome. I'm slim and probably of average height. I glance at the backs of my hands to get an idea of my age and am at once taken by the elegance of my long fingers and shell-pink, manicured nails and – oh, goodness, a gold band on the third finger of my left hand. A *wedding* ring. I'm married? A stab of horror momentarily paralyses me. If I'm married, will I have to share a bed with a husband? Will

I have to . . . ? I shudder at the thought. I don't want to think about that. I'll face it when the moment comes and fake a headache. If there's a husband, I'm going to have to really be on my mettle to pull off this pretence!

My heart sinks and I curse the vocation I've chosen for the lengths I have to go to to settle souls!

I sweep my eyes over the room. I'm standing in a square-shaped sitting room on a fine Persian rug. There's a white, marble fireplace in the centre of one wall, but the grate is empty. Above it, on a generous mantelpiece, is a big brown clock with a gold face. Its black hands mark the time: eleven o'clock. I have one hour to find out where I need to be. Of course, I have no way of knowing whether the woman I have possessed would *want* to be there. *Let me explain.* It feels very much like a letter from a man. Have they had a row? Is she having an affair? A note like this is unlikely to be from a husband. It reeks of subterfuge. Good Lord, I find myself in the most mysterious of situations. Why can't things ever be simple?

The room is naturally warm. I glance out of the sash window and notice a mature cherry tree with bright, almost phosphorescent leaves. Cherry trees usually blossom in April, so it must be May. Sunshine is tumbling in with the blithe abandon of spring. I hear the rumbling sound of a car in the street below, and the merry tweeting of birds. Tuning in now, I can also hear a dog barking in the distance and the sporadic laughter of children, followed by the loud patter of scampering feet, which gradually dies out. I turn my attention back to the room. I suspect that it's mine because why otherwise would I be in it with a letter in my hand? It's cosy and decorated with an eye for colour: bold wallpaper depicting thick green vines, fat purple grapes and hummingbirds; an apple-green sofa with scatter cushions, purple upholstered chairs, occasional tables displaying trinkets and books, standard lamps with fringed shades and a wide bookcase against the back wall. Framing the window are heavy green curtains with an elaborate tasselled pelmet. Through the glass I can see elegant Georgian town houses opposite, typical of provincial southern English towns. I'm pretty sure I'm in Seacombe.

I need to find out who I am, and the date.

I begin to race about the room looking for clues. There's a round table in front of the window upon which stands a glass vase of cut flowers – alliums, lilies and green, leafy foliage – and various magazines: *Time & Tide*, *The Lady*, a fashion mail order catalogue and *The Times Weekly Edition*, mercifully displaying the date, Friday 4th May 1923.

If the fire that kills Nessa Blunt happens on the 9th May, I have five days in which to investigate how and why it happens in order to persuade her to move on. I suspect, however, that the root cause of her compulsion to create mischief in spirit lies *beyond* the events of the 9th of May. That the fire is, to use the popular idiom, just the tip of the iceberg. I need to find out what lies beneath – what kind of woman is Nessa Blunt?

To orientate myself, I focus a moment on the date: 1923. The Conservative Bonar Law is prime minister, King George V is on the throne. Tutankhamun's tomb has been discovered in Egypt – totally irrelevant detail, but it's surprising the things one remembers from reading *National Geographic* magazine.

That settled, I now need to find out about *me*. Who am I?

My eye falls upon a wastepaper bin. It's tucked beneath the wooden console table to the right of the fireplace. I have a suspicion that the envelope the letter came in might have been thrown in there. I stride hopefully across the rug and glance inside. I'm right. She didn't even screw it up. I fish it out. The name is written clearly in the same black ink. *Mrs Tom Skipton. By hand.*

I wonder where Tom is and question how I'm going to manage five days being married, when in my own time I haven't had much luck with relationships. In fact, the only one that lasted more than five days was handsome, albeit feckless, Pablo whom I caught in bed with another woman. Perhaps marriage is like living with Ulysses, only with sex. I vigorously shake my head at that thought, because it's unimaginable. I will simply have to wait and see. Then another horrible thought arises: what if I have children?

I frantically look about for a mirror. I need to see what I look like; faces reveal an enormous amount about a person's character. But there doesn't seem to be one.

I'm on the point of leaving the room to further explore the house when the door opens and in walks a harassed-looking maid in a black dress and white apron. She's large-boned and wide-hipped and has the careworn face of a woman who has worked hard all her life and has little time for vanity, or self-indulgence. Judging by her greying hair and wrinkled skin, I guess she's about sixty. 'Ma'am, the scissor-grinder is at the door. What shall I tell him?' She speaks slowly with a soft, West Country accent and seems irritated at the interruption. 'Would you like the clocks attended to?'

'Yes, please,' I reply, doing my best to sound authoritative.

She sighs heavily and shakes her head. 'The range is playing up again and Cook says that if Bunsen doesn't mend it well and good this time, she'll give in her notice. How is she to provide for yourself and two hungry young women without a range?'

'Two hungry young women?' I repeat dumbly, wondering who the hell is coming for dinner.

'Sorry, Ma'am, young *ladies*,' she replies with emphasis.

I smile weakly. How can I squeeze more information out of her? But she is gone.

I decide to find my bedroom. I step out onto a landing. I'm on the first floor. I peer down the stairs. There's a hall where the maid is talking to the scissor-grinder. It's got a tiled floor – white squares and black diamonds – and a large, gilt-framed mirror which hangs above a wooden console table. Upon it is a silver plate full of letters. My heart thuds in my chest at the prospect of finding out who I am via those letters.

I wait for the maid to escort the scissor-grinder off, to the kitchen perhaps, and then hurry downstairs. Halfway down, on the landing, is a big arched window that lets in lots of light. Through it I see a sumptuous garden, lovingly tended with tidy borders of clipped box, pink and purple delphiniums and an assortment of shrubs. At the bottom of a neatly mown lawn is an old apple tree, beneath which a round table and four chairs promise peace and shade. I continue down to the hall and seize upon the letters. Before I open them, I grab the opportunity to look at my reflection in the mirror. It always knocks the wind out of me the first moment I see a strange face staring back. A face that moves according to my will, but which doesn't belong to me. I blink a few times in astonishment, liking very much what I see. I'm beautiful but no longer in the bloom of youth. My beauty is neither classical, nor obvious. It lies in something deeper than perfect proportions and pouting lips, and I run my fingers over the contours in fascination, taking in every detail.

Mrs Skipton is undoubtedly a woman of intelligence, sensitivity and charm. Her grey-blue eyes are the colour of washed denim. Her eyelashes are long and naturally dark. Fine laughter lines fan out into her temples and the skin on her eyelids is a little slack. What strikes me, above all else, is the gentle, compassionate expression that shines out of her eyes. I can see that she's a woman of empathy and kindness, and I'm glad that I've taken possession of someone who is good. I remind myself of the apparent rules of timesliding – that, by the Law of Attraction, I'm drawn to possess someone of a similar vibration to me. Mrs Skipton must be in her late thirties or early forties, which is older than I am, but she must be of a comparable character.

Her hair is dark brown and gently greying. It's pinned carelessly into a low chignon at the nape of the neck, with loose strands curling prettily about her heart-shaped face. Her nose is long and slightly aquiline, her lips curling by nature, which, together with the laughter lines around her mouth and eyes, suggest she has a good sense of humour. Her skin is slightly tanned from the sun with a light sprinkling of freckles over her nose. She has altogether a very appealing face.

Satisfied that I now know something of this woman I have embodied, I peer through the door and notice a flamboyantly decorated dining room with a big oval table and six high-backed chairs, upholstered in fuchsia pink and green velvet to match the walls. There's a fireplace, a mantelpiece with the ubiquitous clock, two gold cherub candlesticks at either end, and an array of stiff white invitations, embossed in swirly gold writing, leaning up against a brightly coloured abstract painting. There's something magical about physical letters and invitations. In my time everything is sent via email and paperless post, which feels cold and impersonal by comparison.

There's another room beyond the dining room with double doors leading out onto a terrace and the garden. It's a light and airy sitting room with wicker armchairs and a sofa arranged around a fireplace. It's decorated in greens and yellows with big potted ferns. But I must not get distracted by the allure of the house. I have a job to do.

I use the silver knife lying beside the tray to slice open one of the envelopes and pull out the letter within.

5 Chelsea Square
London SW3

My dear Eddie. I cannot thank you enough for the wonderful week you gave me in Seacombe. You were so right, the sea air and brisk walks have done me the world of good and I feel much restored. Ready to fight again! Your advice was most welcome, and I will take it all on board, every word. What a wise owl you are! With everything that is going on in your life, I am astonished that you have so much time for other people and their woes. But what would we do without you? I will keep you abreast of every stage of this miserable divorce, and perhaps return in the summer for more beach and theatre, an unbeatable combination.

Speaking of which, The Aphrodite was at its best. The company is second to none – all thanks to your dear husband, of course, for having championed amateur drama with such passion, and to you, for having kept it going during those dark years of war. In spite of your misgivings, I think Mr Bentley is what the place needs. A firm and steady hand, and handsome too!

I am sure Macbeth will be a great success with the inimitable Gilda Garrett stealing every show! Those Americans have a certain glamour, don't they? Do let me know. How I wish I could be there for the opening night.

Hey-ho!

I hope you will give me the opportunity to return your hospitality with a visit to London. My little Chelsea home is very quiet now that I am a woman on her own. Your presence here would be most cheery!

With much affection,
Rose

Macbeth! This is no coincidence, of course. Nessa Blunt's spirit began to make mischief at the theatre during the opening night of *Macbeth.* I sense immediately that this is significant. And Gilda Garrett, the leading lady, is American, like Isadora Nash. That isn't a coincidence, either. I feel invigorated, suddenly. Like fog slowly clearing to reveal the outline of a landscape, I'm beginning to see a vague pattern emerging in this drama.

From Rose's letter I deduce that my husband has something to do with the theatre. I imagine Mr Bentley must be the manager, or director? I swiftly read the other letters. There are bills to be paid and a postcard from the South of France from someone called, simply, Lady B. Nothing particularly illuminating. I replace them on the silver tray.

I wonder then whether Eddie Skipton writes a diary. Many did in those days – Constance Fleet, the woman I took over in my last slide, wrote an excellent journal that told me a great deal about her life. Ignoring the guilty feeling of snooping about in someone else's house, I make my way upstairs. I reach the first-floor landing and the now familiar drawing room on the left. There's a big sash window right ahead of me which looks out onto the cherry tree and the street. There are various paintings hanging on walls papered in an indigo and white floral design, polished pieces of antique wooden furniture and two big white panelled doors to my right, separated by a half-moon table bearing an extravagant hydrangea in a blue and white china pot. I hear a creak and wince. I remind myself that I'm *not* Pixie Tate. That this is *my* house now, and I must play the part. Still, I can't help feeling like a thief, prowling around someone else's property.

I turn the brass knob of the door nearest the flight of stairs. As soon as it opens, I know that it's Eddie's bedroom. It's feminine, decorated in dusty pinks and apple greens with two windows opening onto the garden. The sweet scent of wisteria wafts in on a warm breeze, carrying with it the salty smell of the sea. There's a big bed covered in a pale green quilt and tasselled scatter cushions; tall green lamps on bedside tables; charming seats tucked into window recesses and floor-length satin curtains in a sumptuous pink. There's an elegant dressing table upon which sits a triple-folding mirror, lotions and potions in fancy cut glass bottles with elaborate silver lids, and a spherical vase of pink roses. There's no trace of a man in here.

I look closely at the books piled neatly on one of the bedside tables beside a green water glass and matching jug: Oscar Wilde's plays, *Night and Day* by Virginia Woolf, Thomas Hardy's *Tess of the D'Urbervilles, The Age of Innocence,* by Edith Wharton, and Agatha Christie's *The Mysterious Affair at Styles.* Mrs Skipton is obviously an avid reader. There is no sign of a journal, however.

I notice a tapestry handbag thrown over the green chaise longue at the end of the bed and open it. I find a lipstick in a gold case, a green satin purse, reading glasses in an embroidered sleeve, keys on a silver ring and a small vial of perfume. I put the vial to my nose. It smells strongly of carnations.

I rummage about for anything else, but besides a small pink notebook and miniature gold pencil, there's nothing in the handbag that helps me work out where the 'usual place' might be, or the identity of the person who is expecting Eddie to be there.

I enter a bathroom, decorated in the same pretty colours as the bedroom. I notice the claw-footed cast iron bath and stunning brass taps. How Ulysses would love those. At the other end of the bathroom is a white panelled door leading into what appears to be a man's dressing room: a high bed with a dark mahogany frame, simple beige walls adorned with framed cartoons, a built-in wardrobe and a sturdy chest of drawers. There's a collection of silver-backed brushes arranged neatly on the chest of drawers and an oval mirror, slightly tarnished, on a pole. The window behind it opens onto an ornamental courtyard and beyond it, through an iron gate, is the street. I peer down. The street is paved rather than tarmacked and there are no markings at all. It's also quiet. Only an elderly woman in a brown coat walks slowly along, carrying a shopping bag. I wish I had access to the internet, then I could find out where the theatre is in relation to this house.

I open the wardrobe. Mr Skipton is very tidy. Jackets are arranged on hangers in an orderly row according to colour – black to navy to beige and finally brown, and are made in all sorts of fabrics. I finger them curiously, trying to get a sense of the man who wears them. Wool, silk, cotton, velvet and tweed. Below the jackets is a rail for trousers. I'm quite mesmerised by the choice. Ulysses would kill to have a cupboard like this! I push my nose into the jackets and inhale the scent of sandalwood.

'Is everything all right, Mrs Skipton?' I jump as if caught with my hand in the safe. It's the maid again. She is standing in the doorway with a sequinned green dress hanging over her arm. Her tone is gentle and a touch fearful, and she's looking at me with concern.

'Everything is just fine,' I reply, and smile, closing the cupboard. I feel my face burning guiltily.

Her concern turns to pity. I'm not sure why she's looking at me like that. My blush deepens.

'Your dress for tonight,' she says. 'I managed to get that stain out, although it took a fair bit of elbow grease. I'm not sure what that dog had to eat.'

I can't imagine what the hell she's talking about. But I agree with a nod. 'Thank you very much. I'm so grateful.' Then I remember what she said about Cook. 'When will Bunsen mend the range?'

'You know Bunsen!' She laughs cautiously. I don't think she's one to easily give in to joy.

I laugh with her. 'Oh, I do,' I reply, wishing I knew her name. 'Well, let's hope he manages to fix it before supper.'

'Indeed, or it will be cold meat and cheese again. The young ladies won't like that, two nights in a row.'

Are the young ladies Eddie's daughters? 'We can't have Cook giving in her notice, can we?' I add.

She shakes her head and clicks her tongue. 'She's all bark and no bite, that one. Don't you worry, ma'am, she'll manage. We all will.' She hesitates and looks past me to the wardrobe. 'Were you looking for something?'

'No, no. I'm about to go out.'

She nods slowly, but her eyes narrow suspiciously. 'I do keep it clean and tidy in here, you know, even though . . .' She gives a little sniff and lifts her chin, then turns and walks back into Eddie's bedroom.

I follow her. I watch her carefully lay the dress on the bed. 'You'll look lovely in this tonight,' she says, and her voice is full of pride. 'Perhaps the black headband with the green feather, and those pearl earrings Mr Skipton gave you that time he took you to Paris.'

'Ah, Paris,' I repeat and smile at what surely must be a lovely recollection.

She regards me with such sympathy, I'm taken aback. I wonder whether I shouldn't be quite so enthusiastic about Paris. She purses her lips. 'Damn the war,' she says, then adds quickly, putting a finger to her lips, 'Pardon my French, ma'am.'

I glance at the gold clock on the mantlepiece. There seems to be a fireplace in every room, and a clock too. It's now twenty to twelve. Twenty minutes to the mysterious rendezvous. I'd like to ask the maid, but I doubt she'd know. The letter seemed secretive. I sigh. There's nothing for it. I can't go to 'the usual place' so I'll have to go to the theatre instead and see what's going on there. 'I'm heading out,' I say, and leave her staring at me with a strange look on her face.

She must think me very odd. I don't even know her name.

Just before I set off down the stairs, I remember the possibility of Eddie writing a journal and pop back into the room to ask her about it. 'I can't remember where I put it,' I tell her hopefully.

She frowns. 'I wasn't aware that you wrote a journal, ma'am.'

I shrug. 'Oh, I've only recently started. I thought it would be fun to record the minutiae of my life,' I say. 'If you come across it, do let me know.' I feel her confused gaze boring into my back as I turn and walk away.

The scissor-grinder is working on the clock in the dining room. I decide to see if I can elicit some information from him. 'Good morning,' I say cheerfully, trying to convey the appropriate confidence and authority of the woman who owns this house. 'Will you do the clocks upstairs as well, please?' I add in order to start a conversation.

He doffs his cap. He's a rough-looking man with weathered brown skin, bushy eyebrows and a thick, woolly grey beard. His eyes are very blue, shining out of his face like sapphires in rock. 'Yes, madam,' he replies. His West Country accent is tightly wound, like his clocks.

'If you need anything, you know whom to ask.'

'I do, indeed, madam. Mrs Crocker says she will escort me upstairs when I'm ready.'

I silently congratulate myself. Smoothly done! I smile at him. 'Very well.'

I leave him to it, satisfied that my skills are being honed with each new slide. No doubt about it, I'm getting quite good at this.

There are hooks by the front door upon which various coats and hats are hanging. I choose a bright red, brimless hat because Eddie Skipton is clearly a woman who likes colour, then stand before the mirror to put it on. It complements the light tan on my skin and is very becoming. I admire myself a moment. Pixie Tate is not beautiful like Eddie Skipton. It's a delightful novelty to be so good-looking, and I make a mental note to bask in it while I can.

I take a deep breath, then open the door and step out into this strange new world of 1923.

Chapter Nine

I'm not sure which way to go. If I can find the hotel, or the station, I can easily work out the way to the theatre from there. Before I set off, I take a good look at the house and commit it to memory. I don't want to forget where I live. I immediately recognise the building as Queen Anne. Ulysses would like it, for that's his favourite style. It's charming, as Queen Anne houses tend to be, set a few yards back from the road behind an iron gate. It's built in red brick with two big windows either side of the front door, five in the row above and three dormer windows peeping out of the grey tiled roof. There is a row of tall chimney stacks. Wisteria scales the brick around the door, right up to the first-floor windows. Its purple flowers tumble over each other in extravagant heaps of fragrant petals. On the York stone paving between the house and the gate, intrepid weeds have begun to poke out of the cracks in the pointing, their bright green foliage basking greedily in the sunlight. There are giant terracotta pots of hydrangeas slowly blooming, and the cherry tree I saw from the sitting room window has shed its blossom and is now a bright green. It is, without doubt, a stunning property.

I take a left and set off up the cobbled street. No reason for choosing that way, just following my nose and trusting my instinct. Seacombe is incredibly pretty. The houses are painted in a rainbow of colours, with grey slate roofs and window boxes full of bright spring flowers. The breeze is fresh and damp, and smells of brine. I sense the sea is close.

As I stroll on, my mind turns to Cavill. I haven't had a moment to think about him, but I think about him now. My heart strains with longing, and the desperate hope that I will be given another opportunity to see him – a *final* opportunity, perhaps; one I will not squander. The last time I laid eyes on him was in the hall in the Aldershoffs' mansion in New York, in April 1912. It is now eleven years later. He'll be sixty-six.

Sixty-six.

An anguish takes hold of me as I sense the grains of sand running out of the hourglass, for I'm now reaching the final part of our story. I've been sliding forward in time – we met in 1895, then 1912, and now, if our paths cross again, 1923. There seems to be an indefinable pull that is drawing me to a certain destination. I don't know what that destination is, but as that word implies, it has a ring of destiny to it. What is our destiny? Is there a greater design?

As I wander over the shadows, from dark to light, I fear that perhaps I'm reading too much into it. That I'm overthinking, because I *want* there to be a greater design – a purpose. I want it very badly to be significant. But the more I think about it, the more impossible it seems that he will be here. Why would he be? He lives in America! Why would he be in Seacombe? I worry now that I've been a fool, that he's on the other side of the Atlantic, thousands of miles from here. My blind belief in the Law of Attraction bringing us together stalls horribly. Perhaps I haven't started anything at all. Maybe it's just wishful thinking – putting undue significance on the fact that we met in two different slides. Perhaps they were just coincidences? I slow down to an amble as my dreams crack like mirrors, splintering the beautiful images I'd cultivated in my mind into a hundred pieces. I have to accept that there's a strong possibility Cavill will have *no* part to play in this slide.

My heart shrinks and I lose courage. Have I been so blinkered by love that I've created a possibility where there isn't one? Perhaps there will be no last encore.

With these gloomy thoughts the street ceases to look so pretty, and the sun slips behind a cloud, casting me in shade. But I lift my chin and rally, as I always do. It's in my nature to look for the light, always. I remind myself that this is my job. This is what I do – I settle lost souls, and poor Nessa Blunt needs my help, even though she doesn't know it. I must forget Cavill and focus on *her*.

I walk down cobbled streets, following my nose, not having a clue where I'm headed, trying to shake off the feeling that this isn't real, that it's an Agatha Christie film set. The odd car motors by. It's fascinating to see those beautiful old vehicles which are so small and elegant compared to our large, chunky four-by-fours. But cars are still rare in 1923. Most people walk, or cycle, and there are horsedrawn carriages, and carthorses pulling all sorts of things, from vegetables to barrels and building equipment.

I jump at the sudden hooting of a motor car and step out of the road to watch it pass. A woman in a ruby red convertible, sitting at the wheel in a hat and veil, waves at me enthusiastically. I wave back gamely and smile. As she rattles on up the street, I brace myself for the inevitable 'stop and chat'. In a town of this size, Eddie Skipton is bound to know a lot of people. I'll have to keep my wits about me in order not to expose myself as an imposter or let the real Eddie down.

I take my time. Apart from the occasional car, the pace of life here feels slow and unhurried. Seacombe in 1923 has the energy of a large village rather than a thriving town. It's sleepy beneath the big blue sky and the lazy white clouds that drift idly across it.

Eventually, I emerge onto the sea front. The air smells marshy. There's a gusty breeze. I set off up the promenade, taking everything in. Various people mull about. There are a few shops whose awnings give shade to the wares stacked tidily beneath them. A pair of elderly women converse on a bench while fat gulls waddle about their Mary Jane shoes, hoping for crumbs. Two young children play with a bucket full of something exciting, for they're dipping their fingers inside then extracting them quickly to squeals of delight. I can't see where their mothers are, but various women stroll arm in arm beneath parasols, deep in conversation, while others browse the shops. Fishermen tend to their boats moored in the harbour, their sails down, the masts pointing skyward like toothpicks. Seabirds circle them, both in the air and on the water. The sea is calm. The waves gently lap the shore. The scene is one of early summer, of enjoying the warm sun while it shines.

It must be well after midday now. I wonder where the 'usual place' is and who is waiting for me there. I feel sorry for them. I hope I haven't let Eddie Skipton down.

I want to ask directions to the theatre, but I can't be sure that I won't wind up asking someone who knows Eddie, and that would be very odd. As in all slides, I must be mindful of the woman I'm inhabiting. I will leave once this job is done and Eddie will have to deal with whatever situation I've left her in. It's paramount, therefore, that I act responsibly.

I come across a sign that reads *Town Centre*. It's likely that the theatre is there, so I follow it. I'm setting off in that direction when a young woman in a pair of tweed knickerbockers, thick ribbed socks, lace-up brown shoes and a baggy brown sweater detains me. 'Tallyho, girlie!' She comes to a breathless halt in front of me. I'm taken with her eyes, they're very big and round, like blue marbles, and fiercely animated. I notice too that her eyebrows are drawn in thin arches above them and her lips are ruby red and bleeding into the edges of her mouth, giving her a dishevelled look. Her black hair is cut in a fashionable bob, and she has what appears to be white paint beneath her fingernails. She must be in her thirties. She grins, revealing small, crooked teeth. 'Darling, are we ready for tonight?' Her accent is cut glass, like our Queen's, and her voice shrill.

'I think so,' I reply, mimicking her accent. She doesn't seem at all surprised by it, so I must have got it right.

'Jolly good. It's going to be tremendous. Have you decided what to wear?'

I recall Mrs Crocker laying the dress on the bed. 'Green sequins, I think,' I answer. 'And perhaps an ostrich feather in my hair.'

'Too magnificent!' she cries, clapping her hands gleefully. 'I can't wait to see what Gilda is going to do. She's built it up into a tremendous surprise, so it had better be spectacular or everyone will be frightfully disappointed. All to raise money for the theatre.' She smiles wickedly. 'But don't be fooled that she's being altruistic. She'll make it all about her beneath the guise of selflessness. That poor long-suffering husband of hers. Truly, I don't know how he puts up with her. I bet he secretly rues the day!' She laughs mischievously, crinkling her large nose. 'Still, we all need to support her, don't we? For the good of darling old Aphrodite.'

'We most certainly do,' I reply, feeling quite out of my depth. 'Where are you off to?'

'Meeting Aunt Wallie for lunch.'

'Oh.'

My tone must have surprised her, for she pats me on the arm and pulls a face. 'Come now, Eddie. She's a good egg, you know.'

'I know.'

'She's just outspoken. One of those women who thinks it's her duty to be honest, and, in her position, entitled to be. She'll berate me for reading low-brow books and lecture me on finding a husband, and I shall listen patiently as I always do and then ignore everything she's said. That's the only way to deal with a narcissist. But we must keep her sweet. We simply can't do without her patronage.'

'You're so right, my dear,' I reply evenly, trying not to sound stupid.

'Anyhow, see you tonight, girlie. I'll be suffering in blue. How I hate a dress!'

'You will carry it off beautifully,' I reply, then take a punt. 'Blue is your colour.'

She laughs again and widens her sapphire eyes theatrically. 'God didn't give me much choice, did he?' she says and sets off towards the quay with a bounce in her step. 'Tallyho!'

Who the hell is *she*?

I follow the signs to the centre of town and wind up, quite by chance, in front of the Brambling House Hotel. I stand, staring up at it in amazement and relief. But it's not a hotel. It's a private home. And a beautiful private home, at that. Ulysses will be so jealous that I'm seeing it in its original splendour, freshly painted and gleaming white. There are pink roses scaling the gorgeous Georgian façade, borders of leafy shrubs growing beneath the sash windows and potted bay trees either side of the door. It's sumptuous. How wonderful to live in a house as splendid as this one, and how sad that in the future, the very heart of it is ripped out so they can modernise and reshape it, without an ounce of taste or sensitivity to its heritage. I wish I had a camera so I could photograph it for Ulysses.

Now I'm in familiar territory, the relief turns to a strange feeling of discombobulation. It's like a weird dream. The building is the same, but *not* the same. I feel as if the world has turned upside down. I wonder who lives here, for they must be very grand. The mayor perhaps, or some other local dignitary.

Just then I hear the whirring sound of a car behind me. I turn, expecting that woman in the hat and veil to accost me, but it's not her. She was driving a red car. This one is racing green, and the roof has been lifted like a lid, revealing a sumptuous pale leather and polished wood interior. It draws up beside me. I glance at the man driving it. He's wearing a cream-coloured jacket, an open neck blue shirt and a straw trilby. It takes me a beat to recognise the face behind the beard.

I look again. It can't be.

Cavill?

'Don't look so surprised,' he says. 'Get in.'

I'm paralysed with astonishment. I stand staring at him like an idiot. He looks at me and frowns. 'Well?'

I can barely contain my joy. So, I was right. I *have* drawn Cavill into my slide, or he has drawn me. Either way, we are here, together. I've been given a final opportunity to see him again. I'm overcome with gratitude and resolve to savour every second.

I hurry round to the other side of the car, while he leans over and opens the passenger door for me. I climb inside and turn to him expectantly. I'm aware that I'm grinning like a fool. He doesn't greet me like a long-lost friend, however, and for a second I'm baffled. Then I remind myself that I'm no longer Constance Fleet, I'm Eddie Skipton, and I don't know what the nature of our relationship is. Nevertheless, his behaviour is that of someone who knows me very well. *How* well does he know me, I wonder?

I reach behind me for the seatbelt only to find there isn't one. Cavill doesn't notice my blunder. He speeds off without another word, as if he can't get out of town fast enough. I turn to look at him. His profile is set in a serious expression. He's staring at the road ahead through the glass windscreen, his brow furrowed. He looks nervous. One arm is resting nonchalantly on the rim where the window has been wound down, the other hand on the steering wheel. But there's nothing nonchalant about his demeanour. I avert my eyes. Pixie Tate wants to take him in, every inch of him, but Eddie Skipton must be restrained. He's not looking at me, so I must not look at him. I remind myself that he doesn't recognise me Hermione, or me Constance – he certainly doesn't know me, Pixie, at all. Oh, how I wish he did!

He drives on in silence, leaving the town for narrow country lanes that wind their way between thick hedgerows of mayflower and cow parsley. I'm intoxicated with happiness that I'm here, with the man I love, even though he has no idea who I really am. Right now, it doesn't matter. I sigh contentedly, lean back against the head rest, and allow the sun to gently caress my face. I will this drive to go on forever.

I resist the urge to look at him, to reach out and touch him. I know I mustn't. But it's all I can do not to give in to my impulses, and I turn my eyes to the sea which comes into view in the gaps in the hedges, and focus my attention on the role that I'm playing. He must take the lead, and I must blindly follow, and hope that I can pull it off without letting myself, or Eddie Skipton, down.

The silence between us is killing me. I have so many questions, but I can't ask them. How come he is in Cornwall? When did he return from America? Is Josephine here too? At last, he drives into a farm entrance and brings the car to a halt in the field behind the hedge. We won't be seen from the road. The air of adultery intensifies. I give a quick thought to Eddie's poor husband, but just as quickly dismiss it. Whether or not she commits adultery is really none of my business, and it's not my place to judge.

Cavill turns to face me, and I suddenly notice how much he has aged. The crow's feet at his temples are deeper and those that furrow his forehead are more pronounced. His hair is still thick, but fair has darkened to grey, and his skin is rugged now, although much of it is concealed beneath his short beard. Eleven years have passed since I last saw him and even then he was no longer the young man I fell in love with, but a man of mature years and greater experience that I loved still. He's in his mid-sixties now, and it shows, not just in his appearance but in the weight of his personality, which seems heavier with gravitas, as if he carries a hefty sack of troubles on his back. However, he's still handsome. He will always be handsome to me.

His blue eyes gaze at me and as I fall into them, I see him in his depth. In his soul. And I suffer a pang of dread, for how can I sever so unique and profound a connection? How can I bring myself to do it? How *will* I?

He takes a steady breath. He's had the drive to think about what he's going to say and yet it takes him a while to find the words. 'I know why you didn't come,' he says at last. I make a stammering attempt at answering, but thankfully he cuts me off. 'No, let me explain, Eddie.' There it is. Those three words. So, the letter *was* from him.

He glances out of the window then back again. He gives me a bashful smile as if about to apologise for something about which he doesn't feel remotely guilty. 'I kissed you last night because I wanted to.'

I blush, not with embarrassment, which is how he'll interpret it, but with the surprise of finding myself in this extraordinary position. It's as if the Universe has conspired to give me exactly what I want.

If he kissed Eddie once, might he kiss her again?

'It must not have come as a surprise,' he says. Then chuckles and looks at me fondly. 'You knew that was the way it was going, didn't you? We both did.'

'Well . . . I . . .'

'I know I'm married,' he says.

Now I'm really surprised. He's married? To whom? My heart

sinks, although, I don't know why it matters. I'm here for a short time only – to end it – why should a wife make any difference to *me*?

But it does.

'It is *I* who am in the wrong.' He sighs despairingly.

'Oh, Cavill, don't . . .'

'You have been a widow long enough, Eddie. You deserve better than me.'

So, Eddie Skipton's husband is dead. No wonder Mrs Crocker looked perplexed when I was opening cupboards in his dressing room. I'm relieved I don't have to deal with a Mr Skipton. Eddie is free to love Cavill, but Cavill isn't free to love her. Sod's law.

I take his hand. It's premature, I know. But I can't stop myself. It feels warm and familiar in mine. We knit our fingers as if we've knitted them a thousand times before. 'I deserve no one but you,' I reply, and gaze at him with all the longing that has been building up over these achingly lonely months. He cannot imagine what I have gone through. There's so much I want to tell him.

He's thrown off. He wasn't expecting this. But he doesn't withdraw his hand. 'Oh, Eddie. You don't know what you've done to me. You've brought light into my life after so much darkness. What a fool I've been.'

The expression in his eyes changes and I respond to it without thinking. I follow my heart, its will is very strong. Too strong. It seems that I have lost control of it. I'm no longer Eddie Skipton, but Pixie Tate, leaning forward to kiss him.

He presses his lips to mine, and I close my eyes and savour the sensation of being pulled into his arms and kissed deeply. I can hardly believe that I have slid into the body of a woman he loves, and who is free to love him. How is that possible? Have I somehow manifested this?

I inhale the familiar scent of his skin, even though the feel of his beard is novel. I bask in the familiar intimacy, the familiar energy, the familiar touch. Everything about him is familiar. It's as if I've come home.

*

He cups my face and gazes upon me with such affection that my stomach overturns. He no longer looks nervous or troubled, but peaceful, as if he's been released of that hefty sack, at least for the moment. 'If I explain myself now, will you listen?' he asks softly. I nod. He pulls away. 'Let's walk.'

He gets out of the car and comes round to my side to open the door for me. He takes my hand, and we set off slowly down the field of buttercups and dandelions that slopes towards the coast. The navy sea sparkles ahead, and in the distance I can see rugged cliffs jutting out into the water. Gulls wheel and cry, cotton clouds float across a bright blue sky. I might as well be in a dream, for the colours seem heightened somehow, and I have to squint in the glare of so radiant a beauty.

'As you know, I was married before.'

'Yes, to Hermione,' I say, hoping that Eddie would know that. I haven't a clue how long she and Cavill have known each other and how much he will have told her about himself.

'Our daughter, Josephine, is now twenty-seven years old, married and with two young boys. What you may not know is that we were married only thirteen years before Hermione died of consumption, leaving our daughter motherless.'

'No, I did not know that.' Another punt which pays off.

'I loved Hermione very much, Eddie,' he continues. 'I never thought I would love another, but I did, and she, too, was taken from me.'

'I'm sorry,' I mutter, and imagine he's referring to Constance.

His jaw stiffens. I can see the muscles tense beneath his beard. 'She had an accident and died.' He looks deeply saddened. 'It was a long time ago, over a decade.'

'You have, indeed, suffered,' I say, and my heart aches for the pain he has endured because of me, for I was possessing both Hermione and Constance when he fell in love with them.

'I should never have remarried,' he continues, his voice heavy with regret. 'But I wanted to turn my back on the two women I had loved and lost. I couldn't bear to put myself through that anguish again.' He chuckles sadly and grips my hand more tightly, as if anxious I might let go and run away. I want to tell him that *I* was those women whom he loved and lost. I want to tell him that I've come back, that I'm not going anywhere, for now. But I remain silent, holding on to the truth with all my strength lest it slip out of my grasp and ruin everything. Now is not the time to reveal it. 'Therefore, I married a woman I *didn't* love,' he goes on. 'Whom I was in no danger of loving. Who was shallow and charming and amusing. Who was glitter, like a bauble on a Christmas tree. I didn't want to give of myself again, as I had given of myself in the past. Giving of myself only brought me pain and unhappiness.' He looks across at me and smiles in the way one does when one is about to share a delicious secret. 'Then I met *you*, Eddie my darling, and I wanted to give my *whole* self.' His eyes caress my face, as if loving every contour, and my heart soars like a kite on the wind. He is Cavill Pengower in the garden at St Sidwell; Cavill Pengower on the deck of the *Titanic*.

My Cavill Pengower.

I smile back with affection, encouraging him to expand, yet knowing that I will have to leave him a third time. However, this situation is very different. He already loved Eddie Skipton before I possessed her and will likely love her still after I have gone.

This is a love story I will not influence. Will that make it easier for me to let him go?

He shakes his head and continues in a quiet, reflective voice. 'I didn't expect to love again, Eddie. I had shut down that part of me and thrown myself with as much enthusiasm as I could muster into my new life. I had closed the door on the past and committed to the present with all its shallow pleasures. Who knew that I would meet *you*? Who knew that I would be ready to love again?'

'Fate, indeed,' I reply. He couldn't possibly know how busy that hand of fate has been.

'Perhaps.' He stops and turns to cup my face in his large hands. He seems to devour what he sees, and I catch my breath because he has looked at me like this before – as Hermione and as Constance, and I search his gaze in the hope that he is able to see *me*, Pixie, behind the façade. I so want him to be looking at *me* with this tenderness, but he is not. He is looking at Eddie. 'Your physical beauty is undeniable, Eddie,' he says softly. 'Any fool can see that. But you are so much more than beautiful. When you grow old, your inner beauty will continue to shine out of those lovely eyes of yours and I want to be there, in your gaze. I want you to be in mine. Eddie my darling, I want us to grow old together.'

My eyes fill with tears, because I know we will *not* grow old together. When I return to my time, he will have grown old without me and already departed the world, and I will have all those years ahead of me. Will I grow old on my own?

'We are in an impossible situation,' I say. He cannot imagine how impossible the situation is.

He seems surprised at my shiny eyes. His face softens with affection, and he runs a thumb across my cheekbone where a tear has escaped. 'Nothing is impossible, if one wants it enough.'

Again, I am in his arms, and we are kissing with an urgency that surpasses those kisses in St Sidwell. It seems as if, on a subconscious level, there's a deep knowing that understands the journey we have taken, that is grateful for this reunion and, at the same time, painfully aware of its transience.

Or is it only *I* who feels it? How can I possibly know?

We walk down to the beach and stroll hand in hand over the dunes. I ask him about Hermione and Constance, and he is surprised by my keenness to hear about them. I don't suppose many women are enthusiastic to know about the women who precede them. I listen with rapt attention as he opens his heart and allows me to know what's in it, even though I *already* know.

Everything is rendered more enchanting because I'm with Cavill. The sea appears to glitter in a blaze of jumping stars, the sky has enriched to a magnificent imperial blue and the very air seems to shimmer with tiny flecks of gold. Gulls ride the wind with their white wings outstretched and their desolate cries pull at my heart. This place could not be more beautiful. Nothing of the modern world mars its splendour. I think of the horror to come in the decades ahead and realise that this moment is but a brief respite after the Great War, an inward breath before the exhale that will blow out fire like a terrifying dragon, to scorch the earth. Cavill has no notion of what is to come. No one does. That is the terrible burden of the timeslider – to know and not to be allowed to tell.

I wonder whether this beach is the 'usual place'. Have he and Eddie strolled up this strip of sand before? For how long has he been married? How long has he loved Eddie? There is so much I want to know that I cannot ask.

We sit on the bank among the long grasses and out of the wind. He draws me to him, and I rest my head against his chest, fighting to stay in the moment while my mind strays into what-ifs and if-onlys.

'We'll make it work, Eddie darling,' he says. 'If I know you love me, I'll move mountains.'

'I do love you, Cavill,' I reply. *You don't know how much I love you.*

He squeezes me tighter. 'Then watch those mountains move.'

How romantic those words are, but the mountains that lie between us are impossible to move, even with the power of love.

Chapter Ten

We cannot remain long on that secluded beach, for Cavill must return to his wife and I, Eddie, must return home too, to prepare myself for the party I know nothing about. As I climb back into the car, I feel as if I'm waking from a dazzling dream and returning to the dull complexities of real life. I need to find Nessa Blunt and focus my attention on my mission, but my whole being rejects it. I feel as if I'm having to turn my face from the sun and step into darkness. I crave the bright light of Cavill's presence. I don't know how I can do without it.

I watch him as he backs the car and then swivels the steering wheel to drive out into the lane again, and I wonder whether I will be able to finish it – I don't have a clue how it can be done. Must I tell him the truth? Does he have to know who I really am in order for *him* to let *me* go, too?

I started this, but truly, I have no idea how to end it without breaking my heart.

The sun shines with all the vigour and enthusiasm of spring. It is pleasantly warm, and in that warmth nature basks. The ferns unfurl, the flowers open, the leaves unfold in all their glorious splendour, and among them dragonflies dart, songbirds frolic and bees buzz. It reminds me of St Sidwell. The English countryside at its most extravagant, at its most lavish.

We reach town and he pulls up outside Eddie's Queen Anne house. I wonder why Cavill is so relaxed about being seen with her in his car. He's certainly not concealing their friendship. 'I'll see you later,' I say as he climbs out and comes round to open the door for me once again. I'd like to find a man in my own time who is chivalrous like this, but I fear feminism and the woke ideology have all but erased it.

We stand a moment facing each other, and I feel the unbearable urge to kiss him. He smiles and his eyes linger a moment on my lips. I know he feels it too. 'Until later,' he says, and I'm left no alternative than to return through the iron gate and up the stone path to the front door. I turn and watch him start the engine. He doesn't look at me again but drives off. I wonder where he lives and what his wife is like.

I delve inside Eddie's handbag for the keys, but the door opens and Mrs Crocker is standing there with a face full of complaint. 'Miss Blunt is in the morning room, ma'am. In distress.' She arches her eyebrows which add a silent 'again' to the sentence. By Mrs Crocker's expression I gather that Miss Blunt is often in distress.

My encounter with Cavill is swept aside as my energies come together in a single beam of intention, which I train resolutely on my mission. I'm going to meet Nessa Blunt.

And so it begins.

I have no idea where the morning room might be. Mrs Crocker puts out her hand and I realise that she's expecting me to give her my hat. I take it off. 'Thank you, Mrs Crocker,' I say. She frowns at me, and I wonder suddenly if I've misnamed her. I swiftly think back to my conversation with the scissor-cutter. I'm sure he said Crocker.

'I don't think you've put Mrs in front of my name for ten years!' she exclaims.

'So I haven't,' I reply swiftly, feigning nonchalance. 'My mind is doing funny things today, Crocker. You'll have to bear with me.' I shrug apologetically, hoping she will excuse any other blunders I'm sure to make.

'Let's go and see what Miss Blunt is weeping about today,' she says, and I'm grateful to her for inadvertently showing me the way.

*

The morning room is situated up the stairs and leads off, by way of big double doors, from the drawing room in which I first found myself when I slid. It's a light, airy room decorated in vivacious greens and purples, with sash windows giving out onto the garden below and a big fireplace with a green marble mantelpiece and a purple and green patterned club fender. I'm getting the measure now of Eddie's style and her love of colour. In front of the fireplace, curled into a velvet armchair like a miserable dog, is Nessa Blunt. I recognise her at once. She looks up at me with big, shiny grey eyes, her lips trembling. Even with her pale, tear-stained face I can see that she's pretty and full of character.

'Nessa,' I say, leaving Mrs Crocker in the doorway and stepping into the room.

'Skippy,' says Nessa, and I'm surprised at the nickname; we obviously know each other well. 'It's just too horrendous!' she exclaims, holding up a letter. 'Papa is coming to the opening night of *Macbeth* and I'm Lady Macbeth's understudy and an apparition. The first time he sees me on stage, I'll be an apparition. Barely a part at all! My lifelong dream has led me to *this!* I might as well give up now and do as he demands.'

'That's defeatist, Nessa,' I reply. 'You're not one to give up so easily.'

'I am when everyone is against me! Bentley promised me Lady Macbeth, but once again Gilda has stolen the limelight. Will I never be the lead? Am I destined to always shadow other actresses who are more beautiful than me? Because that's what it's all about, you know, Skippy. Beauty. I'm far more accomplished than Gilda. Everyone agrees she's a rotten actress. If she wasn't married to the man who owns the theatre, she'd never get further than the chorus. It's so unfair.'

I perch on the armchair opposite her then turn to dismiss Mrs Crocker, but she has already slipped away. 'It *is* unfair,' I agree, then wait for her to give me more information.

'She's not even that beautiful,' she continues bitterly, twisting a white handkerchief in her hands. 'She's artificial. It's all make-up and glamorous clothes. If she were English I don't think people would consider her special. Besides, they're all fawning over her because her husband owns the theatre.'

I realise I need to know more about Nessa Blunt, and I'm inspired suddenly with a cunning idea. 'This is all very distressing, darling,' I begin, hoping Eddie is the sort of woman who would use that term of endearment. Nessa doesn't flinch so I take it that I'm on the right track. 'I think you need to let it all out. All of it. There's an interesting new therapy I read about recently that encourages people to heal from trauma by talking it out.'

She looks at me askew. 'You mean Carl Jung, Skippy.'

'Maybe. I can't recall. But I think it would help if you had a good rant.' She's doubtful, but not opposed. I sense that, with my encouragement, she'll go along with it. 'Tell me about Gilda, from the first moment you met her. Pretend I know nothing.'

She inhales through her nose and gives a little shake of her head. 'Very well, but Carl Jung is not new, Skippy.'

'I don't think it was Carl Jung, I simply can't recall. But let's give it a go all the same, shall we? It might help to get it off your chest.'

'I'd like to get *her* off my chest.' She sighs dramatically and drops her hands into her lap. 'Very well. The first time I met her, I was dazzled by her like everyone else. It was my first day at the Aphrodite and I was nervous. As you know, Papa was against me going on the stage. To him it's akin to prostitution.' She chuckles joylessly and rolls her eyes. 'Mamma secretly supported me, but she would, wouldn't she, being your sister.'

So, Eddie Skipton is Nessa Blunt's aunt. The fog is clearing some more.

'I was fortunate that you and Uncle Tom were so passionate about amateur dramatics. If it wasn't for you keeping the theatre going during the war, I wouldn't have had the opportunity to act.' Her eyes shine as new tears glisten. 'I know how fortunate I am.' Her lips curl at a recollection. 'I remember when we were little, you'd help us put on plays at The Hallows for Mamma and Papa and their friends. We all enjoyed rehearsing and dressing up, but none of my siblings loved it as much as I did. I adored performing and was good at it too. The seed was sown, and Papa curses you now. It's not ladylike to be an actress and goodness, how he minds about that! But as you're always telling us, times are changing. Women's role in the world is changing rapidly. The war gave us independence and social freedom, and things that were deemed unseemly are now accepted as normal. But Papa is a stuffy old sofa. There's no moving him. He doesn't mind other women enjoying their newfound independences, but he won't tolerate his daughter. It doesn't help that Flossy and Clemmie have toed the line. They've both made good marriages and are still stuck in the Edwardian age, which pleases Papa enormously. One would have thought that, as the youngest child, he wouldn't give a toss what I do. But he's terribly concerned about appearances, and I'm letting the family down. As if the Blunts are anything special. But that's the heart of the problem, isn't it? The Blunts *aren't* special. He's trying so terribly hard to keep up. Now he's been persuaded to come . . .' she glances at me slyly. 'I don't know whether you're behind it, or Mamma, but he's been persuaded to come and see me perform and I'm an apparition. It's too horrendous for words!'

I give her a knowing smile, although I have no idea what Skippy knows! 'But it's wonderful that your dear Papa is coming at all, isn't it?'

She frowns, and then a light dances in her eyes and she grins mischievously. 'What did you have for lunch, Skippy? *Dear* Papa, indeed! You've never made a secret of disliking him. It's usually Horrible Humphrey or "that man".'

I laugh to mask the mistake and hastily think up a reason for making it. 'I'm trying to be nice,' I explain.

She chortles. 'That's novel.'

'The way to win him over is not by being brutish, but by being so wonderfully sweet that he can't help but give in.'

'Was that in the article you read too?'

'Very likely,' I reply with a grin.

She hangs her head and looks at the letter forlornly. 'I do so want him to be proud of me.'

'May I read it?' I ask.

She sighs in defeat and holds it out.

My dear Nessa, I will not waste ink in repeating what I have already made perfectly clear numerous times, so I will be brief. I do not condone your choices and do not understand why you have wilfully made them when you know very well how I feel. But for the sake of your mamma, this froideur between us must come to an end. I have been persuaded to attend the first night of Macbeth and hope you do not put me , or your mother, to shame.

You cannot live off your aunt indefinitely and I am ready and willing to welcome you back into the fold. Do be sensible, Nessa, and consider your future.

Your father

'What do you make of it?' I ask.

She takes the letter back and scrunches it up crossly. 'He's coming under duress. Make no mistake, he still expects me to step off the stage and come home.'

'While threatening to cut you off financially if you don't,' I add.

'Of course,' she replies. She looks at me longingly. 'Seeing the tiny part I will be playing will simply give him more ammunition. He will tell me it's hardly worth it, damaging my reputation for that! If only I could play Lady Macbeth and impress him with my talent, then he might change his mind.' She throws the ball of paper towards the grate, but misses. 'Damned Gilda Garrett!'

'I really don't understand why he's so against it,' I argue. 'It's 1923, after all.' I'm hoping she'll expand a little more on her father, but she assumes I know him.

'That's why I'm here, Skippy. Because *you* understand.'

'And your poor mamma?'

She sighs and drops her shoulders in defeat. 'Always been compliant, that one. No help at all.'

I'm now extremely curious about Nessa's parents. What sort of people are they? Why is her father so against his daughter treading the boards? But I cannot ask what Eddie would most certainly know.

'Tell me about Gilda, your nemesis,' I ask instead.

'But you know Gilda, Skippy!'

I laugh. 'Of course I do, but this is all part of the therapy. You must talk it out.'

'Talk it out?'

'A problem shared is a problem halved.'

'Very well,' she says with a sigh. 'Gilda Garrett.' She almost spits the words out. 'She married her husband for his money and then made him buy the theatre so she could be an actress. She's so much younger than him and spends like it's going out of fashion.'

'There's nothing new about that,' I interrupt. Even in my own time marriages are not always founded on love.

'Of course not. The point is that she pretends she loves him, but she's as cunning as a fox. She's devious. She's an avaricious fraud. I know she loathes provincial life because Lavinia overheard her telling Bentley that her ambition is to eventually act on the London stage. She thinks very highly of herself, doesn't she, but anyone can see that she doesn't have what it takes. She's just beautiful, that's all, but without talent beauty will only carry one so far. And beauty fades as one gets older. It won't last forever.' That thought appears to give her comfort, for her lips twitch at the corners.

'And Mr Garrett?' I ask, trying to find out a bit about him.

At that Nessa laughs. Her hilarity takes me by surprise, and I wonder what I've said that's so amusing. 'Oh, that's so funny, Skippy! I'm going to call him that now behind his back. Mr Garrett! Well, you're not wrong. Poor Mr Garrett. I bet he wishes he wasn't married to her. He sometimes has the look of a beaten dog, I think. Gilda craves the bright lights and he, poor dear, probably just wants a cosy armchair, a warm fire and a good book. He's only interested in the Aphrodite because he has to be, to keep her happy.' She looks at me with narrowed eyes. 'I think he would rather be married to you.'

'Oh, surely not!' I exclaim, hoping that's the correct response considering I don't know who any of these people are.

She smiles knowingly. 'I think he comes to the theatre to spend time with you.'

'What nonsense!'

'You should marry again, Skippy. It's been seven years since Uncle Tom died.'

'My dear Nessa, if I ever do marry again, it will be with a man who is not himself married.'

She shrugs. 'A man who is married can quite easily *un*marry, you know. Goodness, you sound like my sisters. The word divorce horrifies them to their marrow!'

'I'm sorry you're Gilda's understudy,' I say, changing the subject.

'And an apparition. Not even a witch! It's just horrendous. I wish Gilda would break a leg then I could perform.'

'I don't imagine that's likely.'

She sighs loudly. 'And as long as she's here, in Seacombe, she'll take every leading role. I have the talent, but she has the face. What can I do?'

'You're a pretty girl, Nessa.' Indeed, she *is* pretty. I haven't seen Gilda, so I can't compare, but Nessa, with her soft brown hair, aquiline nose, sensual lips and smooth olive skin has the sort of face that would be considered beautiful in my time. Maybe her strong eyebrows are not fashionable now, and perhaps her expression reveals too much character, I don't know, but if she were alive in 2014 she'd probably be on the cover of *Vogue*.

'I cannot compete with Gilda,' Nessa says dispiritedly.

'How long have you been living here with me?' I ask, hoping she doesn't reply a week, in which case I'll look very stupid.

She sighs and lifts her eyes to the ceiling as she works it out. 'Fourteen months,' she answers. Before I can comment, she adds, 'I know what you're going to say, and I've told you not to in the past because I believed I had to prove my worth. But maybe you can talk to Mr Bentley now on my behalf. After all, it's in his power to give me better parts.'

'Of course, I will,' I reply.

She gives a small smile. 'Thank you.' She uncurls her legs and gets up off the chair. I follow her lead. 'I wish you still ran the theatre, Skippy,' she says sadly. 'Then I'd be the leading lady, and ghastly Gilda would be in America.'

'If it's her ambition to be on the London stage, perhaps we need to make that happen,' I suggest.

Nessa is delighted by that idea. 'We need to persuade Mr Garrett to buy her a theatre in the West End,' she replies, arching an eyebrow. 'At the ripe old age of thirty-four, I'm not sure she'll make it on her own, and I dare say he's rich enough – if he doesn't allow her to spend it all first.'

As we walk through the drawing room and out onto the landing, another young woman is hurrying up the stairs. She's breathless and flushed. 'Lavinia!' Nessa cries out.

'I'm not late, am I?' the young woman replies, an anxious look on her freckled face. She has long curly red hair that reminds me of Botticelli's Venus, and hazel eyes.

'We were just going to dress for the party,' says Nessa.

'Oh, good!' Lavinia exclaims.

'But we had better hurry,' Nessa adds. 'We don't want to be late.'

'No,' I agree blindly. 'We don't want to miss a moment.'

'*Gilda's* moment,' Nessa sneers.

'You need not worry about that,' Lavinia adds, meeting us on the landing. 'She won't begin until everyone is present to see her in her glory, and you can bet on it being *exceedingly* glorious.'

The two young women catch eyes and smile shrewdly. I'm more than curious now to meet this infamous Gilda Garrett.

I glance at the clock on the drawing room mantelpiece. It's four thirty. I'm not sure what time the party starts. 'Shall we meet in the hall at . . .' I hesitate on purpose, knowing that Nessa will probably interrupt me. I'm right. She does.

'It starts at six, so let's meet in the hall at a quarter to the hour,' she says briskly.

'Perfect,' I reply and watch the girls head on up the stairs.

I open the door to my bedroom and find Crocker running me a bath. How luxurious it is to have someone to look after my every need, although I don't think I could live like this permanently. When would I get any privacy? But Eddie Skipton is used to it, so therefore I must not look like a bewildered sheep. I affect nonchalance and allow her to fuss about me, folding my clothes as I shed them, and hanging my dress in the wardrobe.

As I wallow in the warm, scented water, I remind myself of the characters I'm likely to meet tonight: Mr Bentley, the manager or director of the theatre – perhaps he's both as it's am-dram, after all. I doubt they have the funds to splash out on positions they don't desperately need; straight-talking Wallie, whoever she is, and the woman in knickerbockers who accosted me in the street on her way to meet Wallie for lunch and called me 'Girlie'. There's also the lady in the car who waved at me as she drove past.

Then there's Cavill. I shiver with nervous excitement at the anticipation of possibly seeing him tonight. I close my eyes and indulge in a moment's reflection. He kissed me. He really kissed me. And it was blissful. If I have manifested this, then I've done a marvellous job. I bask in the warm water and contemplate the five days leading up to the fire that stretch out before me. Five days of kisses. For a while I see nothing but those kisses. Perhaps we'll visit the beach again. Maybe we'll find a small hotel hidden out of sight where we can spend more time together, just the two of us. A room with a big soft bed where we can be alone. That delicious thought occupies me until I feel the water getting cold and my fingertips puckering.

I open my eyes and Nessa's anguished face floats into my mind like a bright moon, eclipsing Cavill's. My joy evaporates in the glare of what is to come. In five days, she will die in the fire. There's no avoiding it. What a horrible way to go. What an unbearably horrible way to go.

Once again, I will have to stand aside and allow a story, whose ending is within my ability to rewrite, to take its natural course. I must not interfere. It's the primary rule of a timeslider. Do *not* alter the past. Leave the smallest possible footprint on the timeline so as not to influence the future. Of course, I'm aware that everything I do and say will influence the future to some degree. It's unavoidable. But saving Nessa Blunt from the fire would make too great an impact. I know that. I will have to stand aside and allow it to happen.

I dread growing fond of her as I grew fond of little Felix Pengower. After that slide, I told myself I wouldn't get attached again. I would remain coldly impassive. But how is that even possible, when one so easily gets lost in the dream?

I wash myself with the bar of soap. I think it's tallow. I appreciate the Victorian taps again. They're those classic brass crosshead ones which, in my time, are copied in chrome to give a vintage feel. Where I come from they'd be highly sought after by collectors and fetch a high price. In fact, most things here would, were I able to take them home with me. They're nothing special now, however. Everyone takes these things for granted, as we take things for granted in our time. Perhaps decades into the future iPhones will be collectors' items.

My skin is wrinkled like a prune. I climb out of the bath and wrap myself in a towel.

With Crocker's help I get dressed in front of a full-length mirror. I'm delighted by the lingerie Eddie wears. It's a kind of cream-coloured silk teddy – a combination of a camisole and knickers in one. Beneath is a suspender belt that holds up silk stockings. I feel incredibly sexy and my eagerness to see Cavill intensifies. I want him to see me like this. How can a man resist a woman when she looks like *this*?

Except *this* is not *me*. *This* is Eddie Skipton. I swat that thought away like an annoying fly about to drop into my most delicious dessert. I won't allow a minor detail to ruin this slide. Possibly, my *final* slide with Cavill. So what if he's not seeing *me*? Does it really matter? I'll enjoy being in his arms. I'll savour him kissing me and loving me, even though I'll be living vicariously through another. Does it really matter?

I stare at my lovely reflection in the mirror. At the face gazing back at me that isn't mine, and I'm accosted by a stark realisation. Yes, it *does* matter. It matters very much. I wish it didn't, but it does. There's no escaping the fact that I yearn with all my soul for him to know me. That yearning is so powerful that for a moment my heart aches so severely I put a hand against my chest to nurse it.

I recognise then what it is that is tying our destinies together. It dawns on me like a blood-red sunrise breaking onto the sky. It's not Cavill. No, Cavill is powerless. He's helpless against a force he's not even aware of. It's *my yearning*. By the Law of Attraction, my yearning is a magnet, and while it burns with this ferocious intensity, it will draw Cavill to it over and over again. He cannot resist it, and I cannot dampen it.

But it *must* burn itself out or we will be fated to live a kind of Groundhog Day, meeting and leaving each other over and over again. But how?

I sit at the dressing table as Crocker curls my hair and arranges the headband and ostrich feather. Avril said that Cavill must know the truth of who I really am in order for the love that I have started to fulfil itself. That's the only way this terrible yearning in my heart will be satisfied and the connection severed. But if I tell him, I will risk everything – not just for me, but for Eddie.

Crocker stands back and admires her handiwork. 'There, ma'am. Don't you look handsome?'

I smile at her in the mirror. 'I do, Crocker. Thank you.'

She places a gentle hand on my shoulder, and I sense that she and Eddie are very close. 'I wish Mr Skipton could see you looking so fine,' she says, and the gaze she settles upon me is maternal.

I put my hand on hers. 'So do I,' I reply in the same sorrowful tone.

She's satisfied with that and withdraws her hand after a moment's pause. 'You had better get going or you'll be late,' she says, blinking away the mist in her eyes. 'Those young ladies will want to arrive on time. They do love a party.'

'Then I must not keep them waiting,' I reply and get up off the chair with a twinge of apprehension. I will recognise no one tonight besides Cavill, yet I will have to pretend to know them all.

Nessa and Lavinia are in the hall. I descend the stair slowly, taking in Nessa's scarlet dress embellished with fringes and Lavinia's green one adorned with sequins that catch the light and sparkle festively. They both wear glittering headbands and plush feathers to match their dresses. To my modern eye they look like they're in fancy dress on their way to a 1920s-themed party. but of course, this *is* the 1920s. This is the fashion. How colourful and fun it is.

As I approach the hall two other women come into view, hovering in the corridor. One is a corpulent woman of about sixty, in a white apron with a white cap covering her hair. I guess she's Cook. The other woman is small and skinny with an angular, wan face, in a black dress and white apron. I guess she's a maid. It seems that everyone at this time dresses appropriately for their station or form of employment. In my time you simply cannot judge a person by what they wear. A duke can dress like a vagrant and a vagrant can dress like a duke. There's often no telling who anyone is.

Cook and the maid give me appreciative glances as I alight into the hall. 'You all look smashing,' says Cook and her soft Cornish brogue curls warmly around her words. From her hard features I deduce that she's the sort of woman who can be curt and abrasive but who, nonetheless, has a big heart. 'What do you say, Nancy, or have you lost your tongue?' she adds brusquely to the maid, and my analysis proves correct.

Poor Nancy is forced to give an opinion. 'Beautiful,' she repeats shyly, and I sense she's a little afraid of the cook.

'Now off you all go,' comes Crocker's voice behind me. She's making her way down the stairs with the air of a headmistress in a boarding school. 'And have a lovely time.'

'Oh, we will,' cries Lavinia excitedly.

Nessa grins at me. 'I think your silly therapy might have worked,' she says. 'At least, I'm feeling much better.'

'I'm happy to hear it,' I reply.

We walk out of the gate into the street and Nessa links her arm through mine. 'We must encourage Gilda to move to London,' she says. 'Then you can buy back the theatre and Lavinia and I can be your leading ladies.'

'What a good idea,' I say, knowing that Nessa is only including Lavinia because she's here.

Nessa giggles. 'Either that or she must break a leg.'

'Oh, really, Nessa. That's wicked,' says Lavinia.

'Then she must move to London,' Nessa declares. 'I'm glad we're all agreed.'

Chapter Eleven

We walk through the town. The sun is still bright, the air warm and sugar-scented. Spring's uplifting energy infuses Seacombe with a blithe, careless feeling, and I wonder whether this sense of innocence and leisure comes from my knowing what darkness lies in the future, or whether it comes from the community itself; after having suffered a terrible war there's an appreciation for the simple things. Certainly, the place has a picturesque charm.

The streets are uncluttered with the modern paraphernalia of bollards, traffic lights, cones, bins and speed signs, and the tarmac free of yellow lines, zebra crossings and the like. There are street-lamps and tram lines, but besides those the town looks tidy. There are no plastic bottles and bags littering the pavements; indeed, plastic has yet to be invented. The main streets are busy with bicycles and the odd car that motors by. People are leaving work and heading for the pubs or making their way home. A draught horse pulling a cartload of rubble plods past. The moustachioed man in a jacket and cap leading it by the reins waves at a friend on the other side of the street who is winding up the awning outside his hardware shop. They exchange a round of repartee before the shop-keeper retreats back inside and the horse plods on. People seem to have time to stop and chat. I notice gaggles of women in hats laughing together on the pavement, and clusters of men in caps having a smoke on the street corners. Everyone wears a hat and the men sport jackets and ties, and all look the same, as if in uniform. A group of young boys in shorts kick a ball in the road, moving casually out of the way when confronted by a horse or car. There's a breezy, holiday atmosphere, and everyone seems to be friendly. I suppose communities are closely knit in the 1920s. There's less movement, people have grown up together – and old together. It's hard not to see it all through rose-tinted glasses. One is always more critical of one's own time and place, and nostalgic about the past when one is yet to explore beneath the pretty surface. It's a sobering sight, then, when we pass the war memorial. There are wreaths of poppies at the foot of it. A stark reminder of those brave young men who died for their country – and to me, a sad forecast of what the late 1930s will bring.

I'm surprised when we turn into that magnificent white mansion, which in my time is the Brambling House Hotel. Does Gilda Garrett live *here*?

We are not alone. Others are making for the door, which is wide open. I glimpse a butler in a black tailcoat and waistcoat holding it open and, beyond him, a maid, also in uniform, waiting to take guests' coats, although I suspect most come without, for the weather is fine. I feel a squeeze on my stomach as I anticipate the inevitable faux pas I will almost certainly make tonight. I must keep my wits about me and deflect any questions I'm unable to answer. It's going to be a challenge.

I anticipate seeing Cavill. I'm already looking out for him. If I can stay close to him, I know I will be fine.

No sooner do we step inside the house than the girls leave my side and rush off into the grand drawing room which can be seen from the hall. It barely resembles the hotel of the future, unlike the Aldershoff in New York where Henry Stirling worked so hard to hold on to its heritage. Here, only the mouldings on the ceiling take me back to Brambling House, the rest is a sumptuous home filled with treasures. I'm staggered at how gorgeous it is.

The floor in the hall is made of shiny black-and-white marble, laid in a bold, geometric design. The walls are white, adorned with giant works of art ranging from the traditional to the contemporary. There are tall palms in big pots, vases of lilies and roses, glass chandeliers, gleaming black fireplace surrounds, gilt-framed mirrors, and furniture made of palisander wood. I think of Ulysses suddenly. How he would love this extravaganza of Art Deco. I wish he could see it. He wouldn't believe his eyes. I can barely believe mine. It seems so *un*-English. Might Gilda have imported it all from America?

I follow the crowd into the drawing room. I take in the sun-pattern gold and teal-blue wallpaper. It's bold and brash but utterly ravishing. Above me two giant chandeliers sparkle as if crafted from diamonds, and everywhere I look is gloss and shine and polish and, quite simply, immaculate taste. She might be ghastly, but Gilda's style is beyond reproach.

At the other end of the drawing room I can see a stage. A pair of scarlet curtains have been drawn in front of it to conceal what lies behind. I wonder whether Gilda is already in position there, waiting for everyone to arrive before revealing herself. There are rows of gold-coloured chairs with red velvet seats, ready for the guests to watch the show. I'm itching with curiosity to see Gilda. Nessa has already given me her opinion, but I want to see this leading lady for myself and make up my own mind.

I strain my neck in search of Cavill and spot him in the garden which lies beyond the drawing room through a pair of large, glass-panelled doors. Everyone is assembling on the lawn with crystal flutes of champagne. For a moment I feel dizzy, for the scene is so reminiscent of my last slide where elegant men and women in evening dress gathered in the ship's drawing room with the same style glasses filled with champagne, and the same air of excitement. The only difference, besides the place, is the length of the women's dresses which reach mid-calf. This is 1923, not 1912, after all. The fashion has changed and so has women's place in society, quite dramatically. They have lived through the First World War and it has changed them profoundly.

I don't recall there being a garden at the back of the Brambling House Hotel, but the garden in which I find myself now is ablaze with the abundance of spring. It's large for a house in the middle of a town and boasts as its centrepiece a spectacular dogwood whose white flowers resemble snow. I feel sorry that in the future this lovely garden is dug up for some build. I help myself to a flute of champagne proffered on a silver tray by a young waiter in a black tailcoat with greased-back blond hair, and bravely launch myself into the crowd. I hope I can carry this off. Who knew timesliding would require me to be a skilled actor?

The first person I encounter is an elderly lady in a long Edwardian dress. She looks quite out of place in this garden of flapper dresses that reach just below the knee. Her thick grey hair is swept up in a voluminous pompadour and crowned with an elegant diamond tiara. 'My dear Eddie,' she says in a cut-glass accent that makes our Queen sound common. 'You're wearing Tom's pearl earrings.' She appraises them with hooded green eyes. 'Fetching.'

'Thank you,' I reply, wondering who the hell she is. I lift my chin and feign confidence I do not feel.

'But don't you think it's time to move on and find another husband? One really shouldn't be without one for too long or you'll find yourself left to gather dust on the shelf. I was talking about you to Lydia earlier today. A woman without a husband is like a pot without a lid. The two go very nicely together for a reason. You're still fine-looking, but beauty doesn't last. You won't be able to rely on that lovely face of yours forever.'

This has to be Aunt Wallie!

'Oh, I'm in no hurry to remarry,' I tell her.

She sniffs her disdain. 'That is the response of a woman who has had no offers, and I know you better than that . . .'

She's cut off by a handsome young man with dark brown hair, chiselled cheekbones, a tidy moustache above a wide, attractive mouth, and a pair of round glasses, which exaggerate the size of his clear, toffee-brown eyes. 'Countess,' he says in a rich, confident voice, taking her gloved hand and bowing politely. 'How kind of you to come and support our little theatre.' He turns to me and his wide mouth extends into a dashing smile. 'Mrs Skipton, lovely as always to see you.'

'And you,' I return, guessing he's Mr Garrett, but not daring to say the name in case I'm wrong.

The countess gives the imperious smile of a woman who is used to being a benefactor and receiving thanks for it. 'You will always have my support, Mr Bentley,' she replies, correcting my assumption that he is Gilda's husband and the man who owns The Aphrodite. I sway a little at how close I came to making a terrible mistake. 'My husband simply adored the theatre,' she goes on. 'And I admire Mrs Skipton very much for valiantly keeping it going during the war years while her poor husband was doing his duty at the front. It is a tragedy that he paid the ultimate price, but we are so grateful to him, and to other young men like my own grandson, Charles, who gave their lives for our freedom. May they never be forgotten.'

'May they never be forgotten,' I repeat, and I don't have to feign a heavy heart.

'But this is a jolly evening,' she continues, her solemn voice lifting. 'And I am happy to pay handsomely for the pleasure of seeing our very own American import perform solo. She does bring much-needed glamour to our small community, does she not?'

'Oh, she does, indeed,' Mr Bentley agrees keenly.

'I am not one of those dusty old relics that is unable to appreciate the bright young things now setting the world alight. After the darkness we need light, and we elderly people must keep up.' She smiles smugly. 'You know, in my day, I was something of a novelty myself.'

'Do tell, Lady Faversham,' Mr Bentley says encouragingly.

'While not chaining myself to railings and defacing property, I was a most ardent supporter of women's suffrage. I still am, in my own quiet way. Influencing where I can behind the scenes. You theatre people know all about that. Much goes on off stage, does it not?'

'It does, indeed,' Mr Bentley agrees.

'We still have a way to go,' I add, aware that the Equal Franchise Act is not introduced until 1928. 'But I am confident that we will get equal voting rights in the end.' I want to add that in fifty-six years' time Great Britain will have a female prime minister.

Lady Faversham smiles at me approvingly. 'I admire your optimism, my dear. Women must and will have equal rights to men. But I stand by my opinion that a woman of your age should not be without a husband. It is just the natural way of things, and that will never change however much the hemlines rise.' They are going to rise much higher than she can imagine!

'Would it not be greedy to have two husbands, when so many young women are unable to marry even once due to the dire shortage of men?' I ask, aware of the war's dreadful losses and of Eddie, whose position on the matter is unknown to me.

The countess laughs and taps me lightly on the arm with her fan. 'Oh, Eddie dear, sometimes one must be selfish in order to survive in the world!'

Lydia, the young woman with big blue eyes who had lunch with Wallie, now rushes up to join us. Her smile is uninhibited and her blue dress, covered in tassels and sequins, appears to move all on its own, even though she looks decidedly uncomfortable in it. She carries a glass of champagne in one hand and between the fingers of the other, a cigarette in a long ebony holder. 'Thanks to Aunt Wallie's generosity,' she gushes, 'darling Aphrodite will steam on for another year. Isn't that marvellous?'

'Oh, it really is,' I reply, smiling broadly to show how very excited I am. 'You are incredibly generous, Lady Faversham. I can't thank you enough.'

The elderly lady frowns at me. 'Good Lord, we're not standing on ceremony now, Eddie dear.'

I assume she's referring to my use of her title. I laugh and shrug off yet another faux pas. 'Habit,' I state simply. But would Eddie call her Wallie? It feels wrong somehow, akin to calling our Queen Elizabeth, Lilibet. I decide not to call her anything.

Lydia draws on her cigarette and exhales a puff of smoke. In spite of the elegant ebony holder, she fails to make the action feminine. 'Owning a theatre is an expensive hobby,' she continues. She looks beyond Lady Faversham and puts her cigarette holder between her lips again. I follow the line of her gaze. She seems to be looking at Cavill, who stands head and shoulders above everyone else in the middle of the garden. He senses he's being watched and lifts his gaze off his companions. Those familiar eyes find mine and we lock together with the almost audible click of a pot whose lid fits to perfection. I watch his face light up and, without pausing his conversation, his lips curl at the corners into a small smile. At the sight of it, my stomach flips over with joy, and I have to restrain myself from fighting my way through the crowd to be with him.

I return to my senses. Does this woman mean that Cavill owns the theatre? Surely not.

Is *he* Mr Garrett?

'My dear Lydia,' says Lady Faversham in the tone of a teacher talking to a rather dim student. 'Even Pengower's wealth has limits. His wife is doing her best to burn her way through it. Poor man. Keeping her happy is an expensive hobby, indeed.'

I find it hard to believe they're speaking of Cavill Pengower, but what other Pengower could it be? I try to remember his references to his wife while Lydia and Lady Faversham move on to discuss the merits of marriage. It's clearly one of Lady Faversham's favourite subjects and one that Lydia is only too happy to indulge.

It's a relief when the butler announces in a loud voice that the show is about to begin and can the esteemed guests please make their way into the drawing room. The crowd moves obediently back into the house and people begin to take the seats set out for them in front of the stage. I find myself drawn into brief salutations with various people who obviously know Eddie well. Mercifully, the dialogues are short, owing to the movement of the guests which, like a stream, carries me forward, and are little more than enquiries after my health, comments on the glorious weather and the anticipation of the up-and-coming performances of *Macbeth*. I want to talk to Cavill, but I don't know where he is. My heart sinks. I'm lost in this sea of strangers who greet me with familiarity, expecting the same level of familiarity in return. It's a disconcerting feeling. I imagine this is what it must be like to lose one's memory. It's a shame I can't feign a fall and then claim amnesia.

I spot Nessa and Lavinia in one of the middle rows and make my way towards them. They seem surprised when I sit with them. I say nothing but notice them put their heads together and speak in low voices. The row fills up. The middle-aged man who takes the chair beside mine is porcine with red hair and a red face and bushy yellow eyebrows that remind me of hairy caterpillars. He bows and greets me enthusiastically. 'By Jove, this is a fine way to spend a Friday evening, is it not?' he exclaims in a fruity voice. 'Ever since Gilda Garrett came to Seacombe, it's been one long party. Viva L'Americana,' he says in a very English accent and chuckles heartily.

Just then Cavill walks up the aisle. I spot him at once. He's looking at me with a perplexed expression on his face. 'Eddie, what the devil are you doing there?' he asks.

I try not to look lost.

'Come on, your seat awaits you at the front.'

I turn to the girls. They are looking at me with the same bewilderment. 'I'm not sure what Skippy had for breakfast,' says Nessa and laughs. Lavinia laughs with her, not unkindly.

I get up and the porcine man has to get up also. I only just manage to squeeze past his barrel belly. Cavill puts out a hand and I take it, allowing him to guide me into the aisle. He shakes his head and lets me go. 'You're beside *me*,' he tells me softly. 'Where else would I seat you?'

He stands aside and I make my way to the front row, the fond way he looked at me still creating butterflies in my stomach. I can feel my face burning. I'm not sure Eddie Skipton would blush so easily. There are two empty seats. One is beside Lady Faversham, the other on the aisle. I take the latter, assuming that Cavill will sit next to Lady Faversham. Thank goodness I get that right. No one seems surprised when I take that chair. I cross my legs and try to calm my frantically beating heart.

Cavill goes and stands in front of the stage. The chatter dies down and the room eventually goes quiet. He sweeps his blue eyes over the audience and then speaks. 'Lady Faversham, lords, ladies and gentlemen, it gives me great pleasure to introduce my wife Gilda Garrett, who needs no introduction, to be sure, and to thank you all for your continuing support of the Aphrodite.' I feel the blood drain to my feet. So Cavill is married to Gilda! *She* is the glitter, the bauble on the Christmas tree, the woman he *doesn't* love. Gilda Garrett is obviously her stage name. 'As you know,' he continues. 'I bought it a year and a half ago for Gilda so that she could realise her dream of being a leading lady of the stage. And a leading lady she most certainly is. I am very proud of her, and grateful to you, my dear friends, for welcoming us so warmly to Seacombe, for making us feel at home in this new town, and for generously giving, so that our small band of dramatics enthusiasts can pursue their art and their dreams.' He drops his eyes onto me, and I flinch at the sudden unexpected beam of attention. 'The theatre is new territory for me,' he says without averting his gaze. 'And I have had to learn the ropes. Therefore, I thank Mrs Skipton – Edwina, Eddie, Skippy – she has various names, because you are all so terribly fond of her, as are my wife and I – for her guidance, support and tolerance, because we arrived from America and took it over. She has never once shown impatience or, indeed, regret. It is with great respect to Tom Skipton, who was a cherished member of this community, that we keep the Aphrodite going, so that you may enjoy many evenings of entertainment, and my dear wife many opportunities to express her art. Tonight she expresses it in a slightly different manner. I do hope you enjoy it. Thank you.'

There's an enthusiastic round of applause as he takes the seat beside me. I feel the pressure of his arm pressed to mine and am acutely aware of his every movement. I'm not sure I'll be able to focus on the show, so intense is his presence. There's a brief pause as the audience takes an expectant breath and I mouth thank you. He holds my gaze for a lingering moment and then the curtains part.

There, seated serenely in a rowing boat in a white dress with her long Titian red hair tumbling over her shoulders and down her back is Gilda Garrett as, unmistakeably, the Lady of Shalott. At once I recognise the echo of the famous painting by John William Waterhouse for it hangs in the Tate, which Ulysses and I have visited on many occasions. Gilda sits upon a pink patterned throw similar to the one in the painting which is draped over the side of the boat, and the backdrop is rendered to resemble the trees and the stage floor the river. As the audience show their admiration with another round of applause, Gilda lifts her chin and begins to speak. 'On either side the river lie . . .' she begins, and I wonder whether she's going to recite the entire poem by Tennyson, which has about twenty stanzas, or whether we might be spared, for as beautiful as she undoubtedly is with her milky white skin, high cheekbones, full, sensual mouth and vivid green eyes, she simply cannot act. Her voice is flat and her movements wooden. I want to see whether I'm the only one who has noticed how talentless she is, but I dare not take my eyes off the stage. Surely Cavill cannot be so blinded by her beauty to fail to see how very bad she is.

She drones on and I sit frozen on the chair. I remind myself that I come from a culture of television series and blockbuster movies, of CGI and sophisticated special effects and animation. I can even watch a movie on my phone! These people have only recently begun to go to the cinema to watch silent films in black and white. For them theatre is one of the few forms of entertainment they can enjoy, and while I feel a moment's smugness at the marvel of modern technology which they will never know, I realise that *they* enjoy something that is later lost to *us*. Something special that *we* will never know: the close-knit community life of family and friends who share pastimes that bring them constantly together, whether it be circus, fair, theatre, fête, card games, treasure hunts or picnics. Our wonderful technology seems to be thrusting us more and more into isolation and society is suffering a plague of loneliness in spite of the many gadgets that are meant to make communication easier. I sit stiffly as Gilda makes her way tediously through each verse – truly, it's like wading through concrete – and reflect upon the differences between this time and mine and feel a little ashamed of my initial sense of superiority. I'm not sure having a smartphone and internet makes me better, it just makes me different, and possibly more alone.

What hasn't changed is the human heart. In an ever-changing world love remains the same. Perhaps it's the only thing that always has been, and always will be, constant.

I want to reach out and take Cavill's hand, but I cannot. I fold mine in my lap and wait with increasing impatience for Gilda to finish. When she finally ends with a dramatic pause, everyone claps. She climbs out of the boat and takes a graceful bow. The clapping seems to last a long time. I pray no one shouts 'Encore'. Thankfully they do not.

The curtain closes and Gilda disappears behind it. I turn to Cavill. 'She was magnificent,' I say, trying to mask what I really think.

He smiles knowingly. 'Wasn't she, indeed,' he replies, and I'm sure I detect a hint of sarcasm in his voice.

We stand and are immediately gathered into a group of enthusiastic guests, who are keen to congratulate Cavill on his wife's performance. 'Well, wasn't that a delight,' says one, and I stare at him in disbelief. How could it have been a delight? It was excruciating.

'Wasn't she marvellous,' enthuses another. 'A mesmerising Lady of Shalott.'

An elderly man with fluffy sideburns pats Cavill heartily on the back. 'My dear fellow, I look forward to *Macbeth* with bated breath,' he says. 'To see the dazzling Gilda Garrett play Lady Macbeth will be a veritable treat. Capital!'

Can they really think she's so marvellous? I mean, she's as far from Meryl Streep as it's possible to be!

Cavill accepts their praise with dignity. I agree, because I must. It's only when Gilda steps into the room, changed out of her costume and wig, into a stunning white and gold floor-length dress, with strings of pearls on her wrists and diamonds in her short blonde hair, that I understand this audience's enthusiasm. She looks every inch the American film star. She oozes glamour, wealth, charm and joy. She's like a dazzling star in a universe of rocks, and she eclipses everyone.

I watch her face light up when she spots her husband, and she makes her way gracefully through the throng towards him. I'm struck by a stab of jealousy, which is irrational considering he's in love with Eddie. The very fact that Gilda gets to share his life is enough to give me pain, when *I* am parted from him by almost a century and can never share more than days with him. I should be jealous of Eddie too, but right now I *am* Eddie, so my jealousy is also felt on her behalf. Eddie and I are one, for the moment, at least. I glance at Cavill. His expression reveals nothing of what he really feels. He smiles and holds out his hands.

Gilda tilts her head this way and that in response to people's compliments, and her smile is truly radiant. Each person she speaks to looks as if they've just been given the sacrament. I'm dumbfounded. I didn't expect this. No wonder poor Nessa doesn't get a look-in. Gilda might not be a great actress, or even a good one, but she is obviously much admired.

She takes Cavill's hands and offers him her smooth cheek, as pale and silken as cream. He kisses it dutifully. My stomach clenches but my smile is fixed upon my face like a mask. It's the first time I've seen him intimate with another woman, for in my past two slides, I *was* that woman. I can barely endure it.

I wonder how Eddie feels. Whether she suffers as much as I do, or whether she's confident of his devotion. After all, *I* have merely five days, *she* might have a lifetime. Perhaps she can afford to be patient. But I have to end it, while for her it's only just beginning. Unless in ending it for me, I end it also for her.

How can I sever my connection with Cavill without ruining it for Eddie?

Do I want to?

Chapter Twelve

I walk home from the party with Nessa and Lavinia, both relishing Gilda's appalling performance and resenting the audience for giving her such a hearty applause. 'It's because they like her,' I tell them. 'It had nothing to do with her rendition, which, I agree, was wooden.'

'Finally!' Nessa screeches gleefully, grabbing me by the arm. 'We get you to admit what you really think.'

Oh dear! Have I let Eddie down *again*?

'If you admit that she's wooden, Skippy, you must surely admit that she shouldn't have been cast as Lady Macbeth!' Nessa continues.

'You can't deny it,' Lavinia adds. 'The great Gilda Garrett is wooden.'

'Don't quote me on that,' I tell them seriously. 'She has great appeal and will fill the theatre because of it.'

'Beneath the gilt she's as plain as a plank of wood,' crows Nessa. 'Don't you agree, Lavinia?'

Lavinia laughs. 'But we have a plan, don't we?' Nessa links her arm through Lavinia's, and they come closer in collusion.

'Are you going to share this dastardly plan?' I ask, but a shiver courses down my spine because in five days' time Nessa dies in a fire. Does her plan go horribly wrong and result in her death?

'It's secret,' says Nessa. The girls laugh, then Nessa offers a chilling teaser. 'But I think you'll find the understudy will get her moment to shine!'

*

We eat in the dining room, the three of us. Bunsen has managed to mend the range, and we are offered vegetable soup followed by baked potatoes and ham with peas and cabbage. Outside, the sky has darkened, and Nancy draws the curtains and serves the food. Fortunately, Nessa and Lavinia are both overexcited and chatty as a result, which gives me the opportunity to learn more about this world into which I have slid. Like a spy, I seize upon the pieces of information that are important for my quest.

Nessa is staying with her aunt Eddie because her father, who is married to Eddie's sister, has basically disowned her. While her brother and two sisters have all made good marriages, Nessa has shunned the 'wet rag' her father wants her to marry in order to pursue a career on stage. She's hoping that amateur theatre will lead to her becoming a professional actress. She has no doubt that she is good enough. Her father, Humphrey Blunt, is a successful businessman who made his fortune in tobacco. As Nessa goes off on a rant again, I begin to get the measure of him. The aristocratic world to which he aspires looks down on people who work, for they have all inherited their wealth; work is for the working classes. But he is desperate to be accepted. Therefore, appearances matter tremendously. His family must do everything with the utmost decorum. Nessa is letting the side down – well brought up young ladies do not become actresses. You could say that Humphrey Blunt is *nouveau riche* and upwardly mobile and, as Nessa airs her frustrations and really lets rip, a snob as well.

She told me in spirit that no one loves her and I'm beginning to understand why she believes that. 'Mamma is terrified of Papa,' she says, forking a pile of ham and potato into her mouth. 'She'll never stand up for me.'

I sigh and take a punt. 'I've tried, my dear . . .' I begin, after all, her mother is Eddie's sister. Surely, Eddie has fought her corner?

'I know you have, Skippy,' Nessa interrupts. 'But she's not strong like you. I will have to take matters into my own hands. There's nothing else I can do.' She takes a swig from her water glass and grins over the rim. 'You and I are the black sheep of the family, Skippy. At least I'm in good company.'

It's only after supper, when we drink tea in the drawing room upstairs, that I learn more about Lavinia. Lavinia Bedworth, who's around the same age as Nessa, has been living here too, since September, and works as secretary to the pharmacist here in Seacombe. Also passionate about theatre, she is playing the part of a witch. Her mother is Lady Bedworth, Lady B who wrote the postcard Eddie received today from the South of France, her father the recently knighted Sir Clive Bedworth. I managed to glean all this from one evening without Nessa laughing at me and asking me again what I had for breakfast!

I also glean that tomorrow, being Saturday, is a big rehearsal day and we will spend all of it at the Aphrodite. This will be a great opportunity for me to really find out what's going on between Gilda and Nessa – and to see Cavill again, for surely he will be there.

By the time my head hits the pillow – the deliciously soft pillow – I'm exhausted. I close my eyes and allow my mind to drift on rosy-pink clouds to Cavill, in spite of the fact that I know this story can have no happy ending.

I awake to the sound of birdsong. White beams of sunshine stream in through the gaps in the curtains, illuminating this pretty bedroom with the innocent vigour of a spring dawn. I luxuriate a while beneath the sheet and blankets and remind myself where I am and what I'm here to do. Today is going to be a big day. I'll have to have my wits about me.

I glance at the clock that ticks softly on the mantlepiece, above a fireplace that must be a lovely treat in wintertime. I'd like to fall asleep to the golden glow of dancing flames. Correction: I'd like to fall asleep *in Cavill's arms* to the golden glow of dancing flames. At that thought my heart aches for him while my mind pushes away any allusion to the terrible decision I'm going to have to make. I'm determined to enjoy every precious moment with him, while I still can.

It's seven thirty. I'm wondering what time they have breakfast when I hear a light knocking on the door as it opens and Crocker walks in. 'Morning, ma'am,' she says, then briskly opens the two sets of curtains. I squint in the glare. 'Another lovely day,' she declares.

'Morning, Crocker,' I reply and stretch.

She goes into the bathroom and I hear the gush of water as she turns the taps to run a bath. How very luxurious to have a bath in the morning, especially when I don't have to run it myself! When she comes back into the bedroom, I strike up a conversation. 'It's going to be a busy day at the Aphrodite,' I begin.

'Only five days to go until first night,' she replies, taking a purple silk dressing gown off the hook on the bathroom door and laying it over the bed. 'I hope Ned Pollock has learned his lines.'

'I'm sure he has,' I reply blindly.

She frowns at me doubtfully. 'Ever the optimist, if you don't mind me saying. Still, you'll be there to prompt him if he dries up.'

I take that on board. Am I the official prompter?

'Well, he has just five days to learn them,' I add, wondering whether Ned Pollock will be playing Macbeth.

She laughs and puts her hands on her hips. 'Poor Nessa. A drama queen she might be, but she did have her heart set on playing Lady Macbeth, didn't she? And Mr Bentley assured her back in the autumn that the part was hers. Poor lamb. Not fair to be let down like that. Still, whatever you said to her yesterday evening seems to have lifted her spirits. It's nice to see her smiling again.'

'Yes, I'm going to have a word with Mr Bentley today. I think he's treated her badly.'

Mrs Crocker shakes her head. 'In more ways than one,' she says cryptically.

I want to ask what she means, but she's giving me a knowing look, as if we're both in on a secret. 'Yes, that too,' I add and arch an eyebrow, hoping she'll elaborate. But why would she elaborate on something she believes I already know?

'You enjoy your bath, ma'am. I'll tell Cook you'll be down in half an hour for breakfast. I suppose I'd better wake the girls. Those two sleep like bears.'

*

Eddie's wardrobe is limited. I count five day dresses, two short evening dresses, one very elaborate long one, a pile of woollen sweaters, a couple of pairs of trousers – they would call them slacks – and shirts. I'm not sure what Eddie would wear to the theatre, but I follow my instinct and choose a pair of beige slacks and a white shirt. No such thing as trainers, but there is a pair of brown lace-up shoes. I appraise myself in the long mirror and like what I see. Indeed, I like being Eddie Skipton. She has style as well as beauty. I think I look quite chic and head on down to breakfast with a bounce in my step. I sit at the head of the dining table and Nancy comes in with a pot of hot tea and a rack of toast on a tray. As Pixie I seldom eat breakfast, but I'm Eddie Skipton now, and she clearly enjoys toast with butter and marmalade for the two are arranged in front of my place. I'm tucking into my second piece of toast and glancing at the front page of *The Times* when the girls appear, looking like a pair of marmots whose hibernation has just been interrupted. They mutter good morning and then take the chairs either side of me.

Nessa is wearing a cream-coloured, drop-waisted dress and a long cardigan while Lavinia is wearing slacks, and a rather lovely short Fair Isle knit sweater in taupe and green. Nancy brings them porridge and coffee and they gradually begin to perk up. The subject of conversation turns once again to Gilda, and Nessa's resentment of her, and I try to remain neutral in spite of having admitted to finding her acting wooden. Lavinia agrees with everything Nessa says, like a trusty lady-in-waiting. For all her bluster, Nessa is a fragile soul. I pity her for her unsupportive family and for having been let down by Mr Bentley, but I pity her most for her terrible end. It's hard to imagine that in just under five days' time she will be dead.

I watch her as she spoons porridge into her mouth and sips her coffee, and hope that I manage to find out what it is that later prevents her from returning home to spirit. The limbo between worlds is a dark place to be, even though she claims to like it there.

We walk to the theatre, which is only ten minutes away. I'm now getting my bearings, but it's lucky the girls are with me to show the way. The outside of the Aphrodite hasn't changed at all. It stands majestically with its grey stone façade, twin domed towers and lofty windows. I half expect to meet Emma and Leila in the foyer. But no sooner do we walk through those heavy wooden doors than I realise that it's changed a great deal. The fire that happens in just over four days' time guts the place and sometime in the future they will renovate it in the Art Deco style that Ulysses loves so much. But right now, it's the original Edwardian theatre, built in 1901 by Randolph Brown for the woman he loved, Aphrodite Allen. The floor is black-and-white chequerboard, the walls panelled in dark, shiny wood. The ceiling is mock Tudor, divided into squares, each of which contains a fleur-de-lis motif painted in gold. The effect is lavish but heavy and I reflect on the Art Deco interior of the future and consider it superior.

We walk through the foyer and on into the auditorium. There are various people milling about. I recognise Mr Bentley immediately. He's on stage in a blue shirt with the sleeves rolled up, holding a clipboard, a pencil lodged behind his ear and his steel-framed round glasses giving him a professional air. He's deep in conversation with Gilda, who wears a slim-fitting ivory-coloured dress to mid-calf with a thin black belt around her tiny waist. Her short blonde hair, cut in a fashionable bob, is so luscious, it shines like silk. I feel a pang of envy. It doesn't surprise me at all that Cavill married her, but really, I've got no business being envious. It's of no consequence to me, Pixie, if he's married or not. Maybe the fact that he's attached will make it easier for me to sever our connection. As for Eddie Skipton, she will continue on once I have slid back to my time, and the manner in which she conducts her relationship with Cavill will have nothing to do with me. I remind myself that this has already been played out. I'm simply rewinding the tape and playing it again. It sounds simple in theory, but even I can't get my head around *that*.

We approach, and they break off their conversation. 'Skippy!' Gilda exclaims in a voice as sweet as honey. Her smile is dazzling. Really, her energy lights up the stage. It's just a shame she can't act.

I wonder where her husband is, and my eyes stray in search of him.

'And there's my understudy,' Gilda adds, turning her radiance onto Nessa like a golden spotlight. I watch the two women closely. There seems to be no animosity from Gilda. If she's aware of Nessa's jealousy, she does a great job of ignoring it. Nessa pulls her energy inwards and her whole body stiffens. It's subtle and I doubt Gilda notices for she's blinded by her own luminosity. But *I* sense the resentment beneath Nessa's outward politeness. It fumes like embers at the base of a wooden pyre. Mr Bentley is brisk. He's got a job to do, and he doesn't waste any time with pleasantries. He declares that he wants to rehearse Act 1 scene 7 with Gilda and Ned. Not being familiar with the play, I haven't a clue what this scene is about.

Mr Bentley summons Nessa and a young man with floppy brown hair and a long, earnest face who's sitting in the front row of the stalls. He jumps up on stage with the agility of a big cat. 'Miss Blunt, Mr Neil, I want you both to watch closely. Then I'd like to see you perform it. If for any reason Miss Garrett and Mr Pollock are unable to act, you will take their places. I need you to be sure of your parts.'

'Right-oh,' says Mr Neil, giving a comical salute. He's clearly a character. He grins at Nessa, exposing crooked teeth, and gives her a jaunty wink. 'Come on, Miss Blunt. We're going to have our moment in the spotlight, at last!' He laughs cheerfully. He doesn't appear to be at all put out that he's not playing the lead himself.

The two of them go and sit on wooden chairs at the edge of the stage. Mr Neil pops a cigarette between his lips and strikes a match to light it.

'Mrs Skipton, can you prompt, please,' Mr Bentley adds. 'We might as well do this properly. We've only four full days until the first night, and a limited time in which to rehearse. Did you bring your copy?'

I did not. He looks at my hands, then flicks his fingers as if summoning a waiter. 'Mrs Gladstone, a script, please.'

A middle-aged woman with dark brown hair and glasses who's

been sitting in the front row of the stalls gets up and passes me hers. I take one of the chairs on the other side of the stage to Mr Neil and Nessa, and flick through the pages to find the right place.

I glance at the stalls. There are various people dotted about. I search their faces for Cavill and feel my spirits sink when I don't find him. I have a terrible sense of urgency, for I know the sand in the hourglass is running out for me. But Cavill will have no such pressure. I wish I could tell him who I really am so that these precious hours would not be wasted.

Gilda and Ned begin their scene, and I turn my attention to the script, which is lucky because Ned hasn't learned all his lines, and I have to prompt him quite regularly. He's a talented actor, however, and I'm impressed with his interpretation of Macbeth. He commands the stage with his baritone voice and confidence. Gilda, on the other hand, is terrible. No wonder Cavill had to buy the theatre in order for her to perform. If she had auditioned in the ordinary way, I doubt very much she'd have got the chance to step onto the stage at all. I wonder then whether she had failed in her attempts to become an actress in America and believed she had more of a chance over here. Certainly, with Cavill's wealth, and perhaps his keenness to make her happy, the probability of realising her dream was more likely in the UK – especially in provincial Cornwall. It's hardly the West End. As I watch Gilda's lacklustre performance, I conclude that she will *not* be hitting the London stage, as Nessa hopes. However, that will not matter to Nessa. I look at her watching her nemesis with dismay, and suffer a pang of sorrow, for tragically, she will not live to see what becomes of Gilda Garrett.

Something pulls at me then, and I turn absentmindedly to the stalls. There, in the front row, is Cavill. He must have slipped in while I was absorbed in the script. My spirits ignite and I feel full of vigour again, as if my very soul is on fire. We catch eyes and he nods and smiles, and I revel in that smile which is specifically for me. It's intimate and knowing, the smile of a man in secret collusion with a woman he trusts. I can barely tear my gaze away. I can scarcely remain on my chair. It takes every ounce of resolve to turn my attention back to my job and not give in to my impulses.

The scene is interrupted once again by Ned forgetting his lines. Mr Bentley makes them go back and do it again, giving instruction every now and then, encouraging Gilda to be less stiff, and I grind my teeth in frustration because no amount of coaching can loosen her. My eyes follow the words as they're recited, but my mind, and heart, are in the front row of the auditorium with Cavill. I can't look at him, but I can feel him as if he's glowing like the sun. I can feel the warmth on my skin. I can sense his breath, even his heartbeat. And I feel not an ounce of guilt that his wife is only a few feet away, because, like her, I'm playing a part. *She* is not Lady Macbeth, and *I* am not Eddie Skipton; I'm simply going along with her script.

That gives me licence to love him, doesn't it?

But as heady as that licence is, it only accentuates the fact that Cavill doesn't see *me*, Pixie. And I cannot help but *want* him to see me. Those tender looks, that colluding smile, those stolen kisses, are all for Eddie Skipton. How I long for them to be for *me*.

At last, Mr Bentley is satisfied. He announces that we'll take a short break and he and Gilda leave through the back of the stage. I imagine they're going to get coffee from the kitchen. I wonder whether there's a character like Madge who is making sandwiches and cake.

Cavill stands and I go down to meet him. He puts his hands on his hips and smiles at me. The fondness in his gaze is so bare I feel my stomach flip over. Does anyone else notice it? How can they not?

'How is it going?' he asks.

'Let's just say it's going,' I reply, and he laughs. He slides his eyes to left and right and then adds, in a low voice, a little pitifully, 'It makes uncomfortable watching, doesn't it?'

I nod. 'There is only one person to blame for that.'

He shrugs. 'Anything for peace.'

I want to warn him that in just over four days' time his theatre will burn to the ground. In four days' time there will be no peace at all.

'Come, let's go and get a cup of coffee.' He nods in the direction of the foyer, and I follow him up the aisle.

'We must be quick,' I add. 'Mr Bentley said a short break . . .'

He puts his hands in his trouser pockets and chuckles. 'Bentley won't need you for a while. Nessa and Robert never forget their lines.'

'That's very true,' I reply, and it doesn't surprise me that Nessa is competent. Anyone who wants the part that badly will make every effort to know it through and through.

There's a small café round the corner from the theatre and we go in there. It's warm and full of cigarette smoke. It's obviously a place Cavill regularly frequents because he's greeted enthusiastically by a waitress in a pale pink apron carrying a tray of tea and scones. We take a round table against the wall and sit down. The waitress brings us a couple of menus and I'm amused to read what's on offer: Bovril with biscuits 9d. What's Horlick's malted milk, I wonder? And Chocolate Digestive Biscuits each 1d. That amuses me, considering *we* buy them in packets at any supermarket. Cavill asks me what I fancy, and I ask for Russian tea just to see what it tastes like.

Cavill smiles in surprise. 'I didn't know you drink Russian tea,' he says.

I shrug. 'I don't.' Which is true. 'I thought it would be fun to try something different.'

We grin at each other like a pair of school children playing truant and knowing they're getting away with it. 'I love that about you, Eddie darling.' He settles that fond gaze on me again and I can't wipe the smile off my face.

'You do?'

'Yes, I love the way you see the world.'

'And how do I see the world?'

'As a place of opportunity and adventure. There's a fearlessness about you that I admire.'

'Life is precious and it's short,' I tell him, and I'm no longer playing the part of Eddie Skipton, but being me, Pixie Tate. 'If you consider your mortality, you'll appreciate every moment of life. Because you blink and it's over. That's how quick it is.'

My heart contracts because in *my* time his life is already over. This is just a replay.

He looks at me sympathetically and I realise he believes I'm alluding to Tom Skipton dying in the war. 'Death certainly focuses the mind,' he replies softly, and he puts his hand on the table as if he's reaching across to take mine. But my hands remain in my lap. I daren't reach back in case we are seen. But how I want to.

'We have both suffered the loss of those we love,' he says. 'A wise friend once told me that those we love and lose are always with us. That we have to accept what life throws at us, both good and bad. Because without sorrow, we can never know joy.'

Those are *my* words. On the deck of the ship, when I was Constance Fleet. Those are my words *exactly*. I stare at him in amazement. For a brief moment I'm speechless. Then I find my voice, and the words that might bring him back to me.

'We are here to learn and grow,' I say slowly and deliberately. Does he recognise those words? 'If life was simply joyful, we'd be superficial, selfish creatures, for sure,' I add, serious now, gazing deeply into the familiar blue. 'Suffering drives us deeper.'

'Suffering has led me to you,' he says. He frowns, moved suddenly, and his gaze penetrates further into mine.

Once again our words echo through time:

'Will we recognise each other when we no longer have our physical bodies? Will we recognise each other when we are made of light?'

And his reply: *'Of course, I will recognise your soul. I'd recognise your soul if it was a ray of light among a thousand rays.'*

I am a ray of light among a thousand rays. Does he, on some deep level of his being, recognise my soul?

Chapter Thirteen

If it has crossed Cavill's mind that my words are familiar, or the delivery of them at least is reminiscent of Hermione Swift or Constance Fleet, he dismisses the notion as the waitress interrupts us and takes our order. She returns shortly with my tea and Cavill's coffee. Russian tea, I discover, is sweet and spicy, a bit like punch. It's quite pleasant. We don't remain long, however, for we'll be missed, and I must return to my post.

Cavill pays the bill, and we leave. He puts his hand in the small of my back as we step into the sunshine, and we set off up the pavement at a slow stroll. Neither of us wants to reach the theatre any faster than we need to. 'I want to find a way to be alone with you, Eddie,' he says as we turn the corner. 'We are always surrounded by people, and it's killing me.'

'I want to be alone with you too,' I reply keenly, wondering how on earth he's going to swing it, and praying hard that it'll be within the next four days.

'Stolen moments in secret corners are not enough, and you deserve better.' He glances at me and his rugged face, which exhibits in its lines and shadows the vestiges of loss, softens with tenderness. 'I want to give you better.'

'You love me, Cavill,' I reply. 'That is enough.' But it's not enough, and he knows it too.

He briefly takes my hand and squeezes it. Then he lets it go.

I've missed Nessa and Mr Neil's rehearsal, but Mr Bentley doesn't seem to mind. Gilda is sitting in the front row of the stalls, smoking a cigarette and idly flicking through a magazine. Nessa has disappeared, perhaps backstage. Lavinia is nowhere to be seen. But the witches are now preparing to go through their scenes, and I need to do my job. Reluctantly, I return to my chair and to my duty. I'd like to whizz off to the beach in Cavill's car and pretend that I'm not on a mission to save Nessa, but here, in this time, living for *me*.

Cavill goes and says something to his wife, who reaches up and touches him lightly on the arm. I suffer at the sight of their intimacy and turn my eyes away. He leaves and the air is sucked out of the auditorium. It's as if it's been plunged into shade. I find myself in a horribly familiar situation: I must focus on my mission and yet I long with all my heart to be with Cavill. Once again, I have only days before I slide back. I'm reminded of the power of my longing which has very likely drawn us together, and the responsibility I have to deactivate it. I know it's futile as well as painful to reunite time and again. I know what is the right thing to do. What I *don't* know is, in spite of all the arguments in favour of ending it, whether I can actually bring myself to do it. I'm like an addict who is aware that she must quit but cannot. Are my good intentions always going to be followed by a relapse?

The witches perform their scene, and I try to concentrate. I can see Gilda, beautiful, radiant Gilda, like a glitterball she most certainly is, and my envy smoulders in spite of my knowing that I have no real claim on her husband. I wonder whether Eddie feels the same as I do, or whether she is so confident in Cavill's love that she rises above feelings of jealousy because she knows that he really belongs to her, at least in his heart.

I feel sick, suddenly, sick in my soul, because Cavill has never belonged to *me*.

Mr Bentley no longer requires my assistance, and I go backstage in search of Nessa. So far, I've deduced only a few things about her that are significant: she longs to be the leading lady; she's jealous of Gilda taking the part of Lady Macbeth; she wishes that her father were proud of her, and he's coming to the first night on Wednesday, which is four days from today, and she's intent on having her moment.

There is much I do *not* know. I have no idea, for example, how she ends up dying in a fire. I have no idea what she plans to do in order to put Gilda out of action, but I'm sure she and Lavinia are plotting something. They have almost confessed as much. Nessa is the leader in that relationship, so Lavinia will simply do as she commands. But *what* will she command?

I have to stick around in order to find out these things. Without that knowledge, I don't feel I have enough information to persuade Nessa to move on. However, I'm in no hurry to complete my mission, because completion will signal the final good-bye, and I can't bear to leave Cavill. I can't bear to think that there will be no encore.

I hear Nessa's voice rising and falling behind a wooden door. She sounds as if she's having another rant. I enter slowly. She and Lavinia are in a rather shabby sitting room, curled up on green velvet armchairs, hugging mugs of coffee and smoking. Nessa immediately stops talking and stares at me with startled eyes. Then her shoulders drop. 'Oh, it's only you, Skippy,' she says, then starts up again. She's repetitive, but she loves reiterating what I said last night about Gilda being 'wooden'. I wish I hadn't said it. Having my endorsement seems to have given her licence to really let rip! I feel rather sorry for Gilda, whose only crime is taking the lead role. Or is there something else?

I'm struck then with an idea. While both girls are here, the house will be clear for me to snoop around Nessa's bedroom. I decide to grab the opportunity as I don't know when I'll get another.

I leave Nessa to her bitching, and head for home. I hurry over the shadows as the sun plays hide and seek with the clouds and hope that I won't bump into anyone Eddie knows. I'm in complete fear of the 'stop and chat' with people who are supposed to be my friends.

I reach Eddie's pretty house and hurry inside with relief. Mrs Crocker emerges from downstairs, wiping her hands on her white apron. I haven't yet been down there, but I assume it's the servants' quarters with the kitchen and various bedrooms, perhaps. 'Hello, Crocker,' I say cheerfully.

'Can I make you a cup of tea, ma'am,' she asks.

I do need her out of the way while I search Nessa's bedroom. I say the first thing that comes into my mind. 'I would really love some Russian tea,' I reply, hoping she doesn't have any.

Mrs Crocker frowns. 'Oh, we don't have any of that here, ma'am.'

'I know, I thought you might be sweet and go out and buy me some. I tasted it in the café this morning and it's delicious. It's fun to try something new, don't you think?'

'Well, if you don't need me here . . .'

'I don't. It's a lovely day. I'm sure you'll benefit from the sunshine.'

She smiles, surprised. 'I most certainly will. Thank you.'

'And take your time. Enjoy the walk. I'm going to do some correspondence.' I'm sure ladies in Georgian England were always writing letters.

She nods. 'Nancy is downstairs, should you need her.'

'Of course,' I reply. 'But I won't need her. I'd really like some peace and quiet. It's been a busy morning at the Aphrodite.'

Mrs Crocker disappears downstairs, and I head on upstairs. I don't stop on the landing where Eddie's bedroom is but take the next flight to the second floor. There are various white panelled doors with brass knobs. After opening a bathroom door, I try the others. Nessa's bedroom is easily identified by the scarlet dress she wore the night before which hangs on the wardrobe.

My pulse is throbbing in my neck. I'm terrified of being caught. I try to think up a credible excuse as to why I'd be in here, but I can't think of a single thing. I shrug off my lack of imagination and set about searching the place, even though I don't know what I'm looking for. I hope I'll recognise anything significant when I come across it.

The room is square and decorated with delicate blue-and-yellow floral wallpaper. There's a small cast iron fireplace, a long mirror on a stand in one corner, an upholstered chair in a blue striped fabric, a chest of drawers between two sash windows that look out on to the street, and the wardrobe. The bed is a simple brass one covered in a blue quilt. The bedside table carries a lamp, a tattered romantic novel, a glass of water and a small clock. I open the drawer to find postcards – they're more like playing cards, each one depicting a black-and-white photograph of a film star. There's Marion Davies, Gloria Swanson, Bebe Daniels, Alice Terry, Greta Garbo and others. I've never heard of any of them besides Greta Garbo. How fascinating it is that people pop up and shine brightly for a time, and then disappear into obscurity. It's rather amazing that Greta Garbo's fame has endured well into the twenty-first century.

It's clear from Nessa's belongings that she's mad about film and theatre, for there's a cardboard box full of theatre tickets and programmes and various editions of *Picturegoer* magazine stored beneath her bed. Judging from the novel she's reading she seems romantic by nature. I wonder whether she's ever been in love. At twenty-eight, and clearly unimpressed by the men her father would like her to marry, I wonder whether anyone has appealed to her.

I sift through her clothes. She has many more dresses than Eddie. They're crammed into the wardrobe in a mouthwatering display of varying colours and fabrics. At the bottom are two rows of shoes. She's certainly not short of footwear! The drawers are full of blouses and shirts, scarves, handkerchiefs and underwear. Her father might not support her ambitions, but he has certainly bought her a fine array of clothes. Nessa is a girl who wants for nothing, except a career.

I'm at a loss. Besides the usual things one might find in a woman's bedroom, there doesn't appear to be anything that sheds light on why she later chooses to remain earthbound. So, she hates Gilda and wishes *she* were playing Lady Macbeth. But that's not reason enough to shun the next world in favour of haunting this one.

I sit on her bed and look around despondently, wondering where to go from here. The sun streams in, catching little filaments of dust that my searching has released into the air so that they glitter like gold. I'm about to give up, when, on a whim, I try one last thing. I slip my hand beneath her pillow.

Bingo! A journal. Why I didn't think of that first, I'll never know. It's such an obvious place to hide something.

I study it hopefully. It's a cheap grey exercise book. The kind that might be given to school children. She's drawn a big heart on the cover in glue and stuck little pieces of scarlet tissue paper to it, making it into a kind of rough mosaic. I open the first page. There, in large black letters is the name Taran. Who is Taran?

I turn the next page. In her pretty, flowing hand she has listed his date of birth, 26 June 1892 (that makes him 31), followed by the characteristics – both positive and negative – of the sun sign Cancer. There are ticks by some of those qualities: intuitive, creative, moody, home-loving and sensitive. I imagine they are the ones she identifies as his. She's drawn a picture of a crab for the astrological sign and then written down all that she has gleaned about it. On the following page she has gone into his Chinese sign in great detail. He's the Year of the Dragon, and consequently a water dragon, being born in June. Then she pairs Cancer up with her sign, Aquarius. There are pages on this, and I don't bother to read it all. I'm more interested to find out who Taran is, and whether he might be here in Seacombe. Does he have a part to play in this drama?

What follows is quite concerning. She has written pages of repeated sentences, rather like lines one had to write at school as a punishment for misbehaving in class. *I love you, I love you, I love you . . .* on and on and on. Pages! It's alarmingly obsessional. After that, there are lists of his name and then *Taran and Vanessa. Taran and Nessa. T&V.* Hundreds of times!

Oh, my poor, hopeless, broken heart.

I flick through the pages, in search of a last name. There are love poems. Some she has written herself, I think, others are famous, from *Romeo and Juliet* to 'The Highwayman'. They're written in her lovely flowing hand, in black ink. She's taken trouble with every line. But I sense beneath the façade of control is a desperate, compulsive person.

Who is the object of this obsessional passion?

*

I hear shuffling outside the door and in one hasty move shove the book back under the pillow and spring to my feet. The knob turns and like lightening I leap to the wardrobe and grab the dress hanging there.

When Nancy comes in with a basket of laundry pressed to her hip, I appear to be studying the dress.

'Oh, sorry, ma'am, I didn't know you were in here,' she says and blushes with embarrassment.

'That's all right, Nancy,' I reply and smile sweetly. 'I saw a stain on this last night but can't find it now. Will you have a look?'

'Of course,' she replies, putting the basket on the bed and taking the dress off me. She runs her eyes over the fabric, but in spite of finding no stain, she takes it. 'I'll get rid of it, don't worry.'

I want to ask her who Taran is, but that might sound weird if it turns out to be someone I should know. I leave her in the room and retreat to mine, where I stand by one of the windows and gaze out, weighing up what I've just found out. Nessa is madly in love. It has the feel of an unrequited love, for there are no reports of spending time with this man, or even of speaking to him. I wonder whether he's one of the cast members. After all, I haven't met them all yet and one of them might be called Taran. I need to find a cast list from a previous play. A programme perhaps where both first and last names are listed.

A feeling then comes over me. Subtle at first then growing stronger as I consider Taran and his possible part in Nessa's demise. It's the kind of feeling I get when I know I'm on the right track.

Taran is very significant.

I have lunch in the dining room on my own. Cold ham, new potatoes and baby broad beans. It's delicious. Mrs Crocker has returned from the shops with the tea. She offers to make me some now, but I have no time. I must get back to the theatre and find out who this mysterious man is. She looks disappointed. I reassure her that I'll have some later, when I can really enjoy it, and that seems to satisfy her.

I return to the theatre to find them all hard at work. Mr Bentley is giving instructions, the actors are rehearsing their scenes, many are hanging around waiting for their turn, smoking or reading the newspapers, or talking quietly among themselves. Nessa, as it turns out, is doing my job, sitting in my chair and prompting. It's hard to reconcile the smiley girl with the infatuated, obsessive author of the journal. How can she sit here, seemingly so tranquil of mind, when her manic listing of *I love you*s implies a mind that is very disturbed. Or perhaps I'm being harsh. Maybe it's just childish.

When she sees me, she grins. 'I rather like doing this,' she says. 'It's better than being bored, anyhow.'

'Where's Lavinia?' I ask.

She shrugs. 'Not back from her lunch break. She went with Eliza and Tamsin.'

I have no idea who Eliza and Tamsin are. I wish I could just ask where Taran is, but if he has nothing to do with the theatre, I'm going to sound like a right idiot. Eddie Skipton might never have heard of him. The only way I can discover if he is, indeed, connected to the theatre, is by waiting until someone uses his name, or find that old programme. I remember the room at the bottom of the theatre where the costumes are kept and wonder whether I'll find something there.

'Do you want to stay here and prompt?' I ask Nessa.

She beams. 'Yes, if you don't mind.'

'Of course, I don't. I need to nip down to the costume department.'

'Thank you, Skippy!'

I can't imagine why she's so pleased to do such a boring task.

I make my way downstairs, following my nose. Much of the theatre changed after the fire, but I'm surprised by how much is actually the same. It appears that it was the dressing rooms, foyer and auditorium that were destroyed and rebuilt. As I head into the bowels of the theatre, I could be in 2014.

The room still smells of dusty old costumes. I half expect to find Leila and Emma in there complaining about the cold. I switch on the light and am faced with the same rails of clothes, shelves of boxes, trays of accessories and rows of shoes that are present nearly a hundred years from now. I prepare a story in case I'm disturbed: I'm looking for a dress I donated that I want back. I'm sure Eddie Skipton has given clothes to the theatre's wardrobe. I'm sure they all have. This is amateur dramatics, after all.

I start rummaging about. I know what I'm looking for now and quickly dismiss the things that are unhelpful. Being in that room is disconcerting, however. I know I'm in 1923, but I could easily have slipped back to 2014, because this room is exactly the same. It almost has the same old spider webs in the corners. Ulysses could be upstairs in the VIP room, keeping watch, while Joseph rehearses the same play that they're rehearsing here. That's obviously no coincidence. Nessa has started menacing Isadora because Isadora reminds her of Gilda, and both women are playing Lady Macbeth, the part Nessa longs to play. But Gilda doesn't appear to be difficult. In fact, Gilda is charming and delightful. Not at all the diva that Isadora is. There has to be more to it. Nessa doesn't remain earthbound simply because she's jealous of Gilda and wants to play the leading lady. That's not enough. The more I think about it, the more I'm sure Taran has a part to play too.

As I search the room, I ponder on the technological advances in my time that would make this task so much easier. I'd be able to find this Taran person very easily on the internet. He would probably have an Instagram account, or Facebook. The theatre would have its own website and there would be lists of actors and footage of previous productions. Nessa herself would have very likely aired her grievances on Twitter. In short, it's likely I'd be able to do all my detective work on the internet without getting up from my chair.

The door opens and I spin round guiltily.

It's Cavill.

I put a hand to my chest. 'You startled me.'

He chuckles. 'You look like you've seen a ghost!'

'Well . . .' I reply and laugh with him. 'You never know what you're going to find down here.'

He doesn't ask what I'm doing. Why would he? I'm not Pixie

Tate, I'm Eddie Skipton and I belong here, in the theatre. He closes the door behind him and comes towards me with a look of intent. 'Nessa said I'd find you down here.' His lips are curled at the corners as if amused by the success of his plan. 'I was hoping you'd be alone.'

He pulls me into his arms and kisses me deeply. I forget about my search, it's yielded nothing anyway, and give in to my impulses. My entire body aches for him, and it's all I can do to stop myself from putting my hands inside his shirt so that I can feel the warmth of his naked flesh against my palms. But this is not a private place, and we might be disturbed at any moment.

The thought that I have licence to make love to him, because it seems that's what Eddie wants, is like a ball of fire in my mind. It's obliterating all other thoughts that might cast doubt. It's burning up common sense and rationality. It's making me reckless. Because as Hermione I had to hold back. As Constance I wasn't given time. Now as Eddie I don't have to hold back, and I do have time. I'm free to love him and to allow *him* to love *me*. It's intoxicating and I don't want to relinquish it, ever.

He cups my face and looks probingly into my eyes.

Into Eddie's eyes.

I gaze back searching for a sign, however tiny. I wonder, can he see *me*, Pixie, behind these eyes? Does he have any idea that I'm here? That I've come back? Am I a hopeless fool for wishing that he does?

Then he says, 'I feel as if I've waited my whole life for you.'

And I burn with the longing to tell him who I am. It's in my throat and on my breath, but I can't quite form the words. They don't come. I just yield to him again and press my heart against his, and hope that on some deep level, he might feel a memory stir.

Chapter Fourteen

I do not tell him who I am. I cannot risk the revelation ruining my mission. I still have so much to uncover. This is not the time, or the place.

With a heavy heart I return with him to the auditorium, and I resume my duty. Cavill leaves the theatre, once again taking the oxygen with him, and the rest of the day passes slowly and dully, as if with his departure the clock drags its hands in protest. I turn my attention to my task and keep my ear cocked for the name Taran, but it isn't uttered, and Nessa gives nothing away. In fact, I don't see her talk to anyone in particular, and I don't get to see her perform. I get to watch Lavinia, however, who is very good as a witch, and I notice Nessa, arms folded in the front row of the stalls, looking pained. I'm sure she would have been content with the part of a witch. At least, she'd have had more airtime than playing a meagre apparition. A chance, perhaps, to show her father what she can do, and why she's chosen this path. My heart goes out to her. She looks forlorn there on the red velvet seat. I can't imagine why her father would put up such a fight to prevent her from doing what she loves. Why would he care so much about her wanting to be an actress?

In four days' time she'll be dead. I wonder whether he'll regret his behaviour and wish that he had supported her instead.

If we all knew our destinies, would we live our lives differently?

I walk home with Nessa and Lavinia. The shadows are lengthening over the cobbles as the sun dips behind the prettily painted houses of Seacombe. The air is damp with the smell of brine, and growing increasingly chilly as night approaches and the wind picks up, advancing inland over the cold water with a wall of purple cloud. Perhaps it will rain. The girls chatter away like a pair of crickets, discussing the performances with glee and giggling at those they consider abysmal. It's hard to listen to their carefree chatter and not project forward to Wednesday. They cannot imagine what is lurking in their future. None of them will get to perform. The fire will literally steal the show.

There's a dance at the town hall and after dinner the girls go upstairs to change. Nessa notices that her red dress has disappeared, and I explain that it was stained and had to be cleaned. She doesn't question my explanation and chooses another. She certainly has plenty of choice. They dress quickly and set off, and I hear their chirping die away as they walk out into the street.

I'm alone wondering what to do with myself when the doorbell rings. My stomach clenches at the thought of a visitor. I'm tired, and I don't feel up to any more pretence. It's exhausting minding everything I say, everything I do, trying to imagine how Eddie would behave. Not wanting to let her down. I want to lie on the bed and be Pixie for a while.

Mrs Crocker answers the door while I remain upstairs in the drawing room, at the window, trying to see who the visitor is. Shortly, I see a maid hurrying off through the gate, the same way as the girls, and realise with relief that it's not a visitor at all, but a message, perhaps. A minute later Mrs Crocker comes in with an envelope. 'A letter for you, ma'am,' she says and gives it to me. She leaves, closing the door behind her.

I sit down at the round table and glance at the words on the envelope. It's the same handwriting as that on the letter I was holding when I slid into this very room. Cavill. I waste no time in opening it. I pray that he doesn't ask me to meet in our usual place, because I still don't know where that is!

Tomorrow I will steal you after church. I have finessed an entire day. I will explain when I see you.

I'm ecstatic. I can barely contain myself. I press the letter to my chest and close my eyes. Cavill comes to me in wave after wave of memory; in the garden at St Sidwell Manor; on the deck of the *Titanic*; in the carriage in New York; and that dreadful longing tugs at my heart like a begging child.

And like a begging child, it is never satisfied. One day? Two? A lifetime? My longing is unquenchable.

How I wish I could be Eddie Skipton forever.

I tell Mrs Crocker that I don't need her and run the bath myself. I'm weary of being with people and relish the time on my own. I could do with a television but settle instead for one of Eddie's books. I cannot concentrate, however. My eyes trace the lines, but the words are rendered meaningless by my straying mind, which is constantly drawn to Cavill. He's all I can think about. I will spend the day with him tomorrow, but what then?

I want more. I cannot live in the present moment and enjoy it for what it is when I know what the future holds. Fire will consume the theatre, Nessa will die, and I will slide back to my own life with my heart once again in shreds. But this time it will be the *final* good-bye. How can I savour the present moment when I know that every second with him is one more grain of sand that's slipped through the neck of the sand timer?

But end it, I must.

I close the book and lie back against the pillows, staring up at the ceiling, my emotions in turmoil. I go over what Avril told me, trying to make sense of it. She made it clear that in order to sever this invisible force of attraction that keeps reuniting us, I must allow my longing to fully express itself. Like a bud, I must give it the opportunity to flower, to fulfil its destiny, to reach completion. But in order to fully comprehend this, I need to go back to the beginning and work out what exactly it is that I have done.

Undeniably, I have altered time and given Cavill a life he wasn't destined to have. That is the simple truth. But now it's *not* so simple. When Cavill fell in love with me he decided *not* to travel to South America. Therefore, he avoided his destiny and didn't die on the voyage. But in changing his destiny I set in motion something that has gained a momentum of its own. I created a soul connection.

I consider love, not the physical attraction of two people who are sexually drawn to each other, but the deeper, eternal love that is divine. That soul connection we created in St Sidwell in 1895, was found again in 1912 when I embodied Constance Fleet. Of course, Cavill didn't know he'd recognised it. How could he? But he had, on a subconscious level. On the level of *his* soul. Once again, our souls were trying to reunite, to fulfil their destiny, to do what they were never able to do in the beginning because I withheld the truth of who I really was. Now they're trying to come together again, but until Cavill sees beyond Eddie Skipton's eyes and recognises my soul behind them, the force of attraction will be denied, and I don't know how many times I will slide back to him before the truth is finally revealed and our souls can at last recognise each other for what they are.

Is that what Avril was trying to tell me?

I'm fumbling about in the dark for answers. With no one here to guide me, I'm having to follow my intuition. But how do I know that I'm right?

Regardless of whether my theory is true, Cavill loves Eddie, and he deserves to find happiness with her. If I come back again, as someone else, I'll deny him that happiness. I can't do that to him. I can't do it to *me*. I can't do it to Eddie.

Somehow, I have to make him understand who I really am and say good-bye, without changing the status quo. Isn't that like trying to make scrambled eggs without breaking a shell?

The following morning, I wake to the sound of rain. It's like someone's throwing gravel at my windowpanes. I lie in the warmth of my bed, a nervous feeling churning in my stomach. Today I will tell Cavill who I am.

'Will we recognise each other when we no longer have our physical bodies? Will we recognise each other when we are made of light?'

We will see.

The following morning, Mrs Crocker comes in to open my curtains and run the bath. She chooses my outfit and lays it over the upholstered chair. I notice it's a formal skirt suit in gunmetal blue. Perhaps it's what Eddie Skipton always wears to church. Mrs Crocker picks a piece of lint off the lapel of the jacket and brushes it lightly with her fingers. 'You'll need an umbrella today,' she says. 'It's raining cats and dogs.'

'I like the rain,' I tell her, climbing out of bed. 'It's romantic.'

She chortles and shakes her head. 'Only you would think it romantic, ma'am. There's nothing romantic about wet feet and frizzy hair.'

But I think of lying in the arms of the man I love.

After breakfast the entire household gathers in the hall. There's Cook, Nancy, Mrs Crocker, Nessa and Lavinia. When I was at St Sidwell, the cook remained in the kitchen to prepare the lunch. I imagine in *this* household Eddie and the girls spend the day at the Aphrodite, rehearsing, so don't require feeding. With just over three days to go until the first night, they must have a lot of work to do.

The women are all dressed in their Sunday best, complete with hats and gloves. Cook has even applied a little rouge to her cheeks. The rain has diminished to a light drizzle, but the low-hanging, soggy cloud looks as if it's going to stick around for some time. We set off under umbrellas. Lavinia and Nessa link arms, leaving me to walk alone behind them. I'm grateful that they'll show me the way. Behind me Cook, Nancy and Mrs Crocker quietly talk among themselves. I pick up snippets of their conversation, but my hope of hearing someone say the name Taran is dashed. Perhaps he will be at church. I will watch Nessa closely.

The church is an old, grey stone building with a tall, crenellated tower and arched windows. The grassy yard is littered with gravestones. Some must be extremely old for they're blackened with age and listing. I'm reminded at once of Cavill's gravestone in the churchyard at St Sidwell and shiver. I don't want to think of his death. I want to commit to the present moment and live it fully.

Cavill wants to spend the day with me. How is that possible? How has he swung it?

It looks like the entire town is filing into the church and I search the faces for Cavill but without success. I pretend to know everyone and return their greetings with a smile and a brief comment about the weather. Fortunately, the English love discussing the weather, and today they're expecting a storm. 'Love a storm,' says Lydia, who I meet just inside the big doors. She's with her Aunt Wallie, Countess of Faversham, who looks suitably grand in a purple skirt that reaches the floor and a matching jacket worn over a white lacey blouse. Her grey hair is arranged tidily beneath a wide-brimmed hat laden with flowers and her ears and throat sparkle with gems. She looks quite out of place here, as if she's from a different age, but perhaps that's the point; she enjoys standing out.

'My dear Eddie,' she says when she sees me. 'I hear you have all been frightfully busy rehearsing.'

'We have,' I reply.

Lydia grins. She looks uncomfortable in an ill-fitting dress and hat, as if she's worn them under duress. She looked much happier in her knickerbockers. 'I'm nearly finished,' she says cheerfully, and my smile remains fixed because I have no idea what it is that she's finished. 'Cavill says he's bringing you over after the service to have a look.'

'Yes,' I say with confidence. 'I can't wait.'

The Countess cuts in. 'You'll be impressed. Lydia has been working day and night.' She sniffs and gives her niece a sidelong glance. 'However, that is no way to find a husband.'

Lydia laughs. 'No time for a husband, Aunt Wallie.'

The Countess is not amused. She sets off down the aisle and I see her a little later taking her place in the front row, after having smiled graciously at those already seated in the pews as if they're her loyal subjects.

'I hope you like it,' says Lydia. 'Cavill has already seen it and thinks it's smashing, but it's you I want to impress, girlie.' She gives me a sympathetic smile. 'I know how much this play means to you.'

'I'm sure I'll like it,' I reply, wondering why *Macbeth* means so much to Eddie.

More people are coming into the church and we're in the way.

We walk together down the aisle, and I look out for Nessa and Lavinia – and Cavill. I spot Cavill near the front beside Gilda and my spirits immediately soar. Just knowing he's in the same room makes me feel as if I'm suddenly walking on air.

I find the girls and take the place Nessa has saved for me beside her. The church is packed, and I can't help but compare it to my time where most churches are suffering dwindling congregations. Some are so small that parishes have had to unite and share a vicar. There's something rather nice about the community spirit here, where everyone meets on a Sunday. It gives one a warm feeling of belonging.

The chattering stops as soon as the vicar steps into the nave to welcome everyone and I switch off and allow my mind to wander into the past. The last time I went to church was in St Sidwell in 1895. To the Pengower's private chapel on the estate. Cavill was a young man of thirty-eight then, and I was the governess in charge of his small nephews. I remember him well, with his sun-kissed blond hair, his face that barely had a line on it, except for the crow's feet at his temples and the leonine laughter lines around his mouth. He had an air of insouciance. He was untroubled and carefree. Responsibility weighed heavily on his brother's shoulders, but Cavill, being the youngest son, could spend his days in idle pursuits, like painting, riding, and reading. How his life changed, and he with it. I want to run my fingers over the lines tragedy has carved into his skin and smooth them out. I want to press my lips to his forehead so that he forgets the past. And I want to put my hand against his heart and heal the wound that loss has inflicted there. That *I* have inflicted. Because were it not for me, he would have died that summer of 1895. I did what timesliders are not meant to do: change the future. But I changed his.

Is it true that it's better to have loved and lost than never to have loved at all?

The service is long and typically boring. I'll never understand why religions don't make worship more entertaining for their congregations. Why does it always have to be so dull? Where's the joy and the laughter. Why so serious and fearful? God is love and love is beautiful.

It's a relief when we file out into the rain. Cavill finds me beneath my umbrella talking to a stout man about the molehills that have sprung up in his garden. 'An enthusiastic and tireless little digger he is, Mrs Skipton. I'm not sure how to deal with the little fellow.'

'You need to catch him in a trap and then set him free somewhere far away,' I suggest.

The man frowns and appraises me in a condescending manner. 'Why, this isn't *Wind in the Willows*, Mrs Skipton. It's curtains for the miscreant, I tell you.'

Cavill rescues me, politely drawing me away from this bombastic man. I lift my umbrella so Cavill can shelter beneath it, even though he's wearing a hat and coat. 'I'm taking you to Hartismere,' he says quietly.

I nod. Fortunately, I don't need to know where that is as I won't be driving. 'And Gilda?'

'Honing her craft with Bentley.' He gives me a look that suggests he knows full well that her craft, such as it is, needs honing. 'I'll pick you up at midday.'

'Marvellous,' I reply. I can't help but grin because he's looking so serious. 'Are we really going to Hartismere?' I ask.

His face relaxes into a smile. 'For five minutes,' he replies, holding my gaze, and we both laugh. 'I couldn't think of anything else,' he adds.

I return to the house with the girls, and they hurry upstairs to change into what they call 'mufti' – casual clothes – then they set off for the theatre. I rifle through the wardrobe for a less formal dress, although I long for a pair of jeans and trainers. It's not the weather for dresses. Eddie loves colour and is quite chic, so I decide on a forest green dress, a matching cloche hat, T-bar shoes and a camel-colour coat that seems much too big for me, but I suppose that's the look. I've never much cared for fashion, but as Eddie Skipton I rather fancy myself. I certainly cut a dash in this ensemble, and hope that Cavill will be impressed.

As the hands of the clock move slowly towards midday, I feel my excitement rise. I don't know where we're going, but I don't care. We'll be together and that's all that matters. Perhaps this is the only opportunity I'll get to spend time alone with him. The only opportunity to tell him the truth. I'm certain I can persuade him I'm not a fantasist. He's a man who believes in the eternal nature of the soul. Might he be open-minded enough to consider time travel?

Before leaving, Cook asks me what I'd like for supper, and I tell her to leave out whatever is available and to take the rest of the day off. She seems surprised, but thrilled. When I tell Nancy and Mrs Crocker that they will not be needed either, they are equally surprised. Don't they automatically get Sunday off?

Cavill's car draws up outside the gate and I don't wait for him to come up the path and knock on the door but hurry out into the rain to meet him. He walks round to open the passenger door for me, and we smile at each other with ill-concealed joy. It's hard not to throw myself into his arms, but I know that very soon nothing will come between us.

We set off. He reaches over and squeezes my hand. 'Just the two of us,' he says.

'Just the two of us,' I reply, and hold his hand until he requires it back in order to change gear.

The rain does not relent but pelts against the windscreen in an incessant torrent. The small wipers are quite ineffectual and can barely keep up with the bombardment. Cavill drives slowly for the lanes are narrow and the visibility bad, and his car is not like modern vehicles which are robust. The suspension is terrible. Every time we go over a dip or drive through a puddle I bounce up and down as if my seat is made of springs. I feel as if I'm in a rather rickety tin can.

After about ten minutes, I notice an old drystone wall that surrounds what appears to be a large estate. I try not to look too interested; after all, I'm sure Eddie has seen it many times before.

Behind the wall is dense woodland and I try to get a glimpse of the house through it, but my window is too fogged up to see anything more than green and brown smudges. Eventually, we reach the entrance. There's a pretty, fairy-tale gate house and prestigious iron gates, which are wide open. So, this must be Hartismere, although there is no name displayed anywhere. I suppose, with a property this grand, everyone knows what it is. Cavill turns in and we make our way up a long, sweeping gravel drive. On either side is rolling parkland, leafy trees and meadows of long grasses and yellow and purple wildflowers. Then the house comes into view, and I struggle to hide my excitement, because it's absolutely gorgeous. It's a magnificent Jacobean manor built in red brick, with pointed gables and black lead windows. It reminds me at once of St Sidwell and I wonder whether Cavill notices the similarity and what he makes of it. I'm keen to see the interior, but we don't drive up to it. Instead, we take the left fork when the drive splits and enter a farm. Cavill draws up outside one of the barns alongside a van. A couple of workmen in caps are loading into the back of it large objects wrapped in brown paper. 'We'll be quick,' Cavill says, turning off the engine. 'This is simply cover.'

He climbs out and puts up his umbrella, then he comes round to my side and opens the door for me. I take his hand as I step out and then we hurry through the wide-open doors of the barn.

I was expecting farm machinery or haybales, instead I'm faced with an artist's studio on a grand scale. Above us, half the roof has been replaced by glass, which now reveals grey clouds and rain, but still gives light. There are enormous canvases leaning up against the walls along with planks of wood, rolls of hessian, furniture, storage boxes, tins of paint and all the paraphernalia associated with artists displayed on shelving and on the floor. At the end, busy with what is obviously the stage set for *Macbeth*, is Lydia, accompanied by a few assistants. 'Tallyho!' she calls out when she sees us. 'Come on in.' She waves enthusiastically. She's now back in her knickerbockers and smock, with her hair tied up beneath a knotted handkerchief. Her smile is radiant, and she looks much more comfortable than she did in church in that ill-fitting dress.

'You'd have seen more if you'd come earlier,' she says. Then she looks specifically at me. 'But what do you think, Eddie? It'll look better when it's set up on the stage later today, but you get the idea.'

'Goodness, I most certainly do. It's spectacular,' I gush. And it most definitely is. Painted on giant panels are the eerie grey walls of a distant castle being taken over by a dark forest. The twisty-turny branches wind through the walls like snakes, as if they're consuming it. It's brilliant, and I'm full of admiration for this wonderfully creative young woman. She can't possibly have done it all on her own. But I can't ask for fear of undermining Eddie, who would most likely know.

Cavill goes to help her now, lifting the panels and turning them round so I can see the backs.

'Then, hey presto, we have the interior!' she exclaims. 'Smashing, don't you think?'

'It's really stunning,' I tell her. 'You're a genius, Lydia.'

She's clearly relieved. She glances at Cavill, then back at me, and I sense they've discussed this quietly together. 'Oh, I'm so pleased you're happy, girlie,' she continues. 'I've done something very different from when Tom directed *Macbeth*. I was worried. Well, you know. I'm just happy you like it.'

Ah, so now I know why this play means so much to Eddie. 'You've made the right decision,' I tell her. 'I wouldn't want it any other way. It's perfect.'

'We have a long afternoon ahead,' she says, stepping aside so the workmen can reach one of the panels which is already wrapped in brown paper. 'It will all be in place by tonight.'

A vision flashes before my eyes, of the fire ripping through it. All her hard work going up in flames. Everything destroyed. As she smiles proudly, I feel terrible that the play will never be performed, and that this magical set will be reduced to ash.

That Nessa will lose her life.

'I've got a very good feeling about this production,' Cavill says.

'Me too,' Lydia agrees. 'It's going to be the best yet.'

And I can do nothing but agree with them. I wish I didn't know better.

Chapter Fifteen

In the short time that we stay with Lydia, I learn that her aunt, the widowed Countess of Faversham, lives in the big house while Lydia lives with her widowed mother in a cottage on the estate. I also learn that she has had help in making the stage set from the estate workers, especially the gamekeeper and his son who are both good carpenters. She invites us to join her for lunch, but Cavill politely declines. He makes no excuse. We return to the car just as the rain stops and the clouds break momentarily to release a brilliant beam of sunshine.

Lydia waves us off and we motor down the drive and towards the rest of the day that stretches out before us, full of promise. 'She was concerned you might not like the set, being so modern,' he says, as the wheels splash through puddles and we both bounce about like jack in the boxes.

'I do like it, very much,' I reply. It certainly doesn't look modern to me. 'It's important to try different things,' I tell him. 'And she's made this set her own, hasn't she? She's very talented. Do you still paint, Cavill?' The words come out before I can censor them.

He glances at me and frowns. 'How the devil do you know I paint?'

I'm stung. 'You told me,' I reply, realising that I'm going to have to double down. 'You painted birds once upon a time.' I almost hold my breath and stare unblinking at the road ahead. An uncomfortable heat causes the skin on my neck to prickle.

'Did I? I didn't think I had told anyone that. How funny.' He shrugs, accepting my lie. 'I lost the will to paint many years ago, but once, it was a hobby of mine, that is true. I was quite good, on reflection.'

'I think you should take it up again. It's good for the soul.'

He smiles wryly. 'Maybe you're right. I *should* take it up again. I used to keep a sketchbook. I painted ducks, mostly. There's something very appealing about a duck.'

I remember the conversation we had in 1895 by the estuary, when, as Hermione, he told me about his love of teals. 'I like them too,' I tell him, then add, a little manipulatively. 'I especially love the teal. There's something about the curve of the head that's particularly charming.'

'They're my favourite as well,' he says, and his face beams with pleasant surprise. 'You're right, Eddie my darling, I should paint again. The first bird I'm going to paint will be a teal. I'll paint it for you.'

I smile back. 'I'd love that.' But I know I'll never see it.

He reaches over and once again takes my hand. I hold on to his. I never want to let it go.

We drive along the coast for what feels like tens of miles before Cavill turns in to a picturesque yet run down white pub called The Smuggler's Tavern that sits on the top of cliffs, looking out to sea. There's something world-weary about it, as if it's sat there for centuries and is now tired of the monotony of its existence and the harsh winds that whip off the water. 'I think we're far enough away from Seacombe not to be caught,' Cavill says, pulling up and turning off the engine.

'And what if we are caught?' I ask.

He grins. 'I'll think of something.' But I can't imagine what excuse he could give. We have adultery written all over our faces.

The pub is quiet. Only a few locals are sitting around tables beneath a ceiling of old wooden beams and peeling plaster, drinking beer and smoking. When we enter, they look up at us over their pint glasses, appraise us with mild curiosity, then return to their stout and their chat and ignore us. I notice a sheep dog sleeping on the carpet in front of the fireplace, where logs crackle and glow with dancing flames. I'm grateful for the warmth, for the rainclouds have turned the air damp and cold. We choose a small table in the corner by a small, latticed window and order wine and something to eat. There isn't much choice, so I copy Cavill and go for the roast beef with Yorkshire pudding. It's the kind of meal one would expect in a modern pub on a Sunday. Some things never change!

It's cosy in there and intimate. There's something very pleasant about the sweet smell of pipe tobacco and cigarette smoke. And the fug serves as a screen. I feel less conspicuous in it. Soon we're deep in conversation with eyes only for each other. The rest of the pub recedes, and it feels as if we're alone on an island where time doesn't exist.

Having made the mistake of alluding to his sketching, I take care not to put my foot in it again. I encourage him to talk about New York, Josephine, his growing up at St Sidwell, anything so that he doesn't ask about me. It's a minefield, admittedly, because I have no idea how much of his life Eddie knows, and I'm totally ignorant of hers. But he doesn't find my questions strange. In fact, he seems happy to talk and to be listened to. I wonder whether Gilda, as charming as she appears to be, might be a little self-obsessed. He seems grateful that I'm so interested in him.

'I've booked a room upstairs, Eddie,' he says quietly, when we finish lunch. He takes my hand across the table. I glance at the other people and realise that no one is looking at us. We're just a couple, like any other. 'Are you happy with that? You don't have to. I don't want to . . .'

I cut him off. 'I want to, Cavill,' I reply.

He looks deeply into my eyes. 'If you're sure.'

I nod. I can't quite believe that this is happening and that it's okay. At least, I *hope* it's okay. I hope it's what Eddie would want. How can I know?

And then, as if he senses I need reassurance, he adds. 'I wouldn't have been so presumptuous if you hadn't confessed how you felt. How you had felt for some time.'

'I know.' I squeeze his hand. 'I want this. I want *you*.'

*

I'm nervous suddenly. I can't vouch for Eddie, but I've wanted this for so long. I've dreamed of it. But now it's about to happen, I'm riddled with anxiety. Cavill collects the room key from the inn-keeper, a ruddy-faced, impassive woman who has probably seen this kind of thing before, and we follow her to a blackened door. She lifts the latch and tells us the bedroom is at the top of the narrow staircase on the right, number two. Cavill stands aside to let me pass and I go on up. I feel the blood pounding against my temples. My heart seems to beat in my throat. It's not because I'm committing adultery, or, to be precise, Eddie is. That's *not* a concern I allow myself to dwell upon. It's that this will be the one and only time I get to make love with him. Then I'll have to let him go. I'm afraid of it being over before it's even begun. It's like crying over the last page of a novel without enjoying the story. But how can I enjoy the beauty of the present moment when I know that for me, it's an ending. For Eddie and Cavill it's only the beginning, and I envy Eddie that.

Cavill puts the key in the lock, and we enter. The ceiling is low, so he almost has to stoop. The bedroom is plain but quaint and unfussy. There's a double bed, pine bedside tables with brass lamps and a small, lead window that reveals, through the mist and rain, the grey sea and angry grey clouds above it. But I don't linger on the view. I drape my coat over the spindle-back chair placed in the corner beneath it and sit down to take off my shoes. I glance at Cavill and smile. He's standing, watching me, a sweet, pensive look on his face. 'This feels comfortable, Eddie,' he says softly. 'It feels right.'

I remind myself that I'm Eddie Skipton. Eddie was married. She's no ingenue. But I feel like a virgin on her wedding night. There's a mirror on the wall above the chest of drawers and, as I stand and move towards Cavill, I catch myself in it. Eddie's face, pale and beautiful, looks back at me, the skin between her eyes puckered with apprehension. I swiftly shift my gaze and focus on Cavill with determination, but a sharp pain stabs me in the chest. It's Eddie's face he sees, Eddie's eyes he looks into, Eddie's body he now holds. I'm the silent longing in her heart, a whisper he can't hear; a woman he doesn't know who loves him.

I'm in his arms and he's kissing me. I push those dark thoughts away and lose myself in the sensation of his lips on mine. I close my eyes and sink into the familiar scent of him which envelops me in a kind of oblivion. I forget that I'm Eddie. I forget what year it is, and where I am. It's just me and Cavill in the middle of a timeless, eternal space, alone together at last.

The cold bed quickly warms up with the heat of our bodies. There's no need to rush, but we explore each other greedily. My dreams manifest more wonderfully than I could ever have imagined. His touch is gentle, his kisses tender, and the sacred feeling of this moment is not lost on either of us. It's as if I have always been his and he mine. As he enters me, reaching the closest thing to unity that two human beings can possibly achieve, our eyes lock and I'm convinced that he's seeing me, Pixie, at last.

I feel the sting of tears, the welling of emotion in my throat. I'm overwhelmed by the expansion in my chest, this love that is so much bigger than I am. It seems to radiate out of me and fill the room, and I'm carried on it, like a bird on a sunbeam, my spirit soaring with joy. I wrap my arms around him and hold him tightly. I'm in the present moment, not wishing I were anywhere else, and it's a profound bliss I have never known before.

And yet with such intensity of love comes the fear of losing it – and lose it I will. That is inevitable.

We lie entwined, our hearts gradually slowing down, the sweat drying on our skin, the afterglow enduring in the rosiness of our cheeks and the sparkle in our eyes. He kisses my forehead. I put my hand on his chest. I take a breath. We won't have another moment like this.

'There is something I need to tell you,' I begin, lifting my head out of the crook of his neck and propping myself up on my elbow.

He looks at me, and his lips curl into a small smile. He winds a tendril of hair around my ear. 'You're crying,' he says, and his face clouds with concern.

I nod. How do I begin? What words do I use? How can I explain what is really unexplainable?

'Eddie?'

And there it is. *Eddie*. The name pulls me down like a cold stone.

He sees Eddie. He is only ever going to see *her*.

My courage fails me. I press my lips to his, but he's alarmed now. He takes my face in his hands and gazes at me worriedly. 'Eddie, what is it?'

My voice must get past the lump in my throat. I'm wilting in the face of too great a challenge. I simply cannot do it. Not now. Not ever.

So, I don't. I take the coward's way. 'I love you, my darling, and I always will.'

His expression relaxes with relief. 'You don't regret it?'

I shake my head, and tears of defeat blur my vision as the opportunity passes like a ship sailing over the horizon that will never come back. 'It was beautiful.'

We return to Seacombe. The rain has stopped, and valiant shafts of sunlight find holes in the purple cloud and transmute to gold the yellow fields of rape. We hold hands across the gearbox, and every now and then he glances at me and smiles with affection and pleasure. He knows not the heaviness in my chest, and I hide it well.

Eddie has no reason to be sad. But I feel as if my heart is in tatters.

This soul connection I feel is mine alone. Why did I ever think otherwise?

He drops me off at Eddie's house. Before I climb out, he takes my hand and squeezes it. 'I love you, Eddie Skipton.'

'And I love you right back, Cavill Pengower.'

The house is as quiet as a tomb. Cook, Nancy and Mrs Crocker have, on my instruction, taken the day off. I'm glad. I don't feel like talking to anyone. I'm relieved I'm alone. I need time and space to process what has just happened. What I failed to do. And what the consequences of that might be.

I hang my hat on the hook in the hall. I notice a telegram in the silver tray on the console table and open it. It's from a woman called Sylvia. I have no idea who Sylvia is, but she's coming to meet me tomorrow to talk. *Best not meet in the house. I will be at Betty's at ten.* My stomach clenches with anxiety. Where is Betty's?

I stare at my reflection in the mirror. 'Where is Betty's?' I repeat out loud. Eddie's beautiful eyes gaze back at me. I wish she could help me out here, but her consciousness is elsewhere. She can't hear me or help me.

'*Best not meet in the house.*' Well, that implies there's someone in the house Sylvia doesn't want to bump into. Could it be that Sylvia is Eddie's sister, Nessa's mother? I cling on to that hope. If she is, then I can learn more about Nessa and what's in her head. I just need to find Betty's.

I put my hat back on and head out into what is gradually becoming a placid evening. The wall of cloud is heading inland, leaving the sky over the sea washed to the palest of blues. There's a gusty wind, still damp from the rain, and I wrap my coat about me and jump over a puddle that's collected in a hole in the road. Everyone in my path either smiles or nods in greeting. Eddie must be well known in Seacombe, or perhaps people are just polite. It's a small town, after all, not like London where everyone is a stranger.

It's not long before I reach the high street. It's quiet compared to a modern high street. There's a classic Model T Ford parked on the curb, but besides that one vehicle there are only horses pulling carts slowly over the cobbles, people on bicycles, and others going about their business on foot. I notice once again the absence of yellow lines on the street, and the pavements are clear of signs, bollards, traffic lights and the other paraphernalia that clutters modern towns and makes them look so ugly. It's peaceful, charming and innocent, and almost sepia in colour, as if I'm looking at everything through a subduing lens.

It's not long before I find a newsagent. I head inside and search for a map of the town. I find them displayed on a rack on the counter – no Google Maps in this time. The newsagent, a balding man in a beige overall with steel-framed glasses perched on a bulbous nose above a tidy thatch of a moustache, smiles at me warmly. 'What can I get you, Mrs Skipton?' he asks in his West Country drawl, and I'm taken aback because I didn't expect to be known in here.

'I need a map of the town for a friend of mine,' I reply confidently. I always think one can get away with anything if one is confident.

'Indeed,' he says as I reach for one.

'Beautiful day, isn't it?' I add, placing it on the counter.

'Didn't start off that way. Thought the rain would never stop.'

I laugh. 'I agree. It didn't look optimistic, did it?'

I open Eddie's purse and hand over some coins. I have no idea what the value of money is, or indeed, what the coins mean. The newsagent frowns. He takes a couple and gives the rest back. I feel I must say something to justify doing such an odd thing. 'Coins are very fiddly,' I say and drop them back into the purse.

He chuckles. 'Especially those little coppers!'

I change the subject quickly, so as not to look like an idiot. 'My friend is meeting someone tomorrow at Betty's. I need to explain to her how to get there.'

'Then it's a good idea to give her that map. Betty's is a little off the beaten track, isn't it?'

'That's what I thought,' I reply, confident now that I'll find it. 'Well, thank you, and have a good day.'

He frowns again. I don't suppose people say 'have a good day' in 1923!

I walk home with a sense of achievement. I turn my thoughts to Nessa and what I'm here to do. Tomorrow is Monday. The fire happens on Wednesday. That gives me only three days to work out what motivates Nessa to remain in the world after death, when it would be so much more pleasant to leave it.

As for Cavill, I cannot imagine ever managing to tell him the truth. I had an opportunity and I blew it. I don't think I'll be given another. I suppress the rising sense of defeat and shame, for I'm nothing but a coward, and walk on with purpose.

*

That evening, I dine with Nessa and Lavinia on cold meats and potatoes which Cook has left out for us. Both girls comment on the fact that there are no servants in the house. 'It is so unlike you, Skippy, to give everyone the day off.' Nessa grins at me playfully and arches her eyebrows. 'What were you up to while we were rehearsing?'

I smile sweetly. 'I don't know what you're implying, my dear, but it sounds highly inappropriate!' They both laugh. 'Actually, I went to Hartismere with Mr Pengower to look at the sets Lydia has made. They were packing them into a van to take to the theatre.'

They are suitably distracted. 'Goodness, how exciting!' enthuses Lavinia.

'Are they magnificent?' Nessa asks.

'They are fabulous!'

I'm surprised they don't comment on me going with Cavill. Perhaps Eddie and Cavill have been business associates for long enough now for it to be acceptable to spend time alone together.

'Gilda is a shockingly bad actress,' says Lavinia, returning to what is clearly their favourite subject. 'Poor Mr Bentley is having to work extra hours to coach her.'

'One cannot make a silk purse out of a pig's ear,' says Nessa meanly. 'He's wasting his time.'

'Lady Macbeth is not an easy part,' I tell them. Of course, I have no idea as I haven't seen the play.

'Rubbish, Skippy. It's only challenging if one is not up to the job. Gilda should try something else, like gardening, or painting.'

Lavinia laughs heartily at that ludicrous suggestion. 'Can you imagine her getting her pretty white hands dirty in the garden, Nessa?'

'I suppose not,' she concedes. 'Still, she should accept defeat and step off the stage.'

'That will never happen,' says Lavinia seriously. 'She must be pushed.'

At that comment, the hairs stand to attention on the back of my neck. 'Now that's not kind,' I tell her. 'Let's play a game.'

'Snakes and Ladders,' Nessa suggests, getting up and dropping her napkin onto the table. 'One doesn't have to think too hard about that.'

The girls set off up the stairs to the drawing room, their heads together in secretive whispers. I know they're plotting something, I can feel it in that space beneath my ribcage where intuition dwells. But what? I feel rather sorry for Gilda, having these two snapping at her heels. Sure, she's not a great actress, but this is amateur theatre, and her husband is the boss. Gilda can do what she likes. Isn't it just meant to be fun?

I think of the fire, and wonder, with an uneasy feeling building in my belly, whether the fun gets out of hand. Didn't Lelia say that Nessa herself started it? Could it be that a prank to hinder Gilda goes horribly wrong?

The following morning dawns with bright sunshine. The rain has washed the sky to a dazzling blue and the woolly white clouds that trundle beneath it are as clean as freshly soaped sheep. The three of us breakfast together bathed in the light that streams in through the big window. The servants have returned to their posts and the house is buzzing with activity again. We discuss the day ahead. Lavinia has to work. Nessa, I discover, has no occupation. Those who don't have other commitments will be rehearsing at the theatre all day. I tell them that I have a meeting at ten, so Nessa says she'll head over to the theatre alone. She's in a very good mood, almost too good. She has a kind of alertness and vigour that suggests to me that she's up to something that's giving her a thrill. I'll go straight to the theatre after meeting Sylvia so I can keep an eye on her.

I have found Betty's on the map. It's on the other side of town, a good twenty-minute walk from Eddie's house. I set off at half-nine, in a yellow floral dress with a matching yellow jacket, scarf and hat. My stomach is an ant nest of nerves. I don't know what Sylvia looks like. I'm not even sure who she is. I intend to arrive early, so that she has to come to my table; that way I won't embarrass myself by not recognising her.

The café is a small, unimpressive place. The kind of venue frequented by locals and not by tourists who want something more picturesque. It's very clear that Sylvia doesn't want to be seen with Eddie. Is she hiding from her husband, Nessa or people in general? I'm curious as to her motives, but anxious about how I'm going to find out, when I have no idea how much Eddie already knows. If Sylvia is, indeed, her sister, Eddie will already know a great deal.

I open the door and step into a fug of smoke. I'm assaulted too by the savoury smell of fried eggs and bacon. It makes my eyes water. There are about ten wooden tables placed on aged pine floorboards. Only a few of them are occupied; a quartet of bearded fishermen puff on pipes and cigarettes; a trio of elderly women drink tea and gossip quietly; a young couple nervously hold hands across the table. The young woman is blushing. The counter runs along the right-hand side of the room, displaying pastries and cakes, and a pair of women in white aprons work behind it. I take a table at the back and order a cup of tea from one of the waitresses who wanders over the moment I've sat down. She brings a teapot and pours what looks like dirty water into a cup. I don't dare take a sip. I know I'm not going to like it.

I don't have to wait long for my mystery date. The door opens and I recognise Sylvia at once. Pretty with curly brown hair pinned up beneath an elegant green hat, she bears a strong resemblance to Eddie, although, unlike her sister, she is caked in make-up. She smiles when she sees me and comes straight over. She greets me with a brisk, 'Hello, Edwina,' and takes off her green coat and drapes it over the back of the chair. She sits down with a sigh. 'This feels very clandestine, doesn't it?' she says with a chuckle. 'You're probably wondering why I chose to meet here, of all the places. Well, I'll fill you in.' She looks into my cup. 'What are you having? Tea? Hmmm, that doesn't look very nice, does it?' The waitress comes over with the coffee pot. 'I'll have a hot chocolate, please,' says Silvia. 'And a scone. I'm ravenous. You?' She puts her handbag on the table and reaches in. After rummaging about, she brings out a silver cigarette case and flicks it open with a burgundy talon. 'You're not going to eat anything?'

'I had breakfast,' I reply.

'So did I. But, as you know, I have the appetite of a horse.'

One wouldn't know that by looking at her slim figure. Must be the smoking that keeps her so thin.

Sylvia has the jittery, nervous energy of a very highly strung woman. I wonder whether she was always like that, or whether it's a result of being married to Humphrey. It's impossible to know, of course, and perhaps much too easy to blame the man. Maybe she was just born that way. I decide to let her chatter on. Fortunately, that seems to be their dynamic, because Sylvia barely gives Eddie a chance to speak.

She uses a cigarette holder, which seems to be the must-have accessory, and takes a drag, blowing the smoke out the side of her mouth. 'I don't need to tell you that I've come about Nessa.' She shakes her head and rolls her bottle-green eyes. 'Nessa, Nessa, Nessa! Ever since she was a little girl, she's been problematic. I dare say nothing is likely to change. But if anyone can talk sense into her, it's you, Edwina. I'm pinning my hopes on you, for Nessa's sake, for her future.'

My heart sinks at those words, because Nessa doesn't have a future. She has just over two days left before her life will end. I put my hands on the table and lean forward to listen, because Sylvia might hold the key that will unlock the door and allow Nessa to step into her *eternal* future.

Chapter Sixteen

The waitress brings a mug of hot chocolate on a tray, along with a scone, butter and jam, and arranges it all on the table in front of Sylvia. Sylvia takes another drag before stubbing the half-smoked cigarette into the ashtray and putting the holder back in her bag. 'I really don't know why she chooses such a difficult life,' she says, and sighs despairingly. 'Humphrey is prepared to make it very easy for her, if only she would allow him. He loves her very much, you know, even though he sometimes has a strange way of showing it. He only wants the best for her, as do I. You will disagree, of course, but theatre is not a healthy environment for a young lady like Nessa. She should settle down with a good man and busy herself in the home. That's where nice girls belong. You're different, Edwina. Marrying a man who owns a theatre is not the same as treading the boards yourself. Humphrey can't even manage the word "actress" without it getting stuck in his throat. It's embarrassing, and he has a reputation to uphold. It's taken many years, but he has built up a successful business and is now enjoying the fruits of his labour. Nessa is a thorn in what should be a bed of roses.'

'I think that's very unfair,' I reply. I watch her take a sip of chocolate. Her hand is trembling. I sense there's more to this conversation than she's letting on. 'A woman should be allowed to follow whatever path she wants to take. And not necessarily with a man.'

Sylvia puts down her mug with a loud thud and glares at me in horror. 'Have you gone quite mad, Edwina? Not necessarily with a man! I'm not sure what your widowhood has done to you, but surely, you can see that a woman without a man is a lost and vulnerable thing. A woman is nothing without a man.'

I remind myself of the time I'm in. The Suffragettes still have a long way to go. A woman's place continues to be very much in the home. 'Well, Nessa can live with me and realise her dreams of being an actress,' I suggest, and drop my argument.

Sylvia rips the scone in half with her burgundy nails and garnishes it with thick layers of butter and jam. 'And you think you can support her forever, do you? I don't think you understand, Edwina. Humphrey will cut her off. What will she live on when you are gone?'

I feel out of my depth, suddenly, although this conversation is actually irrelevant, bearing in mind the tragedy that is going to befall Nessa. 'Then why is he coming to watch her on Wednesday?' I ask.

Sylvia's jaw stiffens and she doesn't look at me but stares hard into her mug. 'Because I have asked him to,' she says.

'And he'll do what you say?' Humphrey Blunt does not sound like the sort of man who will bow to the will of a wife.

She lifts her chin and stares at me defiantly. 'He has on this occasion, yes.'

'I'm sorry, Sylvia, but this reeks of a lie. It just doesn't add up. Humphrey is about to cut Nessa off because she's disobeying him and playing a part in *Macbeth*, but he's coming to watch her anyway. Not buying it. Sorry.'

She stares at me with startled eyes. I don't know whether it's my language that's surprised her, or my non-cooperation. 'It's true,' she replies.

I laugh. 'No, it isn't. Come on, Sylvia. Out with it.'

She forks a piece of scone into her mouth and chews on it thoughtfully. After a long moment, she washes it down with a swig of chocolate and then looks at me fearfully. 'You are not yourself today, Edwina.'

I sigh. The part I'm playing is far harder than any Shakespeare created. 'I'm just weary of you both standing in the way of Nessa's dream,' I tell her, and hope that I sound more like the sister she knows.

Sylvia sucks in her cheeks, then brings out her cigarette case once more and, as she slips another cigarette into the holder and lights it, she doesn't say a word. She's ruminating on my words and deciding whether to surrender. Finally, she inhales the nicotine greedily. The little end glows crimson. She exhales smoke through her nostrils like a dragon and drops her shoulders in resignation. 'Very well, Edwina. I will tell you the truth. Humphrey does not want a scandal, and neither do I. That is the fundamental truth. We need *you*, no, we *ask* you in the strongest terms, to persuade Nessa to give it up. To walk away. To do the right thing. Humphrey and I will be there to watch her on Wednesday. We will applaud. We will smile. We will be gracious. Everyone will believe that Nessa is stepping away of her own accord. Do you understand *now*, Edwina? Nessa will come home, marry George Cavendish, who is a dear, and give up her silly ideas of being an actress. You must make her do it. We are counting on you.'

I nod slowly, deliberating whether to mention Taran. If I do, will I let Nessa down? Will I set the cat among the pigeons? Will I make the situation so much worse? I make a quick decision and hope that it's the right one. 'Do you know a man named Taran?' I ask and then hold my breath.

She shakes her head. 'Should I?'

I shrug. 'Well, you clearly don't.'

'No, I don't. Who is he?'

'It doesn't matter.'

'Yes, it does, otherwise you wouldn't have asked me.'

'Someone I think Nessa is fond of,' I tell her carefully.

She looks horrified. 'Good Lord! What sort of a name is Taran? What is his last name?'

'That I don't know.'

'How did you come across the name Taran then?'

'I overheard the girls talking.'

'Lavinia and Nessa?'

'Yes.'

'Taran might be Lavinia's lover,' she suggests hopefully.

'Perhaps,' I agree, happy to put her off the scent.

She gives her head a little shake. 'It's academic, really, because one way or the other Nessa will come home, and she will marry someone suitable. I cannot understand why she doesn't like George. She's not a great beauty herself. She should consider herself lucky that he likes the look of her. Suitors are not exactly knocking down her door, are they?' She taps ash into the tray. 'I want to avoid things escalating out of proportion,' she continues. 'I don't want it to get nasty. The washing of one's dirty linen in public must be avoided at all costs. That is frightfully common, and we will not descend to that. Humphrey has not worked his fingers to the bone to be tarnished with that.'

'Very well. I will do my best,' I reply, because she's right, it really *is* academic, but not in the way that she thinks. I watch her tight face and pursed lips as she draws uneasily on her cigarette, and feel sorry for her, because in just over two days' time her daughter will die. It's too horrendous to imagine. And once Nessa is gone, will Sylvia and Humphrey regret their lack of support, or will they blame Nessa's ambitions for destroying her?

That is something I will never know.

Sylvia drops her shoulders. 'Thank you.'

'But Nessa is stubborn,' I add.

She chuckles joylessly. 'You're telling me?'

'Our children don't belong to us, Sylvia.' I want to quote from Khalil Gibran's beautiful book *The Prophet* but I'm not sure whether it's been published yet, so I paraphrase the part about children. 'We bring them into the world and guide them as best we can. But we must allow them to go their own way. To make their own decisions. To fail. That's what life is about. Making mistakes and learning from them. We mustn't make them live in our shadow, as little versions of ourselves. They must be free to be themselves.'

She stares at me, cigarette poised. 'I don't know what you're talking about, Edwina. You don't have children.'

I laugh then, because she has totally missed the point. 'It doesn't matter, Sylvia. Why don't you have another scone? A horse would gobble up at least ten.'

*

She departs as nervously as she arrived. I think I've baffled her with my opinions and the language I used to express them. I obviously didn't sound like the Edwina she knows. It doesn't matter, for I've learned two important things: one, Taran is not someone she has ever heard of, therefore, he must be involved in the theatre. Two, Nessa's parents have no intention of allowing her to be an actress. Her determination to show them how good she is in order to win them over is futile. Wasted energy. They're never going to be won over, because they don't want to be. My heart goes out to her for the limited freedom she has. Right now, she believes she's treading her own path, but the truth is, if the fire hadn't cut her life short, she would probably have been forced to conform. What other choice would she have? Her father would cut her off financially, and how would she then earn a living? Is Eddie's bank account large enough to support the pair of them indefinitely? Would Eddie want to?

As I walk to the theatre, I ruminate on the situation thus far: Nessa longs to be an actress, hence her presence, as a spirit, on stage in Joseph Lightwater's production. She loathes Gilda Garrett, which explains why she transfers that loathing on to Isadora Nash in the present. Both women are glamorous American leading ladies, although one is talented, the other is not. Nonetheless, I'm yet to discover how the fire starts, and I'd really like to know the role Taran plays in her life, if he has a role at all. For a woman so besotted with a man, she is very good at hiding it.

I arrive at the theatre to find that the set has been put up. It's astonishing. I stand at the back of the auditorium and stare in wonder at the magic of it, and that's even without the effects of lighting. The stage has come to life and is now a dark and foreboding forest of tall trees, twisted branches and a spooky-looking castle. Lydia has done a tremendous job.

The stage is busy. They're rehearsing. Mr Bentley is standing to the side while Ned as Macbeth goes through one of his scenes with other members of the cast. I notice Nessa at once. She's sitting in the chair I sat in, script in hand, watching the play with great focus. She's so engrossed, she doesn't even take her eyes off the performance when I walk down the aisle.

I decide to go backstage and see if I can find a programme. Surely, they must have already printed them. And if not, there has to be something with the name Taran on it, if he is in any way involved in the theatre. I have a gut feeling that he is. After all, Nessa is here every day, and she's not required to be. Sure, she's Gilda's understudy, but I'm certain even Gilda has other things to do besides rehearse. She doesn't appear to be here today.

I take the side door and head down the corridor to the back. I come to the dressing rooms. Ned Pollock is written in big letters on his door, Gilda Garrett on hers. I stop suddenly. I can hear the sound of snivelling behind Gilda's door. I press my ear to the wood. Yes, someone is crying.

I knock and enter without waiting to be invited in. I find Gilda alone. She looks up at me from her dressing table, her eyes are red and glassy, and there's a black smudge beneath one of them. She's smoking and I notice from the ashtray that this is not her first. 'Oh, it's you, Skippy,' she murmurs, and blows her nose on a handkerchief with the other hand.

'Are you all right, Gilda?' I ask. She clearly isn't.

She sighs, and I sense from her hesitation that she wants to talk about it. 'I just get down sometimes, you know,' she replies.

I close the door and shift the costumes that are draped over the armchair and sit down. Her room is a total mess. There are clothes everywhere, hanging on the back of the door, on a clothes rail and lying discarded on the floor. For someone so glamorous and beautifully turned out, I'm surprised to see such chaos.

'I'm sorry you're feeling low, Gilda. It's just nerves, probably.'

'Oh, I don't get nervous.' She shakes her head and her golden curls tremble. Her eyes are very green and shiny, and brimming with self-pity. 'Truth is, Skippy, I know I'm rotten.'

I never expected her to say that. 'You're not rotten, Gilda,' I protest. 'You're a fine actress.' It's easy to lie when I'm impersonating someone else.

She flicks ash into the tray and then draws on the ebony holder again. 'No, I'm not. There's no point pretending otherwise. I've been working with Mr Bentley. He's so patient with me.' She smiles stoically. 'Really, he goes above and beyond the call of duty. But even *he* can't make me into a good actress. My English accent is dreadful, for a start. And I'm moderate at best. The only reason anyone applauds me is because I'm beautiful. Beauty is a currency of its own, you know, and I'm rich in it. But I really want to be admired for something more meaningful. I know you understand, Skippy.'

I feel sorry for her, and less sorry for Nessa now, who has been unkind. Gilda is just doing her best. 'If you love acting, you must stick with it,' I tell her. 'The more you practise, the better you'll get. Isn't that so?'

She turns to the mirror to dab her eyes with the handkerchief. She really is lovely to look at. Her skin is translucent and flawless. She has a golden quality to her, like snow in sunshine. I can't take my eyes off her. 'You know, when I met my husband, I was acting in New York. I never got further than the chorus line. I was overlooked in every production. Then Cavill came to the theatre with his cousin Alicia Aldershoff, who was one of our patrons.' She turns and settles her lovely green gaze onto me. 'Of course you know this, Skippy. The point is, Cavill believed in me. Enough to buy me a theatre.' She laughs at the memory and turns back to the mirror to repair her make-up. 'I know what everyone thinks, that the only way I could get a proper role was to marry a man who loved me enough to buy me a theatre to perform in. Well, they're probably right. But I'm living my dream, and Cavill enabled me to do that. Is that so bad?'

I'm not sure what she's getting at.

She sighs, discards the handkerchief and powders her nose with a big fluffy brush. 'Cavill told me that Mr Bentley is going to go work in London.'

I fix my face into a mask so as not to expose my ignorance. This must be something Eddie knows about. I nod. 'He was always going to go on to bigger, better things,' I reply. 'The Aphrodite is a big fish in a small pond. He's an ambitious man.'

Her chin wobbles and her eyes well with tears again. 'Oh, damn it! Just when I'd repaired the damage. I don't think I can do without him, Skippy. He's guided me through every role. If I'm horrible now, imagine what I'll be without him?'

'I'm sure Cavill will find another director who is just as good. Maybe even better.'

'You're so positive. I love that about you, Skippy. Everyone loves that about you. You find light in the darkness, always. But I can't seem to find much light now. Without Mr Bentley, I think I'll have to step off the stage and find something else to do. Nessa can take my place. Truth is, she's a better actress than I am.'

I can't admit that I haven't seen Nessa perform. 'I think you underestimate yourself, Gilda.'

'You would say that, wouldn't you? You're always so nice.' I feel guilty now. As Eddie, I've just slept with her husband! Is that something Eddie would have done? I feel the blood drain from my face as a sick feeling begins to churn in my belly. Would Eddie have taken it that far? Would she have committed adultery? Have I done something with her body that she wouldn't do?

'Believe in yourself, Gilda,' I say through a throat tightening with anxiety. 'Take a deep breath. Dry your eyes. The show goes on. Mr Bentley would not have given you the lead if you weren't up to it. He doesn't want the theatre to suffer, does he? And you got a roaring applause for your performance the other night.'

She sits up straighter and lifts her chin. 'All right, I'll take your advice. I'll look at myself in this mirror and tell myself that I can do it. That I'm good enough. And then I'll go out and kill it.'

She stubs out her cigarette then takes another out of a slim gold cigarette case. There's a pretty green oil lamp on her dressing table. It's the sort of thing Ulysses would love, being Art Deco, and made of a rather stunning malachite. The thought of Ulysses shifts my focus out of the moment, and I have to force myself back into the present. To Gilda, as she lifts the glass and uses the flame to light her cigarette. 'This is my lucky lamp,' she says, exhaling the smoke through pouting scarlet lips. 'I brought it all the way from New York.'

'It's beautiful,' I reply. 'Do you rub it to summon the genie?'

She laughs prettily. Everything Gilda does is pretty. 'Ever since I was given it, luck has found me.' She turns to me and gives me a girlish smile. 'I mean, let's be real, I'm no great talent, am I? And yet, luck has brought me here.' She turns back to the lamp and puts her elegant white fingers to the malachite with a sigh of resignation. 'I need to trust that it will still bring me luck. Sometimes you feel as if a door closing is the end of the world, but then another one opens where you least expect it, and life is rosy again. Maybe rosier than before. I guess, you just gotta have faith, and lots of it.'

I leave her in a happier state, but I'm confused and riddled with guilt. I wish I didn't like her. I wish she was like Isadora, difficult and demanding and not very nice. But she's not. She's sweet and uncertain, and winning. I replay the conversations I've had with Cavill in a desperate attempt to justify my actions. It was what Eddie wanted, wasn't it? Didn't Cavill say so himself, at lunch? That he wouldn't have been so presumptuous and booked a room if she hadn't told him that she wanted it. I hope with all my heart that I did what Eddie would have done. That I'm playing the part, following the script, doing the right thing by her. This isn't *my* life I'm living, it's *hers!*

I wander about backstage, but I'm conscious of looking sneaky. Of course, Eddie Skipton has every right to be prowling about the corridors, but would she really be doing that? There are too many people around to feel safe snooping in all the rooms. I bump into various people Eddie knows well, for they smile and stop for a quick chat. I explain that I've lost a book and am looking for it, but I hate being dishonest. I don't make a very good sleuth. It's hard enough being the imposter that I am.

I return to the auditorium. Nessa is still on the chair, watching Mr Bentley giving directions and striding about the stage with the confidence of a ring master. The dress rehearsal is tomorrow and it's his responsibility that everyone knows what they're doing. These are amateurs, but there are some very fine actors among them. Mr

Pollock plays Ross. He's a big, burly man with black curls and cocoa-brown eyes who's presence on stage is surprising, because he's not especially impressive off it. Mr Swan plays Malcolm. Tall and thin like a leek, with a large nose and blue eyes set close together, he evolves beautifully in the play from weak and timid, to confident and masterful. Mr Patterson is Angus. He's cheeky, with the raw wit of a man who is not well educated but has a natural cleverness. He's short in stature, with wild red hair and mischievous grey eyes, and always looks as if he's about to break into laughter. Mr Bentley is constantly telling him off for mucking about. He's not mucking about today, however. The last of Macbeth's cohorts, Seyton, is played by an older man with a short grey beard and thinning grey hair named Mr Ferris. I wonder whether one of them is called Taran. Maybe he's not an actor, but someone backstage. A lighting man, perhaps, or one of the boys who changes the sets between acts. Eddie knows all these people, so I can't ask them their names.

I take a seat in the auditorium and watch the rehearsal. When they stop for a break, Mr Bentley comes and joins me. 'It's looking good,' I say, as he takes the seat a few away from me, delves into the inside pocket of his jacket and brings out an enamel cigarette case. Everyone seems to own one! He proceeds to light a cigarette with a flint wheel lighter. I'm astonished by the amount of people who smoke. But then it's years before they learn about the connection between cigarettes and lung cancer.

'I'm feeling confident,' he replies, holding the cigarette between his thumb and forefinger and taking a long drag. He blows the smoke out with relish. 'Do you like the set?'

'It's absolutely magnificent,' I reply.

He looks at me with a kind expression in his eyes. 'I didn't realise that *Macbeth* was Mr Skipton's last play. Miss Redcliffe told me.'

'He adored it,' I reply.

'I believe we're doing it justice. We have a terrific cast.'

'Gilda is anxious about her abilities,' I say, deciding to use Gilda as an opening into discussing Nessa.

'Miss Garrett's beauty compensates for her lack of talent.' He puts the cigarette between his lips again and turns his eyes to the stage. 'She's improving all the time.'

'I would like to see Nessa given more of an opportunity,' I add.

He considers this request of mine with a moment's silence, then flicks ash into the little brass ash tray on the back of the seat in front of him. 'As you and I both know, that will no longer be my responsibility.'

I presume he's talking about his leaving and moving to London. I take a punt. 'We will miss you.'

'That is very kind of you, Mrs Skipton.'

'Gilda will miss you the most.'

He keeps his eyes trained on the stage. 'As we discussed, I would like to keep my leaving quiet for the time being, at least until after this run. Mr Pengower will announce my replacement when he's ready. I don't want to upset the cast.'

'Of course,' I reply. 'I haven't breathed a word to anyone.'

'I must say, I will miss this place, and these people. I've grown tremendously fond of it all. But one must take opportunities when they arise. London will be a big change, but I'm confident I will rise to the challenge.'

'As only you can, Mr Bentley.'

He laughs, and the lines around his mouth crease attractively. He's very good-looking when he smiles.

'Righty-ho, onwards!' He stubs out his cigarette in the ashtray and gets up. 'Oh, by the way, I meant to bring the programmes in this morning. They look smashing. I'll bring them in tomorrow. I think you'll be pleased.'

'Wonderful!' I exclaim. Perhaps this mysterious Taran will be revealed at last.

To my disappointment, Cavill does not show up at the theatre that afternoon. I watch the rehearsals for most of the day, turning hopefully every time the door opens behind me. I wonder where he is and why he isn't coming in to see me, but then I remind myself that, for him, there is no urgency. He doesn't know that on Wednesday night the theatre will burn down. He doesn't know that I will slide back to my time. He has no idea how precious these grains of sand are that are slipping through the neck of the hourglass. Grains of sand we can never get back.

I leave the theatre feeling down. It's early evening, almost everyone has left. Nessa, who accompanies me home, is in a lively mood. She has a skip in her step and is full of chatter. I don't tell her that I asked Mr Bentley in a roundabout way to give her a better part in the next production, because I doubt she knows that he's leaving. I'm grateful that he told me it was a secret, because otherwise I would most certainly have let the cat out of the bag! This timesliding business if full of Pooh traps. If I'm not on my guard, I'll step blindly into one!

It's a beautiful evening. The setting sun has turned the sky to a dusky pink and streaks of purple-bellied cloud hover unmoving above it. The first star twinkles faintly in the depths of limpid blue and I know I'm not mistaking it for a plane or a satellite. The quiet is a delight for me too, and I feel resentful, suddenly, that the modern world I know has lost this simplicity, this peace. I feel cross at the devastation to come. At the madness of mankind who will bring so much misery upon itself. How utterly irrational and unwise humans can be! How blind!

And I look across at Nessa, so happy and carefree beside me, and the ache in my heart intensifies. How will I bear to stand aside and let her die in the fire, when I could so easily prevent it?

I will bear it because I have to. Because I'm not here to save her *now*. I'm here to save her *later*. I take a deep breath and try to rise above the sick feeling in my stomach.

I'm here to save her *soul*.

'Oh bother!' she exclaims, putting up her hands. 'I've left my manuscript at the theatre.'

'Do you need it?'

'Yes, I do! I'll run back.'

I suspect she's up to something. 'I'll come with you,' I suggest.

'You don't have to.'

'I want to. I've got nothing else to do.'

'Silly me!' She laughs. 'I don't know where my head is today.'

We set off the way we came at an accelerated pace. When we reach the Aphrodite I follow her round to a side door. I discover that it's locked. Nessa puts out her hand expectantly, and I assume I must have a key in my bag. I rummage around and find Eddie's set on the keyring. I give it to Nessa, and she unlocks the door with the natural ease of someone who has done this many times. We enter into a rather dingy corridor. I haven't come in this way before. She flicks on the lights, then turns to me and says, 'I'll only be a minute,' and heads off down the corridor towards backstage.

I let her go a moment, and then follow. I don't know what I'm hoping to find, but I sense she's up to something. She's a woman on a mission and I imagine it has something to do with Gilda.

It's eerily quiet in there. The old theatre seems to be asleep. Like an arthritic old man in uneasy slumber, it creaks deep in its bones. There are shuffling sounds, probably mice beneath the floorboards. But the theatre sleeps on. I pad softly down the stone floor. I try to work out what I'm going to say to Nessa when she finds that I've followed her. I could use the excuse of my lost book again. I realise that's not a good enough reason. She'll sniff a rat. She's not stupid.

The shuffling and creaking get louder. I realise it's not the sound of mice, or the old bones of the place, but human beings. I stop and cock my ear. Yes, human beings, gasping and moaning. My heartbeat suddenly accelerates. The hairs prick up on the back of my neck. The muscles in my stomach clench. I sense danger. Is it Nessa? Did she return for a clandestine meeting? Could she, while I'm waiting by the door? Would she . . . ?

I follow the sounds.

It doesn't take long. The theatre is not very big.

I see Nessa. She's hiding in the wing, holding her manuscript, staring in horror at something on stage. She turns to look at me. Her eyes are wide and frightened. I hurry softly to her side. There, in plain view, standing up against the wall at the far end of the stage like a strange four-limbed creature, are a man and woman making love. I'm stunned at the brazenness of it. The reckless abandon. The golden hair is unmistakeable, as is the shapely figure and pale pink tea dress. One leg is wrapped around the man, the black top of her stocking shocking somehow against the white of her skin. And he is Mr Bentley.

I hurriedly draw Nessa away, lest we are seen. She grabs my arm, looks miserably into my eyes, and utters in a guttural whisper the word I've been waiting to hear. 'Taran!'

The Present

Chapter Seventeen

Emma found Leila in the foyer, absorbed in something on her phone. 'Right, shall we go and take a look in the library?' she suggested.

Leila slipped her phone into her coat pocket. 'What have you done with Ulysses and Pixie?'

'Left them in the VIP room,' Emma answered.

'How long did they say it would take?'

'Anything, really. Could take half an hour or four.' She shrugged. 'Each case is different, I suppose.'

'Do you believe her?' Leila pulled a face that suggested that, for her at least, the jury was still out. 'I mean, it's hard to prove, isn't it?' she said. 'Speaking to ghosts.'

Emma didn't want to admit that she was apprehensive. 'I do believe her, because I want to believe her,' she confessed. 'But I am worried that I've invited a pair of frauds into our midst. Pixie said she saw the ghost of Nessa Blunt acting on stage last night, alongside Rebecca. The only thing that makes me feel positive, besides my gut instinct, is that every time Nessa seems to appear, the temperature drops. And it *was* very cold in the theatre last night, wasn't it, in spite of the heating and the people?'

Leila was dubious. 'Someone could have left the door open.'

Emma didn't want to look for holes. She was fearful she might find one. 'Look, why don't we go to the library and see what we can find out about Nessa Blunt,' she suggested, making for the door. 'Then, when Pixie is done, we can compare her story with ours. The fire was front-page news, right?'

'Better than the library,' said Leila cheerfully. 'My friend Jenny Pilkington edits the *Seacombe Gazette.* Has done for years. I imagine they'll have records going back to 1923. That paper has been around since the turn of the last century. I'll give her a call and see if we can pop in.'

Half an hour later the two women were standing outside a big white townhouse on Church Street. Leila rang the bell beside the name *Seacombe Gazette* which was listed among a few other businesses on the shiny brass panel. When requested, she gave her name through the intercom and the door clicked open. Inside, the young woman behind the reception desk sent them up to the first floor via a lift.

The office of the *Seacombe Gazette* was small and not very busy. There were a few people sitting at their desks, tapping away on keyboards, and one or two talking on the telephone, or chatting together over mugs of coffee. Jenny Pilkington, petite with intelligent blue eyes and ice-blonde hair gathered into a scruffy bun, was there to greet them. At seventy-seven she was still formidable and full of vigour. She wore a brightly coloured cardigan and scarf over a long purple skirt, and her wrists jangled with African bracelets. She smiled, smoothing out the lines that smoking had etched into the skin around her lips. 'Nice to see you again, Emma,' she said. The two women shook hands. 'I remember the day your husband decided to buy a house in Seacombe.'

Leila grinned at Emma. 'And I hired him to run the theatre.'

'I thank you both,' said Emma with genuine gratitude. 'I had my heart set on moving here, and Joseph was reluctant. I remember I left him for ten minutes while I went to buy something at the pharmacy, and when I joined him in the pub, he was sharing a bottle of wine with the two of you and celebrating his decision to live and work here. Really, you are officially my two favourite people in Seacombe!'

Jenny chuckled. 'Come,' she said, leading them through the office to an airy boardroom that looked out over the grey tiled roofs of Seacombe. 'I'll set you up with tea and coffee and then you can trawl through the archives at your leisure. They've all gone digital.

I'm sure you'll go down a few rabbit holes. I've lost myself many times in old editions. Fascinating to read the minutiae of daily life in the past.'

Emma and Leila sat side by side at the long table with cups of strong coffee and a plate of digestive biscuits, scrolling through the archives on the laptop Jenny's assistant had set up for them. It was connected to a big screen so they could read the articles together. It didn't take them long to find the edition that featured the fire. On the front page was a black-and-white photograph of the Aphrodite in flames, and the headline *Fire Kills Heiress at the Aphrodite.* 'God, it's horrific to read about our dear old theatre,' said Emma, scanning the words quickly to find out whether Nessa Blunt was mentioned.

Leila pushed her spectacles up her nose. 'There it is: *Vanessa Blunt, 28, youngest daughter of wealthy industrialist Humphrey Blunt, was tragically killed in the fire that ravaged the historic Aphrodite theatre in Seacombe on Wednesday 9th May.* Poor lamb. She was only twenty-eight. Imagine!'

Emma was relieved to read that Nessa had been a real person, and that her death in the fire was true. 'Her body was found in Gilda Garrett's dressing room.'

'That name rings a bell,' said Leila ponderously.

'Well, she was an actress, obviously.'

'I've heard her name somewhere. Lord, I can't for the life of me remember where.'

'It'll come if you don't try too hard,' said Emma, clicking onto the next edition.

'Probably in the middle of the night,' Leila chortled and put her coffee cup to her lips, leaving a crimson stain around the rim.

'Let's see if it says anything about how the fire started,' Emma murmured, narrowing her eyes to read the print, which was quite small. '*The blaze interrupted the opening night of* Macbeth, *directed by Taran Bentley, with the luscious Gilda Garrett in the leading role of Lady Macbeth.*'

'Good Lord!' Leila exclaimed. 'That can't be a coincidence.'

Emma's excitement was ignited. 'How extraordinary. Nessa dies on the opening night of *Macbeth* in 1923 and returns to create havoc on the opening night of *Macbeth* in 2014. That's almost ninety-one years later. That has to be significant, right?'

'What else does it say?'

Emma read on. '*In spite of the scheming nature of Shakespeare's most famous play, there appears to be nothing underhand here. Firemen who swiftly arrived on the scene to put out the flames found no immediate evidence of foul play. However, an investigation into the start of the fire has been launched . . .*' Emma scanned to the next paragraph. '*Besides a few who were taken to hospital, no one else was seriously hurt.*'

'No skullduggery,' said Leila. 'How disappointing!'

'Seems not,' said Emma.

She scrolled through the following editions. The two women sat in silence as they read the relevant articles.

'This is interesting,' said Emma, at last. 'They think it *started* in Gilda Garrett's dressing room. An oil lamp. The building was so old, it went up like a matchbox.'

'See if you can find anything about Gilda online,' Leila suggested, sitting back in her chair and draining her coffee cup. 'It's really annoying me.' She sighed. 'I'm getting old.'

'No, you're not,' Emma laughed.

'Old and forgetful.' Leila took off her spectacles to clean them with her scarf. 'Old age is not for sissies, you know.'

Emma typed Gilda Garrett into Google. 'This is disappointing too. There's no Gilda Garrett. There's Gilda Gray, but no Garrett.'

'Gilda Gray was a famous film star in the 1920s,' said Leila.

Emma clicked on the name Gilda Gray and read the first few lines of her entry on Wikipedia. 'Not our Gilda,' she said. 'How annoying.'

'It's irrelevant, really,' said Leila. 'The most interesting thing is that Nessa Blunt *did* die in the fire that night. Madge is right about that. It'll be interesting to see whether Pixie Tate mentions Gilda Garrett, and that they were performing *Macbeth*.'

'Yes, it'll be a test.' Emma gave Leila a sheepish look. 'I do hope she passes.'

*

When the two women made their way back to the theatre, it was just after midday. Fog was rolling inland off the sea, bringing light drizzle and a damp wind. 'Winter is coming,' said Emma in a portentous tone, quoting from the TV series *Game of Thrones*.

Leila pulled her coat tighter about her. 'It certainly is,' she replied. 'At my age, I don't grumble about the weather. I'm grateful for anything I'm given.'

'That's dark.'

'This business about ghosts has focused my mind somewhat,' said Leila. 'Death is a subject we don't want to think about much, even less discuss, but we'll all meet it in the end, one way or another. It's inevitable. It's a comfort to think that there's somewhere we all go to. That we simply don't become dust.'

'I most certainly believe in Heaven,' said Emma firmly.

Leila glanced at her, a thoughtful expression on her face. 'I don't think it really matters whether it's true or not,' she said wisely. 'If you believe it's true, life will be more pleasant. The fact is, none of us knows what happens after we die. That's the one thing we have in common, atheists and believers alike. None of us knows.'

'Pixie sounds like she knows more than most,' said Emma, more confident now that Pixie was the real deal. 'She told me that some spirits get stuck in a limbo between earth and heaven. They're called earthbound spirits. They can't move on and need help. That's what Nessa Blunt is. An earthbound spirit who can't find her way home – or doesn't want to.'

'I don't disbelieve her,' said Leila magnanimously. 'I just don't know anything about it. I find the paranormal world fascinating, but mysterious, and a little scary, to be honest. I certainly wouldn't want to wake up in the middle of the night and see a ghost. I'd rather never see a ghost.'

Emma laughed. 'I'd like to see one. A nice one. Not a mean one. My grandmother, for example. Just to have an experience. To know that we live on. To have proof.'

Leila laughed with her. '*You* can have the proof, Emma, and then tell me about it. I'll believe *you*.'

*

They reached the Aphrodite to find Isadora and her assistant Lezli in the foyer. When Isadora saw them, her eyes lit up like those of a greedy gannet. 'Where's Ulysses?' she demanded, striding across the carpet to meet them. 'And what's her name, Pinkie . . . or Pixie,' she added as an afterthought. 'They haven't left, have they?'

'No, they're doing their job,' Emma replied.

Isadora laughed scornfully. 'What does that mean?'

'I'm not entirely sure,' said Emma. 'But I've given them a private room, and Pixie is hopefully getting rid of the ghost.'

'Here?' Isadora asked. When Emma nodded, Isadora wanted to know how long they would take.

'I'm not sure,' Emma answered. 'How long is a piece of string?'

Leila took in Isadora's painted face and blow-dried hair and deduced that she had tarted up especially for Ulysses. She felt sorry for her. It wasn't likely to get her anywhere. 'Can we help you with anything?' Leila asked.

'Yes,' said Isadora. 'You can come and have coffee with me while we wait. They won't be much longer, will they? How long have they been in there?'

'Since about half ten,' said Leila.

'God! How long does it take to get rid of ghost?'

'I have no idea,' said Emma, finding Isadora's impatience grating. She wondered what the woman wanted with Ulysses.

'Okay, so let's go to a coffee shop and wait it out together.' Isadora rolled her eyes at Lezli. 'Ghost, my ass! Still, as long as nothing disturbs my performance tonight, I don't care what you all want to call it. My money is still on those witches, though. It really is quite simple.'

They settled around a table in a small café which was a few streets down from the theatre. It was warm in there, out of the fog, and smelt pleasantly of freshly ground coffee and baked bread. Isadora insisted on sitting in her big white coat until she warmed up. It took only a few seconds for people to recognise her. Emma noticed the ripple effect as customers sitting at the other tables lowered their voices to excited whispers or stopped their conversations altogether. Everyone stared at her. Isadora ordered an oat milk flat white from the waiter, who was the only person in the place who seemed not to know who she was, and ignored the attention. It was what she had signed up for, after all, and she liked it.

'So, do you both believe in ghosts, too?' Isadora asked. She put up her hands, revealing long tapering fingers and buffed nails. 'I'm doing my best to keep an open mind, but boy is it a challenge!' She laughed.

'I'm keeping an open mind, too,' said Leila. 'Emma is more accepting of things we can't see.'

Isadora looked at Emma expectantly, and a little condescendingly, as if she pitied her for being so unworldly.

Emma, being a natural people-pleaser, felt the need to win her over. 'We've just been to the office of the *Seacombe Gazette*, to read about the fire that destroyed the theatre in 1923.'

'Really? Was there a fire?' Isadora asked, only mildly interested.

'It gutted the place and one of the actresses was killed.'

'She was called Nessa Blunt,' said Leila.

'She's our ghost,' Emma added.

Isadora said nothing and looked bored.

Lezli, on the other hand, was thrilled. 'Gripping!' she exclaimed. 'That would make a good film, wouldn't it? A woman who died tragically in a theatre fire, haunting it years later.'

'How do you know she's haunting the theatre?' Isadora asked.

The waiter brought their coffees, and they suspended their conversation while he handed them out. He blushed when he gave Isadora hers, which suggested someone had alerted him to the identity of their famous customer. He lingered a moment, asked her if she wanted anything else, and appeared visibly disappointed when she said she didn't.

Emma continued the story once the waiter had reluctantly left the table. 'Madge's father worked in the Aphrodite when he was a young man, and apparently everyone knew of Nessa Blunt's ghost,' she said. 'There were many sightings.'

'They could have made it up,' said Isadora, putting her coffee cup to her lips. 'If it was in the newspapers that she had died, then everyone would have known about her.'

'The fascinating thing is that the fire happened in May 1923, on the opening night of *Macbeth*,' said Leila.

Isadora perked up a little, but it might have been the coffee. 'Interesting,' she said.

'What *I* want to know is, why she went quiet for so many years, and then came back,' Leila mused. 'If, indeed, she is haunting the theatre, why is it that in the last twenty years, which is as long as I've been involved with the place, no one has ever seen her or even mentioned a ghost?'

Emma thought it obvious. 'Because we're putting on *Macbeth*.'

'Do you think that's relevant?' Isadora asked.

'Seems a little coincidental,' Emma replied.

'How did the fire happen?' Lezli asked. 'Was it arson?'

'Apparently not,' said Emma. 'It was started in the dressing room of the leading lady Gilda Garrett. We tried to find her on the internet, but there's no mention of her anywhere.'

Isadora sat up with a start, as if she'd previously been asleep and was now fully awake. 'Did you just say Gilda Garrett?' she demanded.

Emma nodded. 'Yes, she was playing the part of Lady Macbeth.'

'Gilda Garrett?' Isadora repeated. She gave her head a vigorous shake. 'No, must be another one.'

'Why, do you know a Gilda Garrett?' Leila asked. 'I've been trying to remember where I've heard her name before and it's driving me mad.'

'My great-grandmother was called Gilda Garrett,' said Isadora.

The three women stared at her in astonishment.

Isadora waved her hand as if flicking away a fly. 'Don't be silly. It's not the same one. My great-grandmother was American. She lived in New York. She was married to a man called Taran Bentley . . .'

Emma's eyes widened. 'Taran Bentley was named in the article as director of the play.'

'Get out of here!' Isadora exclaimed. Then she frowned. 'No, that can't be right. But my great-grandfather was English, I suppose.

But no, they lived in New York. My great-grandmother tried to be an actress but failed. It's in my genes, clearly.' She gave a flippant laugh.

'Hold on,' said Lezli eagerly. 'Your great-grandmother was an actress called Gilda Garrett, who was married to Taran Bentley, and you don't believe she was ever here?'

'I would know, wouldn't I?' said Isadora in her little-girl-lost voice. 'I mean, if she was here, as in, here in the Aphrodite! Wouldn't I know?'

'When did she die?' asked Leila.

'It's a sad story. She died of an overdose of sleeping pills when she was in her forties. My grandmother, her daughter, was a small child.'

'Was it deliberate?' Leila asked.

Isadora shrugged. 'I don't know. She was on all sorts of uppers and downers, I think. Most likely an alcoholic too. She was messed up.' She frowned. 'It can't be the same person. I mean, I didn't even know she'd been to England.'

'Why would you?' said Emma. 'You never knew her, and your grandmother was a child when she died.'

Isadora put her hand to her mouth, stifling a gasp. 'Oh my God! Do you think the ghost has it in for *me*, because my great-grandmother had something to do with her death?' Her face paled at the thought. 'This is creeping me out!' She flicked her fingers, and the waiter glided swiftly to their table where he hovered with eager anticipation. 'I need another coffee, make it a double shot, and fast.' Isadora was loving the drama. She was now riding high on it. This was even better than theatre. This was real. 'I think I'm going to faint.' She started fanning herself with the menu.

Lezli put an arm around her shoulder. 'It's okay, Isadora,' she soothed, patting her coat. 'Take a deep breath. In through the nose, out through the mouth. I'm sure it's just a coincidence.'

'Of course, it isn't,' Isadora snapped. 'It's too coincidental to be a coincidence. It's crazy. I mean, proper fucking crazy!'

Leila caught Emma's eye and grinned. 'It *is* proper fucking crazy,' she agreed.

The Past

Chapter Eighteen

Nessa and I stand in the street outside the theatre. Nessa is in tears. She's trembling with shock, and I'm feeling pretty stunned myself. I never saw that coming, and I'm meant to be intuitive. Of course, it all makes sense now. Nessa is in love with Taran Bentley, which is why she's at the theatre from dawn to dusk. But Gilda Garrett is sleeping with him. If Nessa was jealous of Gilda before, she's absolutely beside herself now.

And I don't feel guilty anymore for that afternoon in the inn with Cavill.

I suspect that Gilda loves Taran. But she's married and cannot have him. Plus, he's about to leave Seacombe for London. No wonder Gilda was crying in her dressing room. But what kind of revenge will Nessa plan now? Is this the reason Nessa dies in the fire? Does she plot a revenge that goes badly wrong?

I draw Nessa into my arms and hold her close. She's in complete despair and allows herself to be gathered up and comforted without protest. I recall her journal and the obsessional way she's written the name Taran over all the pages, and begin to understand the depth of her infatuation and the degree of her pain. A nervous anticipation takes hold of me then as I realise where this is all headed. I feel as if my path is narrowing, as if I'm reaching a point, like the tip of a triangle. A point beyond which I cannot go. Something will happen between Gilda and Nessa on Wednesday night that will result in the fire and Nessa's death. I need to find out what that is before I slide back and finish the job in the present.

And what of Cavill?

I feel sick to my stomach at the thought of leaving him, and sick with the sinking feeling of having failed. For that is what I've done. I've failed. It's no coincidence that Cavill is here on this slide. I've drawn him into my experience. I know that I must release him, release us *both*. But I tried at the inn, and I bailed. Do I have the courage to give it another go? Is the problem, really, that I don't *want* to?

We find a bench in a quiet corner of the town, beneath a beech tree, and sit down. No one is around. It's quiet. The light is fading, the stars twinkling through the deepening blue, the evening giving way to night. It's chilly too. A cold, damp wind foretells rain. Nessa is calmer now and she's no longer trembling. She knits her fingers in her lap. 'I hate that woman,' she hisses. 'I wish she were dead.'

'Oh, Nessa. Don't wish anyone dead.'

'You don't understand, Skippy. I love him.' Her shoulders quiver and she drops her chin and starts crying again.

I put my arm around her and draw her close. 'I know you do. And I know what it is to love.' I want to add that I know what it is to love a man one cannot have.

'Papa wants me to marry dull George Cavendish, but I love Taran. I'll never love anyone else. Now Gilda has stolen him from me, and she's married! What right does she have to claim him?'

I'm not sure Taran Bentley has ever belonged to Nessa.

'Does he know how you feel?' I ask.

She shakes her head sorrowfully.

'Does anyone know?'

'No. Just you. But I'll tell everyone what I saw. I'll ruin her.' Nessa's eyes blaze feverishly through the dwindling light.

I think I can see now where this is headed. 'Is that wise?' I ask. 'You won't win Taran that way.'

'Then what should I do?'

I give her the only sensible advice there is, even though I know she won't take it. 'Let him go.'

As I say those words, the irony is not lost on me, and I feel a sharp stab of pain beneath my ribcage.

Nessa stares at me in horror, as if I've just told her to jump off a cliff. 'I can't do that.' She puts a hand against her breast. 'I love him, Skippy. I really love him. I can't live without him.'

I comfort her as best as I can while she lets her sorrow out in sobs and gasps, and many many tears. It's late when we arrive back at the house. Lavinia has been anxiously waiting for us, and Cook and Mrs Crocker are worried.

Nessa takes Lavinia by the hand, and they run up the stairs. I know they're going to plot, but I can't stop them. And I mustn't. I have to allow events to unfold without intervention or influence from me. Cook arches an enquiring eyebrow but Mrs Crocker suggests I eat, or the food will get cold. She tells Cook to leave the girls' dinner on the stove for them to have later.

I'm agitated. I can't relax. I pace the floor of the dining room as the clock ticks loudly on the mantelpiece, reminding me of the seconds lost, never to be regained. Of the time that is running out for Nessa, and for me and Cavill too. I'm overwhelmed suddenly by a suffocating feeling of helplessness. A great weight presses against my chest, and I sit down at the table and stare desolately into space.

I eat alone and my thoughts become ever more convoluted in my head. They're like the threads in a tangled ball of string that I've spent days trying to untangle. They're repetitive, frustrating and seemingly impossible to unpick. How can I tell Nessa to let Taran go, when *I* can't let Cavill go myself? I'm a horrible hypocrite. Weak and selfish.

I can barely swallow the soup for the tension in my throat. I'm filled with self-loathing.

The girls do not appear, and I go to bed. But I'm as restless as a wolf at full moon. I'm wide awake, anticipating what is to come. I lie with my head on the pillow, and every time I close my eyes I see Cavill; I see Nessa burning; I see the Aphrodite in flames, and I foresee my return to 2014 on a wave of despair, having failed to end it with Cavill. I have a terrible sense of doom that I have never had before. It lies heavy and sticky in the pit of my stomach like tar, and I don't know how to get rid of it.

*

The following morning the girls are already at the breakfast table when I come down. To my surprise they are both in a cheerful mood. Nessa acts as if nothing happened at the theatre. I realise then what an accomplished actor she is. It's hard to reconcile the devastated young woman of last night with the carefree person sitting beside me now. She comments on the beautiful day. It has rained in the night but now the skies are a clear, dazzling blue. A blackbird has been singing outside her bedroom window, and the prospect of the dress rehearsal tonight fills her with excitement. My anxiety only increases, because I know that they have been plotting something, and I don't know what it is.

After breakfast Lavinia goes to work, and Nessa and I head to the theatre. The place is teeming with people. Besides the actors, there are sound and lighting technicians, stagehands, seamstresses working on the costumes, carpenters tinkering with the sets, and in the midst of them all is Taran Bentley, as if butter wouldn't melt in his mouth. He has no clue that Nessa and I saw him *in flagrante delicto* with Gilda. I watch Nessa closely as she greets him, but she holds her nerve and gives nothing away. I wonder what terrible revenge she has planned.

Gilda wanders in at midday. She's not radiating her usual glow. Her eyes are red and her face pale. She's been crying. I wonder whether she and Cavill have had a row. More likely, she's still upset at the prospect of her lover leaving. I wait for Cavill to come in after her, but he doesn't. I wonder where he is. I ache to see him.

I tear my eyes away from the door and meet Gilda halfway down the aisle. 'Is everything all right, Gilda?' I ask, in the hope that she might confide in me. I sense that everyone confides in Skippy. I only wish I could tap into her memory.

Gilda gives a wan smile and her eyes shine. 'As all right as it can possibly be.' She sniffs forlornly, like a pitiful child.

'Do you want to talk about it?'

She shakes her golden curls that look unusually lacklustre in the electric lighting of the theatre. 'No, I have a job to do, and do it, I will. Chin up. Isn't that what you English say?'

I smile with encouragement. 'You're a trooper, Gilda.'

She shrugs. 'I have no choice. Everything is out of my hands. I'm as helpless as a dandelion ball on the breeze.'

I wonder what she means. Is she referring to Taran Bentley leaving?

I accompany her to her dressing room. Coming towards us up the corridor is Nessa. She takes one look at Gilda's unhappy face and feigns sympathy. Truly, she is a stunningly good actress. She reveals not the smallest hint of resentment. 'Can I get you anything, Miss Garrett?' she asks. Her voice is soft and kind. 'You look as if you could do with a cup of strong tea.'

Gilda nods. 'Oh, bless you, Nessa. That's exactly what I need.'

Nessa doesn't catch my eye. She turns round and heads purposefully towards the kitchen.

I follow Gilda into her dressing room where she sinks into the armchair with a sigh. 'I don't have a happy marriage, Skippy.'

I'm stunned that she's just come out with that. I'm at a loss of what to say. I take the chair and sit down slowly. She fills the silence with what feels like an attempt to justify her affair, more to herself than to me, who is not supposed to be aware of it.

'Oh, I know what it looks like to everyone else. Loves young dream.' She chuckles cynically and holds my eyes steadily with her shiny green gaze. 'I suppose in that respect, I'm a pretty decent actress, after all. Isn't that ironic? I can't seem to manage it *on* the stage, but *off* the stage I'm swell.'

'Relationships are complicated. Marriage is not the ticket to happiness that most people seem to think it is. It needs to be worked at.'

'You're telling me!' she replies. 'We're very different, you know. I'm like a magpie, attracted to shiny things. Cavill just wants a quiet life. He's old before his time, and I'm young.' She stands up briskly and paces the room, one hand on her hip, the other scratching the back of her head in agitation. 'I miss New York. I miss the city. It's quiet here. Too quiet. I thought a stage would satisfy me. I thought this was all I wanted. Turns out it's a mirage. It's not what I dreamed at all. I'm not cut out for it. I'm not cut out for this place.'

Her voice hardens. 'This deadbeat town where nothing happens but tea parties, and endless games of cards.'

I watch her in fascination and hope that Nessa takes a long time to make the tea, because Gilda is opening up like a water-lily and all sorts of things are flying out. I don't fill the brief pauses as she catches her breath but allow her to fully express her frustration.

She spins round and looks at me in supplication. 'What should I do, Skippy? Tell me what to do!'

I'm caught off guard. I wasn't expecting this. 'Does Cavill know how you feel?' I ask, afraid to hear her response. Guilty again for that afternoon at the inn. Guilty for taking Eddie down that road without being certain of her consent. Even though Gilda is as deceiving as I am.

'No. Cavill doesn't know how I feel. But I have to tell him, or I'll lose my mind.'

I decide to take a plunge. 'Is there someone else?' I ask.

She stares at me suddenly, like a cornered fox, eyes wild and fearful. 'No,' she lies, and looks away. 'Of course not. I'm not that kind of girl.'

Not such a bad actress, after all. 'I'm sorry,' I reply. 'I shouldn't have asked you that.'

'It's all right, Skippy. We're friends, you and I.'

There's a knock on the door. Gilda goes to open it. Nessa comes in with a cup of tea and a plate of biscuits. 'I hope I'm not interrupting,' she says. 'Would you like one too, Skippy? I'm sorry, I should have thought of that.'

'I would, thank you,' I reply in order to get rid of her.

Gilda takes the cup and thanks her. Nessa leaves, closing the door softly behind her. Gilda turns to me again. 'I'm sorry for burdening you with my problems,' she says, and takes a sip. 'Life is hard, isn't it? Can one ever be happy?'

'Happiness is a state of mind,' I reply, repeating the cliché that always pops up on Instagram. 'The trick is to find a deep, inner contentment that's permanent and unaffected by superficial surface emotions. And to prevent anything from disturbing that inner contentment.'

She chuckles. 'I don't imagine many people achieve that. Monks maybe.' She sighs and takes another sip of tea. 'The truth is, Skippy, I don't think I can be happy here, in Seacombe.'

'Would Cavill move back to America? After all, his daughter lives there.'

'I haven't asked him.'

'Perhaps you should.'

If Cavill loves Eddie, I doubt he'll leave her and move back to the States. If Gilda loves Taran, I don't think she'll want him to.

There's another knock on the door. It's Nessa with my tea. She's made it quickly this time. 'Miss Garrett, Mr Bentley wants you on stage.'

Gilda drains her teacup and gives it to Nessa. Then she leaves the room.

Nessa turns to me. 'Is she unwell?'

'No, just anxious about tonight.' I lie as well as Gilda does.

Nessa nods. 'She doesn't look well, though, does she?'

'She's pale, I agree.'

'I'd better prepare myself,' Nessa says, straightening her shoulders and lifting her chin. 'I have a feeling I might be required to play a bigger part on stage tonight.'

I narrow my eyes and then drop them into Gilda's empty teacup. Did Nessa put something in her tea?

Mr Bentley wants Nessa to act as prompt while Gilda rehearses. I sit in the front row of the stalls and observe them both. Now I know how Nessa feels about Mr Bentley, I notice the pink in her cheeks and the sparkle in her eyes as she watches him. I don't know how I missed those signs before.

I'm so engrossed in the action on stage, that I barely notice when Cavill comes and sits beside me. I turn to him in surprise. He looks at me and smiles. 'Hello, stranger.'

'Where have you been?' I whisper. Every nerve in my body

quivers with aliveness. Cavill is sunlight and I'm drinking him in like a solar panel.

'I had business in London . . .' He begins to tell me, in a hushed voice, what that business was. Something about investments, his broker, a meeting, lunch at the Ritz – I don't listen. I'm too busy watching his lips move and wanting so badly to kiss them.

'Shall we go to our usual place?' he asks, and his eyes glint with mischievous intent. He's Cavill at St Sidwell Manor sneaking into my bedroom at night.

I nod eagerly and we both get up. I doubt anyone notices us leave. There's too much going on both on stage and off it. It's like a hive of busy bees as they prepare for the dress rehearsal tonight.

I'm curious as to where our usual place is and follow him out of the theatre and into the sunlight.

It's a twenty-minute stroll out of the town to a small, stony beach hidden among the rocks. We reach it by way of a snaking path that meanders down a grassy slope, and then via narrow steps built into the cliff. It's a secluded spot, and one that can't be reached any other way, and due to the precarious nature of the descent, not a place for dog walkers. Snugly embraced at both ends by cliffs, it's horseshoe in shape and sheltered pleasantly from the wind. The sea stretches out to the far horizon, where it blurs into a hazy blue line.

'Do you remember the first time you brought me down here?' he asks and takes my hand.

'Of course,' I reply. How curious. I assumed that it was *he* who brought *Eddie* here.

'I asked you to show us a secluded beach and Gilda felt unwell due to the steep descent and remained up on the cliff.'

'That wasn't very gallant of you to leave her there,' I say, taking another of many punts.

He chuckles and squeezes my hand playfully. 'She insisted.'

'You were very quick to agree.'

'*You* didn't protest.'

I smile, hoping he will continue reminiscing so I can learn something of their past.

'The truth is, even back then, I wanted to be alone with you,' he continues.

'And I you,' I reply, wishing I shared a history with him. Wishing that I was creating one now. One we would reminisce about well into the future.

'All those times we came down here to discuss plays, I just wanted to kiss you.'

'Why didn't you?'

He smiles across at me and pulls me close. 'Because I wasn't sure you wanted me to.'

'Was I that inscrutable?'

'You're everyone's best friend, Skippy.'

'And you were, *are*, married,' I add.

'That too. I fought with my conscience for months. Until I lost the battle.'

How relieved his conscience would be if he knew what I know about his wife. 'I don't feel good about that, either,' I tell him. It's true, one can never feel good about committing adultery. 'But I have lost that battle too.'

'What we have is stronger than both of us.'

I gaze into the deep blue of his eyes, searching for recognition. Searching for a spark of knowing, however small. Anything, to reassure me that he senses something of me, Pixie, behind Eddie's eyes.

I see love, pure and profound, but how can I know?

He puts his hands gently around my jaw and kisses me.

We walk hand in hand over the pebbles. In the back of my mind a whispering voice reminds me of what I'm here to do. But I can't bear to ruin the moment by telling him the truth. For ruin it, I most certainly will. He might feel deceived and manipulated, or he might simply feel that Eddie has gone mad, and then I'll ruin it for her too.

How to do it and not ruin it for us both?

There seem to be a great many birds here. Gulls, naturally, but other species too that I don't recognise. 'What kind of birds are they?' I ask as we stroll towards the water.

'Most are gulls. Do you see the one with the red beak and legs, and the black face? That's a Mediterranean gull. They're rare in Britain. But I've seen a few here. Especially in this cove. The herring gull with the silvery-grey feathers and pink legs is commonplace, as is the common gull, which is smaller than the herring, with a short green beak and green legs. The one I really love is the kittiwake. They're cheerful little birds who nest in colonies in the cliffs.'

'But you still love the teal best of all.'

He grins at me, pleased that I remember. 'I do.'

'And you're going to paint one, for me.'

'I will paint lots for you.' His lips curl into a winning smile. 'Meeting Mr Tennison was not the only reason I went to London yesterday.'

'Oh?'

'I went to buy supplies. I'm going to paint in earnest, Eddie. And you're my inspiration. Because of you, I've decided to take it up again. And not just sketches, but proper paintings. Unhappiness made me stop doing what I loved. Happiness has inspired me to return to it. Life is meaningless without love, and I don't mean just romantic love, the way I love you.' He smiles tenderly, his affectionate gaze meeting mine. 'But love in all its forms and expressions. Love for what we do, the places we create or find. Love for our friends.' He looks out to sea and takes a deep, satisfied breath. 'Love for life.'

He wraps his arms around me again and holds me tightly. 'God, Eddie. With you, I just love everything about life. It's bursting with beauty. When one's heart is full of love, one sees the world in a completely different way. There are two worlds. The one seen through a lens of tedium, and the one seen through a lens of love. How dissimilar they both are.'

I hold him fiercely and ignore the nagging voice in my head. Tears prick the backs of my eyes, and I close them to stem the tears that threaten to break out. I can't do it. I can't tell him who I really am. I just can't.

I want this moment to last forever. I want to be Eddie.

Right now, I no longer care that he can't see me. I'm content to bathe in his love, vicariously.

But what I'm stealing for myself, I'm stealing from Eddie. And I cannot do that for much longer. Tomorrow night I will discover how the fire starts and how Nessa meets the end of her life, and then I will have to leave her. I will have to leave Cavill. And if I haven't told him the truth, I will be likely to meet him again, in another body, in another slide. In which case, I will never slide again.

He lifts my face and looks at it with concern. 'You're crying,' he says softly. 'Was it something I said?'

I shake my head and give in to the tears. 'It's too beautiful. It's all too beautiful,' I say, and like a thief, I steal another magical moment from Eddie Skipton.

Chapter Nineteen

Back at the theatre, there's an air of intrigue. At first I think the furtive looks on the faces of the company are in response to Cavill and me, who have been gone some time. But it soon becomes clear when Cavill asks one of the stagehands, that Gilda has taken a turn and gone home. Cavill leaves immediately to do his duty as husband. I hope that he's not in trouble for having absconded when he was most needed.

I notice Mr Bentley pacing the stage, looking anxious. He's studying his clipboard and scratching his head. One might put his agitation down to pre-performance nerves, now the leading lady won't be leading, but I know differently. He's worried about his lover.

Nessa rushes up the aisle towards me. I can tell from the exuberance on her face that she's thrilled she's getting the chance to perform. I'm also immediately suspicious that she slipped something into Gilda's tea which put her out of action. Lavinia, who is on stage with a cup of coffee, catches my eye, then looks away swiftly. A thought crosses my mind then. Lavinia works for a pharmacist. Might she have given Nessa a drug to make sure Gilda could not perform?

'Isn't it marvellous!' Nessa declares breathlessly 'I'm going to play Lady Macbeth!'

'What happened to Gilda?' I ask.

Nessa can barely muster up concern for the poor leading lady. 'Oh, I don't know,' she replies dismissively. 'She came over all queer. She's gone home.'

'Oh dear. I hope she'll be all right for tomorrow?'

Nessa gives me sly grin. 'I hope not. Wouldn't it be wonderful if Papa could see me playing Lady Macbeth? He would have to give in then, wouldn't he? He would have to accept that this is where I belong. On stage. My name in lights! Oh, it's all so tremendously exciting!' She rubs her palms together with glee.

How horrendous it is to know that no one will watch her on stage tomorrow night. There will be no performance. In fact, there will be no theatre.

I feel the current of destiny pulling me through time and am acutely aware now of the inevitability of the terrible events that will unfold in the next twenty-four hours.

Nessa hurries off to prepare for her performance. She has a bounce in her step, and I feel sick to my stomach, knowing what will become of her. I focus with determination on my mission, to save her soul in the present, and climb onto the stage to talk to Mr Bentley.

He doesn't smile when he sees me approach him. Fretfulness burns in his eyes. 'You've heard about Miss Garrett?' he says.

'Yes, what happened?'

He shrugs and I intuit his sense of helplessness. I suspect he's wishing he was with her and feeling powerless because he can't be. 'I don't know,' he replies. 'She was fine, going through her first scene, when she went very white and said she felt queasy. She hurried to the bathroom. A while later she returned and said she was going home. She was too ill to perform. Mrs Fry accompanied her.'

Mrs Fry works in wardrobe – elderly, kind, softly spoken, keen to please.

'I hope she'll be well enough to perform tomorrow,' I say, even though I know there will be no performance tomorrow.

'I hope so too,' Mr Bentley agrees, but he looks unsure. He scratches his head again. I know he's not worried about the play. He's worried about Gilda.

*

The atmosphere soon lifts, and the excitement begins to build as guests start to arrive for the dress rehearsal. The curtain is down and behind it last-minute adjustments are being made to the set. I take my place on the chair in the wing and lay the script across my knee, ready to prompt if necessary. Lydia, in her slacks and artist's smock, appears and crouches down beside me.

'What do you think happened to Gilda?' she asks. I can tell from the sparkle in her eyes that she's loving the drama.

'I don't know,' I reply. 'Maybe she ate a bad oyster.'

Lydia grins crookedly like a pirate. 'Only if Nessa gave it to her.'

'Oh, Lydia. I'm sure she wouldn't do something like that.' But I think she's done something *exactly* like that.

'This is Gilda's big moment . . .'

'Tomorrow night is her big moment,' I interrupt.

'Maybe she'll take a turn tomorrow night as well.' She arches her eyebrows suggestively.

'You're a menace, Lydia,' I laugh, but she might be right. Perhaps Nessa put something in Gilda's tea today to find out whether it would work. In which case, what's to stop her doing it again tomorrow?

Lydia pats my arm. 'You know I love intrigue.'

'I do,' I reply.

'I'm going to watch from the stalls. See you after the show. Tallyho!'

I watch her stride across the stage with her mannish gait. She casts another glance at her magnificent set, mutters something to herself, then disappears into the wing.

I can hear people taking their places on the other side of the curtain. It's not a full audience tonight, simply friends of the cast and a few people from the industry. I have gleaned from snippets of conversation that Lady Faversham is always invited to the dress rehearsal but prefers to come to the first night and sit in the royal box with her family and Mr Pengower.

How terrible that tomorrow night Cavill will lose his theatre.

And Nessa will lose her life.

That's the worst part about being a timeslider – being unable to change the future by altering the present.

And falling in love.

Falling in love and being separated by time.

I push away those gloomy thoughts and focus instead on the script. I read the lines in order to distract myself from the feelings of self-pity and frustration that are roiling inside me. I need to calm down. To slow my breathing and, in turn, my pulse. There's no point feeling sorry for myself. It won't get me what I want. It will only make my last hours with Cavill miserable.

My last hours.

I open my eyes wide, willing the tears back, and I say Macbeth's first line of the play aloud. *So foul and fair a day I have not seen.*

The curtains open and the play begins. The three witches in white gowns and bare feet take centre stage to the sound of thunder and the flash of lightening. The set does, indeed, look wonderfully gothic and creepy. The witches themselves are suitably spooky in the mist that swirls around their ankles. The oldest witch is played by an elderly Scottish woman called Eileen McGraw, who is married to the fishmonger whose shop, Seacombe Trawler, is the most popular fishmonger in town. She doesn't have to wear a wig because her wild, curly white hair is already pretty spectacular. She does, however, wear a prosthetic nose with a large wart on the end of it. She's throwing herself into the part with aplomb, waving her arms and spreading her long fingers wide, and being wonderfully weird. When she recites the lines, she hisses like a snake.

Jacqueline Rowe is a less convincing witch. Young and pretty, she's more like a seductive siren in *The Odyssey* than an old crone. Her day job is at the hair salon in town where she works as a beautician, and where, she told me cheerfully, they cut her hair into a fashionable bob for free. Tonight, she's sporting a black wig that reaches her waist and frames her pale face, emphasising her sharp cheekbones and angular jawline most beautifully. She flicks her hair self-consciously and does a lot of pouting. She reminds me of those self-loving influencers on Instagram.

The third witch is played by Lavinia. With her heavy black eye make-up and long wig of tangled red hair – I suspect it's the same wig that Gilda borrowed for *The Lady of Shalott* – I failed to recognise her at first. Unlike Jacqueline, Lavinia is convincing, and I stop keeping track of the script and watch her with a strange fascination. Something about the vigour in her movements is quite compelling. '*Fair is foul, and foul is fair: Hover through the fog and filthy air.*' I can't see the audience from where I'm hidden away in the wing, but I can feel their rapt attention in the stillness and silence of the auditorium. So far, so good.

Enter Lady Macbeth in a gown of emerald green trimmed with gold. She too wears a wig in an elaborate updo of dark brown curls. Her stage presence is off the scale; indeed, nothing has prepared me for Nessa. I suspected she'd be a good actor, because she has that fluid, pliable personality that can take the shape of whatever it fills. Lady Macbeth is the perfect vessel for her. Like water, Nessa fills it right into the very corners. She *is* Lady Macbeth. Now I don't even glance at the script. If she forgets her lines, I'm screwed. I doubt she will forget her lines, though. She's much too professional for that. She's relishing this opportunity to put Gilda in the shade – and put her in the shade she most certainly does! But Gilda is the wife of the proprietor and lover of the director, Nessa doesn't stand a chance however accomplished she is.

If Gilda is back tomorrow, Nessa won't get the chance to perform for her father. I feel sorry for her then, before remembering the fire with a jolt.

No one will get the chance to perform tomorrow night.

I only have to prompt once, when Ned Pollock forgets a line – Mrs Crocker will be amused to hear that! Fortunately, I had the script open on the correct page, and by fluke managed to find the place without delay. At the end, the audience, such as it is, claps loudly and jumps to its feet. The actors take their bows with satisfaction. They know they've done a good job. Nessa gets the loudest applause, and she takes Ned's hand and they bow together. Her face is alight with pleasure. She's soaking up the adulation like a dry sponge. A lump wedges itself in my throat and I feel my eyes sting with tears. She should be on the West End stage. She should be a celebrated actor. But she'll die tomorrow in a fire. It's so unjust. So much talent, vitality, joy – gone.

Surely, if her father were to see her perform he would understand why she wants to do it so badly. He would allow her to realise her dream. Why on earth would he not? She's brilliant. Yet, he'll never get the chance to see her on stage. He'll never get the chance to be a better father. A better man. It makes me so angry, because I imagine he'll spend the rest of his life regretting this silly feud. When his daughter is dead, won't he wish he had been a bigger person?

Why do people wake up to their folly only when it's too late?

The curtain goes down and Mr Bentley takes centre stage. He claps and the cast respond with cries of delight. 'By Jove, you nailed it!' he exclaims happily. 'You really nailed it. What a show! What performances. You, Miss Blunt, were simply sublime!' He turns to Nessa and her face grows red with the warmth of his unexpected attention. 'I don't think I have ever seen a more magnificent Lady Macbeth. Truly, I haven't. You were tremendous!' He seems to be looking at her with fresh eyes, as if seeing her for the first time. She grows taller in the glare of his admiration and for the first time, she looks beautiful. The transformation is staggering. Water taking the shape of the vessel it fills. Right now, Nessa is taking the shape of the woman Taran perceives her to be. Not Nessa Blunt, understudy to the golden Gilda Garrett, but Nessa Blunt, Lady Macbeth. And Lady Macbeth is ravishing.

There are a few things that need tweaking, and Mr Bentley goes through them one by one. There are various lighting issues, and the thunder clapped at the wrong moment, apparently, although I didn't notice. One of the stagehands dropped a goblet and one of the set panels was stiff to turn during one of the scene changes. Minor things that can be easily resolved.

Everyone is enthusiastic about the first night tomorrow. Their joy breaks my heart. I have a constant nervous feeling burning just below my ribcage and I have to bite my tongue in order to withhold what I know. Although, I'm aware that if I told them, they wouldn't believe me. Once again, I'm in the horrible position of knowing what is going to happen but being unable to stop it. An occupational hazard, for sure, but miserable none the less.

When the cast is dismissed, Mr Bentley asks Nessa to wait behind. I pretend I'm distracted fussing over the script in the wing and secretly eavesdrop on their conversation.

'You're too good for amateur theatre, Miss Blunt,' he tells her. 'You should go to London.'

'I wouldn't know where to begin,' she replies. Her voice is as light as flour.

'I can help you. I have contacts. I can introduce you to some casting agents, set you up with auditions. I think you have what it takes to be a great actress.'

'Really?'

She seems to have forgotten what she saw here the other night.

'I mean it.' He sighs and shakes his head. 'I don't know why I've never noticed you before.'

'Because I've been in Gilda's shadow,' says Nessa reasonably, and there's no bitterness in her words. She's much too cunning to reveal what she really thinks. What she saw.

'*Oh, my poor, hopeless, broken heart*' is repaired with hope.

'Leave it with me and I'll see what I can do.'

'If Gilda is unwell again tomorrow, I will be able to perform again,' she says keenly. I see in my mind's eye another cup of tea, and shiver with apprehension.

Mr Bentley nods. 'It's of no consequence, my dear. I've seen you act. That's enough for me.' He pats her arm, leaving it there a beat too long. 'You're London-bound, Vanessa Blunt. The West End awaits you.'

He doesn't tell her that he's going to London as well. I wonder, if Nessa had lived, might they have gone together?

Nessa and Lavinia are in high spirits as we walk home through the dusk. The sun is sinking behind the roofs of Seacombe, leaving a roseate glow in the sky and purple bruises on the clouds. It's a sad and beautiful sunset. I'd like to be sitting with Cavill in that secret cove that's his and Eddie's usual place, watching this celestial show play out over the sea. My mind drifts to the gulls, and I see him there with his paints and easel, while Eddie lounges on the blanket beside him, long after I am gone.

My heart sickens with yearning. How can I bear it?

How can I bear to leave?

Nessa and Lavinia chatter away. They're like a pair of parrots, repeating compliments and squawking with laughter. When we reach the house, Lavinia turns to Nessa and says, 'I hope Gilda is unwell again tomorrow, then you'll get the chance to play Lady Macbeth in front of your mamma and papa.'

The door opens and Mrs Crocker stands aside to let us in.

'That is my intention,' Nessa replies, and her voice is confident, as if she knows it will be so.

'Was it a success?' Mrs Crocker asks as we take off our coats in the hall.

'A resounding success,' gushes Nessa, handing her coat to Mrs Crocker without thanking her.

'The girls did very well,' I add, and watch them bound up the stairs like a pair of witches to their coven. If they did indeed put something in Gilda's tea, how are they going to do the same tomorrow if she doesn't come to the theatre? I make a mental note to read Nessa's journal tomorrow. If she did indeed poison Gilda, she might admit it in her diary. 'Ned only forgot one line,' I add, and Mrs Crocker smiles with pleasure. I wonder whether she isn't a little sweet on him.

She takes my coat and hangs it up. I'm about to go upstairs to change before supper, which is what I know I'm expected to do, when I notice a handwritten note on the silver salver on the hall table. It's the same handwriting as the one on the letter I was reading when I arrived. Cavill.

I take it with me to my bedroom with mounting excitement. While Mrs Crocker is in the bathroom running me a bath, I sit at the dressing table and open it. To my surprise it's not a letter at all, but a beautifully rendered sketch of a teal. Beneath the drawing are the words, *my darling Eddie, my inspiration, my joy, my love.*

I stare at the teal in wonder, feeling a mixture of happiness and sorrow, for I will have to leave it here in the past. Unlike his sketchbook that I found in the library at St Sidwell Manor, this lovely drawing will not turn up in 2014. It will be Eddie's to treasure, commemorating a time she will not remember.

I press the paper to my breast and stare at Eddie's face reflected in the mirror in front of me. None of this is mine. The letter, the sketch, the *love*. Every moment lived as Eddie is a moment *stolen* from her, and Cavill will never know that I even exist. It occurs to me suddenly in a moment of painful lucidity, that I need to tell him the truth, not only for his sake, but for Eddie's too. When I leave, Eddie won't remember the last five days. She'll wake up as if she's had amnesia. The difference this time from when I was Hermione Swift and Constance Fleet is that Cavill and Eddie loved each other *before* I came onto the scene. And they will doubtlessly love each other after I've slid back. I have made no impression at all on Cavill. I haven't made him love Eddie more – I've simply stepped into Eddie's body and enjoyed living vicariously through her. I hoped that he would see me when he looked deeply into her eyes, but he did not. How could he have? It was a delusion. A sad, hopeless delusion of which I am now ashamed. I owe it to Eddie to tell Cavill what I have done, what I've taken, who I am.

And let this charade never happen again.

I slip the teal into the gap in the mirror frame for Eddie to find when she wakes up. I touch it with the tips of my fingers and feel a sharp pain in my chest.

None of this belongs to me.

Chapter Twenty

Today is my final day in Seacombe. I awake to rain. It sounds like someone's throwing shells against the glass. The gale causes the window frames to rattle and the light that usually bursts in through the gaps in the curtains is a weak beam of dull grey. I remain in bed for a moment, warm beneath the sheet and blanket, not wanting to step out into the cold. There's no central heating and the fire in my bedroom is not lit. I can feel the damp in the air on my face, even though the windows are closed. It's no doubt a typical English day in May; low-hanging grey cloud, wind and rain.

Mrs Crocker enters. 'Hardly worth getting up,' she says gloomily as she walks over the carpet to open the curtains. 'Miserable day. Rain and more rain to come.'

I wonder if the rain will prevent some of the theatre building from being destroyed in the fire.

My spirits sink further with dread as I contemplate the fire. I know what's to come. But what I don't know is how I'm going to navigate my way through the events in order to find out exactly how Nessa dies in the fire, while at the same time, finding a quiet moment to tell Cavill the truth, as I realise now that I must.

I get up and hurry into the bathroom. 'It's freezing,' I complain, closing the door behind me.

'I suggest you wear something warm,' Mrs Crocker says, raising her voice so I can hear her above the gushing of water from the tap, and I envisage her going through the cupboard to find a suitable sweater. Oh, for a pair of jeans and a hoodie!

Together we choose a tweed skirt, silk blouse and a gorgeous

Fair Isle sweater, which might easily have been bought at Ralph Lauren were we in my time. I'm grateful for the stockings, because my legs are cold. It's not common for women to wear trousers. Lydia is unusual. I really miss my jeans!

I appraise myself in the mirror and conclude that the 1920s is not the most flattering era for women. The Eton crop and bob are not becoming hairstyles unless one is very beautiful, like Eddie and Gilda, and the low-waisted dresses are shapeless. The Edwardian women in my last slide looked much more attractive, even though the corset and long skirts were uncomfortable and constraining.

Nessa declares over breakfast that she will not be leaving the house in the rain and is going to practise the piano. Lavinia would like to remain with her but has to go to work. 'If I didn't have to start typing Mr Waddle's letters at nine o'clock sharp, I wouldn't have got out of bed,' she says. 'What a morning! I hope the weather doesn't put people off coming to the play,' she adds a little worriedly.

'On the contrary. It's the perfect day for theatre,' says Nessa, chewing on a piece of buttered toast. 'One has to be inside in this weather and where better than the good old Aphrodite.'

'I wonder whether Gilda will be back,' I muse provocatively. I want to get a sense of what these two young women have plotted. For I believe they *have* been plotting. 'Perhaps I should pay her a visit,' I suggest.

Nessa catches Lavinia's eye. She takes another bite of toast. 'I think that's a capital idea, Skippy. Maybe take her some Turkish Delight. There's a box in the drawing room from your soirée last week. You could take her that.' She grins at Lavinia. 'A ribbon around it and she'll be none the wiser.'

'Yes, give her Turkish Delight and encourage her to stay in bed,' Lavinia rejoins.

Nessa gives me a pleading look. 'Oh, please, Skippy. Tell her to stay in bed, just for today. She can play Lady Macbeth every other night. I must have the part tonight, for Papa. You understand, don't you, Skippy? I'm only asking for one night.'

'I will do my best,' I tell her.

*

A while later, I'm in the hall with Mrs Crocker, putting on my hat and coat, when Nessa comes running down the stair with the box of Turkish Delight wrapped in pink paper and tied with a velvet ribbon. My suspicious mind immediately leaps to wonder whether she hasn't injected something into the sweets. I dismiss the idea as silly. How would she do that at a moment's notice? Who would happen to have a syringe on hand, and how could they guarantee that Gilda would eat one?

Lavinia has already left. Nessa skips off to practise the piano, and I head out into the rain. Mrs Crocker shakes her head and calls after me. 'Don't catch cold.' The wind buffets my coat, and I have to hold tightly on to the umbrella to stop it flying away.

Few people are in the streets today. A black car motors by, splashing the pavement as it drives through a puddle. I keep my head down and walk hurriedly. It's certainly not a day for a stop and chat. For that I'm grateful.

I arrive at Cavill and Gilda's house and ring the bell. The building still manages to look splendid, even in the rain. The butler opens it, looks me up and down in an imperious manner, and then welcomes me inside. 'Good morning, Mrs Skipton,' he says solemnly.

'Good morning,' I reply, aware that I should really greet him by name for we are obviously familiar with each other. 'Is Mrs Pengower well enough to receive a visitor?'

He nods slowly. 'If you don't mind waiting here, Mrs Skipton, I will go and ask her if she is at home.'

That sounds contradictory to me. I watch him disappear through the large double doors to my right.

I'm left alone in the silent hall, surrounded by Gilda's immaculate taste, wondering whether Cavill is at home too. I'm painfully aware that today I must somehow make him understand who I really am, but here is not the place, and most certainly *not* the time.

The butler reappears. 'Mrs Pengower is at home.' He takes my hat and coat and hangs them up in the cloakroom. 'Please come this way.'

I follow him through a splendid set of grand drawing rooms,

each connected to the other by big white panelled doors, until he hovers in front of a smaller, more intimate and feminine sitting room decorated in raspberry red and sage green. To my surprise Gilda is not alone. Mr Bentley, Taran, is with her. Hiding in plain sight springs to mind!

Gilda smiles from the sofa. She's lounging there with her feet up, beneath a blanket. Her smile is frail. Mr Bentley is smoking a pipe in one of the armchairs beside the fire, which is lit. When I enter, he stands and greets me warmly.

Gilda puts out her hand, which looks very white against the baby pink sleeve of the silk gown she's wearing. 'Skippy!' she exclaims in a feeble voice.

'I've been worried about you,' I tell her, crossing the sumptuous Persian carpet to give her my gift.

'What is this?' she asks, taking it. Her eyes, a second ago listless, now glimmer with the delight of a child. 'I do love a present. What have you got me, Skippy? Really, you shouldn't have.'

'Oh, it's only a little something,' I reply, taking the chair on the other side of the fire to Mr Bentley. He has a smug look about him, but he doesn't know what I saw the other night.

'Might it be edible?' Mr Bentley laughs, sitting back down and arching his eyebrows at me playfully.

'I do hope so,' says Gilda, pulling on the ribbon and opening the paper. Her eyes light up when she recognises the box. 'Turkish Delight! My favourite,' she cries happily. 'I'm going to have some now. Do you want a piece, Mr Bentley? Skippy? Oh, do!'

I envisage Nessa and Lavinia, like the witches in the play, hovering over the sugared squares with a syringe full of poison, and decline. But Mr Bentley gets out of his chair, takes one and pops it into his mouth with relish.

'Don't they just melt on your tongue?' Gilda says with a contented sigh. She helps herself to another. 'I swear I'll eat the whole box.'

'They're moreish, aren't they?' I add.

Gilda looks at me and frowns. 'I love that word. Moreish. I'm going to use it a lot. Moreish.' I could teach her a few other new words besides.

'Might you be well enough to perform tonight?' I ask.

'I hope so,' she says, glancing at Mr Bentley. 'I must rest today and see how I feel later.'

'Miss Blunt is ready to take your place,' says Mr Bentley. 'There is no pressure. Your health must come first.'

Gilda smiles at him with gratitude. 'You're too good to me, Mr Bentley.' I don't doubt that to her he's usually Taran.

I recall them having sex in the theatre, and then the conversation between Mr Bentley and Nessa, and wonder where he really stands in all of this. Does he love Gilda? If he does, why is he moving to London and leaving her? If he loved her, would he have encouraged Nessa to go too? I watch Mr Bentley closely. Right now, he seems very attentive towards Gilda. Perhaps he doesn't want her to perform tonight, considering the dazzling performance Nessa gave in the dress rehearsal. Maybe he loves Gilda as a woman, but not as an actress, and genuinely wants to help promote Nessa whom he recognises as very talented.

A maid brings in a tray of crockery and Victoria sponge cake and proceeds to pour tea from a pretty floral teapot into delicate china cups. Gilda sips her tea as she makes her way blithely through the box of Turkish Delight. I can barely eat the piece of cake the maid has sliced for me because I'm so worried Gilda is going to suddenly froth at the mouth, poisoned by Nessa with her syringe! But she doesn't froth at the mouth. She doesn't even cough. Her cheeks flush with a rosy glow and she appears much restored.

The butler returns and lays another log on the fire. When he uses the bellows to reignite it, crimson sparks fly out and the logs crackle and burn. Soon the flames are dancing merrily in the grate. I can't help but look into the fire and think of Nessa. I turn my attention back to the conversation to distract me from what is imminent and unavoidable.

'I do so want to go and see *The Rainbow*,' says Gilda. 'Lady Faversham says it's splendid.'

I have no idea what she's talking about but have to pretend that I do. 'I gather it is wonderful,' I add gamely.

'If one enjoys musical theatre,' Mr Bentley says, puffing on his pipe. The smell of his smoke is pleasantly sweet. 'Personally, I think songs get in the way of a good story. I'm afraid I am not a fan of Gershwin.'

'I am not familiar with Gershwin, but I did love *Funny Face*,' I add, remembering the 1950s film with Audrey Hepburn that Ulysses made me watch.

Mr Bentley frowns. 'I'm not familiar with that one,' he says, puffing on his pipe again. 'But it's a snappy title.' I wonder then whether Gershwin has even written it yet.

'We should go to London to see a show,' says Gilda, smiling at him excitedly. 'I know how you love trains, Mr Bentley.'

'I think that's a marvellous idea,' I add, for something to say.

'We should make a party of it,' says Gilda excitedly, looking from me to Mr Bentley like a child wanting approval. 'Wouldn't it be a scream to go all together?'

'Capital idea,' Mr Bentley agrees. '*London Calling!* is on at the Duke of York. I believe that's rather good.'

'We could stay at Claridge's, or the Ritz,' Gilda suggests, eyes gleaming with longing. 'Oh, how I miss the bright lights of a city!'

Mr Bentley chortles. 'I'm not sure the idea of an excursion to London will appeal to your husband, Miss Garrett. I do believe he prefers provincial life to city life. Isn't that why he left New York?'

'Oh, boo!' she exclaims, pushing out her bottom lip. 'Trust him to be a killjoy!' She turns to me and grins. 'Then the three of us can go together and leave the old curmudgeon behind. If you come, Skippy, it will all be good and proper.' She pops another square of Turkish Delight into her mouth. 'Isn't life bonny!'

I glance out of the window and see a pair of blue tits fluttering about a wooden bird feeder. I think of Cavill and I wonder where he is.

I put my teacup on the table beside my armchair. 'I must be going,' I say and stand up.

Mr Bentley stands up too, and I assume that he is leaving with me, but he remains beside the fire. 'Thank you for coming to see me, Skippy,' says Gilda. I notice she has nearly devoured all the Turkish Delight.

Neither she nor Mr Bentley have been poisoned by it.

'I hope you feel better by this evening,' I tell her.

'It's most strange. It came over me suddenly. Nausea, terrible. I don't believe it's nerves, but one never knows. And now I feel tired.' She sighs despairingly. 'Anyhow, you have cheered me up, Skippy.'

'I'm so glad,' I reply, then turn to Mr Bentley. 'I will see you later.'

He nods and puts the stem of his pipe between his lips again. 'It's going to be a triumph,' he says. 'Everyone has worked devilishly hard to make it so.'

I leave, knowing what I know and feeling miserable on account of it. It would be better for Gilda if she doesn't manage to get to the theatre tonight. I wish I could stop Nessa from going, but I can't. I have to stand back, observe, and try not to let it break me.

It's still raining, but not quite as heavily as when I left home. I cower under the umbrella and walk over wet pavements and slippery cobblestones, at one point narrowly missing a steaming pile of horse manure. I feel an urgent need to speak to Cavill, to come clean, but I don't know where to find him. On a day like this he's hardly likely to be outside, and I don't imagine there's anything for him at the theatre. I decide to turn up mid-afternoon and hope that he'll be there. I imagine the place will be teeming with people by then, preparing for the first night.

When I arrive home, Nessa has given up playing the piano and is in the drawing room reading a book by the fire. In spite of the warmth it gives off, the place still feels chilly and damp. Nessa puts down her book when she sees me. 'Is Gilda better?' she asks eagerly.

I can see the dread on her face. 'It's hard to tell,' I reply. 'She's pale, but in good spirits. She says the nausea came over her suddenly.' I go and sit down on one of the upholstered chairs near the fire.

Nessa bites her bottom lip. 'Did you give her the Turkish Delight?'

'She loved it.'

Nessa grins. 'It's her favourite. I hope she eats all of it and then feels sick again.'

'Oh, Nessa. I don't think eating a box of Turkish Delight is going to prevent her from playing Lady Macbeth tonight. But,' I add, and she stares at me with hopeful eyes, 'whatever it was she had yesterday has really knocked her out. She's very tired.'

'Then she must rest,' she says. 'She can play Lady Macbeth every night after, for the entire run.'

I turn my eyes to the flames and watch them dancing merrily about the logs. It's agony having a conversation about the future, when I know Nessa doesn't have a future. I recall her spirit on the stage, playing the part of Lady Macbeth alongside Rebecca, and remind myself that what I'm living now, has already been lived. It's in the past. Nessa has already died. It's like playing a film again and slipping into the narrative. It's all happened already.

But right now, talking to Nessa is very real.

'Mr Bentley was there,' I tell her and watch her face darken.

'He prefers my rendition of Lady Macbeth to hers. He pretty much told me so. I think he knows she's a shocking actress, but as they are lovers, he cannot say no to her.' She narrows her eyes. 'You know, Skippy, he wants me to go to London.'

I feign ignorance. 'Does he?'

'He told me last night that I have talent and that he can help me.'

'Really?'

She nods enthusiastically. 'He doesn't love Gilda. If I can prove to Papa that I am not some foolish girl with dreams of being in a chorus line, but a serious actress, then perhaps he will support me. You would come with me to London, wouldn't you, Skippy?

'Well, I . . .'

'We could stay with Rose. She invited us on numerous occasions. She's lonely in London and would adore to have us to stay. Oh, say you will, Skippy?'

It doesn't matter what I say, because tomorrow Nessa will be dead, and I will be gone. I suppress my distress and tell her what she wants to hear. 'Perhaps.'

Nessa grins triumphantly. She believes she has won me over. 'I will go to London and become a big star, and then Taran will love me. He doesn't love her. He's using her like a toy. And she's so gullible she's believing it. But she's married, so she can't have him anyhow.'

I want to tell her that Taran is leaving Seacombe and heading to London, but what would be the point? Besides, there's plenty of time for her to use that information and expose my indiscretion in the process. I must think of Eddie and not let her down more than I have let her down already.

I put my hand to my throat and rub the skin there, which is prickling with guilt. That beautiful afternoon at the inn is something else I have stolen from her. A memory which I will treasure but which she will never remember.

I turn my attention back to Nessa. I'd like to have another opportunity to read her journal, to see if she did indeed poison Gilda yesterday, but she appears pretty stuck in here. I'm not sure I'm going to get the chance.

'What time would you like to get to the theatre?' I ask, getting up.

'Five,' she replies. 'We can go together. Lavinia will meet us there.'

I sigh, dread causing my very bones to ache. 'Very well. We shall walk together.'

I turn to the window to find that the rain has stopped. To my surprise a sudden beam of sunshine breaks through the cloud and lights up the cherry tree, as if it's taken centre stage. Strangely, that sight encourages me. I take it as a sign. A positive sign. That although we all face death, it's never the end, just the beginning of a new cycle. Tonight, Nessa will leave this world, but she will not die in her essence. There is no such thing.

Chapter Twenty-One

Nessa and I have lunch together and I hold on to the image of the radiant cherry tree and remind myself that we are never alone. We are surrounded, all the time, by those in spirit who are there to help us as we make our way blindly along our paths. Nessa is about to complete her life. She will leave having done what she came here to do, whatever that may be. The only trouble is she doesn't return home; she chooses to stay. Right now, I know that she loves Taran Bentley – or she believes she does. It's either an unhealthily obsessional infatuation, or a childish one. I don't know which. She despises Gilda Garrett. She longs to be a leading lady of the stage. Are all these things enough to explain her remaining here after she leaves her body? I sense that they are not.

There has to be something more.

Souls usually remain bound to the earth plane because they don't realise they're dead – Nessa, in the present, is very much aware that she's dead. They often remain because they hate too much, or love too much, or are afraid of the light that is there to show them the way home. Is Nessa's love too intense? Is her hate too strong? I don't believe so because she, as a spirit, is well aware of time having passed, and that Taran Bentley and Gilda Garrett are both long dead. Additionally, spirits can remain because, for some reason, they can't *find* the way home. But this cannot be the case either, because Nessa claimed to have made fools of the mediums and priests who tried to help move her on, as I did.

The fact is, she doesn't *want* to go home.

Why?

*

At four, I go upstairs on the pretence of going to my bedroom to change. I leave Nessa in the drawing room, playing solitaire at the round table. She declares that she needs to distract herself otherwise nerves will get the better of her. She has managed to convince herself that Gilda won't make it to the theatre tonight and that *she* will be playing Lady Macbeth in front of her parents. She's excited and fearful at the same time. 'This is the biggest night of my life, Skippy. Everything depends on it.'

It infuriates me to know that her parents have already decided that they will not support her. That they'll turn up, play their part, applaud and smile, while secretly intending to force her to give up on her dream. Of course, it's simply academic, because they won't watch her perform. They won't applaud and smile. There won't *be* a performance. There will just be a fire, and that misguided pair will be left with their plans reduced to ashes, along with their daughter.

I hurry up the second flight of stairs to Nessa's bedroom. I know where to find the journal and seize upon it impatiently. Time is running out and I have not a moment to waste. I will leave this house in an hour, and I won't be coming back.

My ears are alert to every sound, but I'm quite alone. I open the diary and flick through the pages to the latest entry. I'm disappointed, however. There's only one line and no mention of Taran and Gilda making love in the theatre, or of Nessa poisoning Gilda, if that's what she did.

I must be cruel, only to be kind. I think of Nessa poisoning Gilda's tea, and shudder.

I return the diary to its hiding place and go back downstairs, dissatisfied. I change into a navy-blue dress with white trimming. It'll be warm in the theatre, so I choose a long cardigan I can shed when I'm in the wing.

Mrs Crocker appears in the doorway. 'I wish you luck tonight, ma'am,' she says.

'Thank you, Crocker. Isn't one meant to say, "Break a leg"?'

'To the actors,' she replies. 'And you gave up on that idea a long time ago, if I recall.'

'I did,' I laugh. 'I'm better behind the scenes.'

'They're lucky to have you.'

I smile at her affectionately. I'm aware that I will be leaving her, too, and that makes me sad. I've grown fond of her as well.

She sighs, that sympathetic look in her eyes again. 'It's a connection, isn't it, ma'am? It keeps his memory alive. Mr Skipton's memory. No one loved the theatre more than him. You've made sure his legacy lives on.'

It pains me to know that it will die tonight.

'I think he would be pleased,' I add. '*Macbeth* is a lovely tribute to him.'

Her eyes mist and she puts a hand to her mouth. 'Sorry, ma'am. The years go by, but they don't make missing him any easier. He was a big presence in this house and without him it feels empty. I shouldn't say this to you, but I cannot pretend otherwise.'

'That's all right, Crocker. I miss him too.'

By the time Nessa and I make our way to the theatre the sun is out and the rainclouds are retreating speedily on the wind. They scud across the sky towards the far horizon, leaving behind a gentle, watery blue. I'm filled with dread. This is the final time I will walk this route. The final time I'll arrive at the theatre. I'm seized with the urge to grab Nessa by the arm and beg her not to come. But even if I managed to convince her that something terrible is going to happen, I believe her desire to play the lead in front of her parents would spur her on anyway. I doubt there's anything I could do to stop her from meeting her destiny. And if I did, perhaps she'd meet it another way. Maybe meeting her destiny is unavoidable, written in the *Book of Life*.

That thought comforts me. It makes me feel less impotent and more ready to accept that there are things I cannot change.

There are two and a half hours before the play commences, but the theatre is already heaving with people. The air quivers with a heightened energy which is thrilling, and for a moment I forget the tragedy that is to come, and my spirits rise on the heat of it, like a paper lantern. Ned Pollock and Lydia are chatting in the foyer over cigarettes. They greet us warmly. 'Tonight is the night, girlies,' says Lydia. She's wearing wide-legged trousers and a colourfully embroidered peasant's blouse with a bright red scarf tied around her head and knotted above her temple so that the tasselled arms fall over her shoulder. She looks raffish and ahead of her time. She can't imagine how in the future women will all wear trousers.

Ned rubs his hands together. 'Tonight is your night, Nessa!'

Nessa beams a smile. 'It's going to be tremendous,' she replies, and trembles with excitement. 'I'm a bundle of nerves.'

'Poor old Gilda,' says Lydia. 'Such a shame to miss the first night.'

'The show must go on!' says Ned.

Lavinia arrives, breathless. 'Mr Waddle let me go early,' she says. Her cheeks are flushed, her curly red hair falling away from the pins that secure it in a low bun.

Nessa and Lavinia disappear backstage. Lydia watches them go, then lowers her voice. 'I bet my right arm that Gilda will be here,' she says.

Ned pulls a face. 'That's a hefty bet, Miss Redcliffe. You can't do without your right arm!'

She blows smoke out of the side of her mouth. 'Trust me, she's not going to let Miss Blunt steal her thunder.'

'I think you're right,' I reply.

I don't know the exact time the fire starts, but I do recall Madge saying that it started during a performance, which means that it won't happen before the play is underway. I'm certain Gilda has something to do with it. Perhaps Nessa is furious that she turns up and thwarts her opportunity to perform, flies into a rage and sets the place on fire on purpose, to punish Gilda. Does Nessa, in despair, commit suicide? Is that what this is all about?

But suicide just doesn't seem likely. Nessa might have an unhealthy obsession with Taran Bentley, but she is not mentally ill.

I go backstage. None of the actors are getting ready yet. The ones that are here, and not all of them are, are making themselves cups of tea and standing about chatting. Mrs Fry has made egg and cucumber sandwiches and is handing them around on a plate. Everyone is excited. It's a sell-out, not a single empty seat. I'm on edge. I need to speak to Cavill, but when? What if he turns up just before the play starts? Then I won't get my chance.

I kick myself for not having told him earlier. I had the opportunity, but I chickened out. I regret that now. I regret my lack of courage. My weakness. So much depends on me coming clean.

Nessa is convinced now that she is going to play Lady Macbeth. There is no news of Gilda. Even Mr Bentley doesn't know whether she'll show up. 'This is very unlike her,' he says when I bump into him in the corridor. 'She's usually punctual and keen.'

'But Nessa is a good Lady Macbeth,' I remind him.

'She's tremendous, yes.' He lowers his voice. 'Between you and me, it wouldn't be a bad thing if Miss Garrett gave Miss Blunt a chance to shine. She deserves it. I see a bright future for Nessa Blunt.'

I hold his eyes steady, disguising my misery. What potential she has. Potential that will never be given the opportunity to flower.

'Have you spoken to Mr Pengower?' I ask, hoping to find out when he'll be arriving.

Mr Bentley shakes his head. 'No. I doubt he is any wiser than us.'

'Surely, it's courtesy to let you know.'

'Come on, Mrs Skipton. You know Gilda Garrett. Have you ever known her to think of anyone else but herself?'

I laugh, because his face has lit up with admiration. He finds that quality attractive. 'I suppose not,' I reply.

'Miss Garrett does exactly what she wants and the rest of us fall into line behind her,' he continues.

'Everyone except Mr Pengower,' I add provocatively.

He grins knowingly. 'Oh, I think Pengower is the most indulgent of all of us.' As he walks away, I'm left wondering what he means by that. Does Cavill know that she's having an affair with Taran Bentley?

I find Nessa and Lavinia with the other actresses in the communal dressing room having their hair and make-up done. Nessa, who is now set to play Lady Macbeth, does not presume to use Gilda's room. That's *her* domain and I'm sure Nessa expects her to return to the theatre tomorrow and resume her role as leading lady. Nessa sits in front of the mirror, lit by the golden lightbulbs that frame it, and applies foundation to her face with a sponge. I catch her eye in the glass, and she smiles back at me nervously.

The room is noisy with chatter and thick with cigarette smoke. Everyone is excited. They drink coffee and gossip. They're all talking about Gilda. How unlike her it is not to show up to the first night! They try to ascertain how ill she really is. No leading lady wants to miss the first night. 'She must be dying,' says Lavinia and the room erupts into laughter.

I glance at the clock on the wall. The second hand is moving at its dogged pace around the big white face, bringing me ever closer to the tragedy. I look at Nessa until I can't look at her anymore. I can't watch her excitement and joy, knowing that this is her final hour. And yet, I can't leave her. I need to find out how it begins. I need to know who starts it, and why.

I sit at the other end of the room and pick up a magazine.

The door opens and the assistant manager pokes his head around it and looks at Nessa. 'Miss Garrett has just arrived,' he announces, and the entire room goes quiet. Everyone looks at Nessa. *I* look at Nessa.

Her mouth falls open and her face turns grey. I can see the change in colour even through her make-up. Her disappointment is palpable. We all feel it. I suspect her colleagues prefer a leading lady who can actually act and are disappointed too.

Nessa fights tears valiantly. She stiffens her jaw and lifts her chin and takes a deep breath. She goes very still. I imagine her mind is moving, though. Moving fast, working out what to do. How to get what she wants. 'I'll finish my make-up,' she says. 'Just in case

Gilda takes another turn, and I have to take her place at the last minute.'

What is she thinking, I wonder? What is she plotting? What is certain, is that Gilda's sudden turning up at the final hour is the flame that ignites the fuse.

It also means that Cavill must be here.

I leave the room to Lavinia's doleful voice. 'Not dying, after all.'

No one laughs this time.

I hurry down the corridor to Gilda's dressing room and knock on the door. I don't wait for her to invite me in, I simply barge in. When I enter I find her at her dressing table. She's not alone. Mr Bentley is standing by the rail of costumes. They don't look happy to have been interrupted. In fact, they look quite pissed off. 'You made it,' I say and smile cheerfully. Even though my heart breaks for Nessa – even though it makes no difference.

'I'm feeling better,' she replies stiffly. She doesn't look better. She appears to have been crying. Her eyes are red-rimmed, and her face is as white as porcelain. She doesn't meet my eye.

'I'm glad,' I reply. 'Time is running out. You need to start getting ready.'

She flicks open her cigarette case and pops one between her lips, which are pale too. Then she reaches for her lucky lamp to light it.

'Can I get you anything?' I ask.

'I have champagne,' she says dully, flicking her hand at the half-empty crystal flute that stands bubbling to the right of the mirror. She lights her cigarette in the flame.

Mr Bentley is keen to get rid of me. 'Why don't you go and see if you can find Elsie, Mrs Skipton. Gilda needs hair and make-up done, *pronto*.'

'Of course.' I smile sympathetically at Gilda. It wasn't so long ago that she opened her heart to me in here. She's not keen to open it to me now. It's as tightly closed as a clam.

I leave and hover a moment in the corridor, deciding what to do. My priority is to find Cavill before he goes and takes his place in the royal box with Lady Faversham. I don't go looking for Elsie but make my way to the foyer instead. I imagine that, if Cavill is in the building, he'll be there, greeting punters as they come in.

I'm not wrong. The foyer is heaving with people. What strikes me at once is that everyone is dressed to the nines. The men are in black tie, the women in evening gowns, their earlobes, necks and wrists sparkling with jewellery. The air is sweet with the smell of perfume and cigarette smoke. I realise that smoking is quite the thing. It's like looking at everything through thick fog.

Cavill rises above the sea of heads. He's always easy to spot in a crowd. I feel a wave of relief, followed quickly by one of trepidation. It's now or never.

I weave through the people with an intense sense of purpose but am detained suddenly by a hand.

It's Sylvia. She's looking at me expectantly. I know what she's thinking: have I managed to persuade Nessa to come home? Her lips are drawn into a thin scarlet line. Beside her is a portly man with receding hair, a fleshy, coarse face, potato nose and small, whisky-coloured eyes. He's standing very straight, puffing out his barrel chest importantly. I notice the thick chain of a gold pocket watch lying against his white waistcoat and the diamond studs that glitter at his chest. Mr Blunt, no doubt. Eddie's brother-in-law and Nessa's father. I get the measure of him at once. His energy is hard and unyielding. The energy of an ego that demands supremacy.

'Edwina,' says Sylvia. Between her fingers is an ivory cigarette holder, and I can't help but wonder what poor elephant had to die for someone to make that.

'Hello, my dear,' says Humphrey, and his weaselly eyes glint like steel. He glances over my shoulder, then lowers his voice. 'Any luck with Nessa?'

Sylvia leans in eagerly through his cigar smoke.

I decide to tell the truth. Of course, whatever I say will make no difference to Nessa. But it might make a difference to them, after she is gone. 'I'm afraid she is determined to follow her heart,' I tell them. I watch Humphrey turn the colour of Bull's Blood.

Sylvia digs her chin into her chest and blinks at me, incredulous.

'You promised you would talk to her,' she says through gritted teeth, the smile still stiff upon her face.

'I did talk to her,' I reply. 'She wants what she wants. Unfortunately, she won't be performing Lady Macbeth tonight, but I wish that she was, so you could see what an exceptional talent she has. Mr Bentley says she's the best Lady Macbeth he's ever seen, and I concur. I'm considering accompanying her to London to see if she can make it in the West End.'

Sylvia's mouth falls open. Humphrey almost has steam coming out of his ears.

I put a hand on his arm. He looks at it with horror, as if I've just laid a dead rat there. 'Humphrey, listen to me. We don't own our children. They come through us to walk their own paths. They're not small versions of us, they're independent souls who are here to have their own adventures. You have to step out of the way and give Nessa space to grow.'

Sylvia looks at her husband, her fixed smile is unable to hide her terror. 'I told you she's not herself.'

I cut in crossly, allowing my contempt for the misogyny of this culture to get the better of me. 'I have always believed women should have the right to choose what they do.'

'Good God!' Humphrey splutters, spraying me with spittle. 'Have you lost your mind, Edwina?'

'No,' I reply calmly. 'My mind is very focused. Nessa is a young woman who knows what she wants. It just happens to differ from what *you* want for her. But aren't you a forward-thinking man, Humphrey?'

Sylvia's eyes dart to her left and right like a startled bird. She's frightened that we're being overheard or observed.

'Forward thinking? What balderdash!' Humphrey exclaims.

Now Sylvia puts a hand on his arm. He shrugs it off.

'I will not be dictated to by a woman.' He hisses the words rather than speaks them. 'No daughter of mine will stoop so low as to work for a living. It simply will not happen. I want Nessa home by tomorrow evening, is that clear, Edwina? And you are not to meddle any more in her life. I insist upon it.'

He sniffs furiously before disappearing into the crowd.

Sylvia turns on me. She's staring at me with round, startled eyes, as if she no longer recognises her sister. Not a surprise to me. I am *not* her sister. 'What has got into you, Edwina?' she demands.

'I don't know what you mean?'

'You know exactly what I mean. How could you speak to Humphrey like that? He has never been spoken to like that before in his life!'

'By a woman?'

'Well, of course.' She looks at me awry. 'What is all this ghastly feminism talk? Tom would turn in his grave to hear you speak like this. You know how he laughed at the Suffragettes. How would he feel to know that you are fast becoming one? I can only assume that you are being led astray. By whom, I do not know. But someone is a bad influence on you.'

'I must get on,' I say. I don't want to get Eddie into any more trouble. 'I need to talk to Mr Pengower.'

She huffs and puts her horrible ivory cigarette holder to her lips with a quivering hand.

I feel a rising sense of panic as I push my way through the throng. Time is running out and I must speak with Cavill alone. I must tell him the truth before I slide back. I need to finish this, for both of us. And for Eddie. I feel sick with anxiety. I fear that I have let Eddie down. That I've put her in compromising positions both with Cavill and with her sister and brother-in-law. But there's no time to dwell on that now. I must talk to Cavill and then go and find Nessa before the fire starts.

I'm going to have to walk a tightrope – witness what happens without affecting the outcome. Oh, for Harry Potter's invisibility cloak. How on earth am I going to do this without it?

Chapter Twenty-Two

Cavill sees me approaching and smiles. I'm too scared to smile back. He reads my expression as an indication that something has gone wrong and breaks off his conversation with an elderly woman in order to come and meet me. 'What is it?' he asks softly.

'I need to talk to you. Can we go somewhere private?'

His face darkens. 'What's happened, Eddie?'

'Nothing's happened. I just need to tell you something.'

We leave the foyer, avoiding getting caught by friends who wish to talk to us, and take the narrow corridor that snakes around the outskirts of the auditorium to a small, quiet back room. Like the VIP room where I sit with Ulysses in the present, it has red upholstered chairs arranged around a low coffee table, and a long wooden console table placed against the wall. Very soon it will be consumed by fire.

Cavill looks at me with concern. 'What is it?'

I don't know where to begin. I wish I could ensure that he'll remain quiet while I speak, but I know he'll interrupt me before I've finished saying what I need to say, that he'll deem me mad the moment I state that I come from the future. I decide to leave that bit to the end.

'Sit down.'

'Eddie, darling? What the devil is going on?'

He's worried now, but he does as I ask. I stand before him and take a deep breath. I know this will change everything. End everything. My grief almost overwhelms me before I've even said a word, because he's already lost to me.

I pull myself together, lift my chin and look at him steadily.

'I'm going to tell you something that might seem very peculiar, unbelievable, actually. Will you promise me you'll listen to what I have to say before you judge me?'

'Of course,' he says confidently. He cannot imagine how peculiar it's going to be.

'Take yourself back to June 1895,' I begin, blindly feeling my way.

'Very well,' he replies. 'I was at St Sidwell.'

'You and Hermione were standing by the window of her bedroom. She took your face in her hands, and she asked you to look into her eyes. She said that when we die, we move into spirit. We leave our bodies behind and live on as souls. She asked you whether you would recognise her when you are made of light. Do you remember?'

He shakes his head in bewilderment. His deepening frown makes him look old, suddenly. 'How do you know what Hermione and I talked about?'

'You said you'd recognise her out of a thousand souls. Do you remember that?' I want him to remember it. I want it to have meant something.

He nods his head slowly, struggling to see a path through the fog. 'Of course, I remember that.'

Hope flares for a second. I continue. My heart is hammering in my chest, the blood pounding against my temples. He doesn't yet understand what I'm trying to tell him. 'Do you remember, after Felix disappeared, Hermione awoke from a faint and didn't recall anything that had happened over the previous two weeks? Do you remember that?' He nods again, very slowly, wondering where I'm going with this. I soldier on. 'Never again did she talk of souls, of life after death, of love that endures beyond time, did she? Hermione seemed quite different after that.'

'What is this about, Eddie? I don't understand.' He's rattled now. He moves to get up, but I lay my hands on his shoulders and make him stay seated.

'Please, you said you would listen.'

He sighs. I know I'm scaring him. This isn't the Eddie he knows.

'Very well,' he concedes and folds his arms. He's now looking decidedly uncomfortable.

I stand back and heave another breath. 'Do you remember the strange song she played on the piano? "Let it Be"? No one had ever heard anything like it.' My throat constricts now, as I feel the pressure building in my chest. I never anticipated that telling the truth would be as hard as this.

'How do you know about Hermione, Eddie?' he asks quietly.

'I will explain. Just hear me out.'

'This is highly irregular, you know.'

'Do you remember, on the *Titanic*, you were on the deck with Constance.'

His eyes widen and stare at me in disbelief. I start pacing the room. I feel as if I'm wading through concrete, trying to explain something that's unexplainable. 'You lent her your jacket because it was bitterly cold,' I continue. 'The stars were the brightest you'd ever seen. She told you she'd had a dream that the ship was going to sink. Then on the night it *did* sink, she seemed to know it before it happened. Do you remember that?'

He's staring at me with growing alarm. I can almost see his mind racing around in his head trying to make sense of the seemingly unconnected pieces of information.

'Constance knew it was going to sink, Cavill. She knew the *Carpathia* was going to rescue those who managed to get into lifeboats. You knew she knew. You questioned her. How did she know? Then she told you . . .' My voice thins. I put a hand to my throat. 'She told you that you were dear to her.'

I've now scared the living daylights out of him. 'Eddie, I don't know how you know all of this, or, indeed, why you're telling me . . .'

I cut him off. I kneel in front of him and put my hands on his knees. I hold his gaze, willing him to see *me*, Pixie, behind my eyes. Willing him to remember what he saw when he looked deeply into Hermione and Constance's eyes. Willing him to see *me* and recognise *me,* at last.

But he doesn't. He's looking at me with distrust, not recognition. He couldn't be further away from recognising me.

I have come this far. I cannot stop now. 'Because *I* was Hermione and *I* was Constance, and now I'm Eddie,' I whisper. My eyes well with tears.

He looks quite terrified now, and furious.

'I come from the future, Cavill,' I tell him. 'I'm sitting in this very theatre on 26th October 2014, in trance. My name is Pixie Tate. I'm a psychic medium with a very strange gift. I can travel through time. I have travelled here to this time to release the soul of Nessa Blunt who is stuck, following a fire that will destroy her and this theatre tonight.'

Cavill pushes me away and stands. I feel his incredulity and his contempt, and they are daggers in my heart. He cannot believe that I'm claiming to be Hermione and Constance and Eddie . . . and I don't blame him. Why ever did I imagine that he would?

I talk very fast now, knowing that in a moment he will leave this room and never want to see me again.

I can't think of Eddie and how this conversation will impact her. I have to end what I started.

I get up and stand before him. 'When I slide back to my time, I will leave Eddie and she, like Hermione, won't remember anything that has happened since last Friday. Constance died on those stairs, but she was due to meet you in Central Park the following day, and she, *I,* was going to tell you the truth. I was going to tell you who I am. But I never got the chance. I never got the chance to come clean. But I wanted to. You said there was something you wanted to tell her. What was it? What were you going to tell her?'

Cavill turns and stares at me with the eyes of a stranger. The cold in them knocks the wind out of me, and, as a consequence, the tears fall freely.

He's lost for words. He's looking at the woman he loves and hating everything she is saying.

'I want you to leave,' he says. He puts his hands on his hips and shakes his head. 'I don't know how you know all of this . . . about Hermione and Constance. I can't explain . . . but it's madness. It's sheer madness. I want it to stop.'

But I can't stop now. I have to make him understand. 'Do you remember the poem Hermione recited? The one Constance recited too? "The King's Breakfast" by A. A. Milne. It hasn't been composed yet. It's a poem from the future.'

His frown deepens with horror. I know he remembers it. I start to recite it, putting on the voices as I did as both Hermione and Constance.

'Stop!'

But I don't stop. I can't. I want to make him understand.

I put on the high-pitched voice of the queen, hoping he will realise the truth. But he resists it. It's too outlandish. Too implausible.

'Stop it, I tell you!' He shouts. His eyes are wild with fear.

He makes for the door, but I hurry and put myself in the way, my back pressed against it.

I'm desperate now. I sense I'm losing him. I put out my hand, but he doesn't take it.

'Step aside, Eddie,' he demands.

My feet remain firmly planted. 'When you fell in love with Hermione, it was *me*, Pixie. When you fell in love with Constance, it was *me*, Pixie. Now I'm Eddie, and you love both of us. I love you Cavill, with all my heart and soul . . .' My voice thins. I clear my throat. I gaze at him longingly and lovingly, but all I get in return is icy distrust. 'Telling you the truth is the only way I can end our connection, so I don't slide back as anyone else and disrupt your life further. You and Eddie deserve to find happiness together.'

'You *are* Eddie!' he exclaims in frustration.

'I am *not* Eddie.' I realise that I'm shouting too. 'I was not Hermione, or Constance. I'm Pixie Tate, in possession of Eddie for the time I need to save Nessa's soul. I'm from the future. From 2014. I didn't expect to fall in love with you when I slid back to 1895. But I started something that gained momentum and now it needs to end. So I'm ending it. It's breaking my heart, but I have to end it.'

He puts his hands on my upper arms and shifts me roughly away from the door.

'Then it's ended,' he says dully. 'I have nothing more to say to you.'

*

He leaves. I'm left reeling from the shock of what I've just done. My heart is splintering into a thousand pieces. I want to slide home and dive under the duvet and not emerge for a week. I want the pain to end. But I have a duty to Nessa, and I can't let her down.

I stumble into the corridor and make my way backstage. I feel suffocated, as if a sack of bricks is pressing down upon my chest, preventing me from breathing properly. I want to cry but I suppress it with a strength I didn't know I had.

A door is open a crack and I see the auditorium, full of people now. The play must be about to begin. I quicken my pace. I don't know where exactly I'm going, but I must find Nessa.

I pass Ned Pollock who is so engrossed in his script that he doesn't even see me. He's reading through his lines in the hope of not forgetting any. But it doesn't matter. He won't be performing tonight. I ignore the stagehands, the prop people, anyone whom I encounter. I'm in a trance and I'm staggering blindly. But everyone is focused on the play. No one has time to notice me. I might as well be wearing the invisibility cloak after all.

The sound of raised voices causes me to stop outside Gilda's dressing room. People are arguing. Nessa and Gilda. They're having a fight. I press my ear to the wood panel to hear better. The words are ejected so quickly, it takes my ears a while to tune in. When they do, one sentence is ejaculated louder and clearer than all the others. 'If you don't let me perform tonight, I will tell him what I saw . . .'

And thus Nessa seals her fate.

Silence.

I sense a presence moving towards the door and scurry down the corridor and dive into Ned's dressing room which is now empty. Through the adjoining wall I hear Gilda's door open, and slam shut.

Did I hear the turning of a key? Could I have, or was it my imagination?

'I'll deal with you later,' Gilda hisses through the door.

Footsteps fade as she makes her way hurriedly up the corridor in the direction of the stage. Gilda has locked Nessa in her dressing room so she can't go out and spoil her performance. So she can't go out and tell Cavill what she knows.

The place falls silent. Everyone has gone. Everyone but me and Nessa. There's an eerie lull. Like the theatre is holding its breath. Like the weird empty beach before the onslaught of a tsunami.

I don't move a muscle. I remain petrified like a statue, my senses alert. Only my eyeballs swivel from side to side, while my ears strain through the strange stillness, anticipating what I know is about to occur.

Then the silence is broken at last by a loud and furious scream, followed by a crash. Breaking glass. In a rage, Nessa has thrown something against the door.

I wait. It feels like time is standing still. As if all the clocks in the theatre have stopped and we are all frozen in suspended animation. I don't know what to do now. Nothing is happening. Gilda has gone to play her part. Nessa is here in Gilda's dressing room. I am in Ned's. I cannot move. My legs have gone numb. All I can feel is my heart thumping dully against my ribcage and the blood throbbing in my temples. I strain my ears for a sound, any sound, but my anxiety deafens me.

And then there's a whoosh. A dreadful whoosh. It's like the roaring of the ocean, or the rush of wind in the trees. The sound of air being sucked into the open gullet of a dragon. Then the fiery exhale and I know it has begun. The fire. It has begun.

Nessa must have thrown Gilda's lucky lamp against the door and the room has caught fire. And she's locked in there.

Through the din of my nerves, and the bellowing of the fire, comes the urgent rattling of the doorknob.

I can't stand it. I can't remain here and witness this part of Nessa's story.

I want to shout for help, to kick down the door, to save her. But I know I mustn't. I can't. This has happened before. The fire, Nessa's death. It's simply being replayed. One cannot edit a movie purely because one doesn't like the ending.

It is written in the *Book of Life*.

*

I leave Ned's dressing room. Smoke is escaping through the gap beneath Gilda's door. Nessa is trying to open it. She then begins to scream.

I clutch my stomach, the bile rising.

I do the only thing I am able to do. Run. I run away and leave Nessa to her fate.

I must save Eddie now.

Panic seizes me like cold hands winding around my neck. I no longer have feeling in my body.

It's time to go.

I stagger through double doors and up the flight of stairs. I follow my intuition, not knowing where it's taking me, but trusting that it's taking Eddie to safety. I blunder down the corridor, tears distorting my vision so that the theatre looks like it's under water. I open the nearest door. The box within is dark. I blink in rapid succession to clear my sight. The play has begun. The witches are on stage. Smoke is swirling around them like spectres. Lady Faversham is watching them through theatre glasses. Cavill is seated beside her. He turns. Our eyes meet.

I hold his gaze for a second, then, drowning in regret and misery, I close mine for the final time.

Good-bye, my love.

I will myself out of Eddie's body. I will myself up up up, into the beautifully moulded ceiling of the Aphrodite, which will now be destroyed by fire. I have done my duty, but at the same time broken my heart. I don't know how I will survive it.

I see Eddie collapse and Cavill rise out of his seat and rush to her aid.

Up I go. Up up up. I leave them all behind. In the past.

I'm a feather on the breeze, light and gentle and free. Into the ether I go, towards the veil that separates their time from mine. Seamlessly, I slip through it. For a blissful moment I am without a body. Without pain and hurt and heartbreak. I'm pure consciousness and it's blissful.

Then I open my eyes, and I'm as heavy as an anvil.

The Present

Chapter Twenty-Three

Ulysses was so engrossed in his film that he didn't notice Pixie opening her eyes. She blinked in confusion, taking in the room and her old friend in front of his laptop. It would take a while to comprehend where she was, and what she'd put herself through. It would take longer to shed the anguish that she had brought with her – the only thing she'd brought with her. Anguish and a heart torn to pieces; everything else was gone.

She took a deep but gentle breath, aware of the pain in her chest and treating it with care, as if she'd just come out of surgery. She felt as if she had awoken from a nightmare and yet was still halfway inside it; one foot in the old Aphrodite, one foot in the new. It was taking longer than usual to orientate herself. For her heartbeat to slow down. For her torment to diminish in the tranquillity of the present and the comforting sight of her dear friend on the armchair.

'Ulysses.'

He lifted his eyes off the screen, smiled in surprise, and took out his AirPods. 'You're back,' he said.

She could not return his smile. 'How long was I gone for?'

He glanced at the clock on his screen. 'Nearly three hours.'

'Five days,' she returned.

'And how was it?' He might as well have been asking about a party.

She shrugged and sighed pitifully. 'Not good.'

'You didn't find out what happened to Nessa Blunt?'

'I found out what happened to *her*. But I told Cavill the truth.'

Ulysses grimaced. 'How did he take it?' He registered her miserable expression. 'Oh dear. Did you fuck up?'

She nodded. Then burst into tears.

Ulysses went to put his arms around her. He crouched down and drew her into his embrace. She was small and wretched enough to be swallowed by it. 'What would you do without me, eh?' he asked, nuzzling her pink hair. 'Always here to pick up the pieces. Dependable old moi!'

He chuckled, but Pixie, usually roused out of sorrow by her funny friend, was inconsolable.

He gave her time. Grief was not something to be rushed. It needed to work its way through her at its own pace. When, eventually, the howling diminished to soft whimpering, he released her. 'Do you want to tell me about it?' he asked.

She nodded and wiped her eyes. He took the chair beside her, crossed his legs and folded his hands in his lap. His compassionate face made her want to cry all over again.

'It was dreadful,' she said. 'I told him who I am, that I was Hermione and Constance, and that I had started something that I had to end. And ending it meant telling him the truth.'

'I don't imagine he believed you.'

'Of course not.'

'If someone told me they came from the future I'd laugh in their face. Except *I* wouldn't laugh, because I know *you*. But if I didn't know you, I'd laugh.'

'Why did I ever think he'd believe me.' She shook her head and took a staggered breath before letting it out in a loud sigh.

'So, who were you?'

'Eddie Skipton. Widow. Pretty. Husband died in the war. He had owned the theatre. Cavill bought it for his young wife, Gilda Garrett.'

'He married again?'

'He did.'

'What was she like?'

'Gorgeous. Beautiful. Sweet. But not talented. In fact, she had no talent at all. Nessa was talented. She could have become a great actress. But her father wanted her to be conventional, marry, have kids. He didn't want her on the stage. God, women had it bad in those days. Gilda was having an affair with Taran Bentley, the director. Nessa was in love with Bentley. I mean, obsessed with him. I read her diary. She was crazy about him. Then she spied him and Gilda having sex in the theatre and was absolutely heartbroken. They were to perform *Macbeth* . . .'

'Get out of here!' Ulysses exclaimed in astonishment, slapping his thigh.

'The plot thickens,' said Pixie, finding a path out of her misery and taking it. She proceeded to tell him in detail about that fateful night. About Nessa being the understudy and Gilda the leading lady. About Gilda and Nessa having a fight, Nessa threatening to tell Cavill about her affair, Gilda locking Nessa in her dressing room and Nessa throwing the lamp at the door in fury. 'I think it must have been the lamp,' said Pixie. 'It was the only flame in the room. Gilda lit it for luck.'

'It didn't bring her much luck that night, did it?' Ulysses could find the funny in the situation because he was so far removed from it. To him it happened ninety-one years ago. To Pixie it was merely minutes and her whole being still reverberated from the shock.

'My theory is that Nessa has been drawn out of wherever she was lingering, to seek revenge on Gilda by tormenting Isadora, who is American, like Gilda was, and the leading lady in *Macbeth*.'

Ulysses nodded thoughtfully and grinned. 'Very good, detective inspector Tate.'

Pixie laughed. Ulysses' smile was impossible to resist for long.

'So, what happens now?' he asked, getting up.

'I confront Nessa.'

'And she trips off into the light, as they all eventually do.'

'That's the idea.'

'Great. I'll go and tell Emma what you've found out and meet you in the foyer when you're done.'

'Good.'

*

When Ulysses stepped into the foyer, Emma, Leila, Lezli and Isadora were just coming through the big doors. Isadora's face lit up when she saw him. 'Ulysses!' she exclaimed, striding towards him with a dazzling smile especially designed to bewitch him. 'Are you done?'

'Pixie's back,' he replied. 'And she's found out some fascinating things.'

'So have we,' said Leila.

They gathered on the crimson and gold carpet to compare notes. 'So, what does Pixie say happened.'

Ulysses put his hands on his hips, finding amusement in the four eager faces staring at him expectantly. They resembled baby birds in a nest when the mother arrives to feed them. 'Well,' he began slowly to make the most impact, 'Nessa Blunt was an actress. Pixie said she had the talent to be a really good actress, but her father didn't want her to have a career on the stage – I imagine he didn't want her to have a career at all. He wanted her to marry well and have kids. Cavill Pengower owned the theatre and Gilda Garrett was his young wife . . .'

Isadora made to speak but Leila jabbed her with her elbow. 'Not yet, Isadora,' she said. 'Let's hear what Ulysses has to say before you add anything.'

Isadora pursed her lips crossly. She wasn't used to being overruled.

'Gilda Garrett was a beautiful but talentless actress. Nessa was her understudy. Nessa was in love with the director, called Taran Bentley, who was having an affair with Gilda. Goodness, you couldn't make it up,' he added with a chuckle. 'Nessa and Gilda were having a fight in Gilda's dressing room on the opening night of . . . wait for it . . . *Macbeth*.' The women didn't seem surprised to hear that. Ulysses was disappointed. 'Well, *I* thought that was an astonishing coincidence, although, if you knew Pixie like I do, you would know that there is no such thing as coincidence. Anyway, they had a fight. Nessa said that if Gilda didn't let her play the lead then she would tell Cavill that his wife was having an affair with the director. Gilda left the room and locked it behind her. Nessa, in fury, threw something at the door. Pixie thinks it was Gilda's lucky lamp. Not very lucky, as it turned out.' He laughed at his joke, but none of the women laughed with him. They were staring at him with wide, incredulous eyes.

'Oh my God!' Isadora exclaimed. 'Can we just process this a moment?'

Emma smiled, relieved. 'This is momentous.'

'Is it?' said Ulysses.

'Emma and I went to the *Seacombe Gazette*,' said Leila. 'We read the newspapers and discovered that Nessa's body was found in Gilda Garrett's dressing room. They later discovered that the fire had been started by a lamp.'

'Gilda's lucky lamp,' said Lezli and grinned at Ulysses.

'And Gilda was my great-grandmother,' Isadora announced triumphantly.

'What the actual f—?' Ulysses gasped, frowning at Isadora.

'Exactly what we said,' Emma laughed at Ulysses' successful stifling of the swearword.

Isadora continued, loving being the centre of attention again. 'Gilda married Taran Bentley, my great-grandfather, and they had my grandmother Judy in nineteen twenty-four.'

'The year after the fire,' said Leila ponderously.

'That makes sense,' said Ulysses. 'Gilda gets pregnant, leaves her husband and runs off to America with Bentley.'

'Wow!' Isadora exclaimed. 'That's awesome. Wait till I tell my mother.'

'So Nessa is sabotaging Isadora because she's Gilda's great-granddaughter?' said Emma.

'How would she know that?' asked Lezli.

'Maybe spirits know stuff,' said Ulysses. 'We'll have to ask Pixie.'

'Pixie!' said Emma. 'When will she be done?'

They all looked to the door at the back of the foyer. 'As soon as she's moved Nessa on,' said Ulysses. 'Shouldn't be long. I imagine this is an easy job. Trust me, she's had harder ones. This one's a piece of cake!'

*

Pixie sat in the upholstered chair once again and stretched out her arms. She moved her hands, turning them this way and that, releasing the ache in her joints from having been in the same position for almost three hours. She pushed the vision of Cavill's stricken face out of her mind and closed her eyes. She had a job to finish. She would think of Cavill and lick her wounds when she was done. Right now, she had to show Nessa the way home.

Pixie took three deep breaths, right into the bottom of her lungs. She focused her attention on her heart and imagined her chest filling with light. Gradually, the light grew, expanding around her torso and slowly building about her entire body. From there it extended out into the room, until the entire space was filled with a radiant, dazzling light. Into that light Pixie invited Nessa to step.

She did not have to wait long; Nessa had never left.

I am here. Where did you *go?*

I went into the past.

Into my *past?*

Yes.

What did you see?

Everything. I saw Gilda lock the door and I heard you throw something against it.

Gilda's green lamp.

Yes. That lamp started the fire.

Gilda murdered me.

Well, I wouldn't say it was murder. She didn't intend to kill you.

She didn't come and let me out. She left me to die behind that locked door.

She was having an affair with Taran Bentley, whom you loved.

I loved him with all my heart, and she stole him from me. She stole everything from me.

Pixie felt Nessa's energy grow anguished and decided to backtrack a little.

You were a talented actress, Nessa.

I was, wasn't I?

Bentley said you were the finest Lady Macbeth he'd ever seen.

He wanted to take me to London. He was going to promote me. If Gilda hadn't killed me, I would have performed in the West End. I might even have been great.

I'm sure you would have been.

And I would have married Bentley.

Perhaps.

But Gilda ruined everything. Because of her I died, and Papa never got to see me perform. He would have understood then why I wanted a career on the stage, and he would have supported me. Gilda stole my future.

Is that why you tormented Isadora?

Isadora is Gilda's blood.

Pixie was blindsided. This wasn't what she expected to hear. *Isadora is related to Gilda?*

Taran married Gilda because she was pregnant with his child.

Pixie remembered Gilda's tears, and tried to recall the atmosphere between her and Bentley when she found them alone together, first at Gilda's house and later, in her dressing room. Did she know then that she was carrying his child?

How did you find that out?

The dead have ears, you know. I stuck around. I wasn't going anywhere. I listened. I watched. I learned.

If Nessa knew that, then she would know what happened to Eddie, wouldn't she? Pixie barely dared breathe for fear of what Nessa might tell her.

What happened to Eddie Skipton after the fire?

Skippy? Skippy left Seacombe. I don't know where she went.

Those words cut Pixie deeply. How she wanted to turn the clock back and reverse the damage she had done. Had it been worth it? She might have found out what happened to Nessa, but at what cost to Eddie and Cavill?

She stiffened her jaw in an attempt to stifle the remorse that now rose into her throat.

After the divorce Cavill sold the theatre and eventually his home. I don't know what happened to him, either.

Pixie knew that Nessa sensed her distress like a hound smells blood and was taking pleasure from it. Unhappy people thrive on the unhappiness of others.

So, you want to punish Gilda through her granddaughter?

Great-*granddaughter,* Nessa corrected.

Are you sure they're related?

I know it. Judy, Gilda's daughter, visited this place when she was a young woman. She wanted to learn about her mother, she said. She came here but she didn't stay long. But she stayed long enough to strike up a friendship with Madge.

Madge? Madge who makes the tea?

The very same. Madge was a child then, helping out about the theatre, sewing badly and assisting her father with the stage sets and props. Judy told them all about her mother, Gilda Garrett, and what an accomplished actress she was. I would have told them the truth, but they couldn't hear me. I tried to make myself heard. Some managed to see me. There are always those who can. But I got tired of haunting the place. It gets boring after a while. After years. Decades.

If it's so dull, why don't you go home?

Because there's nothing for me there.

Life is a stage, Nessa. And you have stepped off it. The people you shared that stage with are now in spirit, waiting for you to join them. There is so much love for you there.

They never showed me love in life, why would they in death?

Because it's not death. It's life, after life. There is *only life. We're all here, on earth, to learn from each other. When we have completed what we came here to do, we go home. You completed your life, Nessa. Now you must go home. I think you'll find that home is a place of love and forgiveness.*

I'll never forgive Gilda for what she did. And love her? Never!

As long as your heart is hard, Nessa, you will only hurt yourself.

I'm not hurting. I'm enjoying hurting Isadora.

But she isn't Gilda.

She is her blood.

She has done nothing to harm you.

She is Gilda's descendant. That is enough. That's as close as I'm going to get. As long as she's playing Lady Macbeth, I will torment her.

How did you discover that Isadora is Judy's granddaughter?

You think you're so clever, Pixie Tate. You have a gift, of that there is no doubt. But it's limited. You're still in your body. I am no longer in mine, and what freedom there is without it. I know more than you can imagine. You may be able to travel through time. You may be able to see ghosts. But you cannot imagine what it is like to be me. Nessa laughed scornfully. *Madge is my informant. She doesn't know it, of course. But those letters that Judy wrote to her right up until her death only a few years ago, were full of information. She was proud of her granddaughter Isadora Nash. She hoped she would become a big star in New York. Madge knows that Isadora is Gilda's great-granddaughter. She knows more than she's telling. She's as sly as an old vixen, that one.*

Why would she keep it secret? What's the point of that?

Because she doesn't like Isadora. No one likes Isadora. And Madge likes having me around. But she needn't worry because I'm not going anywhere. I'm staying right here.

You're determined to get rid of Isadora?

Of course. She won't want to perform again once I've finished with her.

And then you'll move on?

No. I'm staying.

To torment other actors too?

Just Isadora Nash. Gilda's great-granddaughter. She deserves it. She's not a nice person. She was horrid to Madge, and I like Madge. I like Madge very much. She's the only person, besides you and the other useless mediums who have failed to convince me to leave, who talks to me. Madge talks to me a lot.

Please, Nessa. I can't bear to leave you here in darkness, when you can float up on the light.

You all speak about light and dark. Life and death. Spirit and growth. I'm bored of it all. Leave me alone. Leave me to my fun. I can be a great actress here. I am a great actress here. It's all I ever wanted, and no one can stop me. Not even you.

With that she vanished.

*

Pixie opened her eyes. The room felt warm again. And empty. Nessa had gone.

Pixie had failed her. Not only had she failed Nessa, but she had failed Cavill and Eddie too. With a sick heart, she pushed herself off the chair and made her way to the door. She didn't know how she was going to explain to Emma that she hadn't managed to move Nessa on. She didn't care about the money, because of course she wouldn't charge them for her failure. She cared about Nessa's soul. And she cared about Cavill and Eddie, who, had it not been for Pixie's intervention, might have found happiness together. It was dreadful, and she felt guilty right to the marrow of her bones.

She found Ulysses in the foyer talking to Isadora, Leila, Lezli and Emma. They stopped what they were saying and looked at her with eager anticipation. 'Did you do it?' Emma asked.

Pixie shook her head. 'I'm afraid she doesn't want to leave.'

Emma was crestfallen. 'She's still here?'

Pixie looked at Isadora. 'You're Gilda Garrett's great-granddaughter, aren't you?' she said.

Isadora's beautiful mouth fell open. 'How do you know that?'

'Nessa told me. It makes sense. Gilda was the lead in *Macbeth* back in 1923, plus she was having an affair with Taran Bentley, the man Nessa loved. I think Gilda was pregnant with his child, your grandmother Judy. Nessa believes Gilda not only stole Bentley from her and the part she wanted to play, but Gilda also locked her in the dressing room which then caught fire when Nessa threw an oil lamp at the door. Technically, Nessa started the fire herself, but she couldn't escape the room because Gilda had locked the door. Nessa is taking out her anger on you, Isadora.'

Leila shook her head. 'Well, I never. You've got me now, Pixie. You're an extraordinary medium.'

'But what do we do about the ghost?' Isadora demanded. 'Is she going to ruin my performance again?'

'She's going to ruin every performance, as long as you're here,' said Pixie. 'I'm sorry, Isadora. This is the first time I haven't been able to rescue a lost soul.'

Ulysses, sensing her disappointment, put a comforting hand on her upper arm.

Isadora glared at her. 'You make it sound so romantic. Really, she's not a lost soul. She's a bitch! A ghost-bitch! Well, I'm not going to let her ruin my career. I'm going to continue regardless. She can go to hell!'

Their attention was diverted by the sound of someone tactfully clearing their throat. They turned to see a tall, handsome young man of about thirty, with light brown hair and very blue eyes, standing a few feet away. Pixie's breath caught in her throat and her heart lurched. For a second she thought it was Cavill.

'Excuse me. Sorry to interrupt.' He had an American accent, and a deep, masculine voice. 'I'm looking for Pixie Tate.'

Pixie knew she had seen him before, and she knew where. 'I know you,' she said, a moment in her memory lighting up bright and clear. 'You were at the pond in Central Park. Back in October last year. I was on the Bethesda steps. I thought you were someone I knew – or used to know.'

'Pink hair!' he exclaimed and smiled with recollection. Pixie's heart lurched again at the uncanny resemblance.

'Are you Pixie Tate?'

'I am.'

'Okay, here goes.' He looked embarrassed. 'I'm just the messenger, right?' He pulled an envelope out of the inside pocket of his black cashmere coat. The paper looked old, as if it belonged to another age. He handed it to Pixie. She looked at the writing and knew instantly who it was from.

Deliver to Pixie Tate. Aphrodite Theatre, Seacombe, Cornwall, on 26th October 2014. By hand.

Pixie stared at the young man in amazement. 'Who are you?'

'Felix Fairhaven. This letter was written by my great-grandfather, Cavill Pengower, in 1924, and left in his will, with instructions to deliver it here, on this day. He used to own this place, but it was destroyed by fire in 1923. The letter has been kept safely by my family for all these years, but as you can imagine, we are all eager to know what it says. It's not normal to write a letter for someone ninety-one years into the future.' He looked steadily at Pixie and grinned. 'I should really be asking who *you* are.'

Pixie's mouth was dry suddenly. She felt her heartbeat pounding in her throat. She took a breath. 'Your grandmother was Josephine, Cavill's daughter?'

'Yes,' he replied.

Pixie nodded and looked down at the letter then back at him. 'I need to be alone to read it.'

'Of course. I'm staying at The Regency hotel tonight and then heading to London for a week, before flying back to New York. I'll be staying at Claridge's. I'll give you my card, should you wish to speak to me. Like I said, my family and I are really curious to know what this is about.' He pulled out an enamel case and handed Pixie a white card with his name and details embossed in gold lettering. He fixed her with his sapphire blue eyes. 'Anytime. I look forward to hearing from you.'

Pixie watched him leave. She felt light-headed. He had his great-grandfather's walk, too.

'Do you want me to come with you?' Ulysses asked.

'No,' Pixie replied. She didn't feel she was present anymore. She was somewhere between the past and the now, and it was discombobulating. 'I need to be alone.'

'*Who* is it from?' Leila asked as Pixie left the foyer to return to the VIP room.

'An old friend,' Ulysses said. 'A *very* old friend.'

Chapter Twenty-Four

Pixie returned to the chair in the VIP room and sat down. With trembling fingers she tore open the envelope and pulled out the letter. Her vision misted as she felt Cavill's vibration through his handwriting; indeed, the very paper seemed to carry his essence. Thus, he came back to her in a wave of memory, and her heart ached with longing and tenderness, and regret too. Searing regret for the way they had parted.

5th December 1924

To the soul of my soul, Pixie.

I promised you I would recognise you if you were a light among a million lights. But when the moment came, I did not.

But let me start at the beginning. I have time, after all; you are ninety years into the future.

That strange conversation we had last year, on the evening of the fire that destroyed The Aphrodite and took the life of Nessa Blunt, has repeated itself in my mind a thousand times over the last nineteen months. During those incessant examinations, I have analysed with the focus of an obsessive scientist the behaviour of both Hermione and Constance, as you described them to me. I have searched for the truth and every time I have doubted it, another clue has surfaced to prove that that which my mind tells me is impossible, is, in fact, an extraordinary feat of paranormal experience, which no scientist could ever substantiate. It was only when my brother, Ivan, sent me A. A. Milne's book of poetry, When We Were

Very Young, with a note to read the twenty-fifth poem, 'The King's Breakfast', that I realised, without a shadow of doubt, that you had been speaking the truth. That book was only published this year. How could you have known that poem in 1895 if you didn't come from the future? You are, indeed, a time traveller, and I'm sorry I didn't believe you.

I have had many dark nights of the soul, Pixie. Haunted by memories of my beloved Hermione, and of Constance, to whom I lost my heart aboard the ill-fated Titanic. I realise now that it was you I loved. A deep soul connection that I didn't recognise, but felt all the same, in the very core of my being. You asked me what I was going to say to Constance on the Bethesda steps in New York. I was going to tell her – to tell you – that I loved you. That I couldn't explain why so profound a feeling could come over me so suddenly, but that I could only surrender to it. I was going to ask you to marry me.

As you rightly pointed out, Eddie and I fell in love before you 'appeared', and in my blindness, I lost her. In my stubborn refusal to believe you, I blamed Eddie for her moment of what I could only describe as madness, and she left Seacombe and my life, which has, in the months since, been dreadfully dark. I miss her with all my heart.

I miss you, too, Pixie. I fear I will never find you again. You said you had to finish what you started in loving me, and I fear that you have succeeded. I confess, I search for you in the faces of strangers, but so far I have not found you. I am certain now that if you return, I will know you. I will know you as I know myself. We are one.

I will leave this letter in my will, with instructions that my descendants deliver it to you, by hand, on the 26th October 2014, at the Aphrodite Theatre in Seacombe. If it has the good fortune of finding you there, I have an idea that might appeal to you.

Return to me, dearest one, on the 5th December 1924. I am at home, writing this letter at my desk. It is quiet. No one is in the house. I have given the servants the evening off. It is snowing. It is quite beautiful. Feathery flakes fall like fat feathers in the glow of the streetlamps. I call to you from the past with all my heart. I hope

that my longing is enough. I would like to say good-bye.
I wait for you now.
Cavill

Pixie's heart was thumping so hard against her ribs, it reverberated throughout her entire body. Her eyes were swimming in tears so that the words were now smudges of black ink on the paper. Would it be possible to engineer a slide to that specific time and place? Even Avril hadn't known exactly how to do that, and Pixie hadn't yet achieved that kind of mastery over her art.

Avril's words came back to her then: *You won't be free of each other until you allow your love to fully and honestly express itself.* Didn't that mean that both she *and* Cavill had to recognise each other on the level of the soul?

She had to recognise *him*, and *he* had to recognise *her.* Until that moment they were still tied together. Until that moment, the Law of Attraction was still active in its drive to bring them together.

She was quivering with excitement now.

She closed her eyes and took three deep breaths, in through the nose, out through the mouth. She steadied her jumping nerves, focusing on her heart centre, imagining the light expanding into every corner of her body and radiating out into the room. She thought of Cavill, of him writing in his study in that beautiful white house in Seacombe. And she realised then, in a flash of enlightenment, that tailoring her slides was not about knowledge, but about purity of heart and intention. It was about her state of consciousness. About love.

With this awareness dissolving her uncertainty, as sunshine dissolves fog, she was no longer her mind, but her emotions, and on that ray of intense feeling, she floated out of her body and into the realm of the eternal. With her whole being pulsating with joy, she slipped through the veil. To Cavill.

She knew without any doubt that she would find him because he was pulling her to him, and she was willing herself there. With those two forces working in tandem, they couldn't fail to be reunited.

The Past

Chapter Twenty-Five

It is indeed snowing. There are fat, feathery flakes in the golden halos around the streetlamps. I'm standing outside Brambling House. I look down at my red coat and boots, at my hands and wrists, and recognise myself at once. I'm Eddie Skipton. The relief is overwhelming. I feel as if I've come home.

It must be 1924. I've been given another chance.

I hurry through the snow to the front door. The lights of the house blaze through the night, illuminating the frost that's formed in icy designs around the edges of the windowpanes. I imagine Cavill at his desk, writing his letter to me in the future, and my whole being burns with hope.

I pull the bell, and with that my throat tightens. Will he be home? What if Gilda comes to answer the door? Can I have engineered this slide with such precision? Is it even possible?

I wait. The seconds pass with agonising slowness. I had been so certain, but perhaps I'm wrong.

I hear footsteps behind the door. The metallic sound of unbolting and the rattling of a chain. It opens. Cavill stares at me in astonishment.

'Eddie?' he exclaims.

'Pixie,' I reply.

His eyes widen and his lips part, but he cannot find the words, so great is his wonder.

So, I find the words for him.

'"*To the soul of my soul, Pixie.*

I promised you I would recognise you if you were a light among a million lights. But when the moment came, I did not."'

Encouraged by the deep affection in his gaze, I throw myself into his arms and feel him wrapping his around me, pulling me close. So close and so tight that he almost squeezes the air out of my lungs. He nuzzles my neck. 'Soul of my soul,' he murmurs.

Without parting, he kicks the door shut. We remain entwined. I can feel his heart beating against my chest, and my own, quickening to harmonise with his.

'I'm sorry I didn't recognise you,' he says, pulling away so that he can take in my face. However, it isn't my face that draws his attention, but my eyes. 'Oh Pixie, I never saw you before,' he says, sinking deeper into them. 'But now I do. How ever did I not see you before?'

Something warm breaks in my chest and leaks into every part of my body, like the cracking of an egg. His recognition is like a beam of light, penetrating my very soul.

'How long do we have?' he asks.

'I don't know,' I reply. 'Long enough to say good-bye.'

He shakes his head and frowns. 'Will I ever see you again?'

'Not in this life. But I have brought Eddie back to you. I don't know how. But I have. It was because of me that you lost her. I'm happy that I'm able to reunite you.'

'You will always be a part of Eddie, Pixie. As I love Eddie, I will also, at the same time, be loving you.' He chuckles. 'No one but you would understand that. How do you do it, Pixie? How do you travel through time?'

'I don't really know. It's something I've always been able to do. But I never expected to fall in love with you. I never expected to meet you again as Constance, and then finally as Eddie. But you understand now why I must end it?'

He nods. 'I do.'

'There is so much more to our existence than we realise. This earthly life is just a tiny part of our great adventure. One day we will find each other again. Love connects us in a never-ending bond, Cavill. It is so much bigger than we humans can imagine. So much bigger.'

He presses his lips to mine, for words are inadequate in the giant glow of feeling. I close my eyes.

Suddenly I feel as if my heart is on fire. An agonising heat burns me on the inside, consuming me, as if I'm melting. I open my eyes. One final look into those of my beloved and then everything goes black.

The Present

Chapter Twenty-Six

Ulysses panicked. He hadn't realised Pixie was in trance. He hadn't meant to disturb her. He'd simply come in to ask about the letter. Now she was on the floor, having a fit, and he didn't know what to do. A nasty sense of déjà vu came over him. He'd been here before, when Zach interrupted her at St Sidwell. Quickly, he knelt beside her and put his hands on her shoulders to pacify her. What if she swallowed her tongue?

'Pix, it's me, Ulysses. Come back!' He tried to hold her steady, but she was writhing about like an electric eel, eyes wide open but unseeing, mouth agape in a silent scream. It was terrifying to see her like that, possessed. 'Please don't die, Pixie. Please don't die. Just don't die on me, please!'

Suddenly, she closed her eyes and went limp. He stared at her in horror.

'Please don't die,' he whimpered again. 'Pixie, please don't die. Not on my watch. Come on, Pix. Come back!'

For a terrible moment it appeared as if she wouldn't. But then two pink stains spread into her white cheeks.

Pixie opened her eyes to see Ulysses' staring down at her. She blinked hard, not sure where she was. Ulysses' ashen face flushed with colour. 'You're alive!' he exclaimed and cupped her face with hot, sweaty hands. 'Ah, *graças ao Senhor!*' When a tear landed on Pixie's forehead, she was fully roused out of her fit.

'What the hell?' she muttered, pushing herself into a sitting position and wiping her forehead.

Ulysses flopped onto the floor beside her with relief. 'Oh my God, you terrified the hell out of me, Pixie!'

'What happened?' she asked, taking in the room. Returning fully to the present.

'I didn't know you were in trance! You might have warned me. I came in to find out what the letter said . . .'

She put her fingers to her lips. 'Cavill,' she whispered, feeling the remains of his kiss, now cold. 'The letter!'

The letter had fallen beside her chair. She reached to pick it up. Then she gave it to Ulysses to read.

They sat side by side, in silence. Ulysses engrossed in the letter, Pixie in Cavill and the miracle that had just taken place.

She had been given the opportunity to say good-bye, but how fleeting it had been.

'Wow,' Ulysses exclaimed when he had finished. 'So, you went back one last time?'

'I did,' she replied.

'And?'

'It was beautiful.' She smiled softly at the memory of that final meeting. She couldn't begin to explain how she had reunited Cavill and Eddie, so she didn't bother. That story was one she would keep to herself.

'So, is it over?' he asked, handing back the letter.

Pixie could only nod. Her vision misted with tears. She pressed a hand to her heart, which felt confusingly full and broken at the same time.

Ulysses understood. She needed a moment. He drew her into his arms and held her close.

'I think we should leave now,' she said at last, slipping the letter back into the envelope and getting up.

'What are you going to do about Felix Fairhaven?' he asked, pushing himself off the floor.

'I'll tell him the truth.'

Ulysses looked at her in surprise as he opened the door. 'You're actually going to tell a total stranger that you timeslide?'

She shrugged, and grinned. 'Yes. And I have a funny feeling that he'll believe me.'

Emma, Leila, Lezli and Isadora were still in the lobby. Now they had been joined by Joseph.

'We're dying to know what's in the letter,' said Emma eagerly.

'We've brought Joey up to date,' said Isadora. 'And I've told him that I'm not going to let Nessa Blunt win.'

Ulysses chuckled. 'Good luck with that, Isadora. Personally, I wouldn't want to have a fight with a ghost!'

Isadora smiled. 'I've fought with people all my life. This is nothing I can't handle.'

'The letter?' Emma said, her eyes dropping to the envelope Pixie still held in her hand.

'It's a long story,' Pixie replied. 'But let's just say it's concluded a beautiful relationship.' With those words Pixie felt a surge of enthusiasm and positivity, as if she'd shed something heavy that she had been carrying for many months. She felt light, and free.

Pixie turned to Joseph. 'I'm sorry I haven't been able to move Nessa on. It's a first for me, honestly. I've never not been able to solve a case. But this spirit simply doesn't want to leave.'

Joseph didn't care much about the ghost. In spite of his wife's explanation, he still refused to believe it. He just wanted these two to leave, so he could get back to his job. 'You did your best,' he said with a smile. 'That's all anyone can ever ask. Thank you for coming. Emma will drive you to the station.'

Leila insisted on accompanying them. She didn't want to miss a moment, in case Pixie revealed something Emma would later forget to share. The four of them stood on the platform while they waited for the train. 'Madge will be happy you failed to move Nessa on,' Leila said, putting her hands in her pockets to warm them. 'Now I know why she talks to herself all the time. She's talking to Nessa.'

'That's the silver lining,' said Ulysses with a laugh.

'Will she eventually find her way home?' Emma asked.

'She will,' Pixie replied. 'In her own time. What I failed to realise is that she's not lost at all. She knows exactly where to go. And she'll go when she's ready.'

The train came at speed down the track, pulling up alongside the platform in a great gust of cold wind. Emma put her hand on Pixie's arm. 'I feel bad not paying you for your time,' she said.

Pixie smiled. 'I promise you, I got more out of this assignment than you can possibly imagine. More than money could ever buy.'

Emma frowned, longing for her to elaborate. 'Really?'

Pixie embraced her. 'Really.' She embraced Leila, too. 'Thank you,' she said. 'Thank you, both.' But neither knew quite how grateful she was, or what she was grateful for.

Pixie and Ulysses waved as the train moved out of the station.

'This assignment was never about Nessa,' said Ulysses thoughtfully. 'It was about you.'

'It was,' said Pixie.

'Poor Isadora,' he added. 'She's going to get a nasty surprise tonight.'

Pixie looked doubtful. 'Actually, I have a feeling it's going to be the other way round.'

Pixie pulled Felix Fairhaven's business card out of her pocket and looked at it.

'The Universe moves in extraordinary ways,' said Ulysses, grinning mischievously.

'What do you mean?'

'Henry lives in New York. Felix lives in New York. I like Henry. You will like Felix. Just saying. Coincidence? I think not. The Universe brought him to you. You should say thank you.'

Pixie laughed. 'You're always running with the ball,' she said.

'But what a ball!'

'What a ball,' she agreed, turning her eyes to the window. 'What a ball,' she repeated. 'Why don't you listen to your music while I try and make sense of it.'

Ulysses put his AirPods into his ears and nodded. 'I don't think you need to be a time-travelling genius to work it out, Pix. Even I can do that.'

But she needed time. It was a lot to take in. As the train whizzed through the English countryside, she closed her eyes and slowly began to review all the remarkable things that had happened.

Isadora sat at the mirror in her dressing room. She was made up and ready to go on stage. While Lezli had been fussing over her, she had thought of nothing but Nessa Blunt and her great-grandmother, Gilda Garrett. Having dismissed the spirit as a ludicrous figment of the imagination, she was now convinced that Pixie was, after all, right. The ghost of Nessa Blunt did haunt the theatre, and was, most certainly, tormenting *her*. But, in a moment of rare clarity, Isadora believed that there might be a way to stop her.

If her great-grandmother had started it, perhaps it was up to Isadora to finish it.

'Lezli, would you leave me for a moment, please?'

Lezli frowned in surprise. Not because she'd been asked to leave, but because Isadora had said 'please'. 'Sure,' she replied, and left the room.

Isadora remained in her chair. She placed her elbows on the dressing table and knitted her fingers in prayer. Then she closed her eyes and took a moment to steady herself, inhaling deeply and concentrating on relaxing her body, and all the muscles in it. She spoke out loud, because she wasn't sure that, if she simply thought the words, Nessa would hear her.

'Nessa Blunt,' she began quietly. 'I know you've been wrecking my scenes, and that's okay. I probably deserve it. I haven't exactly made friends here, so why should I expect *you* to be a friend? If you've been trying to teach me a lesson, you've succeeded. I give you that, girl. You're a formidable opponent.' She took another deep breath, feeling strangely emotional suddenly. 'For my sins, I'm Gilda Garrett's great-granddaughter. But you know that already, don't you? Look, I'm sorry she stole the man you loved. I'm sorry she locked you in her dressing room and I'm sorry that she didn't help you when the theatre burned down. With all my heart, Nessa, I'm sorry you had to die. Truly, I can't think of a more horrible way to go. You must have suffered terribly. My great-grandmother isn't here to apologise. I hope, if she was, that she would say sorry and mean it. If it's any consolation, she died of alcohol abuse. She can't have been happy. Maybe she was riddled with guilt for what she did to you. Who knows? But I'm here now, and I can say sorry on her behalf. I hope it goes some way to making you feel better about it all. I'd really like you to find peace in a beautiful place. I believe there is somewhere we all go. It's gotta be nicer than here, right? Anyway, I felt I had to say it. I hope you can hear me. I'm not like Pinkie, or Pixie – whatever her name was. I'm not like her. I can't talk to ghosts. At least, I've never tried. I'd really appreciate it if you stopped wrecking my scenes. I'd really like us to be friends. A strange kind of friendship, I know, but we could work together, rather than against each other.' She sat in silence for a moment. She didn't expect to hear anything back, but oddly, she didn't feel as if she'd been speaking to herself, either.

Just before the play began, Isadora found the three witches in the wing, waiting to go on stage. The place was quiet, the curtain was about to go up, the warmth of the full auditorium reached them with the smell of perfume and dust burning on the footlights. 'Girls,' she whispered. They turned to her in surprise. 'Listen, I'm sorry I blamed you for ruining my scenes. I was a bitch.' The witches stared at her in astonishment.

'That's okay,' said Rebecca. 'At least I had an opportunity to play Lady Macbeth.'

'I hear you did a great job,' Isadora replied. 'I hope it goes smoothly tonight. There's no knowing. Anyway, break a leg.'

They grinned, more in surprise than anything else. 'Look, let's have a drink sometime,' said Rebecca. It was in all of their interests that they called a truce.

'I'd like that,' said Isadora.

*

When it was Isadora's turn to go on stage she did so with a shiver of trepidation. Would Nessa do her worst? Might Isadora's words have made a difference? She held the letter in her hand, lifted her chin, and recited her lines more ardently than she had ever done before. The audience was enraptured. Not even a cough broke the silence in the auditorium. Isadora held on to the letter, anticipating it to be whipped out of her fingers at any moment. But it wasn't. The chair didn't move either. Everything was as it should be.

Emma and Leila sat in the stalls, both watching the play closely through opera glasses. To their relief the stage was undisturbed by supernatural forces and the theatre was warm. Joseph was relieved too. When the play ended and the audience leapt to their feet for a rapturous standing ovation, he clapped louder than he had ever clapped. It had been a triumph.

The curtain came down. The actors turned to congratulate each other. Edward Rye embraced Isadora. He had never done that before. 'You were tremendous, Isadora,' he gushed. 'You gave the performance of your life.'

From the captivity of his hold, Isadora looked over his shoulder. Her eyes fell onto the chair. It stood alone at the other side of the stage. She was sure she saw it move. Very slightly. As if someone had just got up from it.

Epilogue

Pixie sat on the train as it made its way from London to Manchester. Ulysses' words about giving her mother the chance to explain her side of the story had made a deep impression. He was right, she certainly would kick herself if she left the world having missed the opportunity to make peace with her. Wasn't the purpose of life to learn and grow from the challenges and obstacles thrown into one's path? This was just one of those challenges that needed to be overcome.

During her journey back to London, Pixie had realised that her experience with Cavill had also taught her much about life and love. Both were complicated. Life was never without trials and love, as we knew it, was never straightforward. But there was a greater love which wasn't complicated at all. A love so powerful that everything orbiting it dissolved into its light: absolute love has no shadow side, it just *is*. Pure and complete. Pixie knew that *that* was the goal we were all aiming for. To love, unconditionally. If one loved unconditionally, forgiveness would no longer be necessary because grievances would simply fall away in the light of that love. Pixie was beginning to understand that it wasn't her place to judge her mother, but to love her. Maybe that was one of the most important lessons Cavill had taught her. That with love, anything was possible.

It had taken a couple of shots of vodka, but Pixie had telephoned her mother as soon as she'd got home from Seacombe. It had been an awkward, stilted conversation, but it was a start. Rome wasn't built in a day, after all. But this meeting was the first brick. The first of perhaps many bricks. They both had a long way to travel to bridge the gap of so many years, of so many *lost* years. But Pixie felt positive about taking this first step.

She was listening to her favourite music, those emotive movie soundtracks that transported her, and gazing idly out of the window, when her thoughts drifted to Felix Fairhaven. She delved into her carpet bag and took out his card. The name seemed so familiar to her, even though she had never heard of it before he'd introduced himself. She remembered being struck by the sight of him in Central Park, how he had reminded her so much of Cavill, how their eyes had met, and how she had been strangely drawn to him, as if she *knew* him. As those memories sharpened, she felt the unmistakeable pull of fate and smiled to herself. This was meant to happen. This was part of her story. She might have severed the connection to Cavill, which had drawn him into her slides, but she would never sever the love, which was uniquely theirs. However, having said goodbye, she knew she was now ready to start living fully in the present, and to embrace the new opportunities which she believed were now coming her way. She slipped the card back into her bag, resolving to arrange a meeting before Felix left London for New York. She would tell him the truth.

She saw Cavill's letter at the bottom of her bag and took it out. She hadn't read it again since she'd left the theatre. She would read it now, in the quiet of the train, with the stirring music to accompany the beautiful words.

She opened the envelope and drew it out. But there was something else in the envelope that she hadn't noticed before. It was pressed up against the side. Intrigued, she pulled it out. It was a square piece of thick white card. She turned it over. There, in watercolour, was the painting of two birds flying into a sunset. Beneath the picture were the words: '*Love connects us in a never-ending bond, Cavill. It is so much bigger than we humans can imagine. So much bigger.*'

Pixie read the words in astonishment and delight, for she knew that she hadn't missed the piece of paper in the envelope, after all

– it hadn't been there. She had said those words to Cavill when she had slid back to say good-bye. He must have painted that picture and written that sentence *after* she had left.

She pressed it to her heart and smiled. Love is, indeed, so much bigger than we humans can imagine. So much bigger.

Acknowledgements

I'm really sad to have come to the end of this trilogy. It's been a wonderful adventure, not only for Pixie but for me! It has also been a massive challenge. Pixie's world was incredibly difficult to create, and at times I was almost defeated. It did my head in. But I wasn't alone. Charlotte Mursell, my brilliant editor at Orion, was really crucial in helping me make the time travel and paranormal world believable. I think it did her head in at times as well. I owe her a big debt of gratitude for her patience, her diligence and her excellent ideas. I also want to thank her team, who have been fantastic to work with, both efficient and enthusiastic: Cait Davies, Leanne Oliver, Sian Baldwin, Snigdha Koirala, Paul Stark, Ellie Nightingale and the eagle-eyed copy-editor Francine Brody. They have all worked hard to make this trilogy the best it can possibly be.

I am so lucky to have the support and guidance of one of the best agents in the business, the doyen of the literary world, Sheila Crowley. We've worked together for too many years to count, and I consider her more of a wise friend than a colleague. She has that rare gift of making each one of her authors feel as if they are the only one who matters, giving her time in a marvellously unhurried way, without the slightest hint of how insanely busy she is. I thank her with all my heart. I also thank her dedicated team at Curtis Brown, especially Krys Kujawinska, Tanja Goossens, Georgia Williams and Helena Maybery.

My interest in the world of metaphysics and the paranormal is inspired by so many exceptional writers and gurus, and I thank them all, but especially Avril Price, who taught me tarot at the

College of Psychic Studies and has become a firm friend and wise teacher, and Susan Dabbs who was my first spiritual teacher and has been a constant and profound inspiration to me. Both of these gifted women have accompanied me along my path and opened my mind. I'm enormously grateful to them both.

There are two incredibly powerful spiritual teachers who, through their books and lectures, have had an incalculable influence on my life and who continue to teach and inspire me every day: Eckhart Tolle and Sadhguru. I thank them for the light they bring into the world.

I would like to thank my father, Charles Palmer-Tomkinson, who fired my interest in the esoteric from early childhood, sharing books and discussing those big, existential questions in the car on the way to school or on long walks around the woods with the dogs. He listened to tales of my spiritual adventures with an open mind and has always been a wonderful example of how to live in a state of positivity and acceptance. 'It's sunny at the top' might be his philosophy while skiing in the mountains, but it is also his philosophy for life. I try to live by that philosophy, too.

I simply wouldn't be a sane person without the support of my family. I thank my mother, Patty Palmer-Tomkinson, my brother, James, sister-in-law, Sos, and their children, Honor, India, Wilf and Sam, for bringing me joy. I thank my late sister, Tara, for reinforcing my belief in life after death.

I thank my husband, Sebag, daughter, Lilochka, and son, Sasha, for bringing the laughter and the love.

Credits

Santa Montefiore and Orion Fiction would like to thank everyone at Orion who worked on the publication of *The Last Encore* in the UK.

Editorial
Charlotte Mursell
Snigdha Koirala
Clara Sokhn

Copyeditor
Francine Brody

Proofreader
Nicky Gyopari

Audio
Paul Stark
Louise Richardson

Contracts
Rachel Monte
Ellie Bowker

Design
Charlotte Abrams-Simpson
Rachael Lancaster

Editorial Management
Charlie Panayiotou
Jane Hughes
Bartley Shaw

Finance
Jasdip Nandra
Nick Gibson
Sue Baker

Production
Ruth Sharvell

Marketing
Cait Davies
Ellie Nightingale

Publicity
Leanne Oliver
Sian Baldwin

Sales
David Murphy
Sammy Luton
Victoria Laws
Rachael Hum
Ellie Kyrke-Smith
Frances Doyle
Georgina Cutler

Rights
Rebecca Folland
Tara Hiatt
Ben Fowler
Alice Cottrell
Ruth Blakemore
Marie Henckel

Operations
Group Sales Operations team